enough space for everyone else
a comic anthology

Published by Bedside Press

bedsidepress.com

Cover Illustration and Interior Design by Eryn Williams
Additional Typesetting by Samantha Beiko

Library and Archives Canada Cataloguing in Publication
Enough space for everyone else / J.N. Monk, Lee Black editor.
Issued in print and electronic formats.

ISBN 978-0-9939970-8-2 (paperback).- -ISBN 978-0-9939970-9-9 (PDF)

1. Outer space–Comic books, strips, etc. 2. Comics (Graphic works)
I. Monk, J. N., 1986-, editor II. Black, Lee, 19XX-, editor

PN6720.E56 2016 741.5'9
C2016-905135-8
C2016-905136-6

table of contents

* * * *

Foreword

Do you know what a generation ship is?

It's a classic element of science-fiction storytelling -- you probably know it best from WALL-E. A generation ship is a kind of space ark, built for a journey that will take so long the crew will eventually have to be replaced by their own children. Then that crew's children will take over for them, and so on until the ship reaches its destination, carrying the distant descendants of those first voyagers who set out so long ago.

It's a neat idea, and one of my favorites, partly because it's just so dang hopeful but mostly because I think that's what the whole genre is, really: one big generation ship set for coordinates unknown, piloted from the first human who told a story about the stars on and on down to the artists and writers who made this book for you. One person alone could never do it! It's like the story about explorers crossing a desert by leaving water caches for the next person, so that one day someone will be able to get to the far side -- and the universe is the biggest desert of all.

The crossing's hard work, too, especially in such an unlikely ship helmed by such an unlikely crew. None of us are what you'd call famous, even in the tiny world of comics. Some of us have never been published before. A lot of us are the kind of people who aren't even supposed to try, because we can't or shouldn't or both -- or at least that's what another, way less interesting kind of person says (but we didn't listen, and you don't have to either).

And there were other obstacles: promising contributors who had to drop out for one reason or another, pretty much everyone being broke, health problems, housing problems, ugh maybe we should just give up and run away to join the circus problems, is that even a thing you can do anymore problems, really just plain old life. And that was before we even launched the Kickstarter campaign! Which took 30 nail-biting, sweating, obsessing-over-the-donation-counter, annoying-everyone-on-Twitter days off our lives. Right up to the last 24 hours it didn't look like we were going to make it after all.

But we did, because truth is? There's no better time for the people who aren't supposed to make books like this to do it anyhow. That's what this book is all about: that there is truly Enough Space For Everyone Else, if they'll dare everything to seek it out. The stars are our inheritance too.

See, when I was a kid, I used to hang out at this used bookstore next to the local pizza place. I'd kill time and my allowance there rifling through its collection of yellowy old paperbacks, always on the hunt for my next favorite book -- and then one day I found something that changed my life. It was the Bank Street Book of Science Fiction, an anthology of classic sci-fi short stories retold by various artists in black and white comics. Y'all, it blew my daggone baby mind. I'd read plenty of comics and plenty of short story collections, but that a book could be both? That you could make a book where each piece was distinct from the next not only textually but visually, each change of writer and artist creating new moods, tones, aesthetics? That Evan Dorkin did stuff other than Bill & Ted's Bogus Journey: the Comic?!

Immediately I knew that making comics was what I wanted to do when I grew up, that I wanted to be part of creating a book like that too. I didn't know people like me weren't supposed to be able to. It wouldn't have mattered. sci-fi had done for me what it's done for so many others, at so many times and in so many places: fired my mind with its vision of imagination, perseverance, and hope.

So here it is, *Enough Space For Everyone Else*, just the kind of book I dreamed of then. It's my dearest wish that this book too will reach across time and space to spark the same feelings in another child somewhere, someday. You're who we made it for, after all. J.N., myself, Hope, all the artists and writers, all the Kickstarter backers, everyone who worked to launch this ship to the stars -- we made it this far, for you.

I wonder where you'll take it from here.

Ad astra per aspera,

Lee

* ※ * ❋

The last time I did one of these I literally put my head through a wall because of the weight of the stress and expectations. No such thing happened this time.

My family apparently has an ancestral motto about facing adversity to reach the stars. And that's what I did here.

I didn't get all the way here by myself, though. There was also the work of those both seen and unseen. We couldn't have made this possible without the solid advice of people like Scott Wegener and George Rohac. Or have an example of what to strive for with the trailblazing efforts of the many comic anthologies that came before us. Or the incomparable talents of Hope Nicholson, who helped push us past the finish line. And let's never forget the hard work of our artists and writers and

my stalwart co-editor Lee Black. Not to mention the tireless McAlister Grant, without whose campaign management we might not have this book at all. The accomplishments, indefatigable optimism, and very generous contributions of our backers cannot be overstated either.

So I didn't put my head through any walls this time around. But we were still able to bust through some metaphorical ones all the same. And now that those boundaries have fallen we might just have Enough Space for Everyone Else.

Hope you enjoy the journey.

Couldn't have done it without y'all.

J.N. Monk

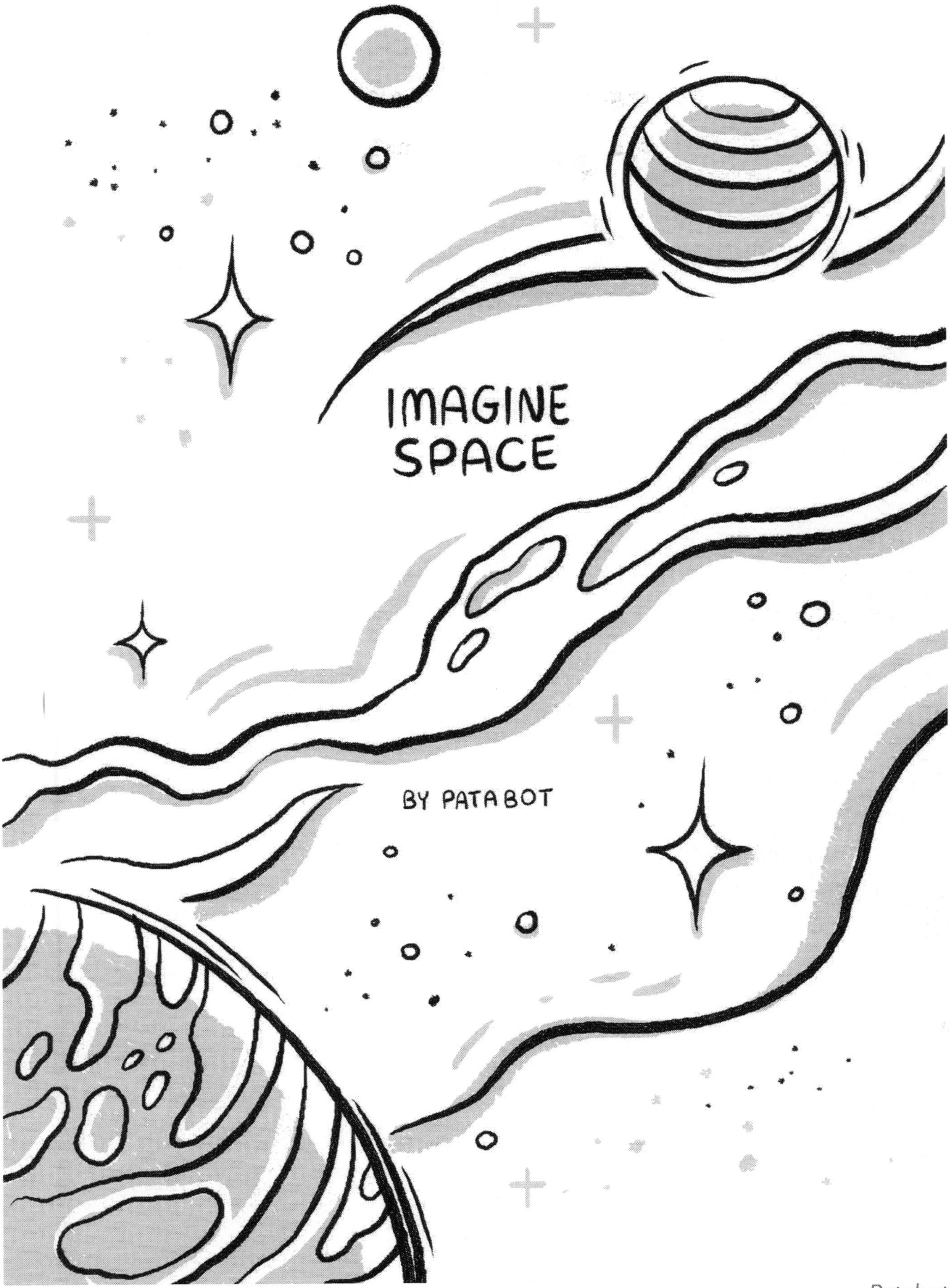
IMAGINE
SPACE
BY PATABOT

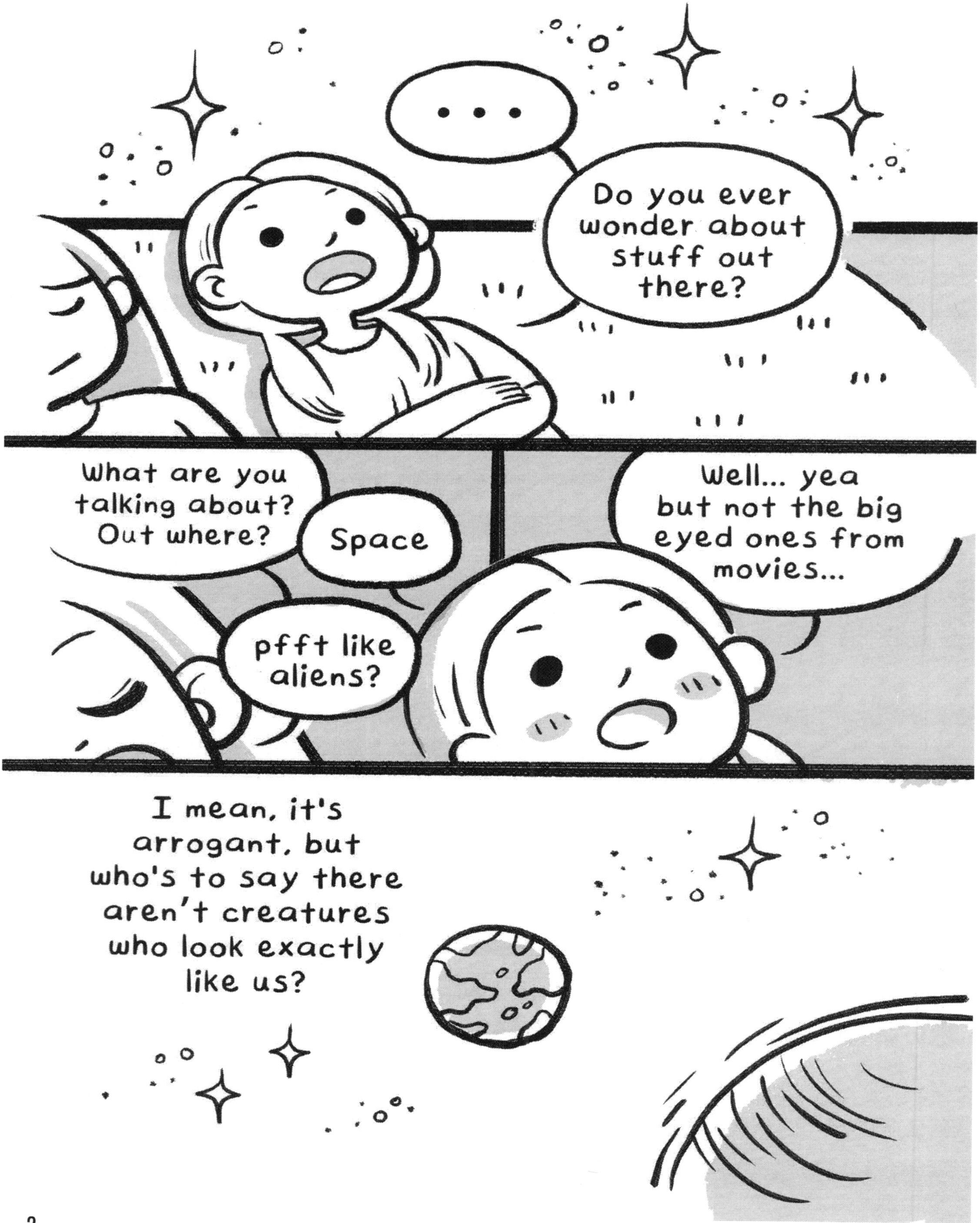
. . .
Do you ever wonder about stuff out there?
What are you talking about? Out where?
Space
pfft like aliens?
Well... yea but not the big eyed ones from movies...
I mean, it's arrogant, but who's to say there aren't creatures who look exactly like us?

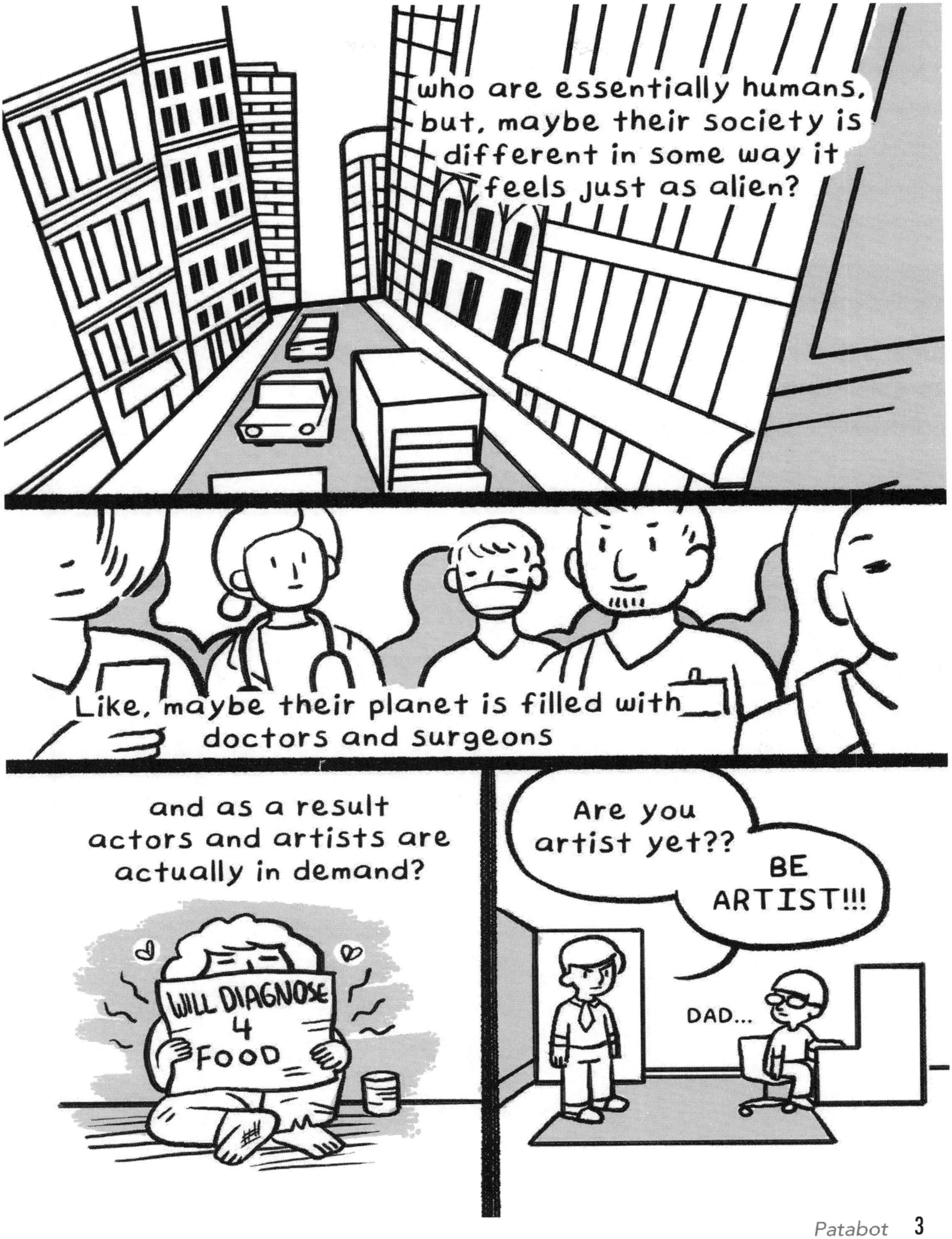
who are essentially humans, but, maybe their society is different in some way it feels just as alien?
Like, maybe their planet is filled with doctors and surgeons
and as a result actors and artists are actually in demand?
WILL DIAGNOSE 4 FOOD
Are you artist yet??
BE ARTIST!!!
DAD...

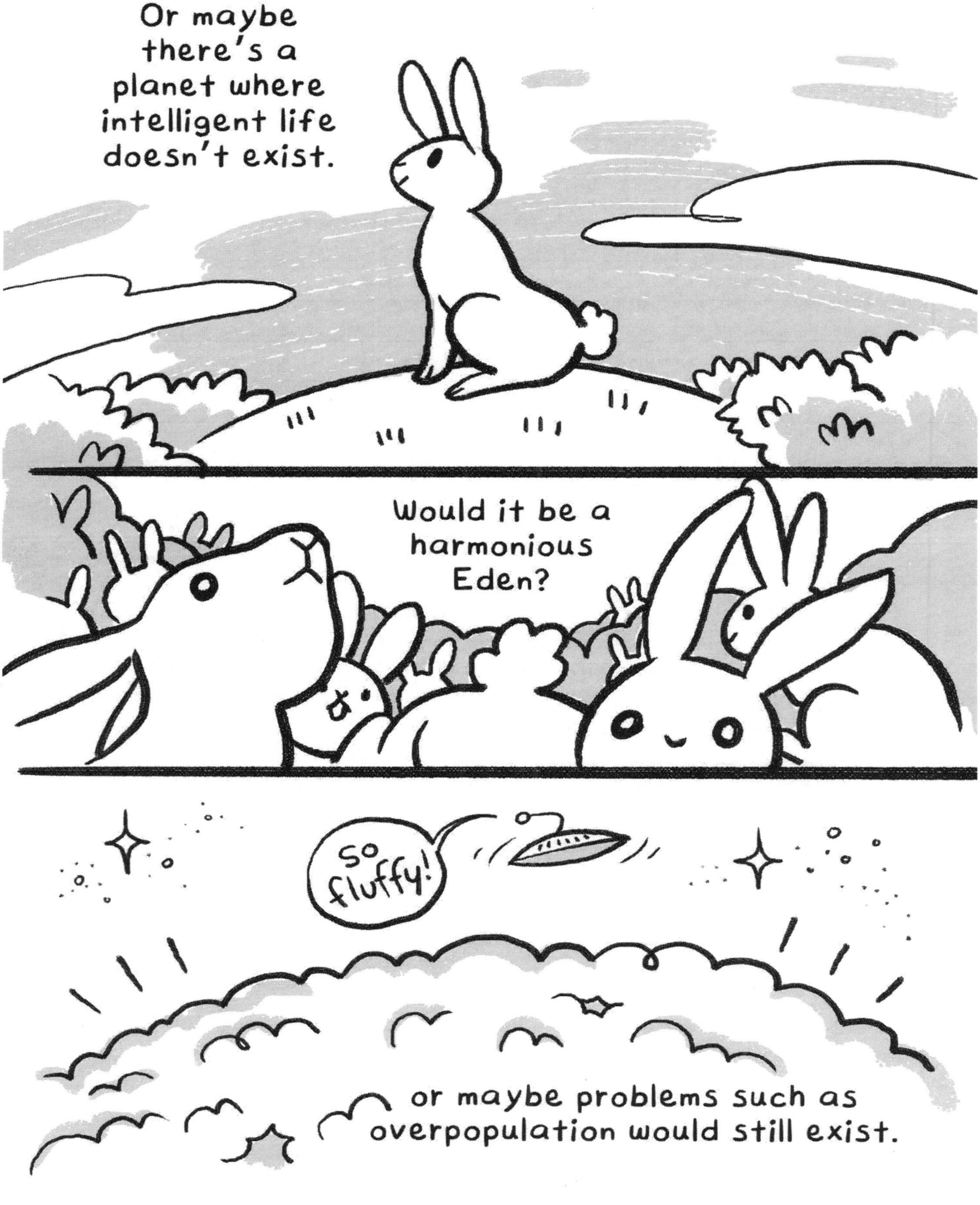
Or maybe there's a planet where intelligent life doesn't exist.
Would it be a harmonious Eden?
So fluffy!
or maybe problems such as overpopulation would still exist.

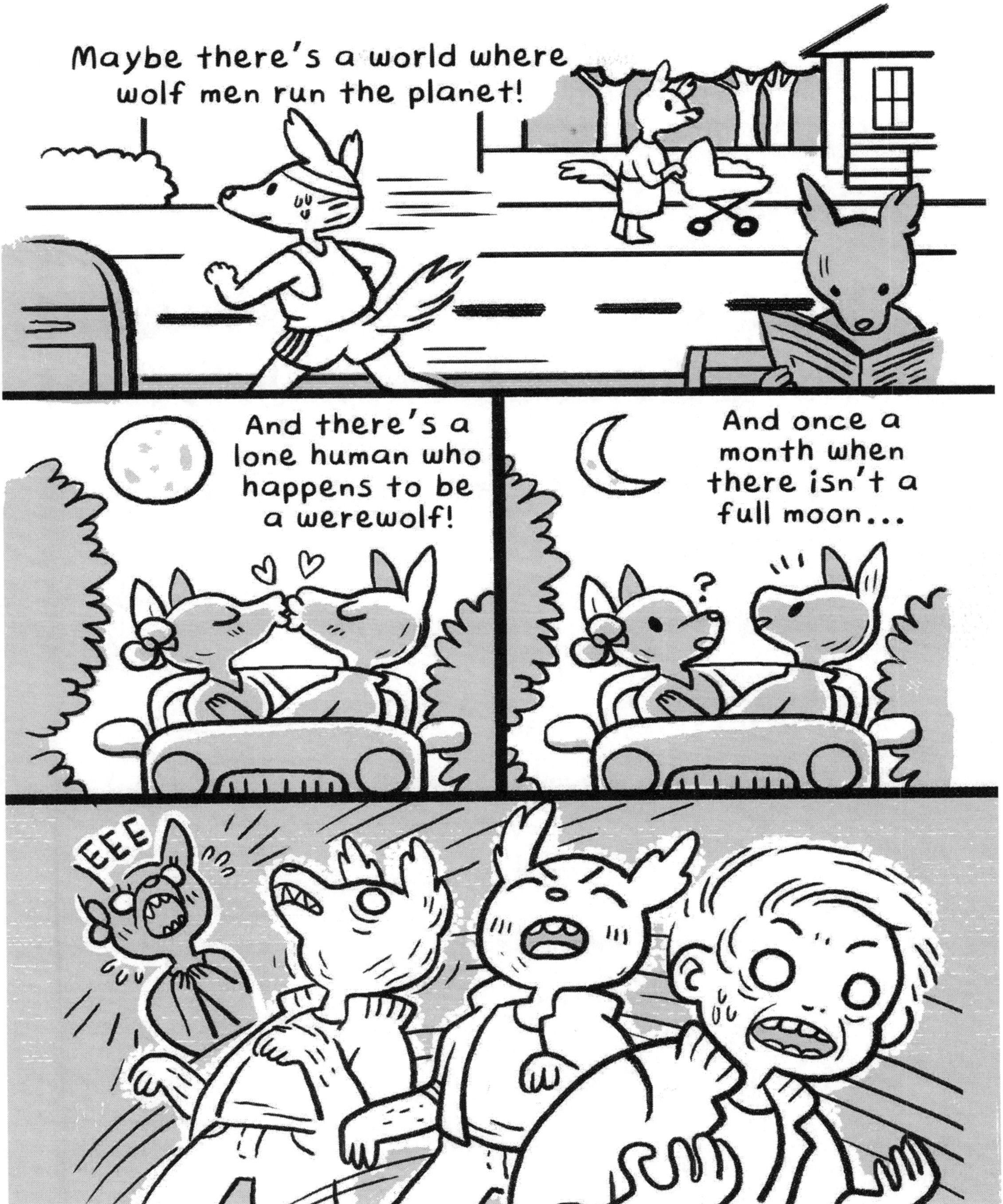
Maybe there's a world where wolf men run the planet!
And there's a lone human who happens to be a werewolf!
And once a month when there isn't a full moon...
EEE
... he un-transforms and it freaks everyone out

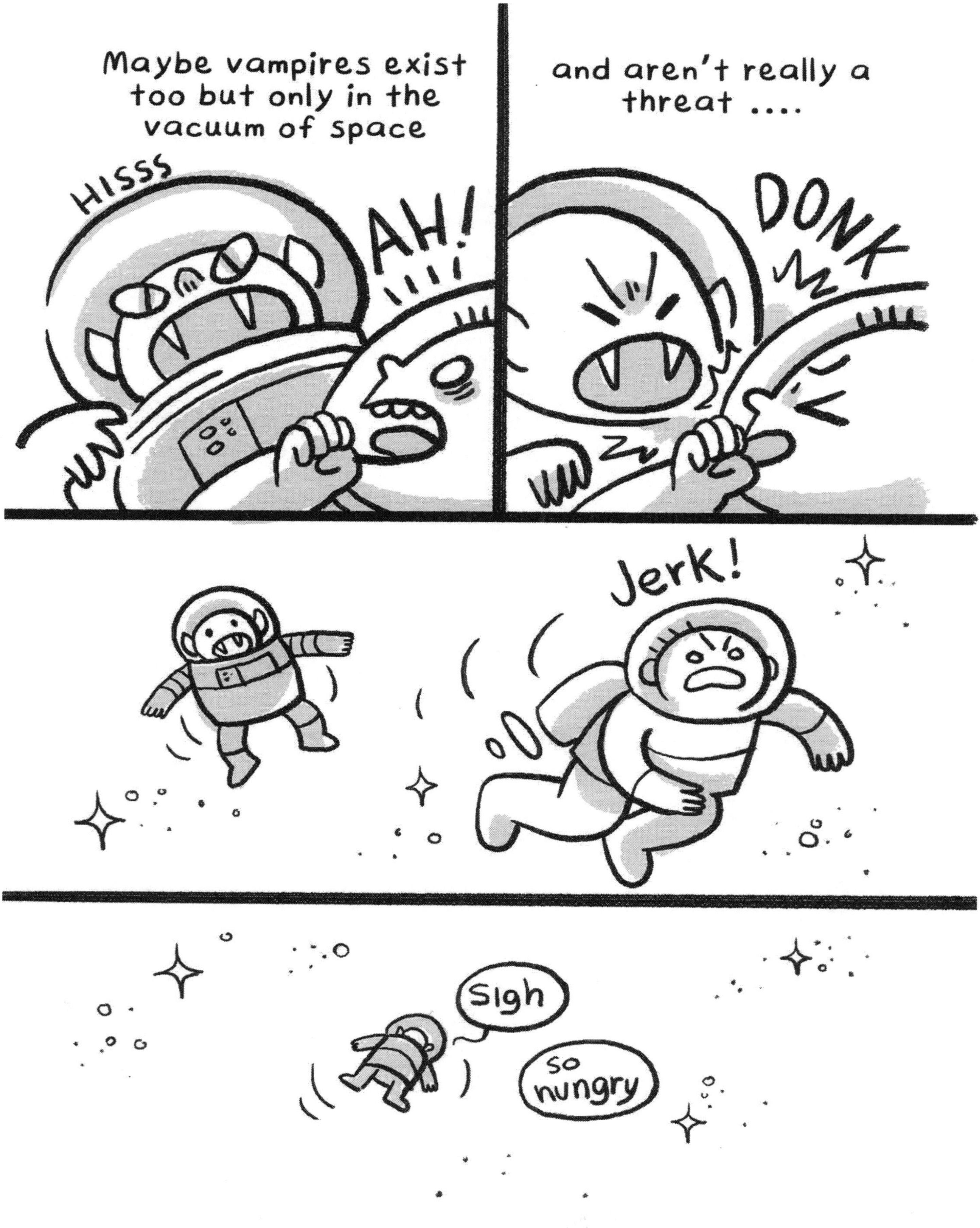
Maybe vampires exist too but only in the vacuum of space
HISSS
AH!
and aren't really a threat ....
DONK
Jerk!
Sigh
so hungry

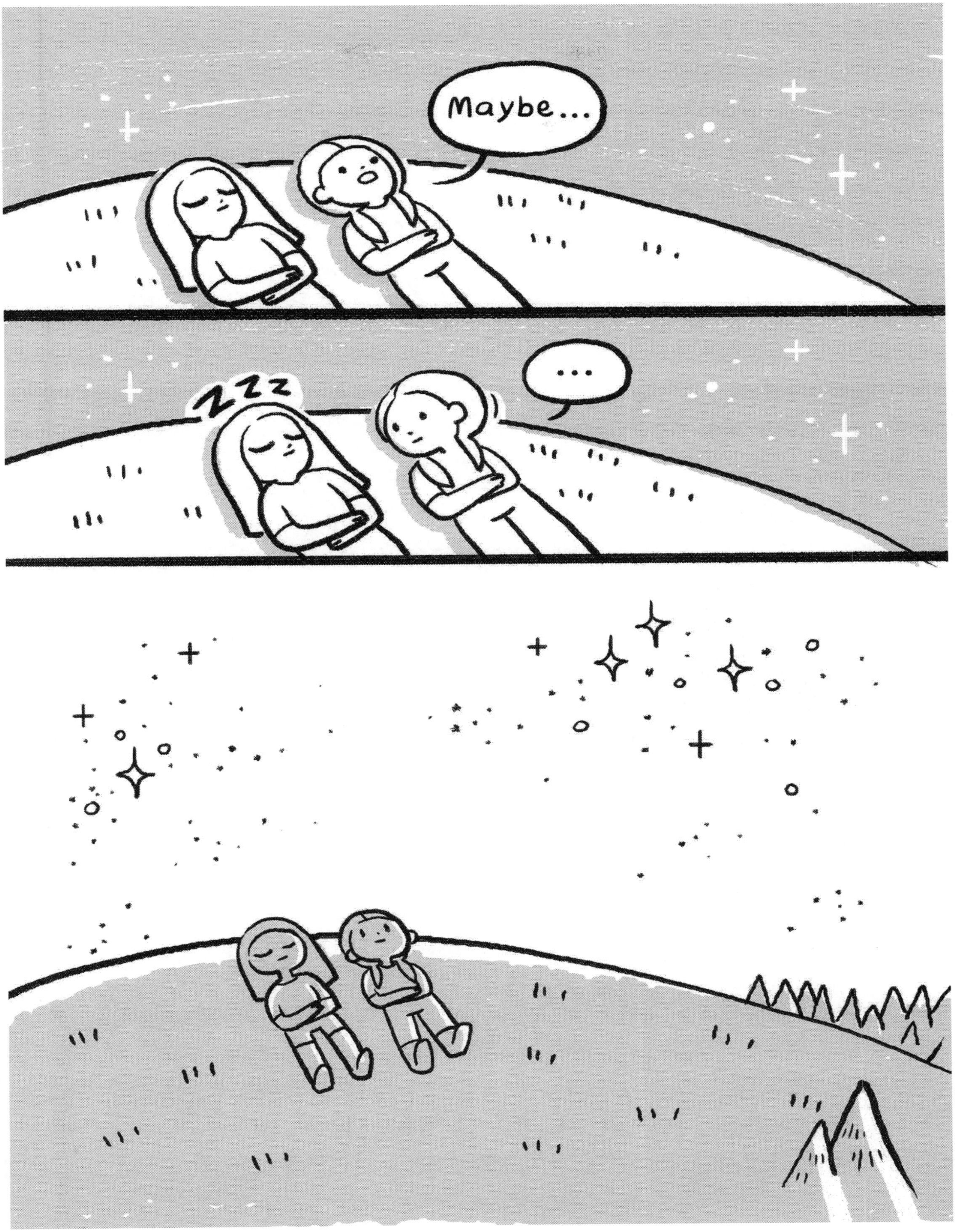
Maybe...
...
ZZZ

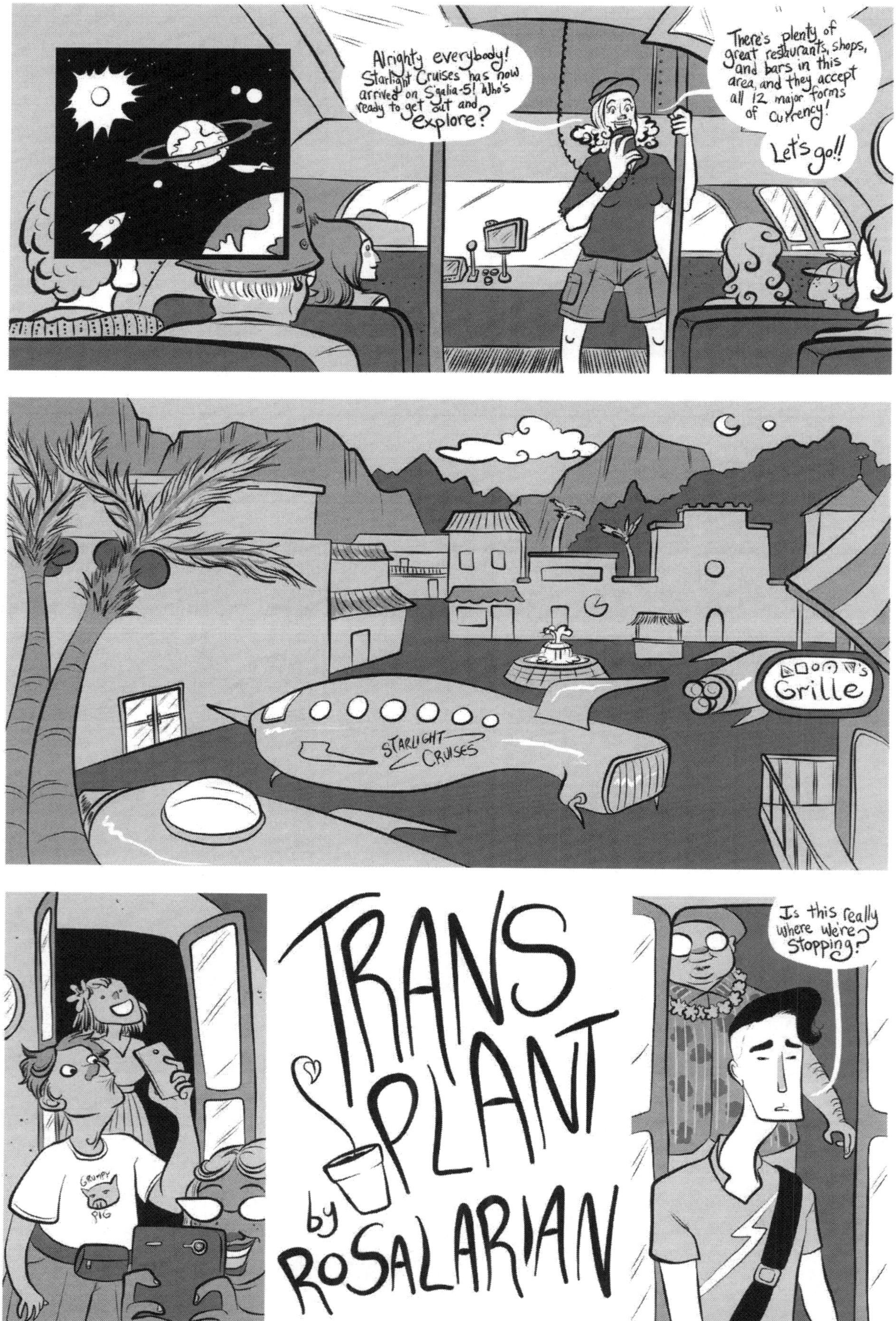
Alrighty everybody! Starlight Cruises has now arrived on S'galia-5! Who's ready to get out and explore?
There's plenty of great restaurants, shops, and bars in this area, and they accept all 12 major forms of currency!
Let's go!!
Grille
STARLIGHT CRUISES
GRUMPY PIG
TRANS PLANT by ROSALARIAN
Is this really where we're stopping?

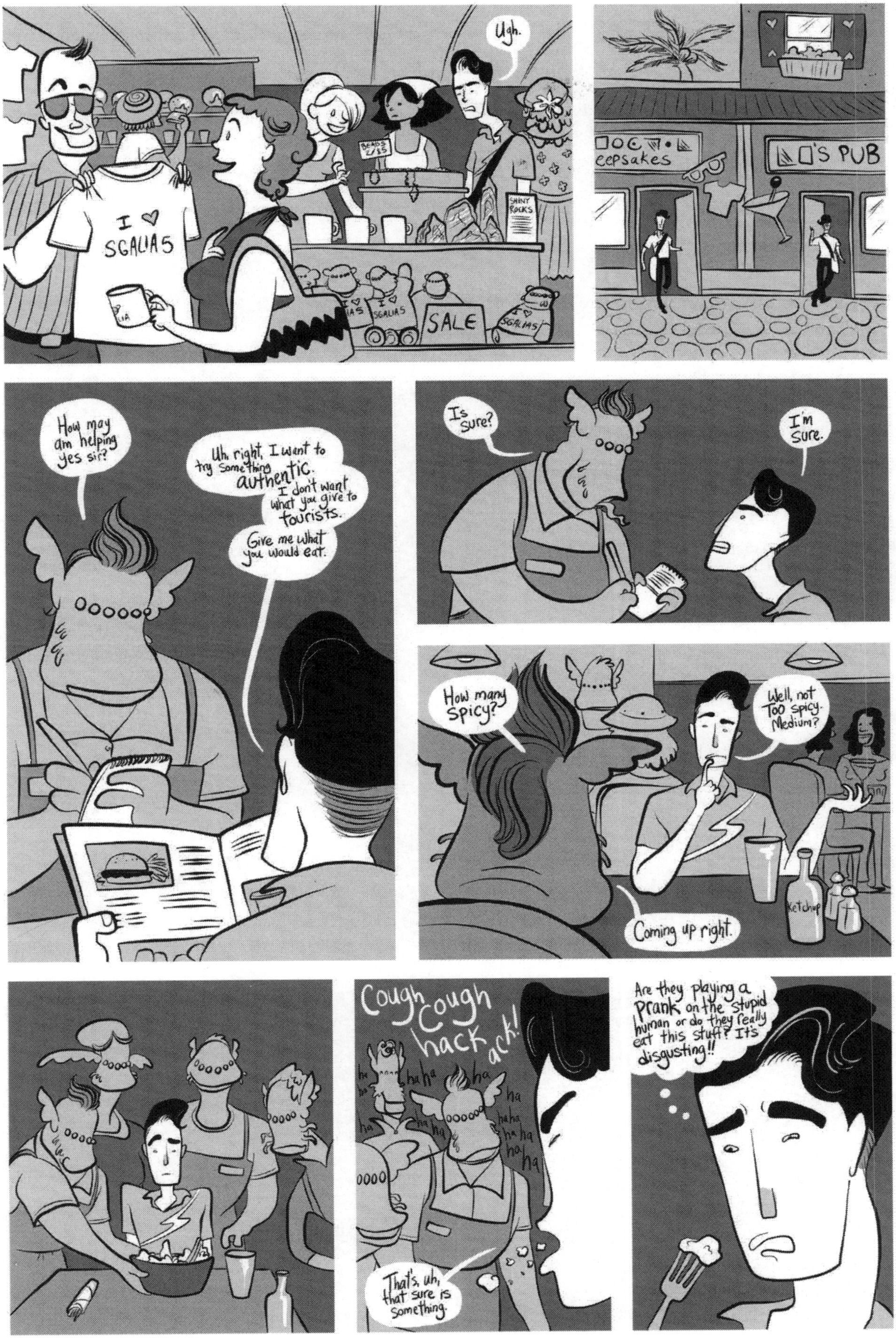
Ugh.
I ♥ SGALIA5
SALE
SHINY ROCKS
eepsakes
'S PUB
How may am helping yes sir?
Uh, right, I want to try something authentic.
I don't want what you give to tourists.
Give me what you would eat.
Is sure?
I'm sure.
How many spicy?
Well, not too spicy. Medium?
Coming up right.
Ketchup
Cough cough hack ack!
That's, uh, that sure is something.
Are they playing a prank on the stupid human or do they really eat this stuff? It's disgusting!!

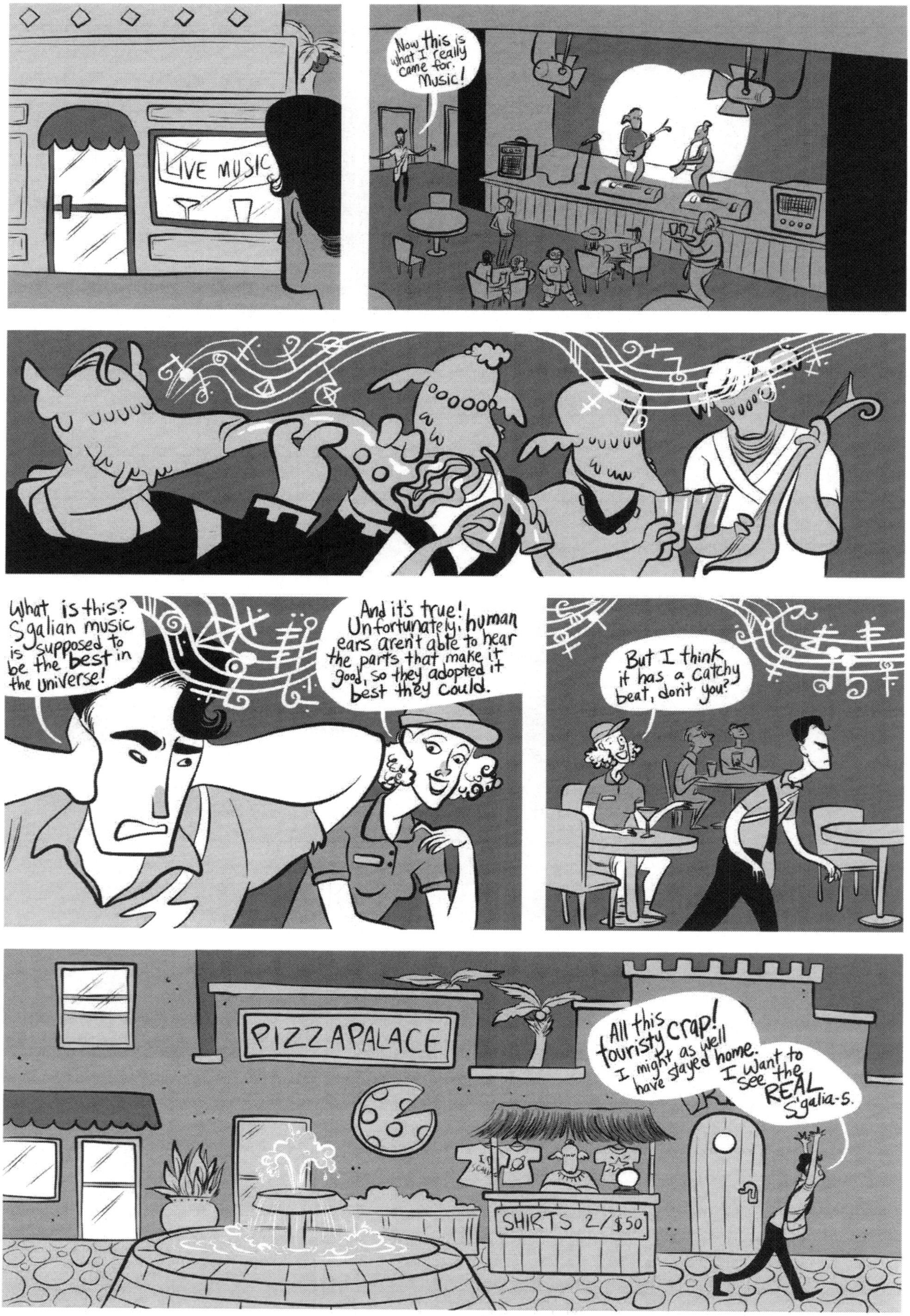
LIVE MUSIC
Now this is what I really came for. Music!
What is this? S'galian music is supposed to be the best in the universe!
And it's true! Unfortunately, human ears aren't able to hear the parts that make it good, so they adopted it best they could.
But I think it has a catchy beat, don't you?
PIZZAPALACE
SHIRTS 2/$50
All this touristy crap! I might as well have stayed home.
I want to see the REAL S'galia-5.

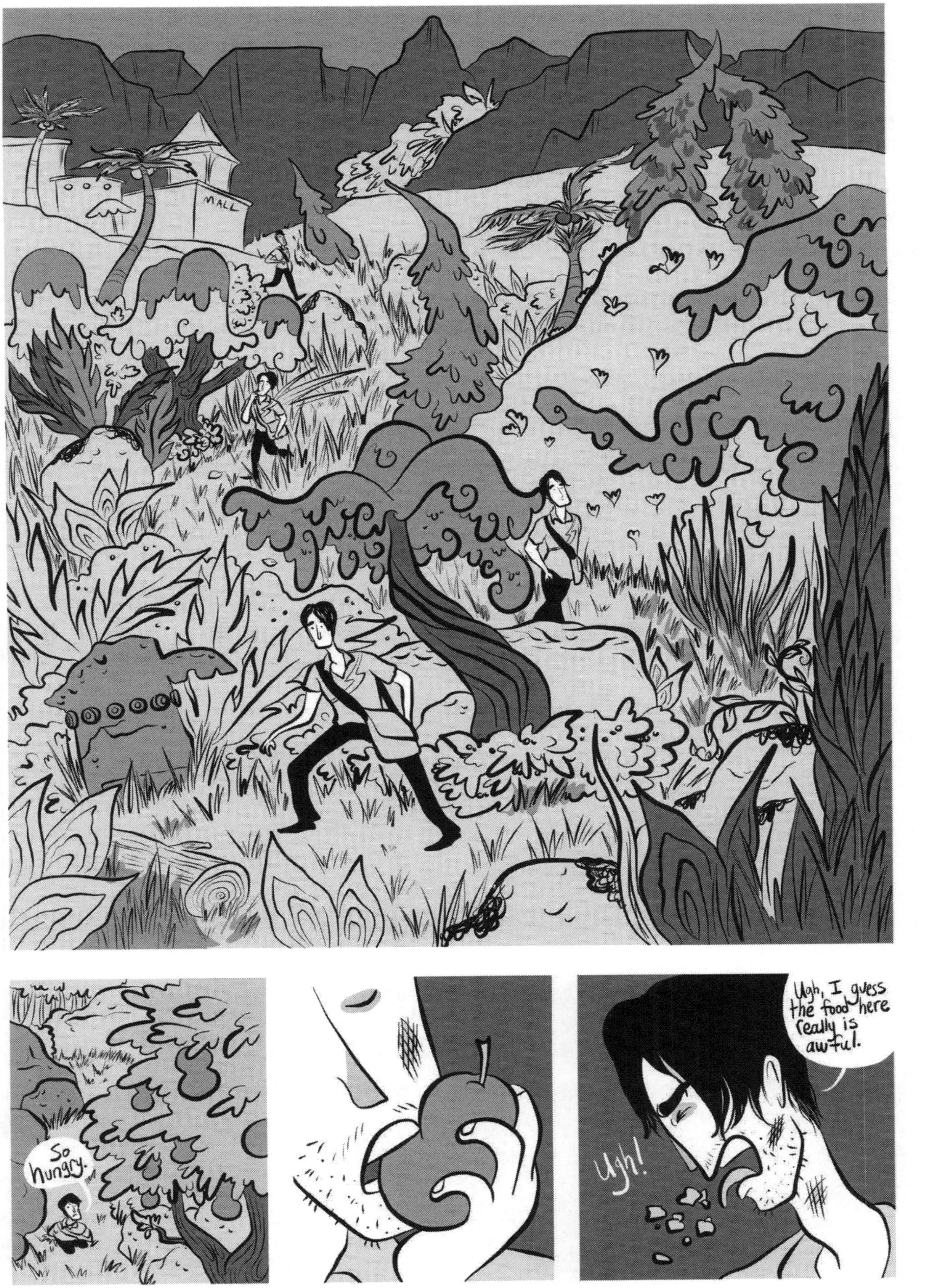
MALL
So hungry.
Ugh!
Ugh, I guess the food here really is awful.

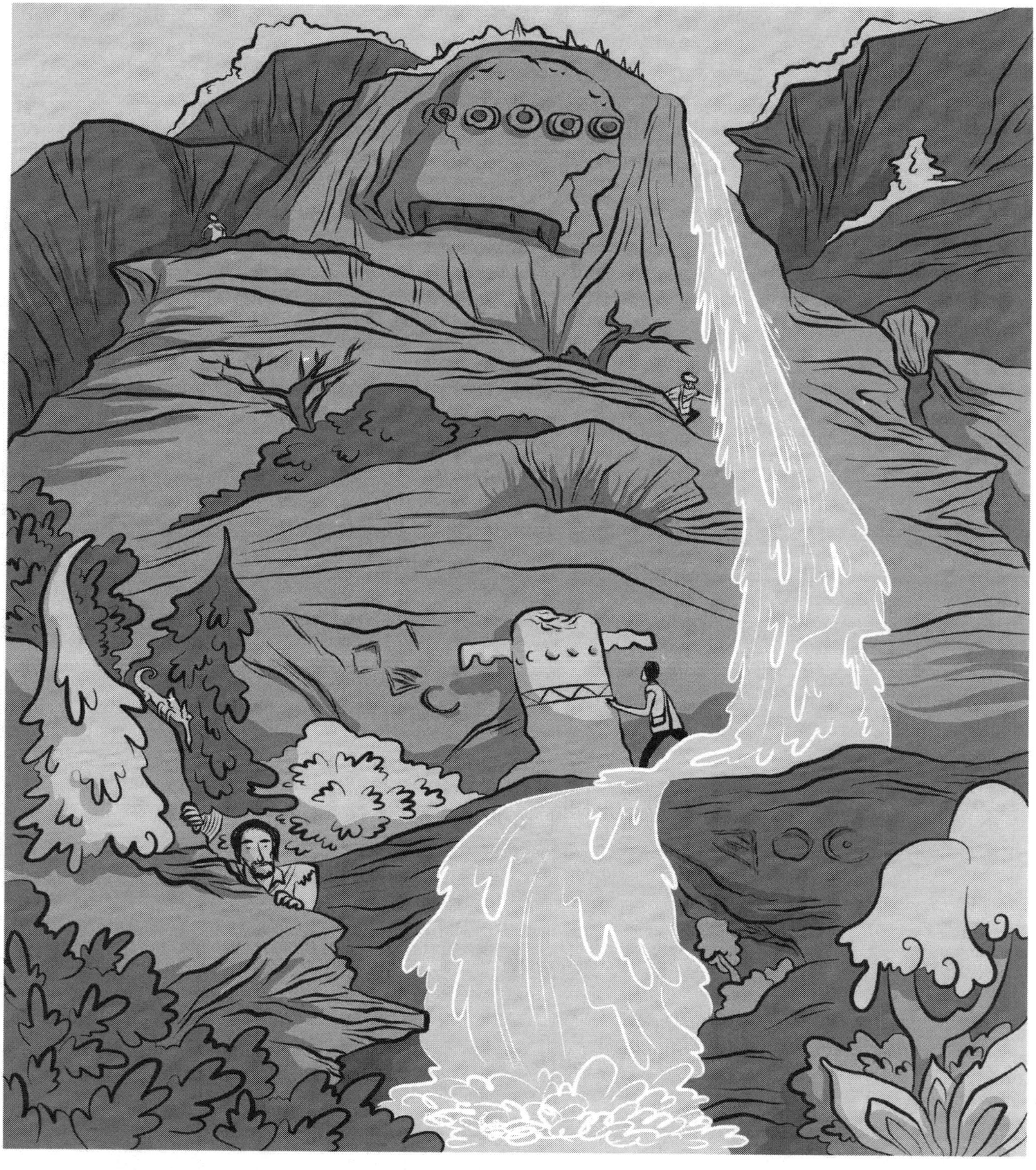

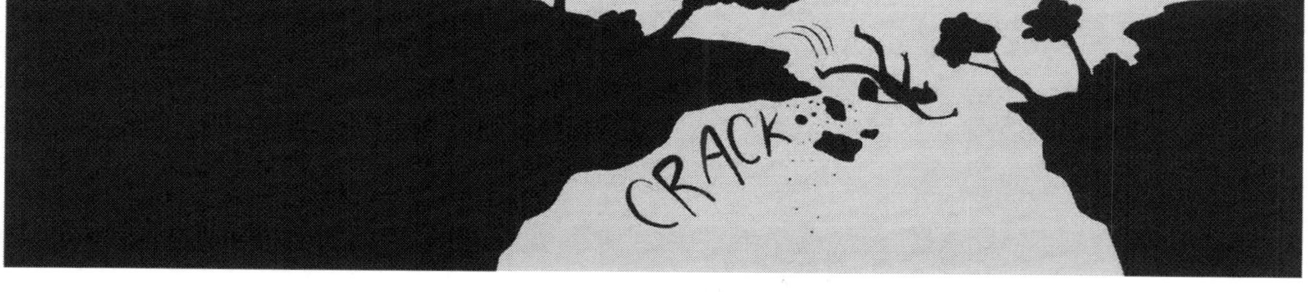
CRACK

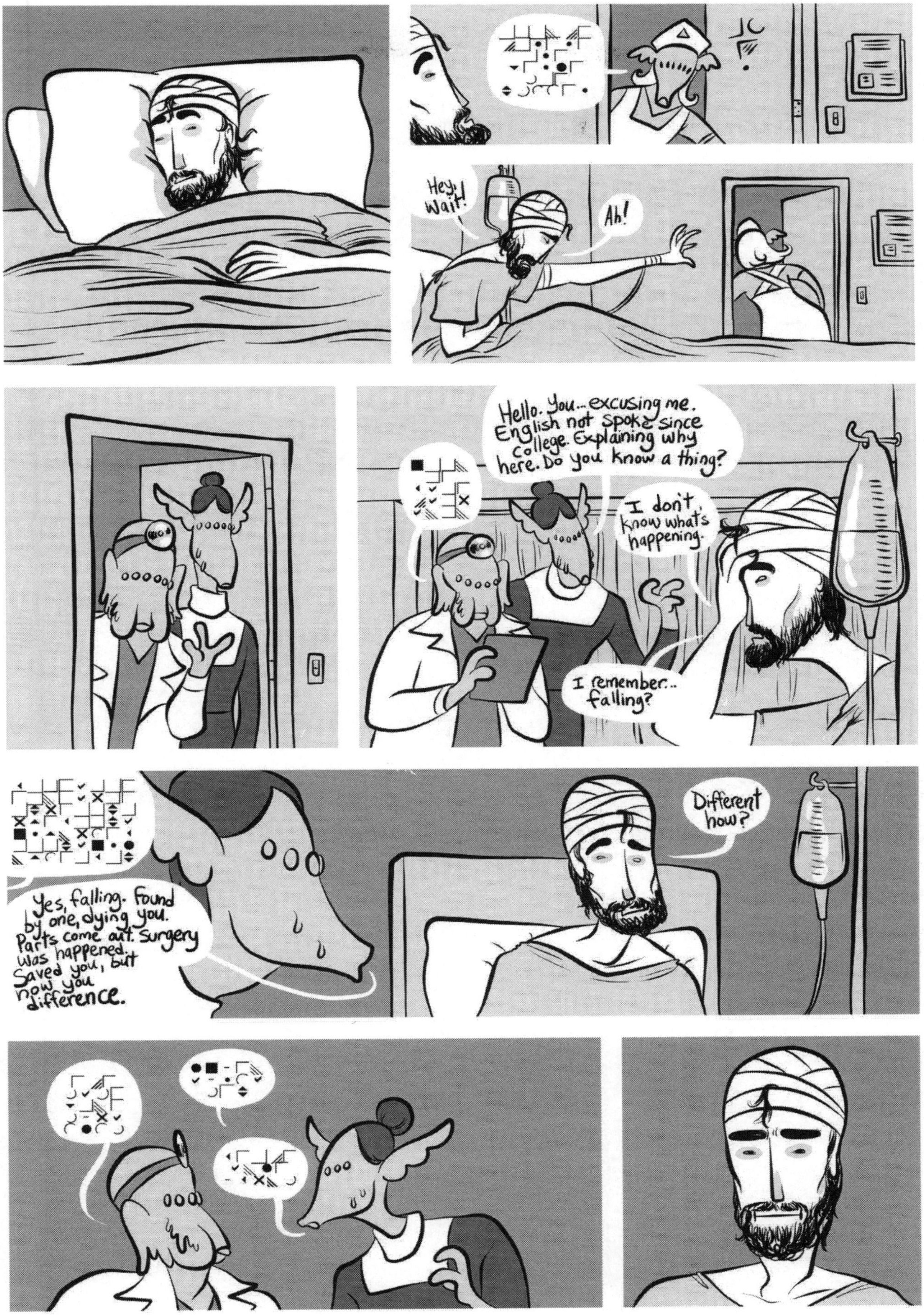
Hey, wait!
Ah!
Hello. You... excusing me. English not spoke since college. Explaining why here. Do you know a thing?
I don't know what's happening.
I remember... falling?
Yes, falling. Found by one, dying you. Parts come out. Surgery was happened. Saved you, but now you difference.
Different how?

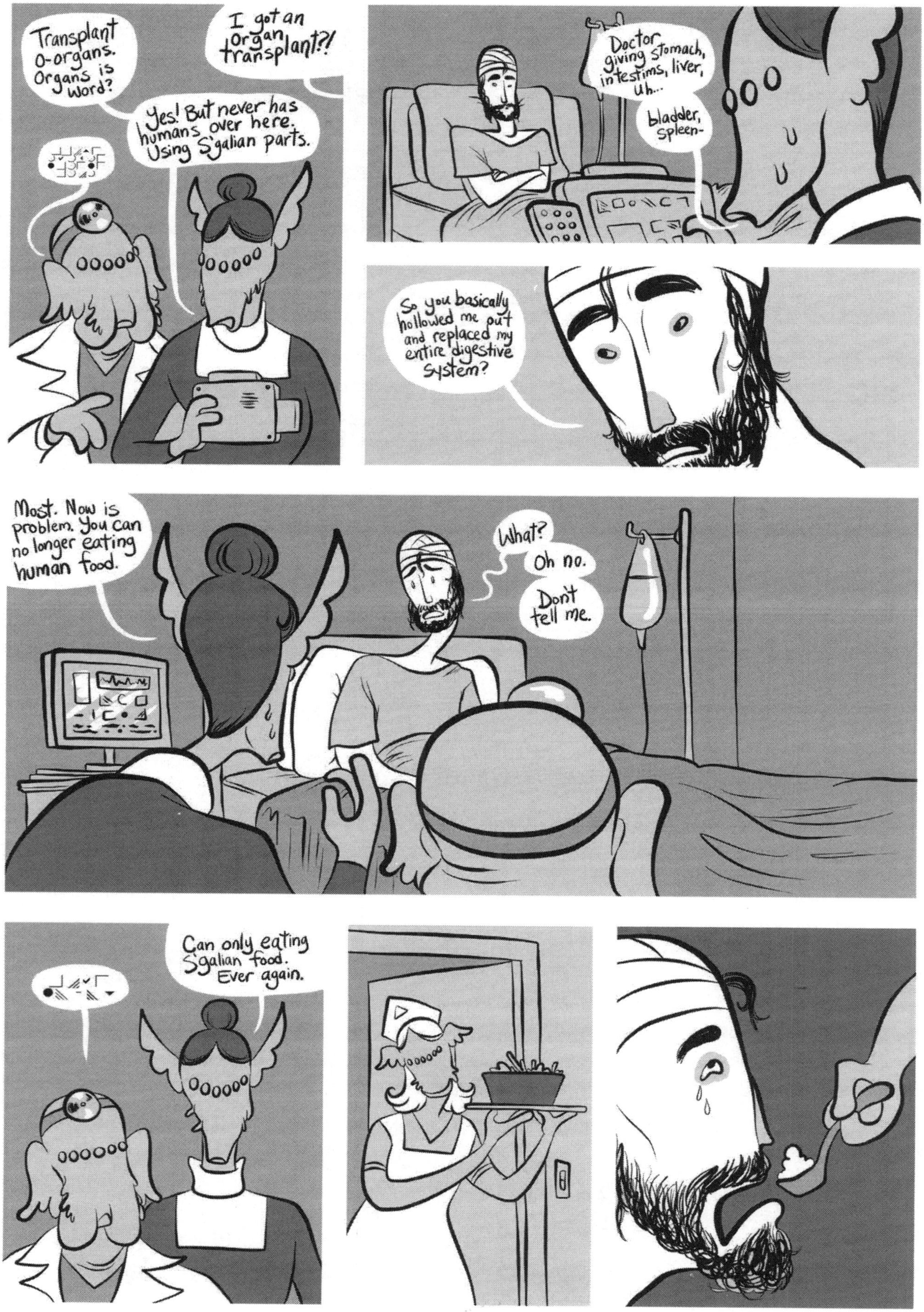
Transplant o-organs. Organs is word?
I got an organ transplant?!
Yes! But never has humans over here. Using S'galian parts.
Doctor giving stomach, intestims, liver, uh...
bladder, spleen-
So you basically hollowed me out and replaced my entire digestive system?
Most. Now is problem. You can no longer eating human food.
What?
Oh no.
Don't tell me.
Can only eating S'galian food. Ever again.

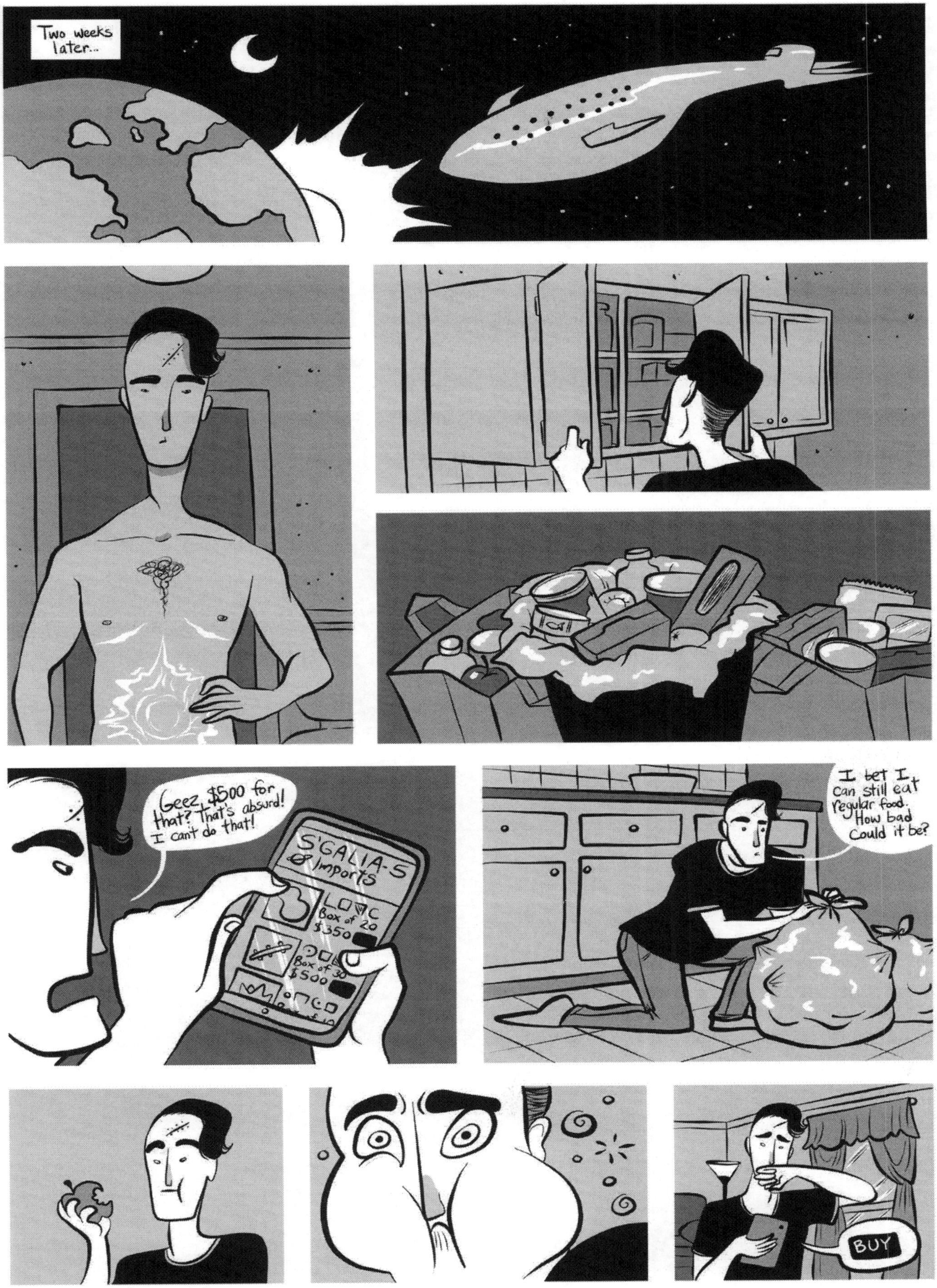
Two weeks later...
Geez $500 for that? That's absurd! I can't do that!
S'GALIA-S Imports
Box of 20 $350
Box of 30 $500
I bet I can still eat regular food. How bad could it be?
BUY

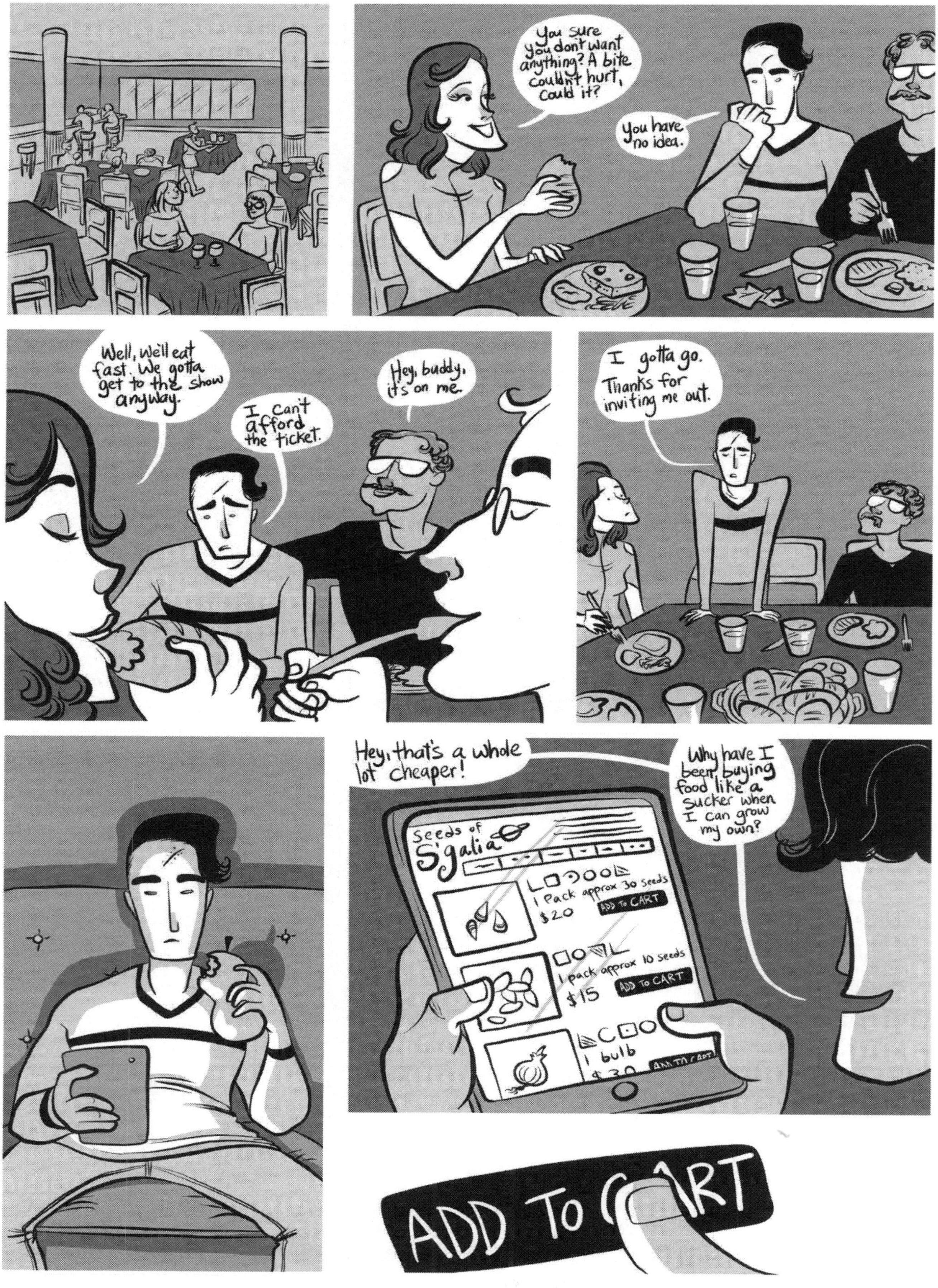
You sure you don't want anything? A bite couldn't hurt, could it?
You have no idea.
Well, we'll eat fast. We gotta get to the show anyway.
I can't afford the ticket.
Hey, buddy, it's on me.
I gotta go. Thanks for inviting me out.
Hey, that's a whole lot cheaper!
Why have I been buying food like a sucker when I can grow my own?
Seeds of S'galia
1 Pack approx 30 seeds
$20
ADD TO CART
1 pack approx 10 seeds
$15
ADD TO CART
1 bulb
ADD TO CART

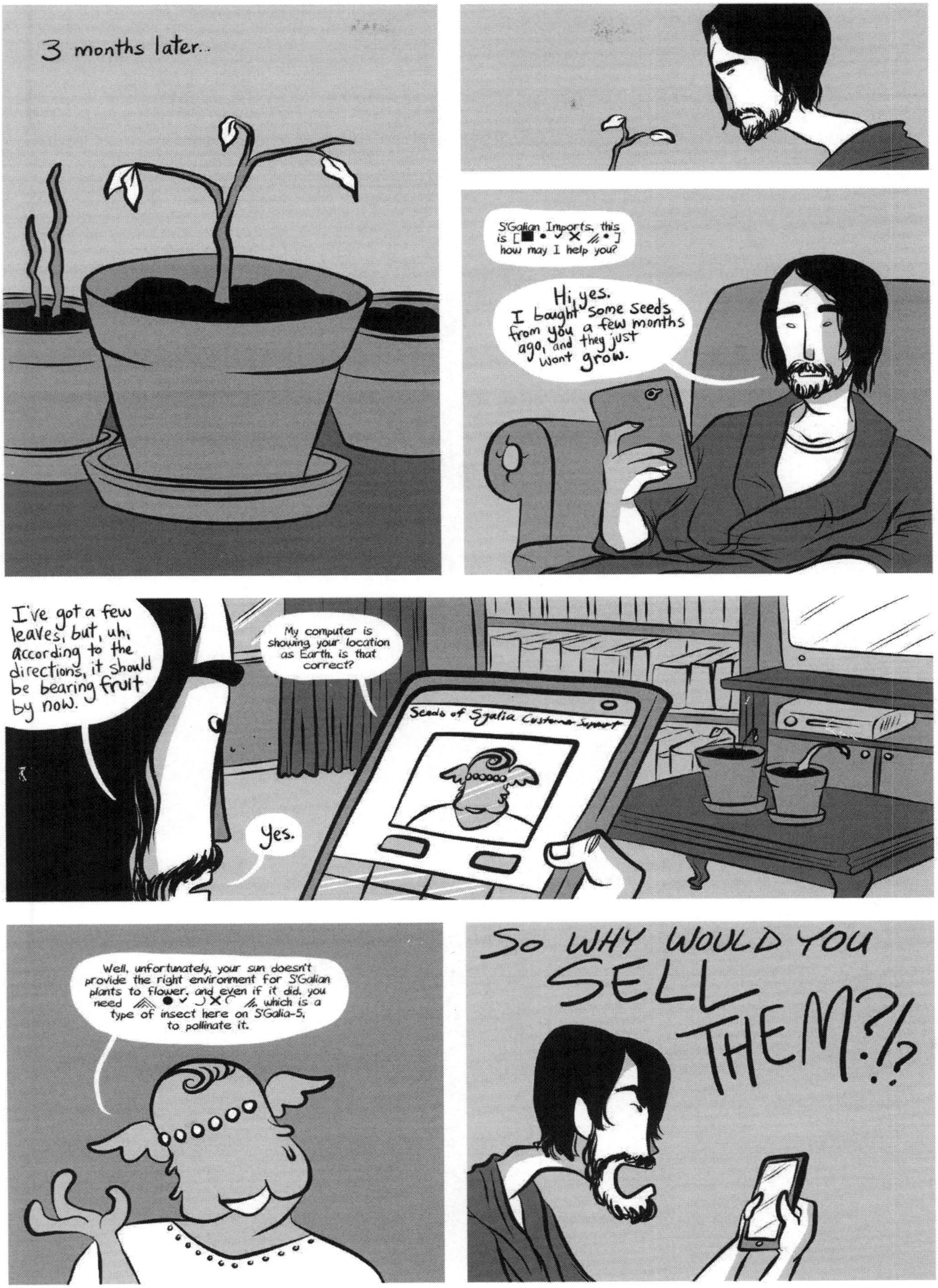

3 months later...
S'Galian Imports, this is [■ • ✓ ✕ ⫽ •] how may I help you?
Hi, yes. I bought some seeds from you a few months ago, and they just won't grow.
I've got a few leaves, but, uh, according to the directions, it should be bearing fruit by now.
My computer is showing your location as Earth, is that correct?
Seeds of Sgalia Customer Support
Yes.
Well, unfortunately, your sun doesn't provide the right environment for S'Galian plants to flower, and even if it did, you need ⩓ ● ✓ ᑐ ✕ ᑕ ⫽ which is a type of insect here on S'Galia-5, to pollinate it.
So WHY WOULD YOU SELL THEM?!?

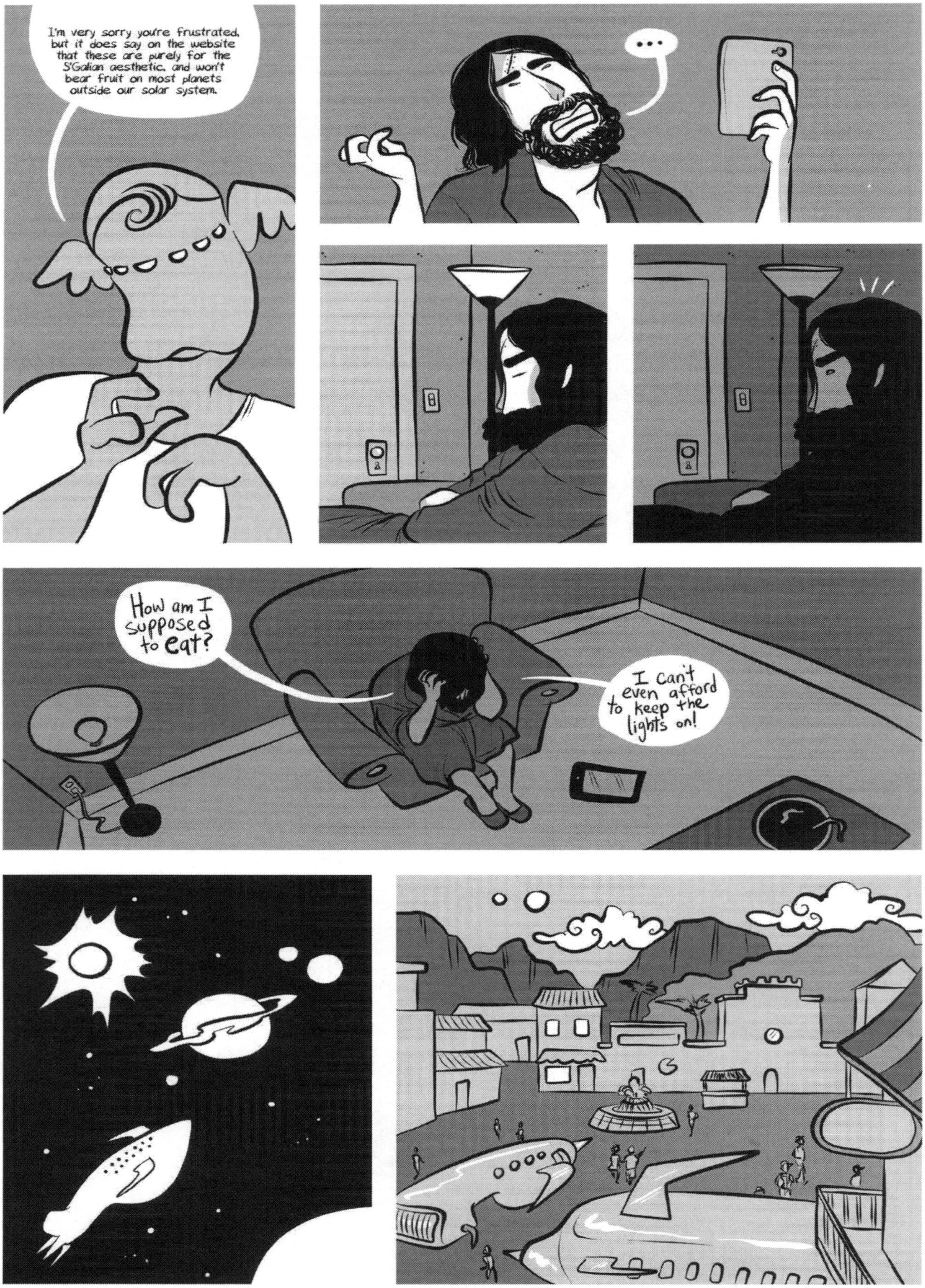
I'm very sorry you're frustrated, but it does say on the website that these are purely for the S'Galian aesthetic, and won't bear fruit on most planets outside our solar system.
...
How am I supposed to eat?
I can't even afford to keep the lights on!

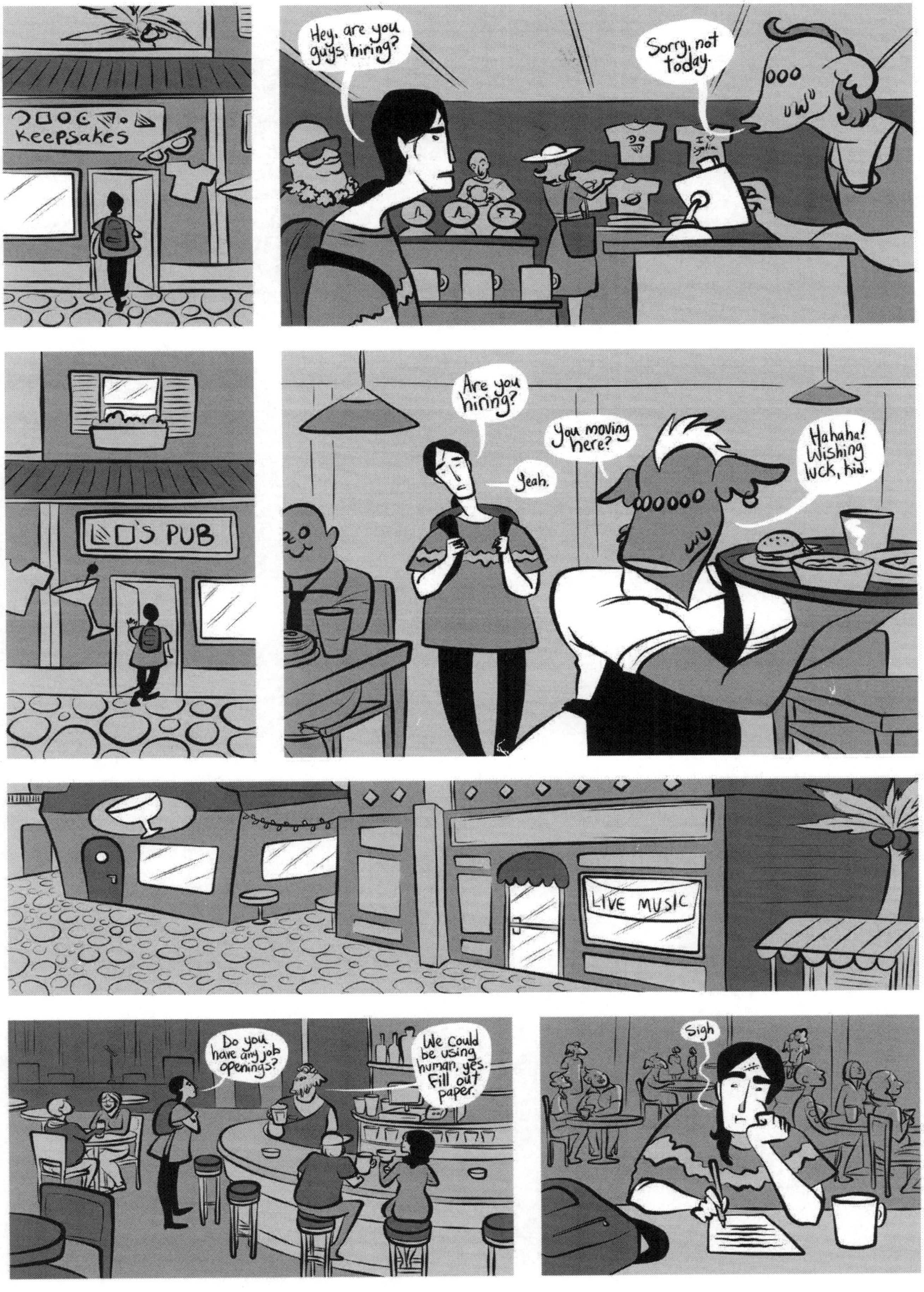
Keepsakes
Hey, are you guys hiring?
Sorry, not today.
'S PUB
Are you hiring?
You moving here?
Yeah.
Hahaha! Wishing luck, kid.
LIVE MUSIC
Do you have any job openings?
We could be using human, yes. Fill out paper.
Sigh

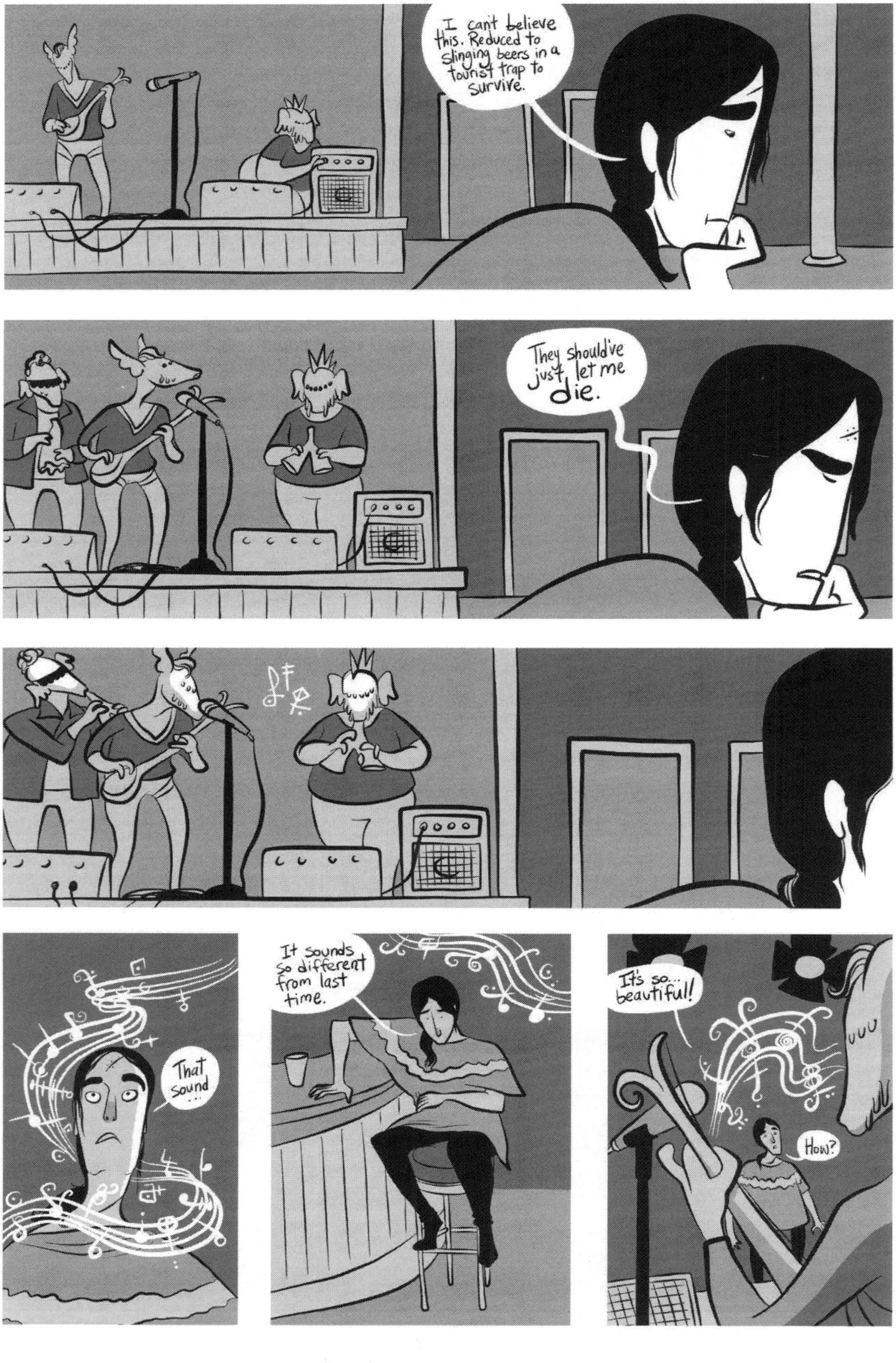
I can't believe this. Reduced to slinging beers in a tourist trap to survive.
They should've just let me die.
That sound...
It sounds so different from last time.
It's so... beautiful!
How?

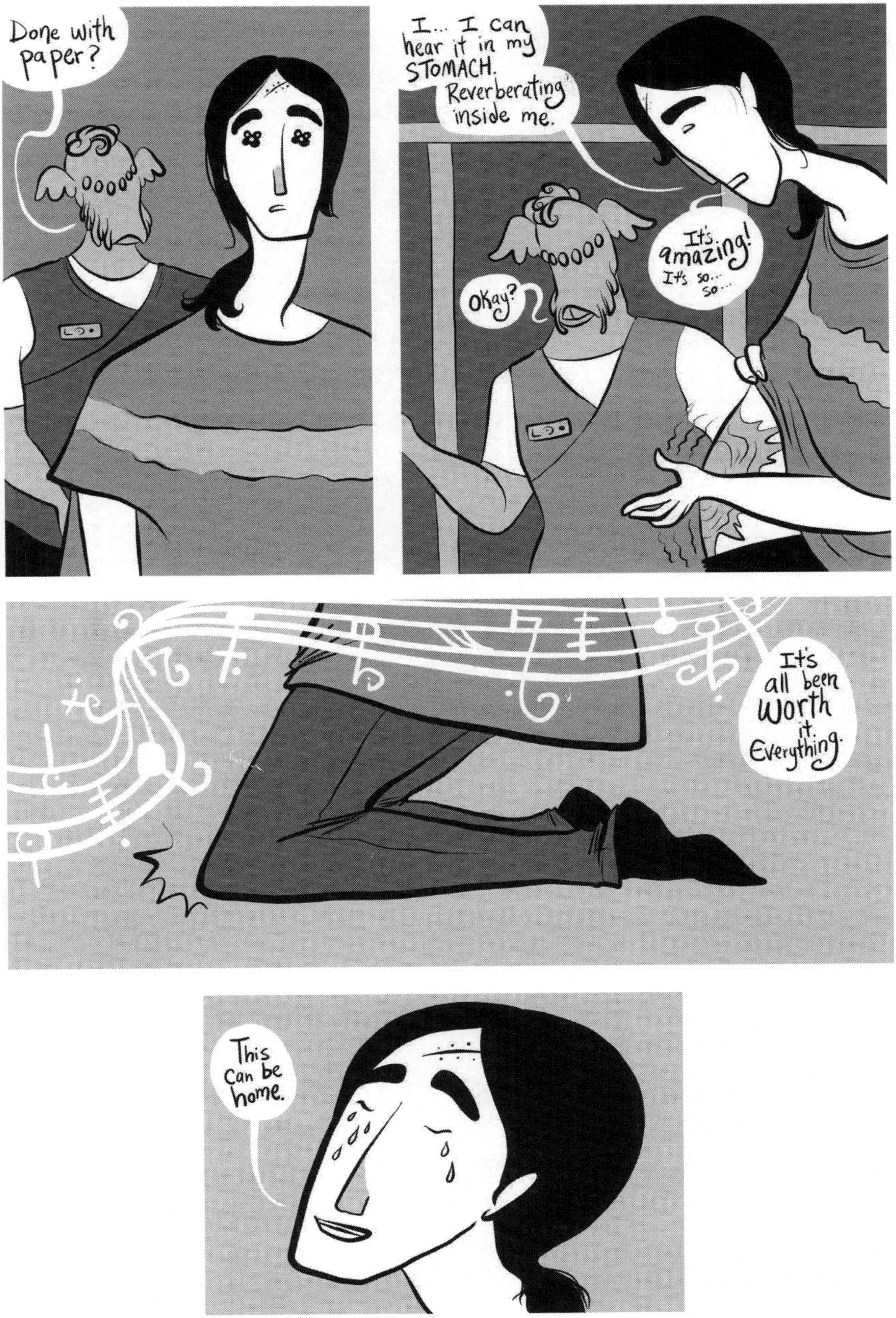
Done with paper?
I... I can hear it in my STOMACH. Reverberating inside me.
Okay?
It's amazing! It's so... so...
It's all been worth it. Everything.
This can be home.

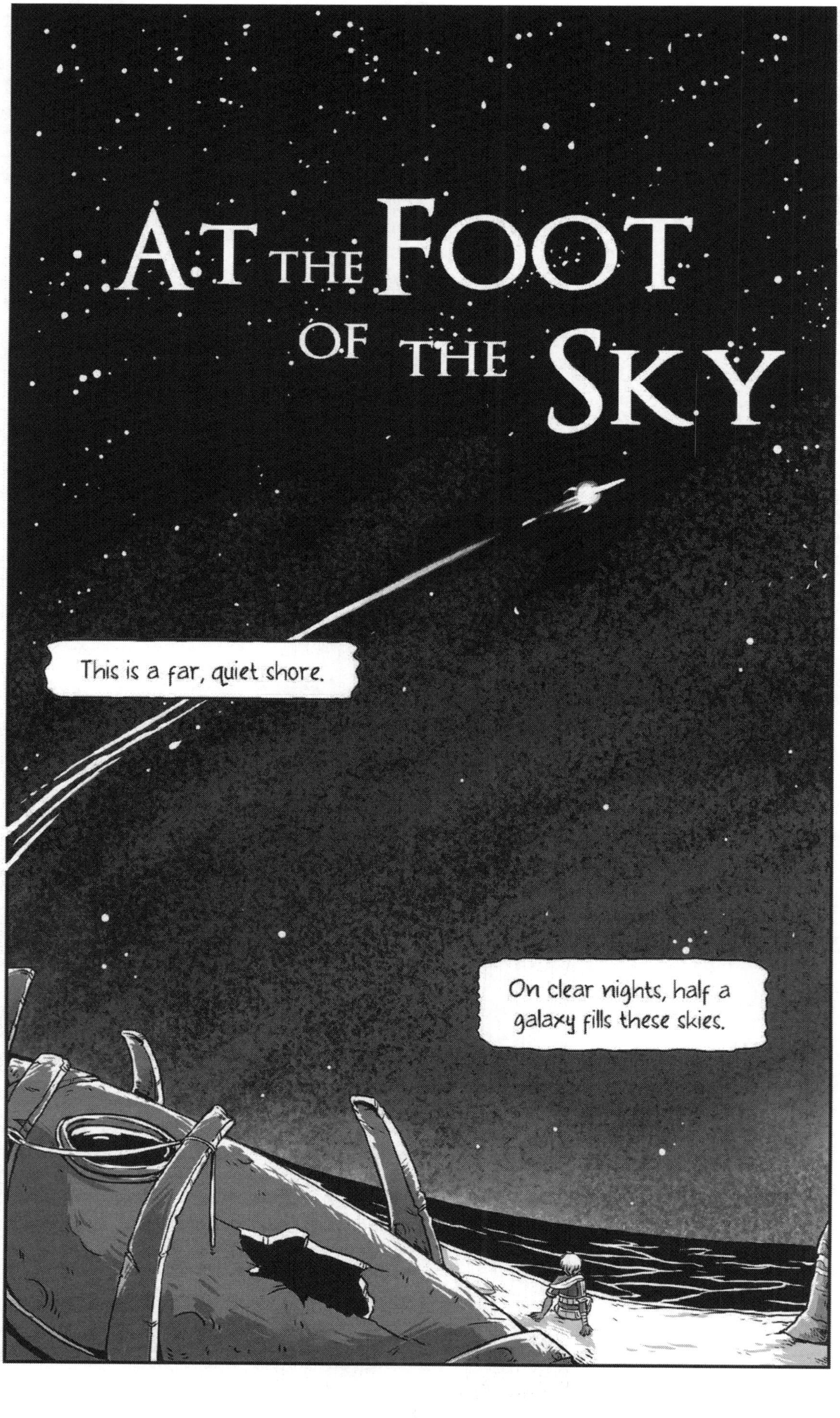
At the Foot of the Sky
This is a far, quiet shore.
On clear nights, half a galaxy fills these skies.

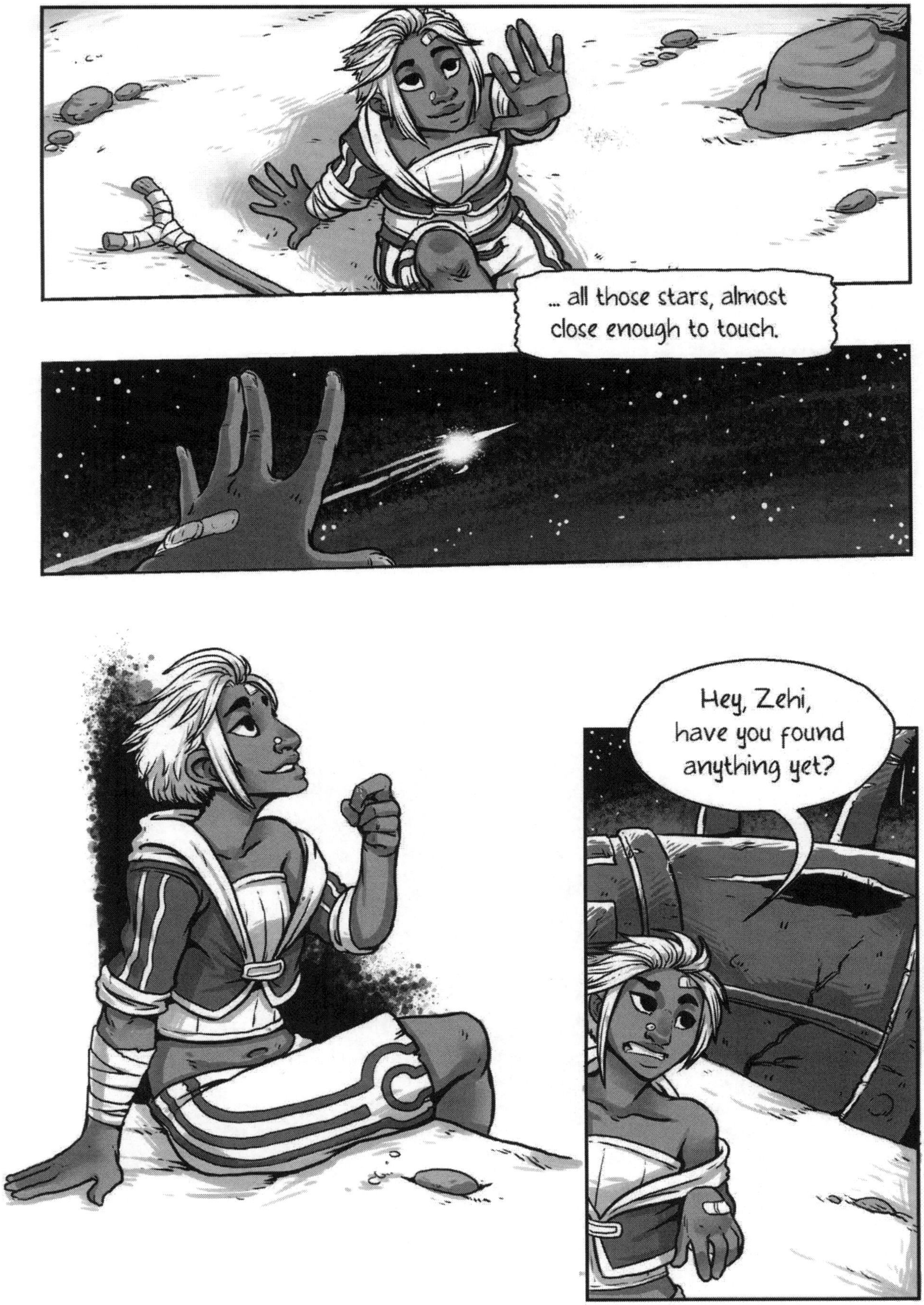
... all those stars, almost close enough to touch.
Hey, Zehi, have you found anything yet?

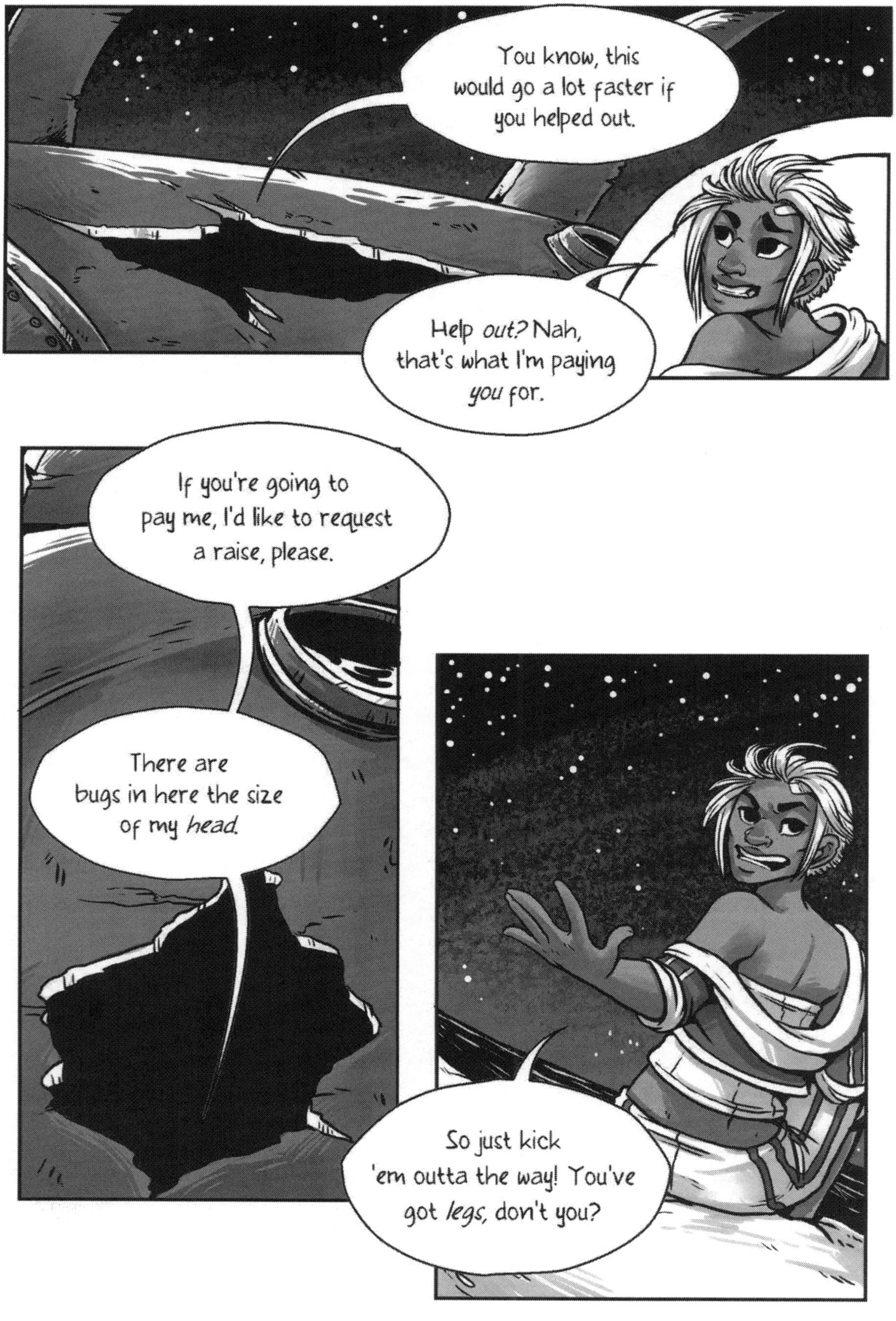
You know, this would go a lot faster if you helped out.
Help *out?* Nah, that's what I'm paying *you* for.
If you're going to pay me, I'd like to request a raise, please.
There are bugs in here the size of my *head*.
So just kick 'em outta the way! You've got *legs*, don't you?

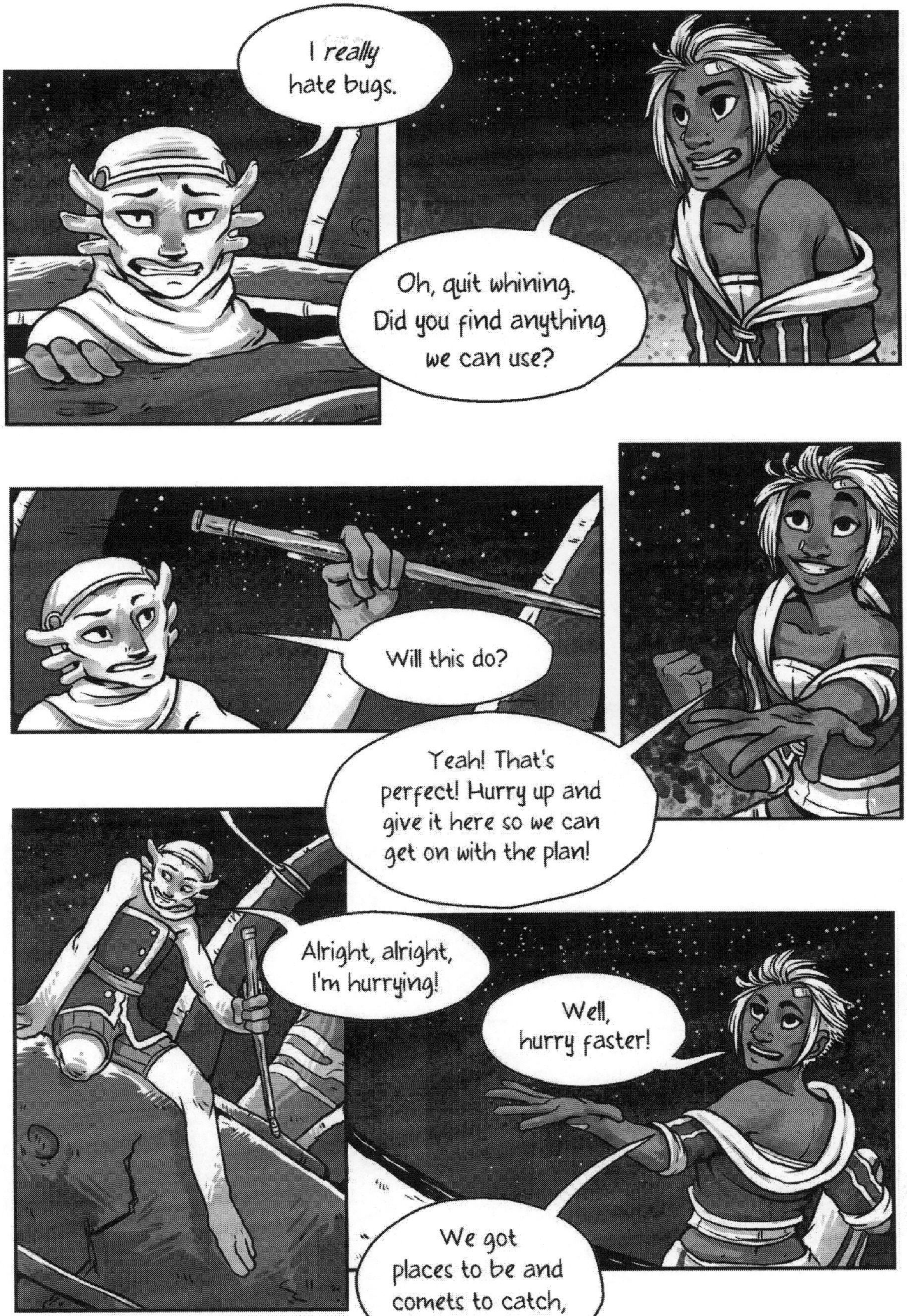
I *really* hate bugs.
Oh, quit whining. Did you find anything we can use?
Will this do?
Yeah! That's perfect! Hurry up and give it here so we can get on with the plan!
Alright, alright, I'm hurrying!
Well, hurry faster!
We got places to be and comets to catch, Zehi!

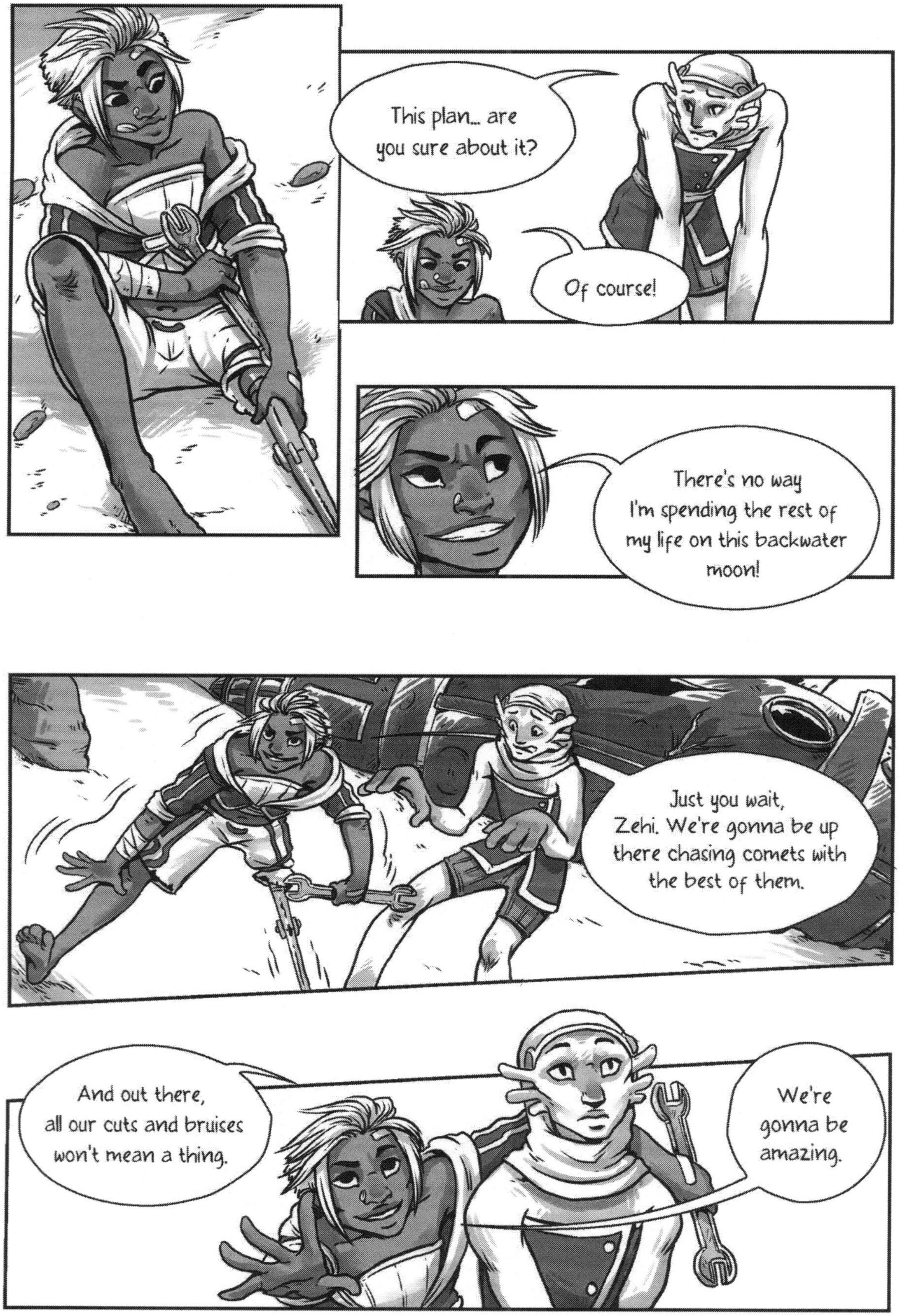
This plan... are you sure about it?
Of course!
There's no way I'm spending the rest of my life on this backwater moon!
Just you wait, Zehi. We're gonna be up there chasing comets with the best of them.
And out there, all our cuts and bruises won't mean a thing.
We're gonna be amazing.

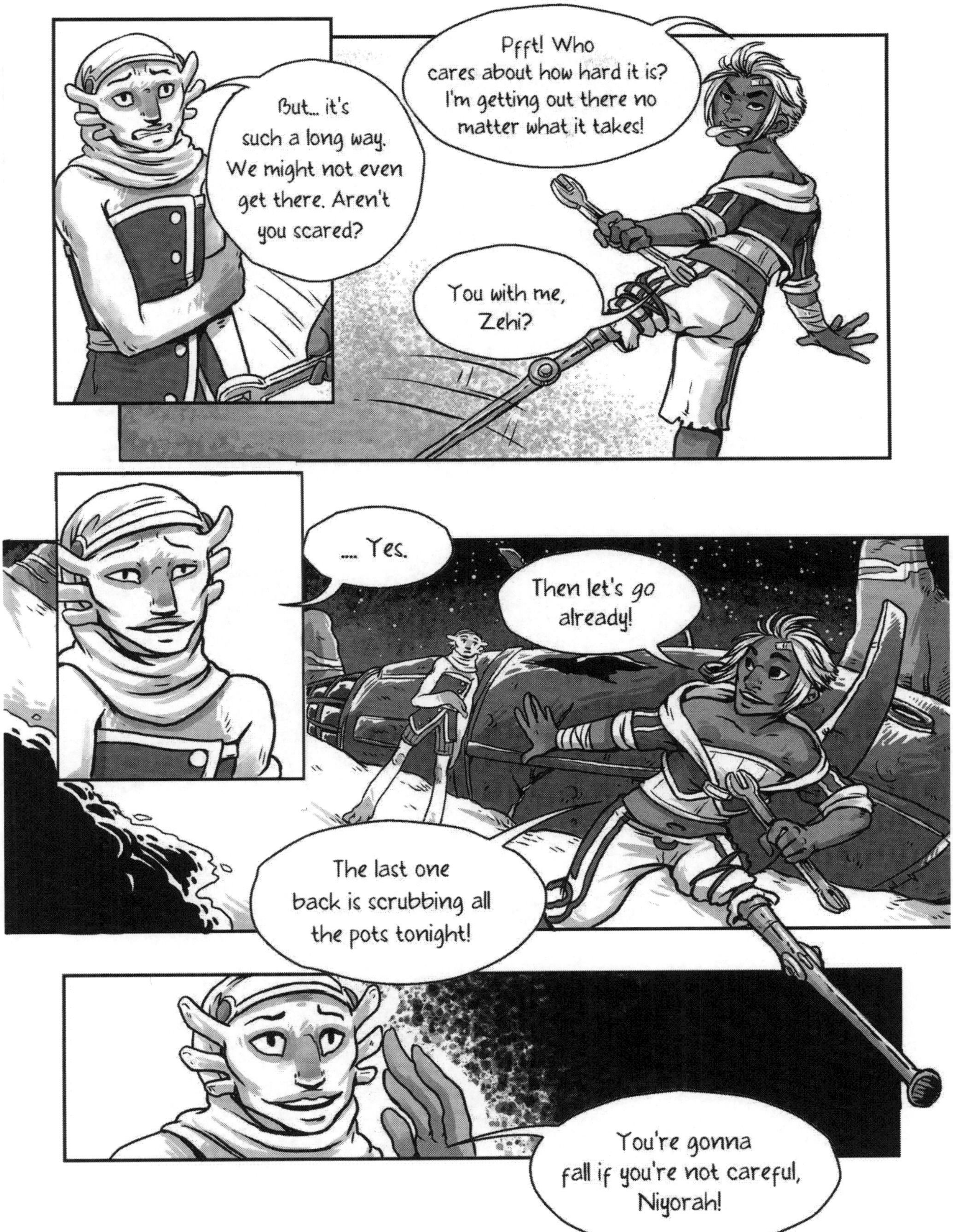
But... it's such a long way. We might not even get there. Aren't you scared?
Pfft! Who cares about how hard it is? I'm getting out there no matter what it takes!
You with me, Zehi?
.... Yes.
Then let's go already!
The last one back is scrubbing all the pots tonight!
You're gonna fall if you're not careful, Niyorah!

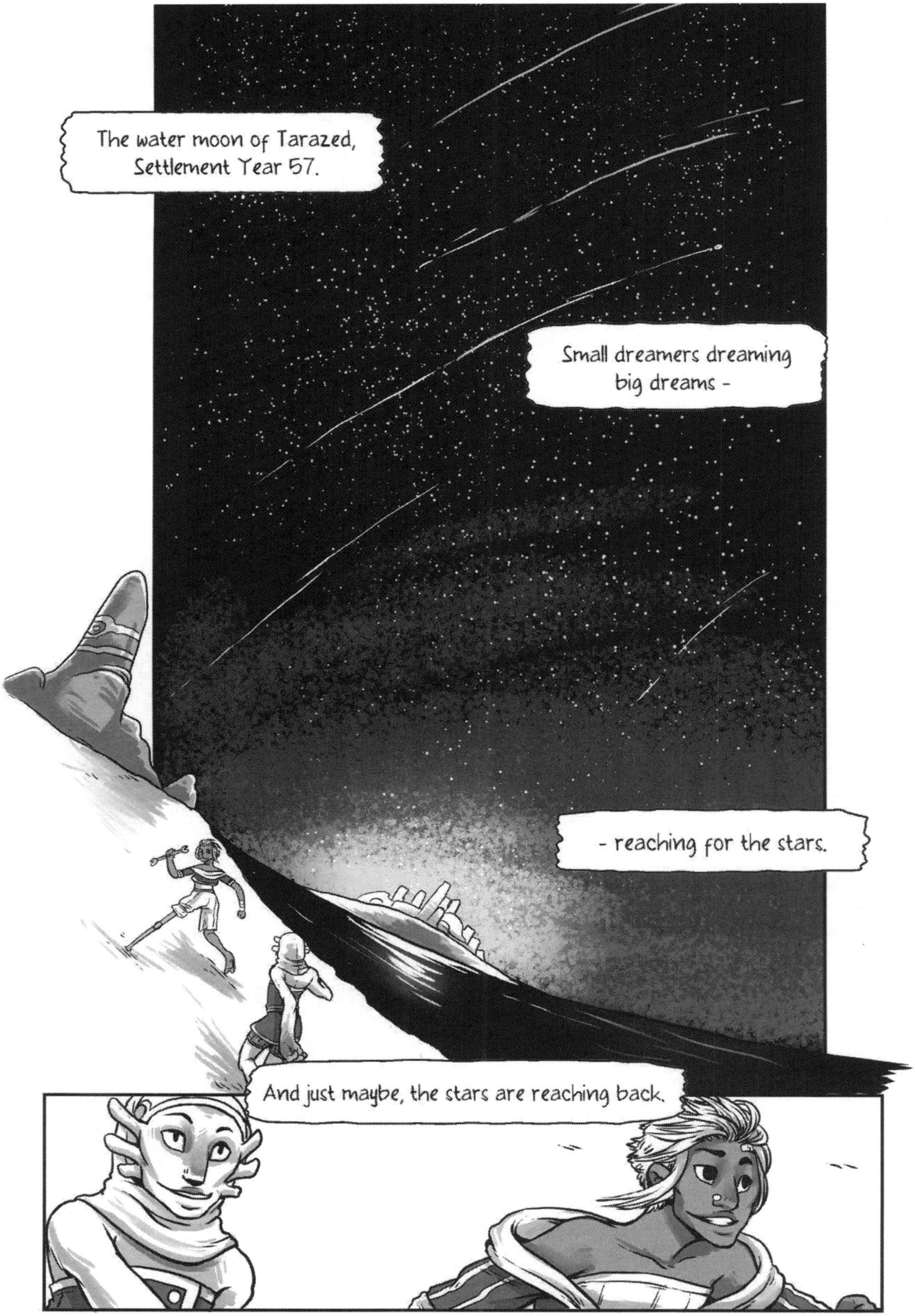
The water moon of Tarazed,
Settlement Year 57.
Small dreamers dreaming
big dreams -
- reaching for the stars.
And just maybe, the stars are reaching back.

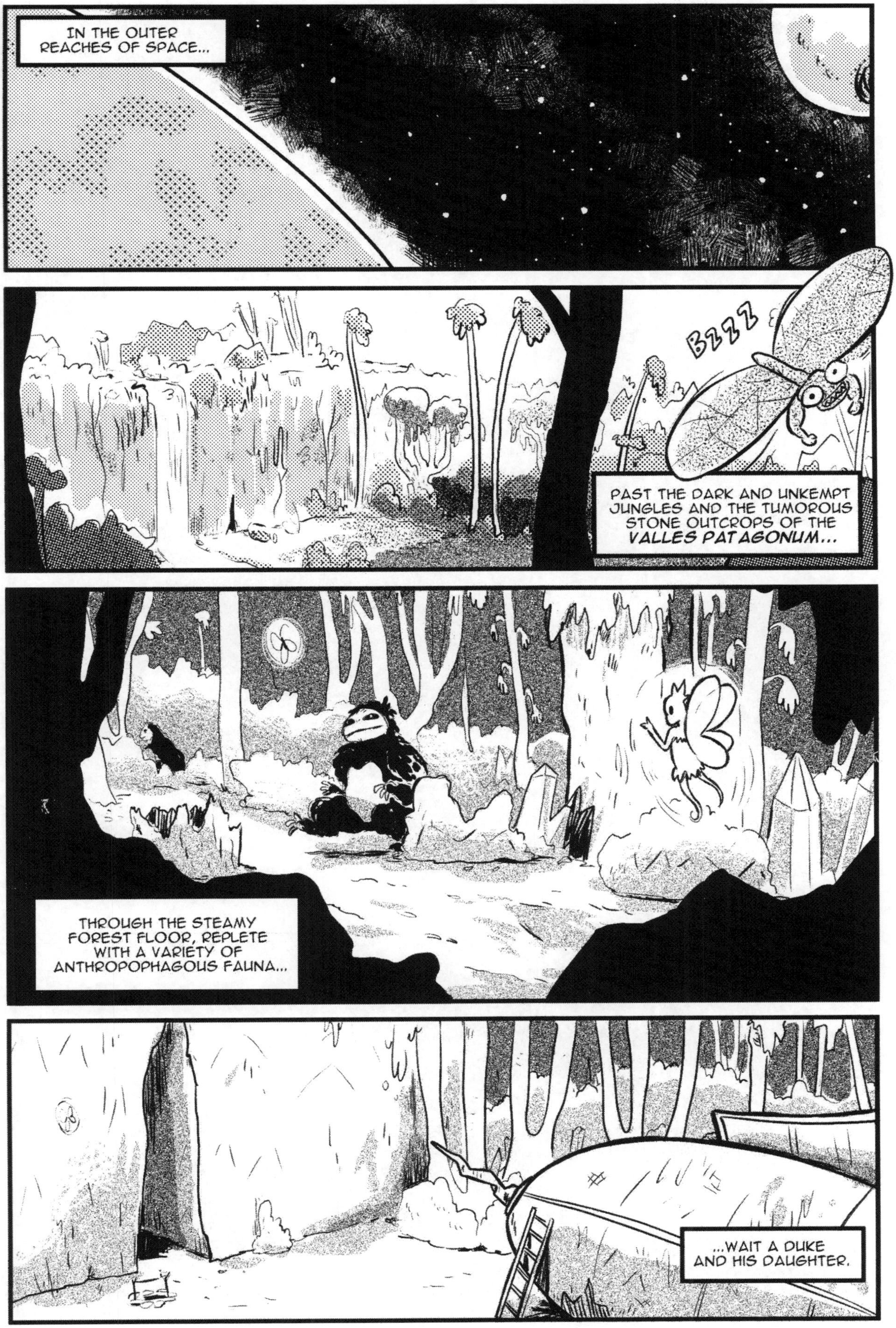
IN THE OUTER REACHES OF SPACE...
BZZZ
PAST THE DARK AND UNKEMPT JUNGLES AND THE TUMOROUS STONE OUTCROPS OF THE *VALLES PATAGONUM*...
THROUGH THE STEAMY FOREST FLOOR, REPLETE WITH A VARIETY OF ANTHROPOPHAGOUS FAUNA...
...WAIT A DUKE AND HIS DAUGHTER.

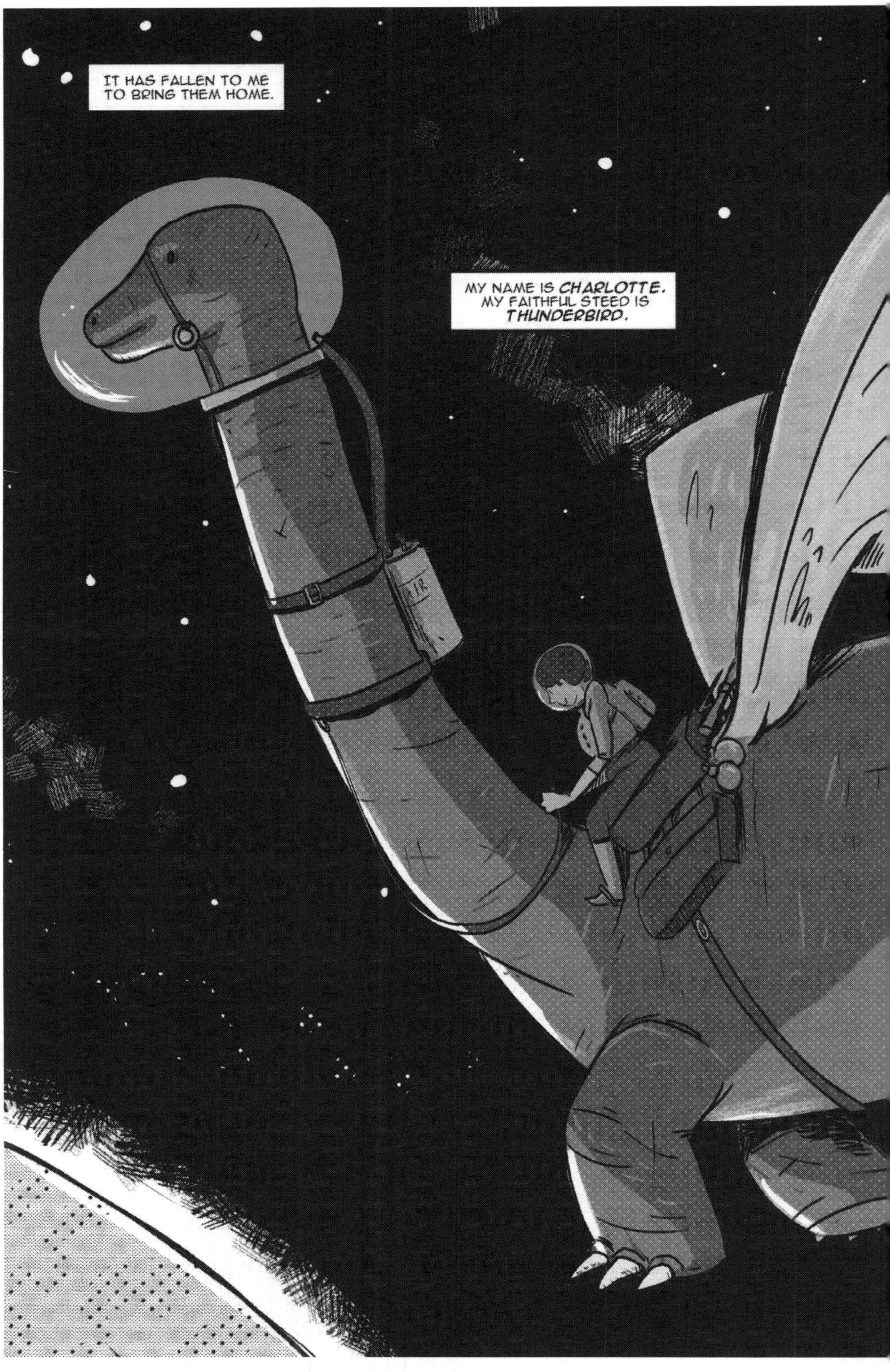
IT HAS FALLEN TO ME TO BRING THEM HOME.
MY NAME IS CHARLOTTE. MY FAITHFUL STEED IS THUNDERBIRD.
AIR

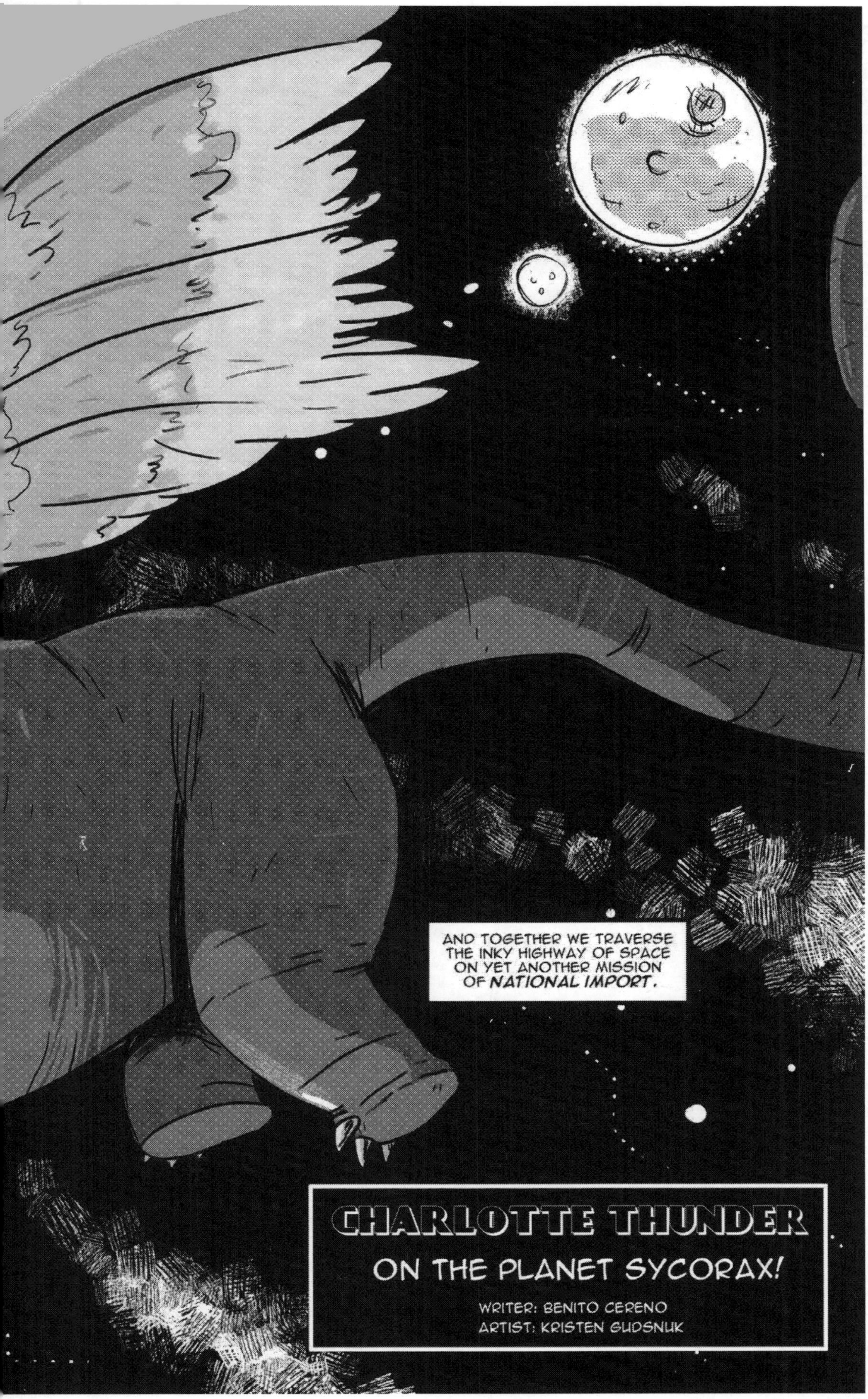
AND TOGETHER WE TRAVERSE THE INKY HIGHWAY OF SPACE ON YET ANOTHER MISSION OF NATIONAL IMPORT.
CHARLOTTE THUNDER
ON THE PLANET SYCORAX!
WRITER: BENITO CERENO
ARTIST: KRISTEN GUDSNUK

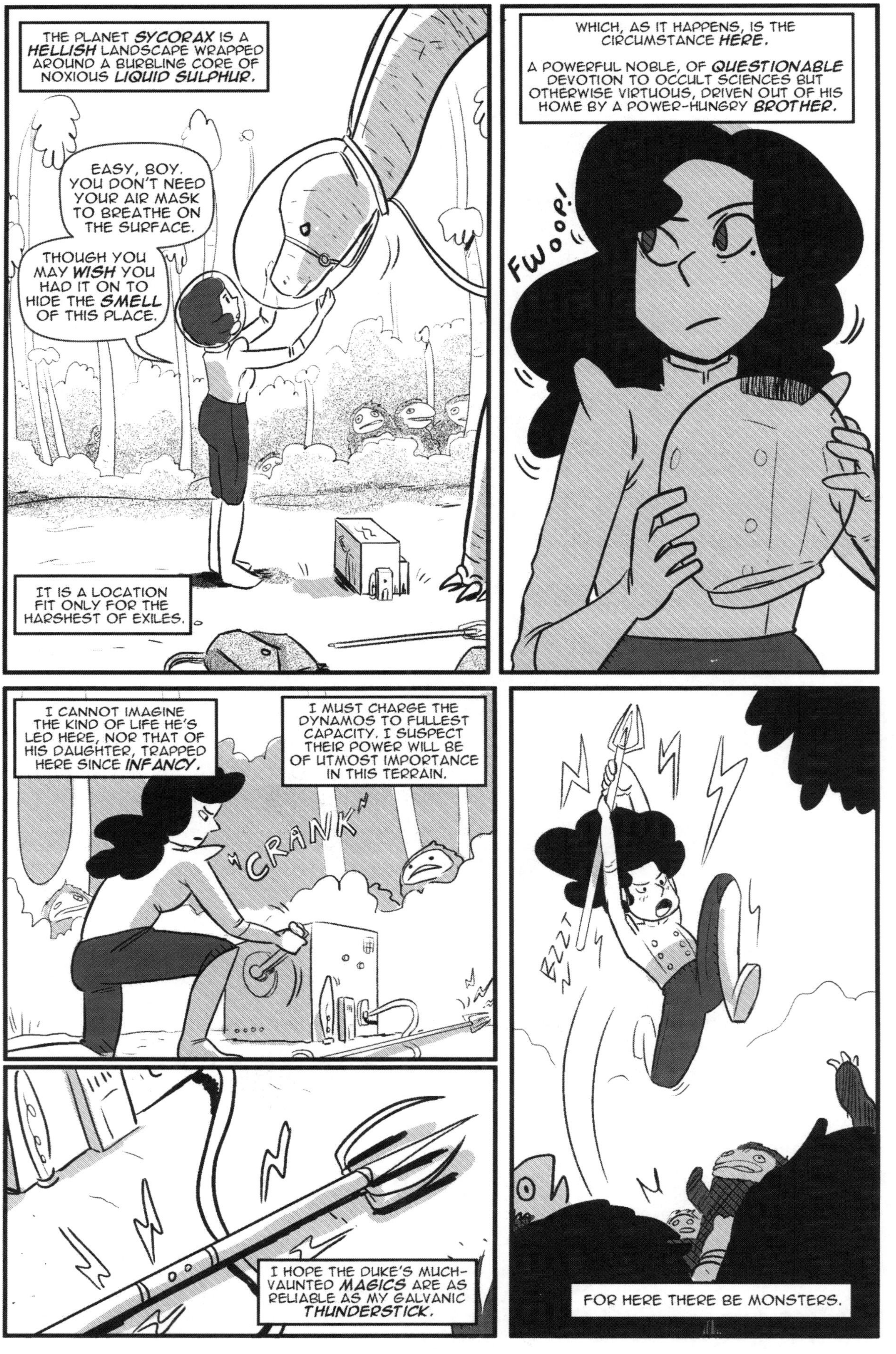
THE PLANET SYCORAX IS A HELLISH LANDSCAPE WRAPPED AROUND A BURBLING CORE OF NOXIOUS LIQUID SULPHUR.
EASY, BOY. YOU DON'T NEED YOUR AIR MASK TO BREATHE ON THE SURFACE.
THOUGH YOU MAY WISH YOU HAD IT ON TO HIDE THE SMELL OF THIS PLACE.
IT IS A LOCATION FIT ONLY FOR THE HARSHEST OF EXILES.
WHICH, AS IT HAPPENS, IS THE CIRCUMSTANCE HERE.
A POWERFUL NOBLE, OF QUESTIONABLE DEVOTION TO OCCULT SCIENCES BUT OTHERWISE VIRTUOUS, DRIVEN OUT OF HIS HOME BY A POWER-HUNGRY BROTHER.
FWOOP!
I CANNOT IMAGINE THE KIND OF LIFE HE'S LED HERE, NOR THAT OF HIS DAUGHTER, TRAPPED HERE SINCE INFANCY.
I MUST CHARGE THE DYNAMOS TO FULLEST CAPACITY. I SUSPECT THEIR POWER WILL BE OF UTMOST IMPORTANCE IN THIS TERRAIN.
CRANK
I HOPE THE DUKE'S MUCH-VAUNTED MAGICS ARE AS RELIABLE AS MY GALVANIC THUNDERSTICK.
BZZT
FOR HERE THERE BE MONSTERS.

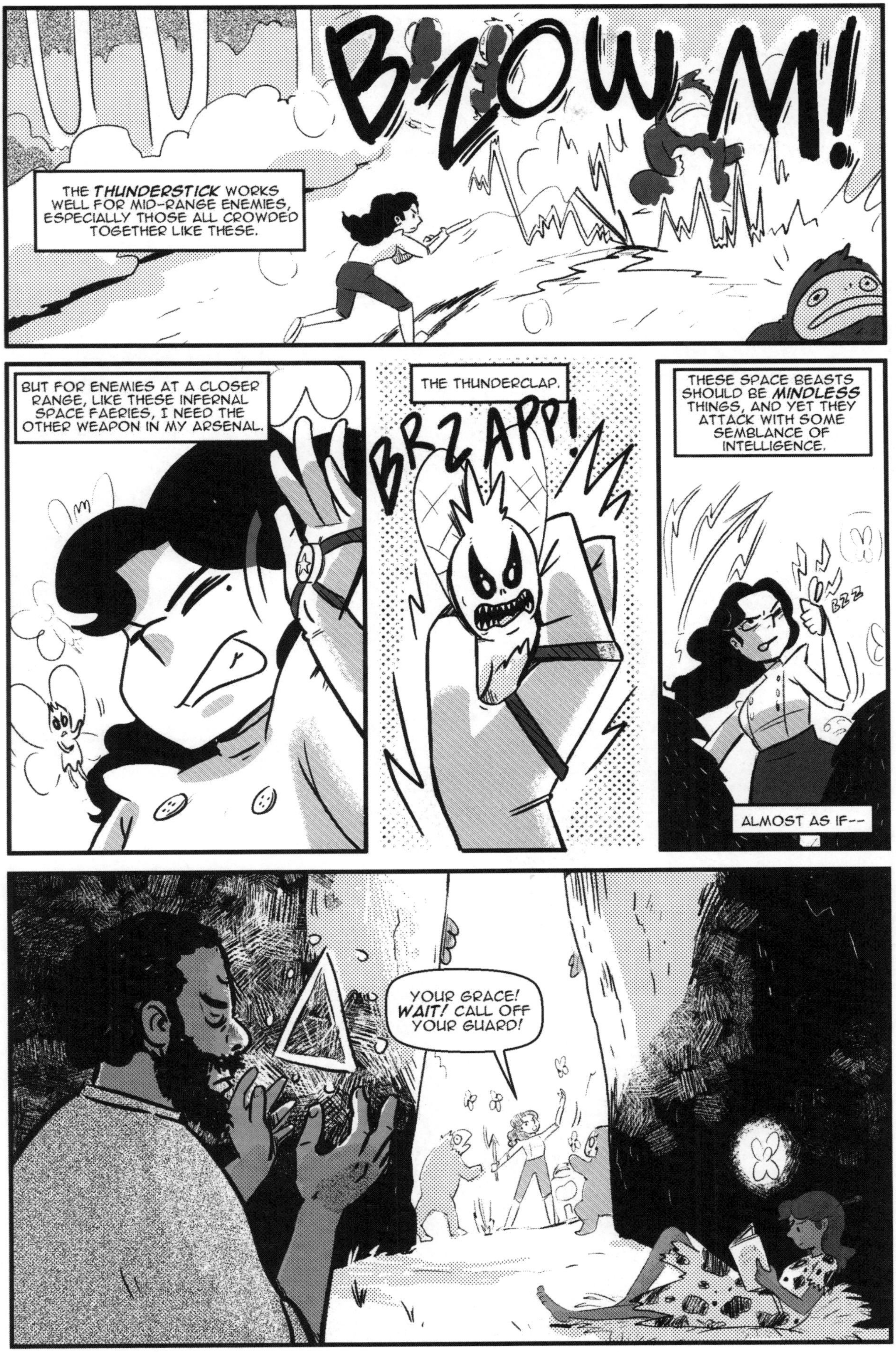
THE THUNDERSTICK WORKS WELL FOR MID-RANGE ENEMIES, ESPECIALLY THOSE ALL CROWDED TOGETHER LIKE THESE.
BZOWM!
BUT FOR ENEMIES AT A CLOSER RANGE, LIKE THESE INFERNAL SPACE FAERIES, I NEED THE OTHER WEAPON IN MY ARSENAL.
THE THUNDERCLAP.
BRZAPP!
THESE SPACE BEASTS SHOULD BE MINDLESS THINGS, AND YET THEY ATTACK WITH SOME SEMBLANCE OF INTELLIGENCE.
BZZ
ALMOST AS IF--
YOUR GRACE! WAIT! CALL OFF YOUR GUARD!

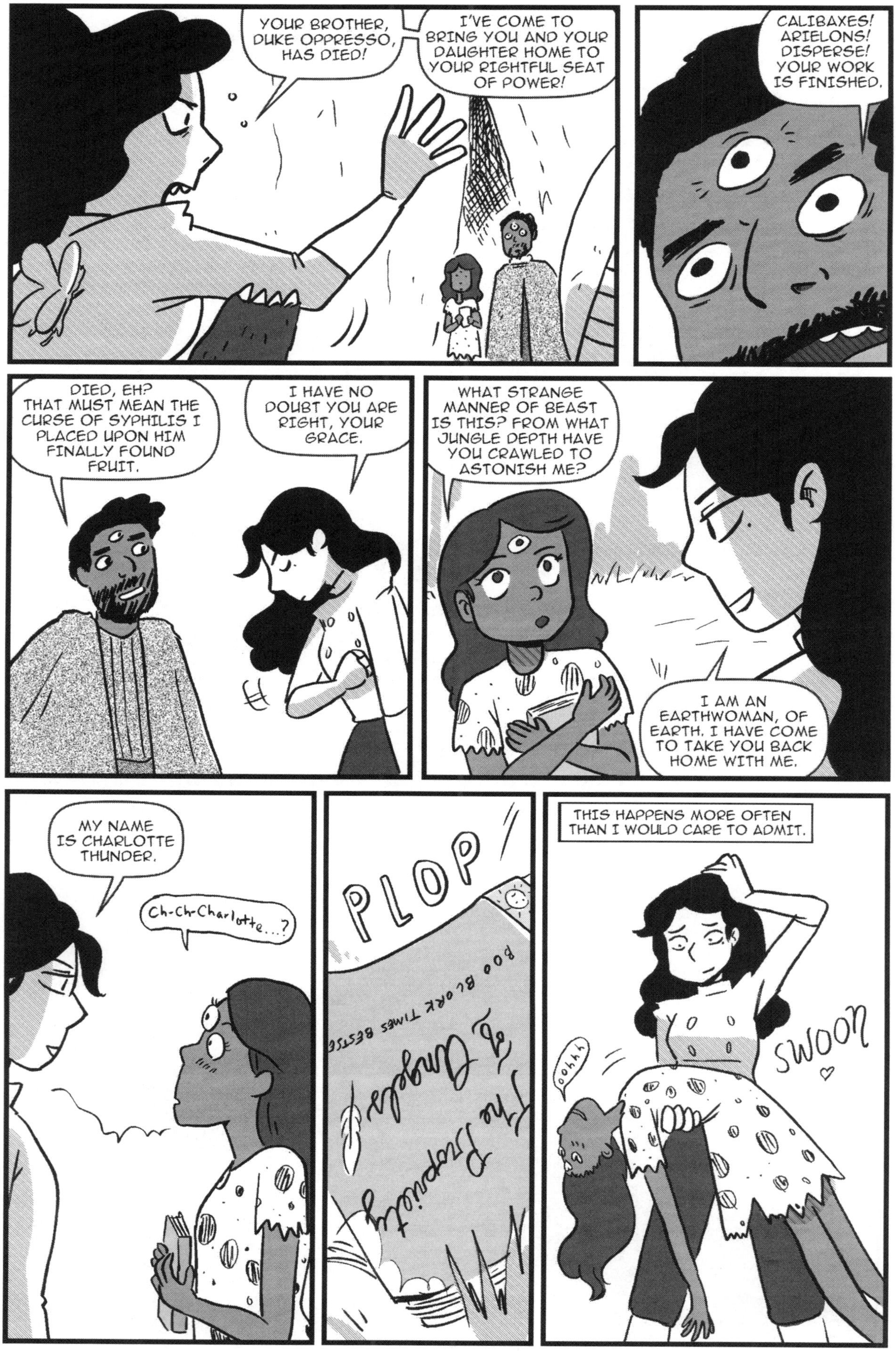
YOUR BROTHER, DUKE OPPRESSO, HAS DIED!
I'VE COME TO BRING YOU AND YOUR DAUGHTER HOME TO YOUR RIGHTFUL SEAT OF POWER!
CALIBAXES! ARIELONS! DISPERSE! YOUR WORK IS FINISHED.
DIED, EH? THAT MUST MEAN THE CURSE OF SYPHILIS I PLACED UPON HIM FINALLY FOUND FRUIT.
I HAVE NO DOUBT YOU ARE RIGHT, YOUR GRACE.
WHAT STRANGE MANNER OF BEAST IS THIS? FROM WHAT JUNGLE DEPTH HAVE YOU CRAWLED TO ASTONISH ME?
I AM AN EARTHWOMAN, OF EARTH. I HAVE COME TO TAKE YOU BACK HOME WITH ME.
MY NAME IS CHARLOTTE THUNDER.
Ch-Ch-Charlotte...?
PLOP
THIS HAPPENS MORE OFTEN THAN I WOULD CARE TO ADMIT.
SWOON

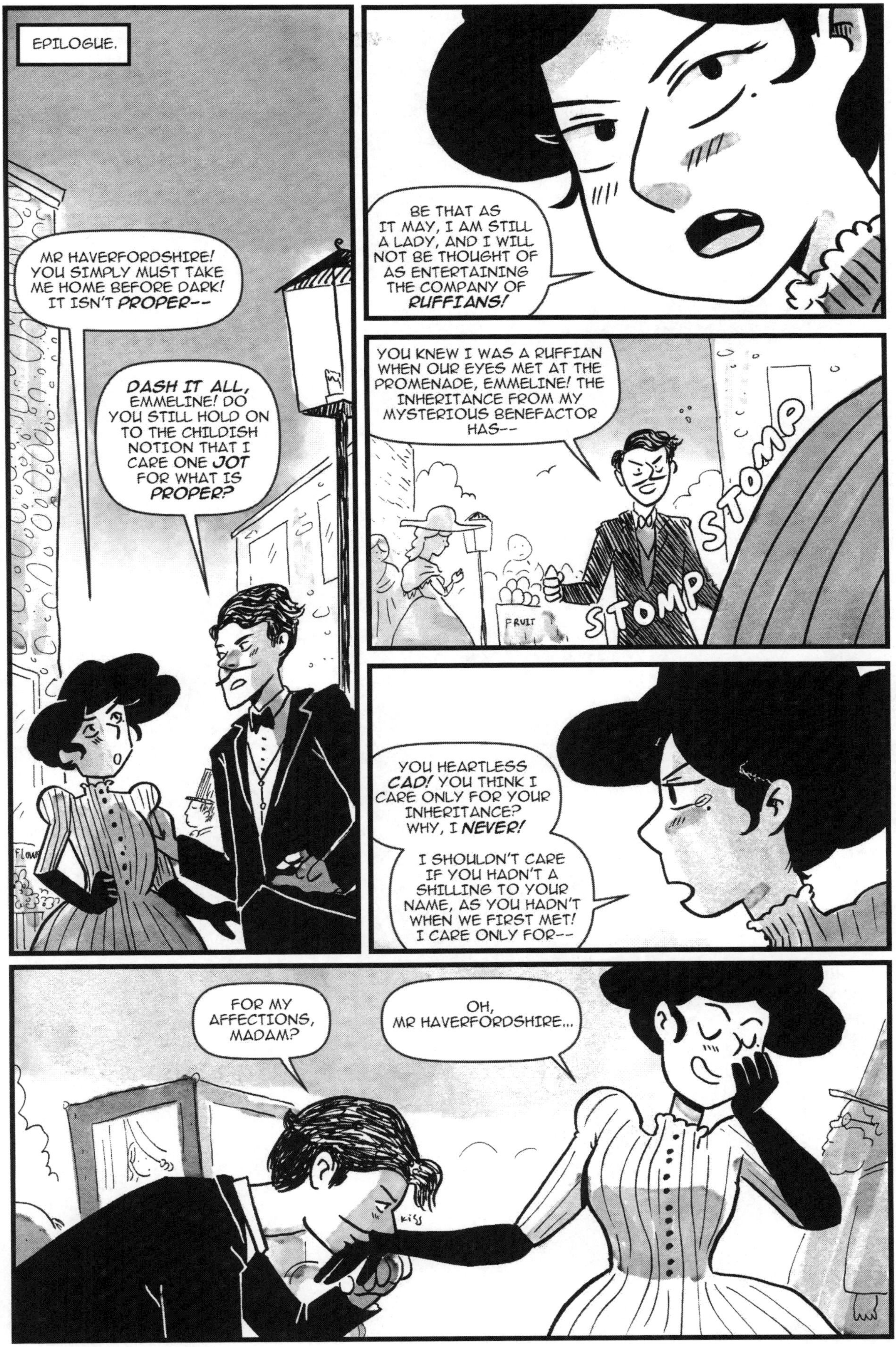
EPILOGUE.
MR HAVERFORDSHIRE! YOU SIMPLY MUST TAKE ME HOME BEFORE DARK! IT ISN'T PROPER--
DASH IT ALL, EMMELINE! DO YOU STILL HOLD ON TO THE CHILDISH NOTION THAT I CARE ONE JOT FOR WHAT IS PROPER?
BE THAT AS IT MAY, I AM STILL A LADY, AND I WILL NOT BE THOUGHT OF AS ENTERTAINING THE COMPANY OF RUFFIANS!
YOU KNEW I WAS A RUFFIAN WHEN OUR EYES MET AT THE PROMENADE, EMMELINE! THE INHERITANCE FROM MY MYSTERIOUS BENEFACTOR HAS--
STOMP
STOMP
STOMP
FRUIT
YOU HEARTLESS CAD! YOU THINK I CARE ONLY FOR YOUR INHERITANCE? WHY, I NEVER!
I SHOULDN'T CARE IF YOU HADN'T A SHILLING TO YOUR NAME, AS YOU HADN'T WHEN WE FIRST MET! I CARE ONLY FOR--
FOR MY AFFECTIONS, MADAM?
OH, MR HAVERFORDSHIRE...
kiss

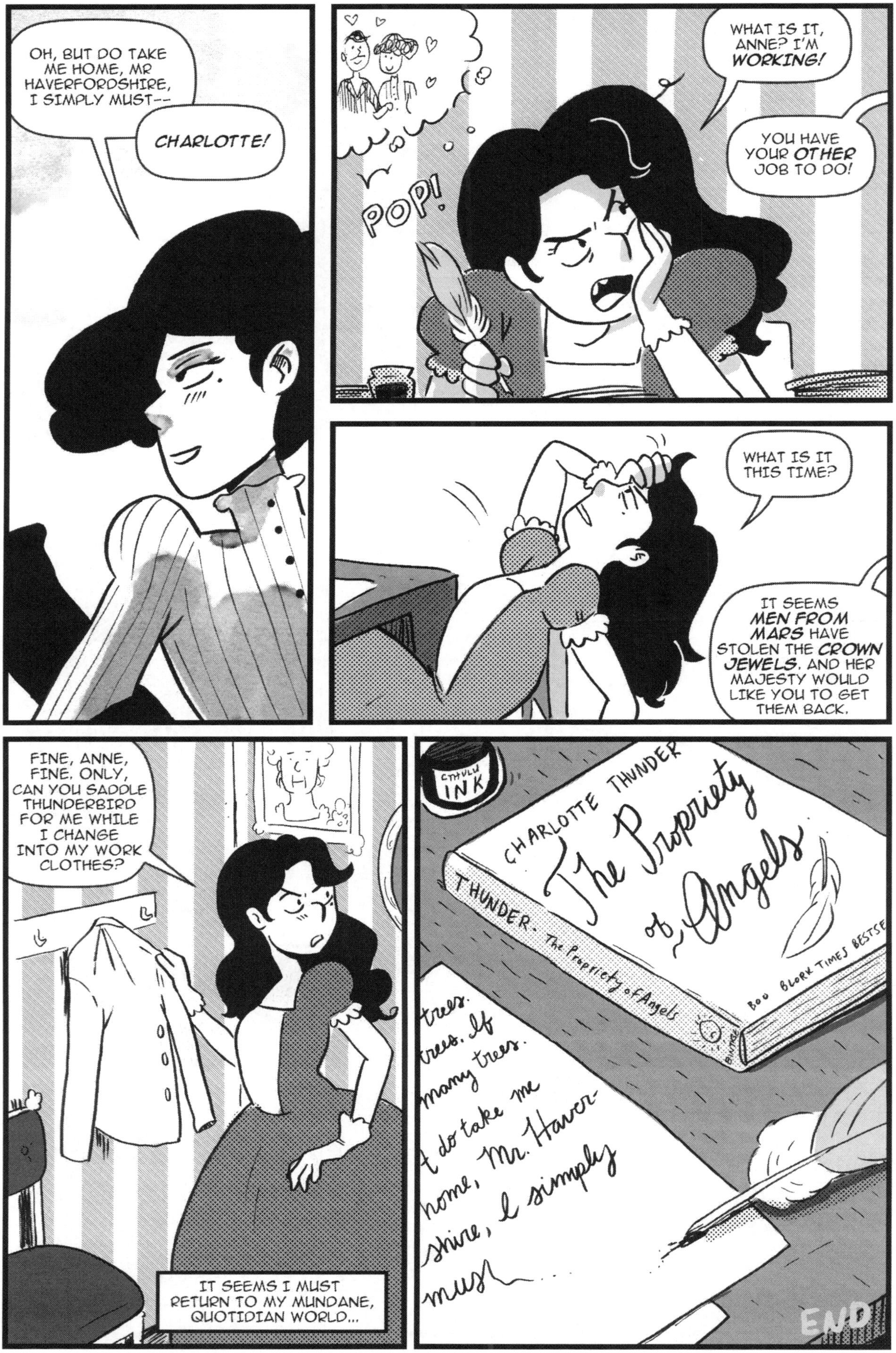
OH, BUT DO TAKE ME HOME, MR HAVERFORDSHIRE, I SIMPLY MUST--
CHARLOTTE!
POP!
WHAT IS IT, ANNE? I'M WORKING!
YOU HAVE YOUR OTHER JOB TO DO!
WHAT IS IT THIS TIME?
IT SEEMS MEN FROM MARS HAVE STOLEN THE CROWN JEWELS, AND HER MAJESTY WOULD LIKE YOU TO GET THEM BACK.
FINE, ANNE, FINE. ONLY, CAN YOU SADDLE THUNDERBIRD FOR ME WHILE I CHANGE INTO MY WORK CLOTHES?
IT SEEMS I MUST RETURN TO MY MUNDANE, QUOTIDIAN WORLD...
CTHULU INK
CHARLOTTE THUNDER
The Propriety of Angels
THUNDER - The Propriety of Angels
trees. trees. If many trees. I do take me home, Mr. Haver-shire, I simply must
END

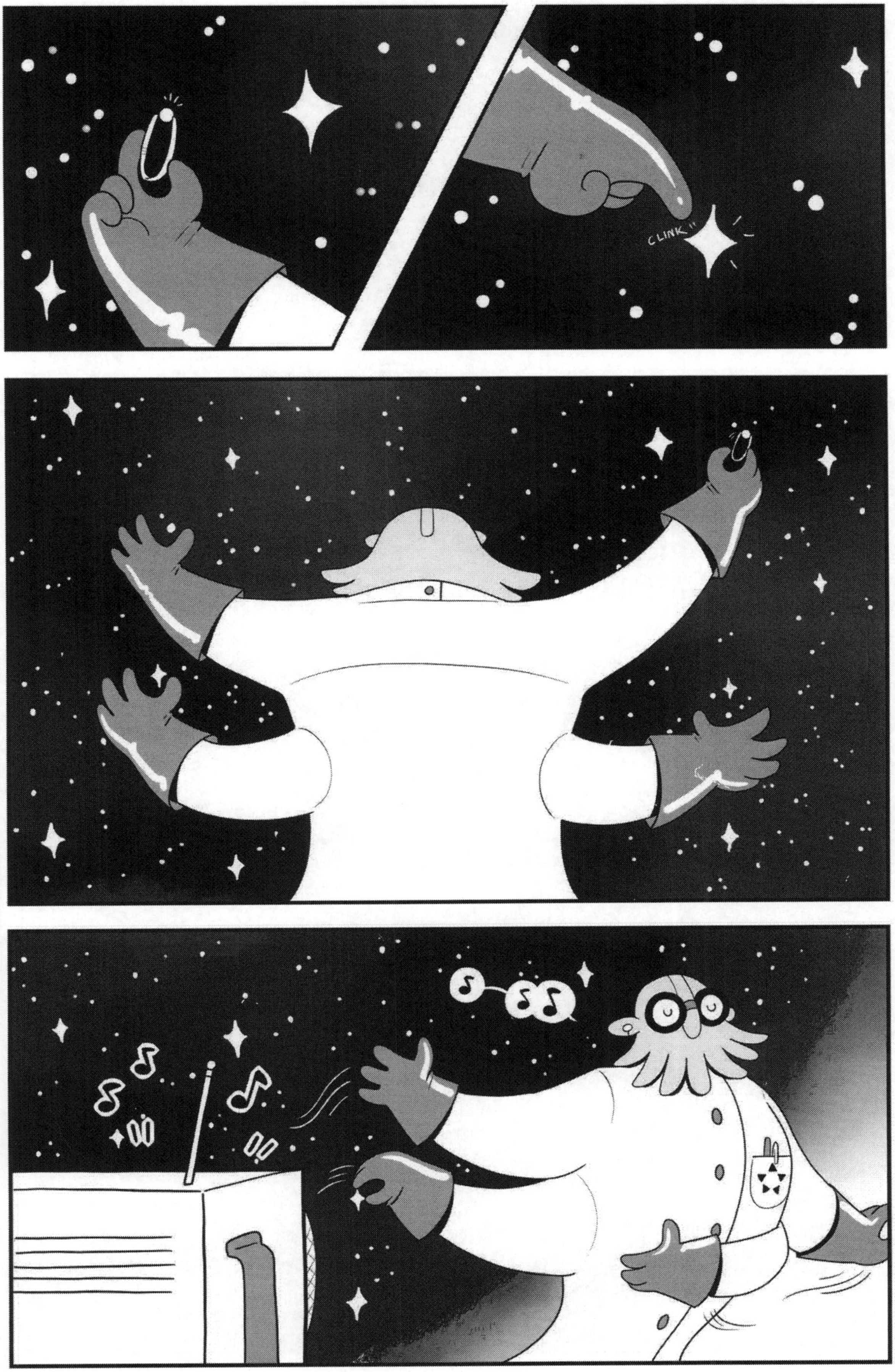
CLINK

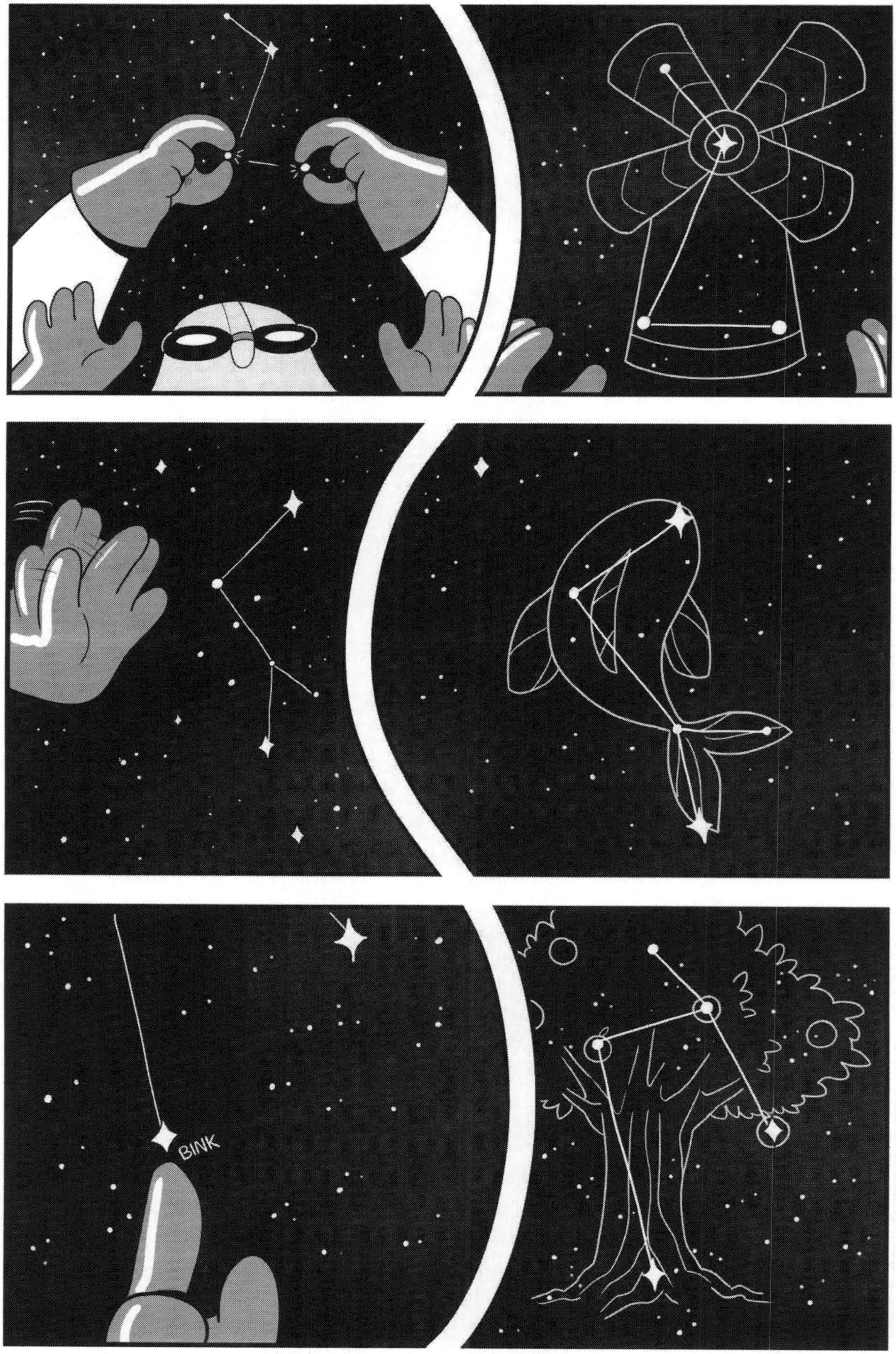
BINK

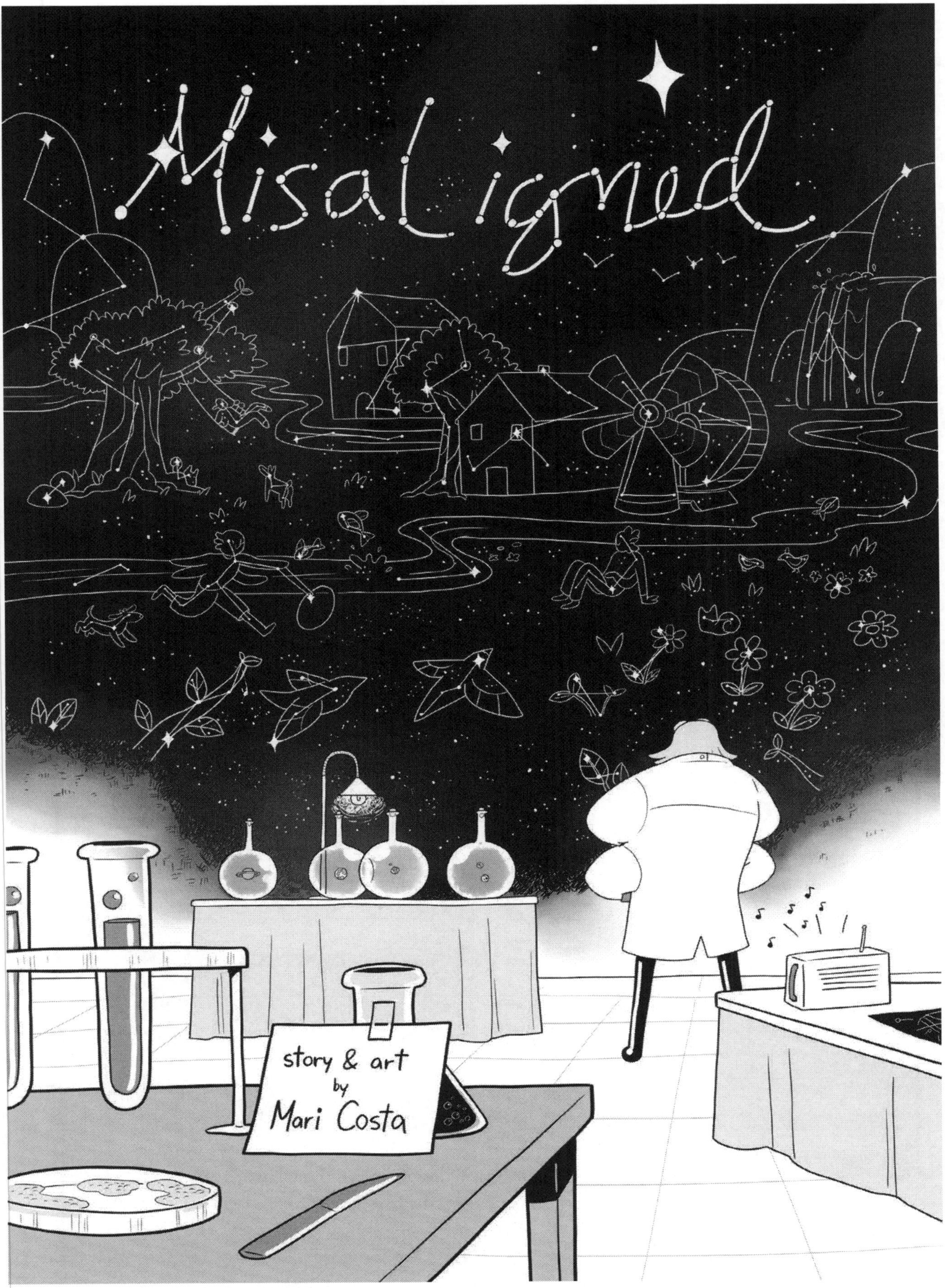
Misaligned
story & art
by
Mari Costa

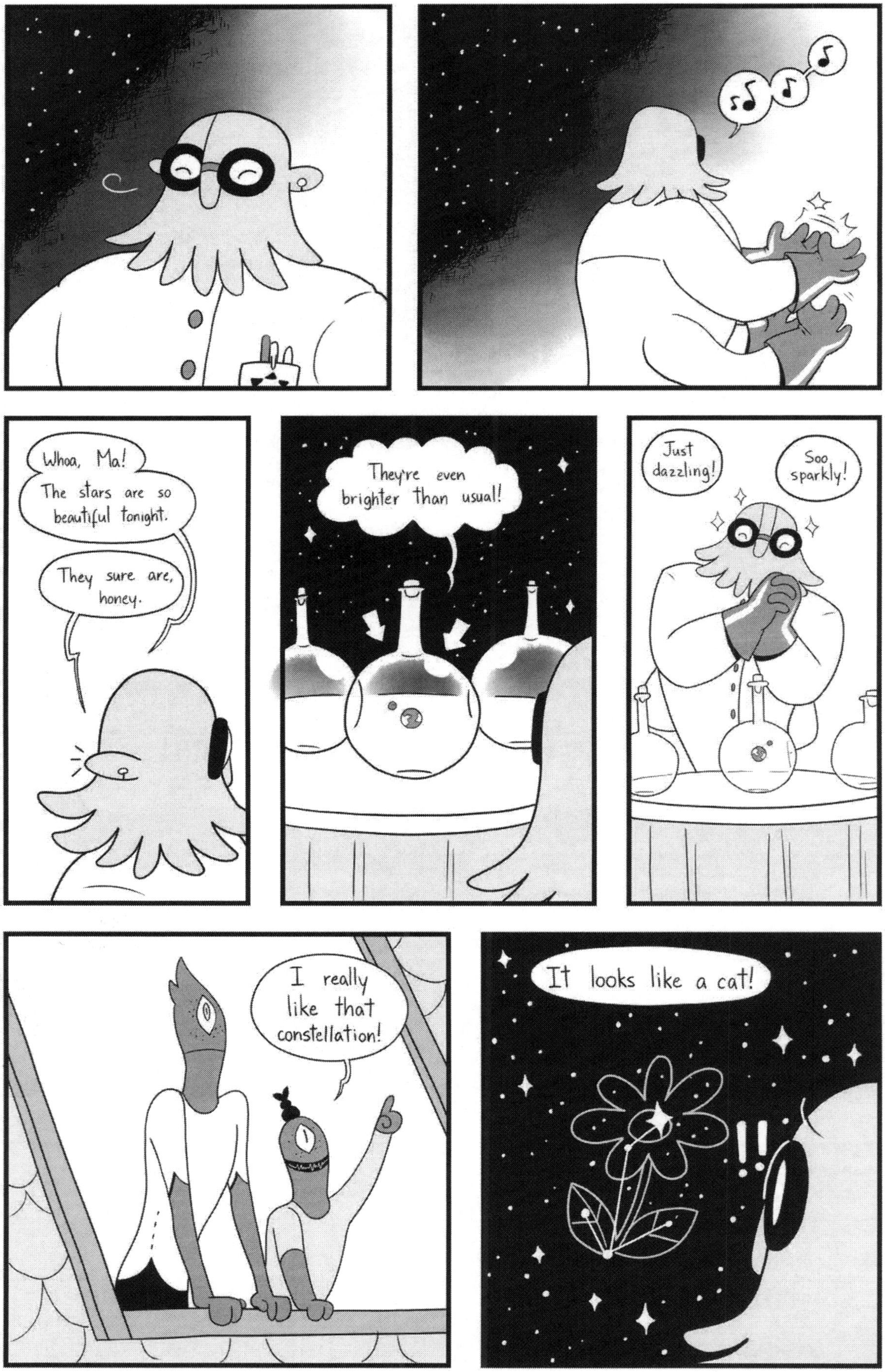
Whoa, Ma!
The stars are so beautiful tonight.
They sure are, honey.
They're even brighter than usual!
Just dazzling!
Soo sparkly!
I really like that constellation!
It looks like a cat!
!!

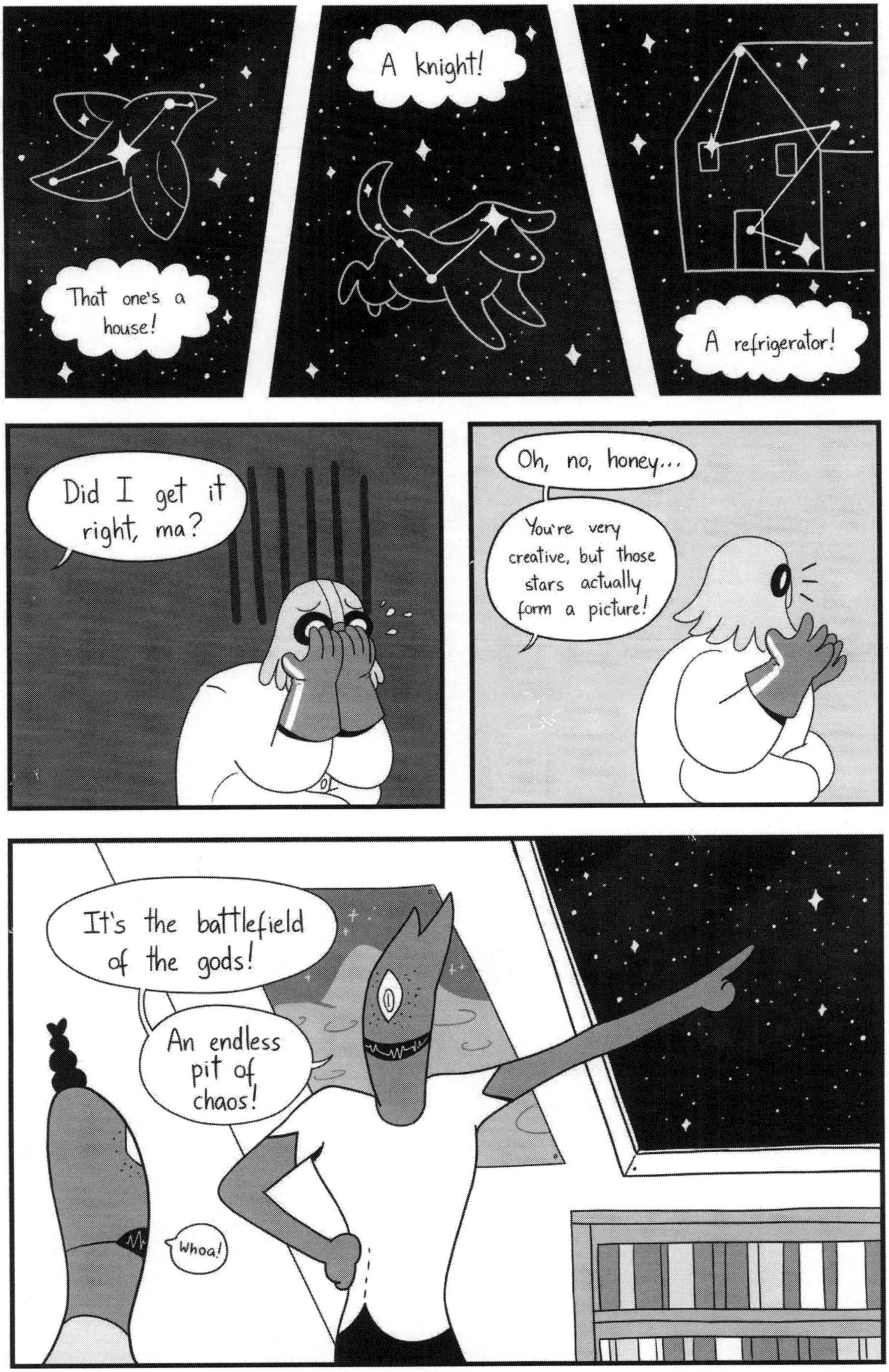
That one's a house!
A knight!
A refrigerator!
Did I get it right, ma?
Oh, no, honey...
You're very creative, but those stars actually form a picture!
It's the battlefield of the gods!
An endless pit of chaos!
Whoa!

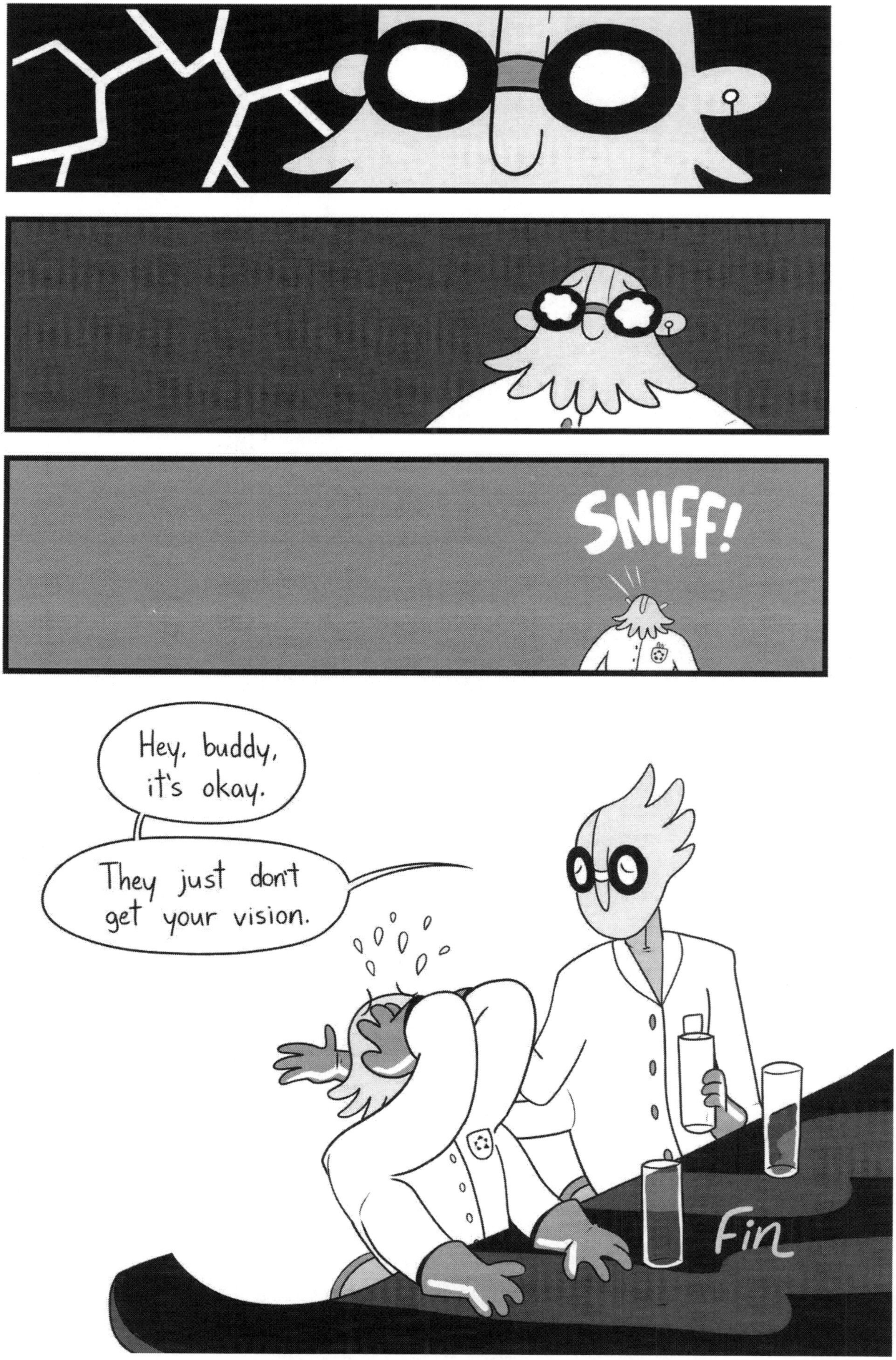
SNIFF!
Hey, buddy, it's okay.
They just don't get your vision.
Fin

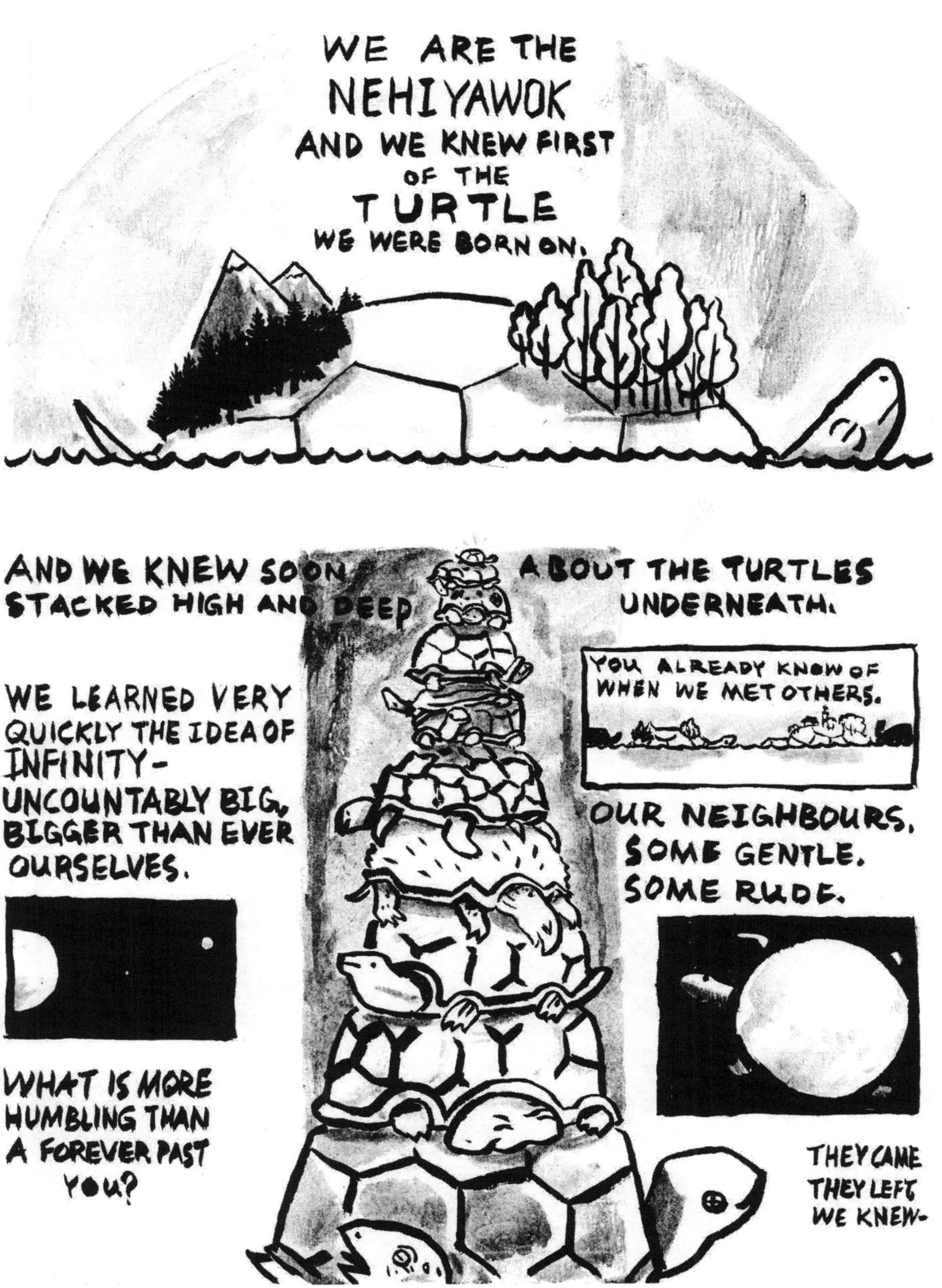
WE ARE THE
NEHIYAWOK
AND WE KNEW FIRST
OF THE
TURTLE
WE WERE BORN ON.
AND WE KNEW SOON ABOUT THE TURTLES
STACKED HIGH AND DEEP UNDERNEATH.
WE LEARNED VERY QUICKLY THE IDEA OF INFINITY- UNCOUNTABLY BIG, BIGGER THAN EVER OURSELVES.
WHAT IS MORE HUMBLING THAN A FOREVER PAST YOU?
YOU ALREADY KNOW OF WHEN WE MET OTHERS.
OUR NEIGHBOURS. SOME GENTLE. SOME RUDE.
THEY CAME THEY LEFT WE KNEW-

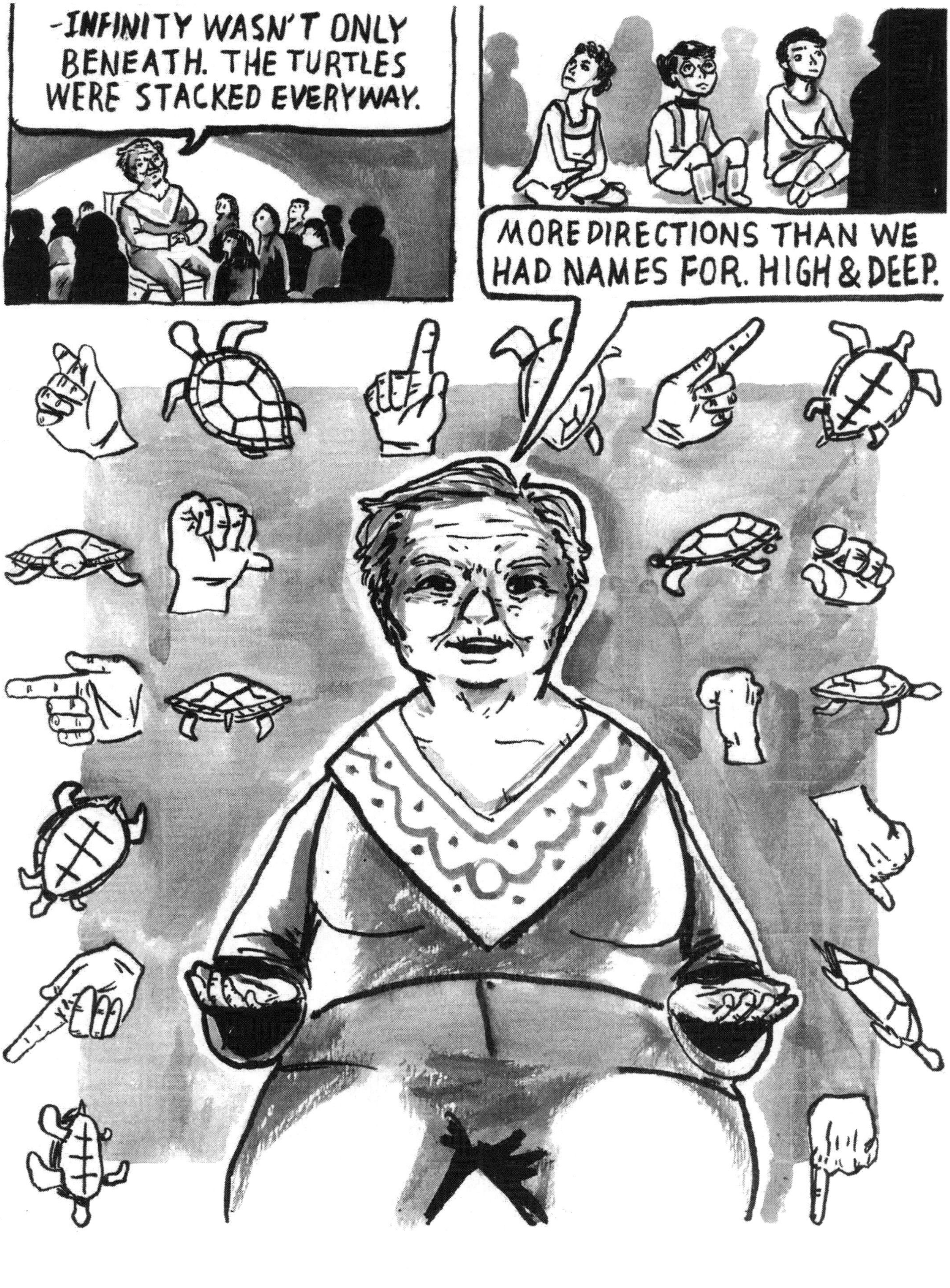
-INFINITY WASN'T ONLY BENEATH. THE TURTLES WERE STACKED EVERYWAY.
MORE DIRECTIONS THAN WE HAD NAMES FOR. HIGH & DEEP.

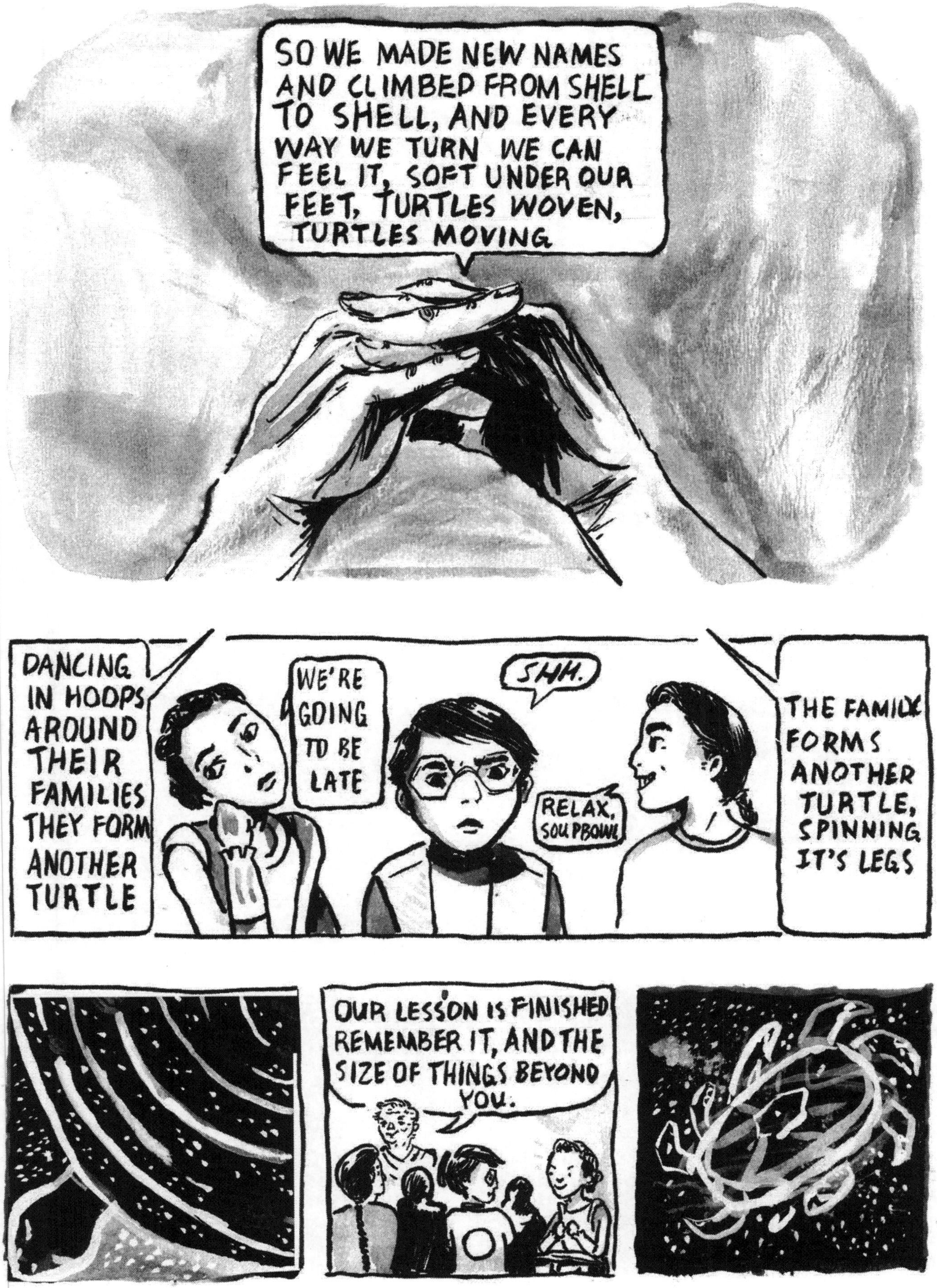
SO WE MADE NEW NAMES AND CLIMBED FROM SHELL TO SHELL, AND EVERY WAY WE TURN WE CAN FEEL IT, SOFT UNDER OUR FEET, TURTLES WOVEN, TURTLES MOVING
DANCING IN HOOPS AROUND THEIR FAMILIES THEY FORM ANOTHER TURTLE
WE'RE GOING TO BE LATE
SHH.
RELAX, SOUPBOWL
THE FAMILY FORMS ANOTHER TURTLE, SPINNING IT'S LEGS
OUR LESSON IS FINISHED REMEMBER IT, AND THE SIZE OF THINGS BEYOND YOU.

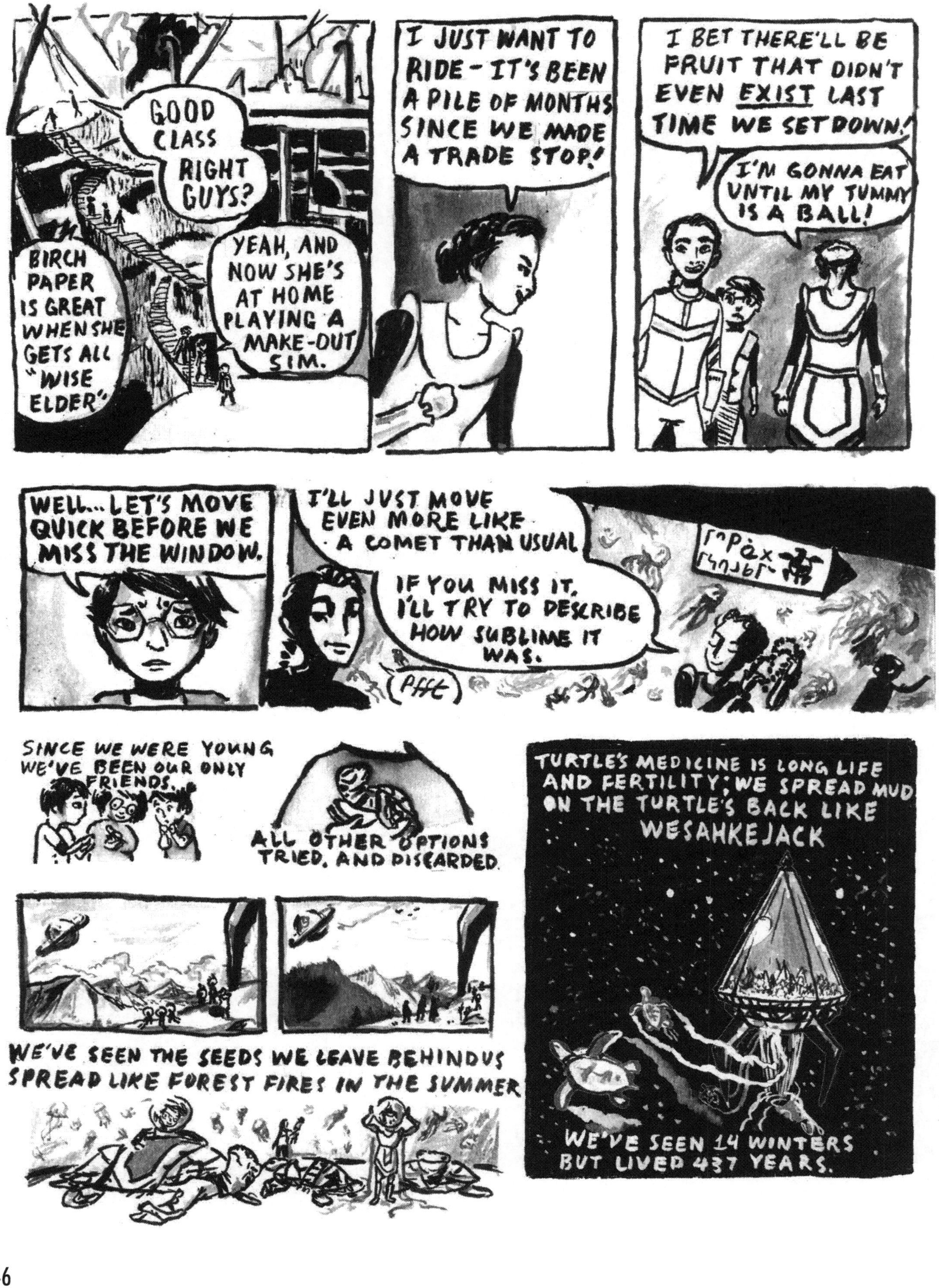
GOOD CLASS RIGHT GUYS?
BIRCH PAPER IS GREAT WHEN SHE GETS ALL "WISE ELDER"
YEAH, AND NOW SHE'S AT HOME PLAYING A MAKE-OUT SIM.
I JUST WANT TO RIDE - IT'S BEEN A PILE OF MONTHS SINCE WE MADE A TRADE STOP!
I BET THERE'LL BE FRUIT THAT DIDN'T EVEN EXIST LAST TIME WE SET DOWN!
I'M GONNA EAT UNTIL MY TUMMY IS A BALL!
WELL... LET'S MOVE QUICK BEFORE WE MISS THE WINDOW.
I'LL JUST MOVE EVEN MORE LIKE A COMET THAN USUAL
IF YOU MISS IT, I'LL TRY TO DESCRIBE HOW SUBLIME IT WAS.
Pfft
SINCE WE WERE YOUNG WE'VE BEEN OUR ONLY FRIENDS.
ALL OTHER OPTIONS TRIED, AND DISCARDED.
TURTLE'S MEDICINE IS LONG LIFE AND FERTILITY; WE SPREAD MUD ON THE TURTLE'S BACK LIKE WESAHKEJACK
WE'VE SEEN THE SEEDS WE LEAVE BEHIND US SPREAD LIKE FOREST FIRES IN THE SUMMER
WE'VE SEEN 14 WINTERS BUT LIVED 437 YEARS.

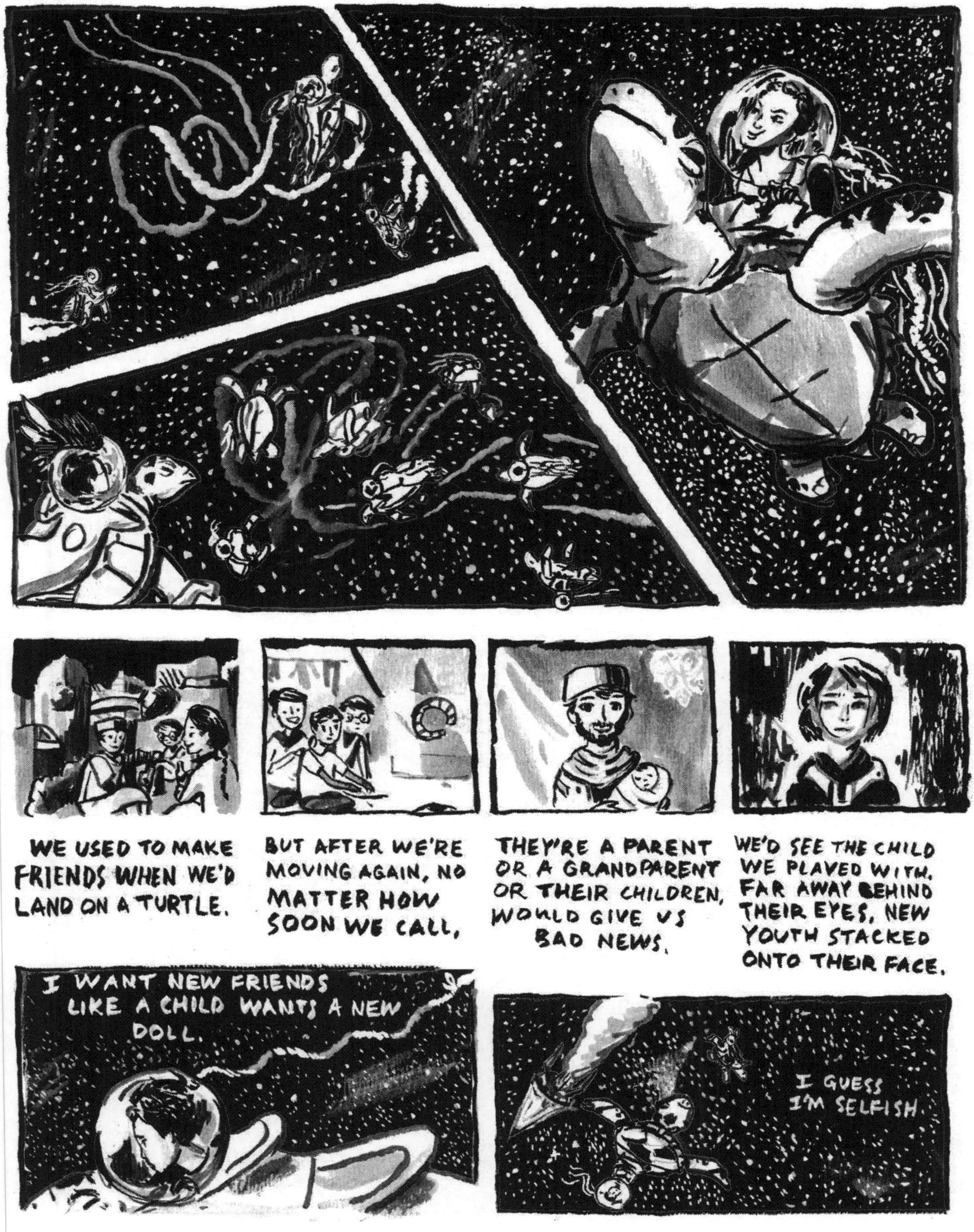

WE USED TO MAKE FRIENDS WHEN WE'D LAND ON A TURTLE.
BUT AFTER WE'RE MOVING AGAIN, NO MATTER HOW SOON WE CALL,
THEY'RE A PARENT OR A GRANDPARENT OR THEIR CHILDREN, WOULD GIVE US BAD NEWS.
WE'D SEE THE CHILD WE PLAYED WITH. FAR AWAY BEHIND THEIR EYES, NEW YOUTH STACKED ONTO THEIR FACE.
I WANT NEW FRIENDS LIKE A CHILD WANTS A NEW DOLL.
I GUESS I'M SELFISH.

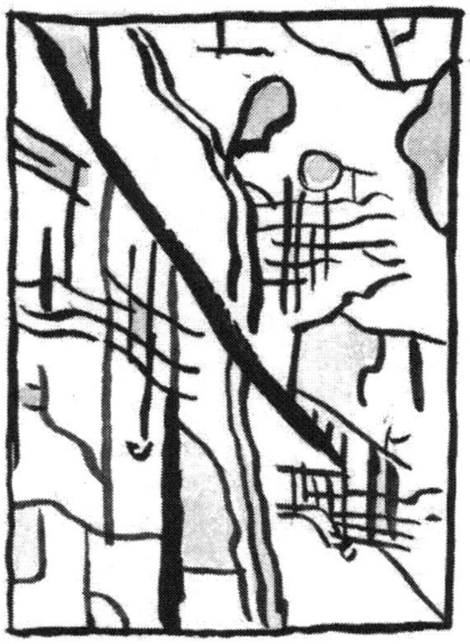

BUT I'M NOT JEALOUS
OF THE PEOPLES
LIVING LIVES ON FLAT MAPS

WE MOVE IN SHAKING WHEELS

RISING, SINKING,
FLOATING
SPINNING

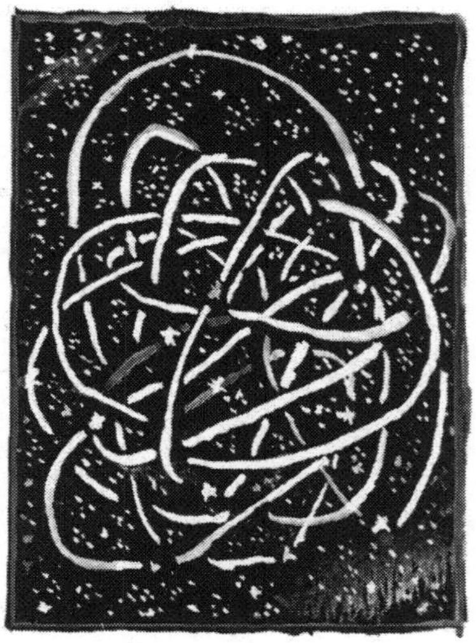

MOVING PROGRESS IN MORE DIRECTIONS THAN THEY HAD NAMES FOR

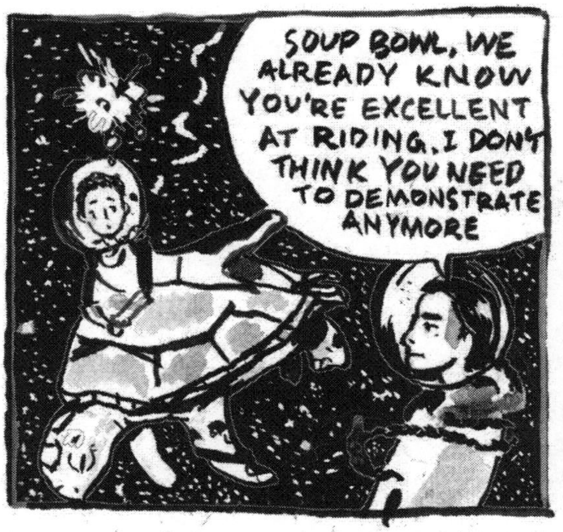
SOUP BOWL, WE ALREADY KNOW YOU'RE EXCELLENT AT RIDING. I DON'T THINK YOU NEED TO DEMONSTRATE ANYMORE

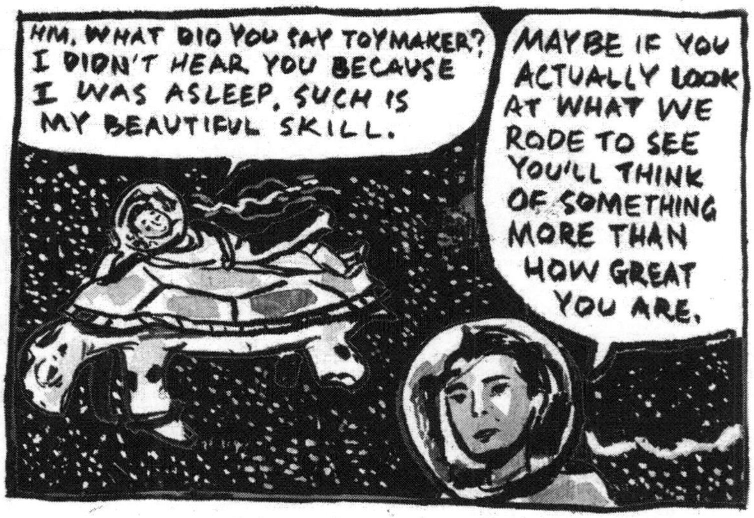
HM, WHAT DID YOU SAY TOYMAKER? I DIDN'T HEAR YOU BECAUSE I WAS ASLEEP, SUCH IS MY BEAUTIFUL SKILL.
MAYBE IF YOU ACTUALLY LOOK AT WHAT WE RODE TO SEE YOU'LL THINK OF SOMETHING MORE THAN HOW GREAT YOU ARE.

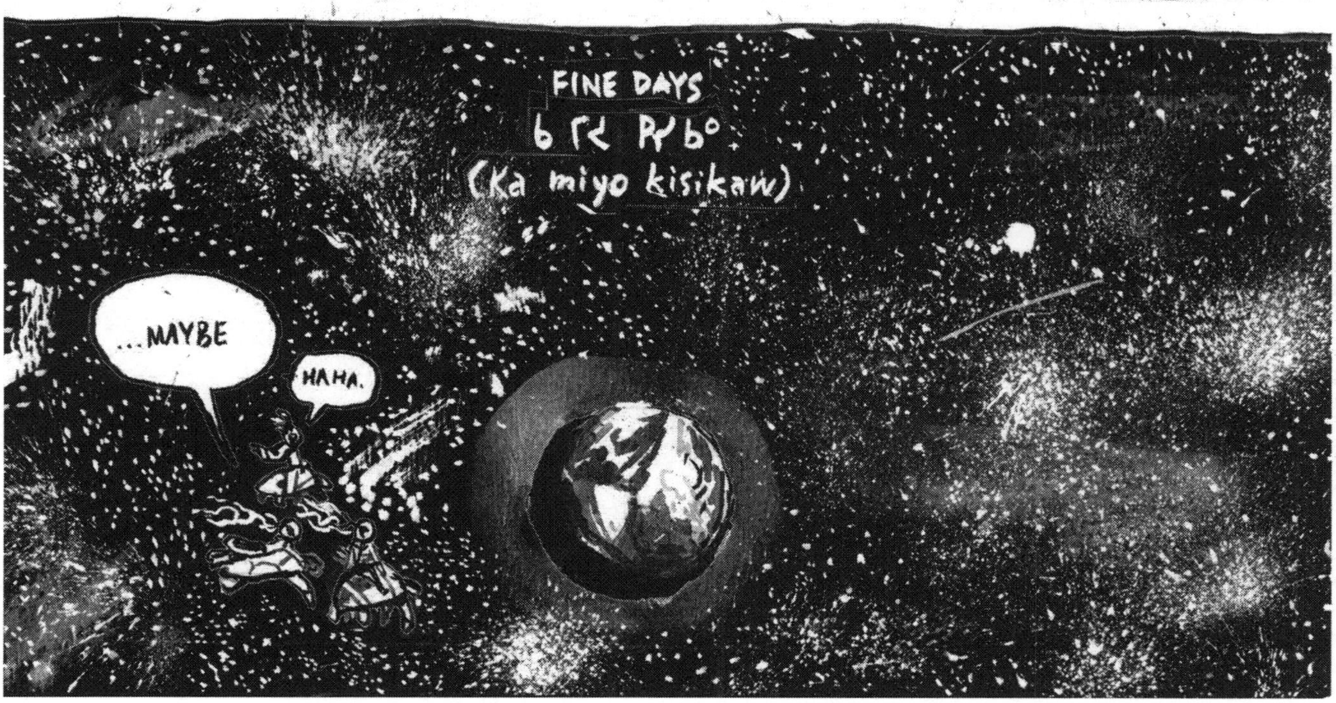
FINE DAYS
ᑲ ᒥᔪ ᑭᓯᑲᐤ
(Ka miyo kisikaw)
...MAYBE
HAHA.

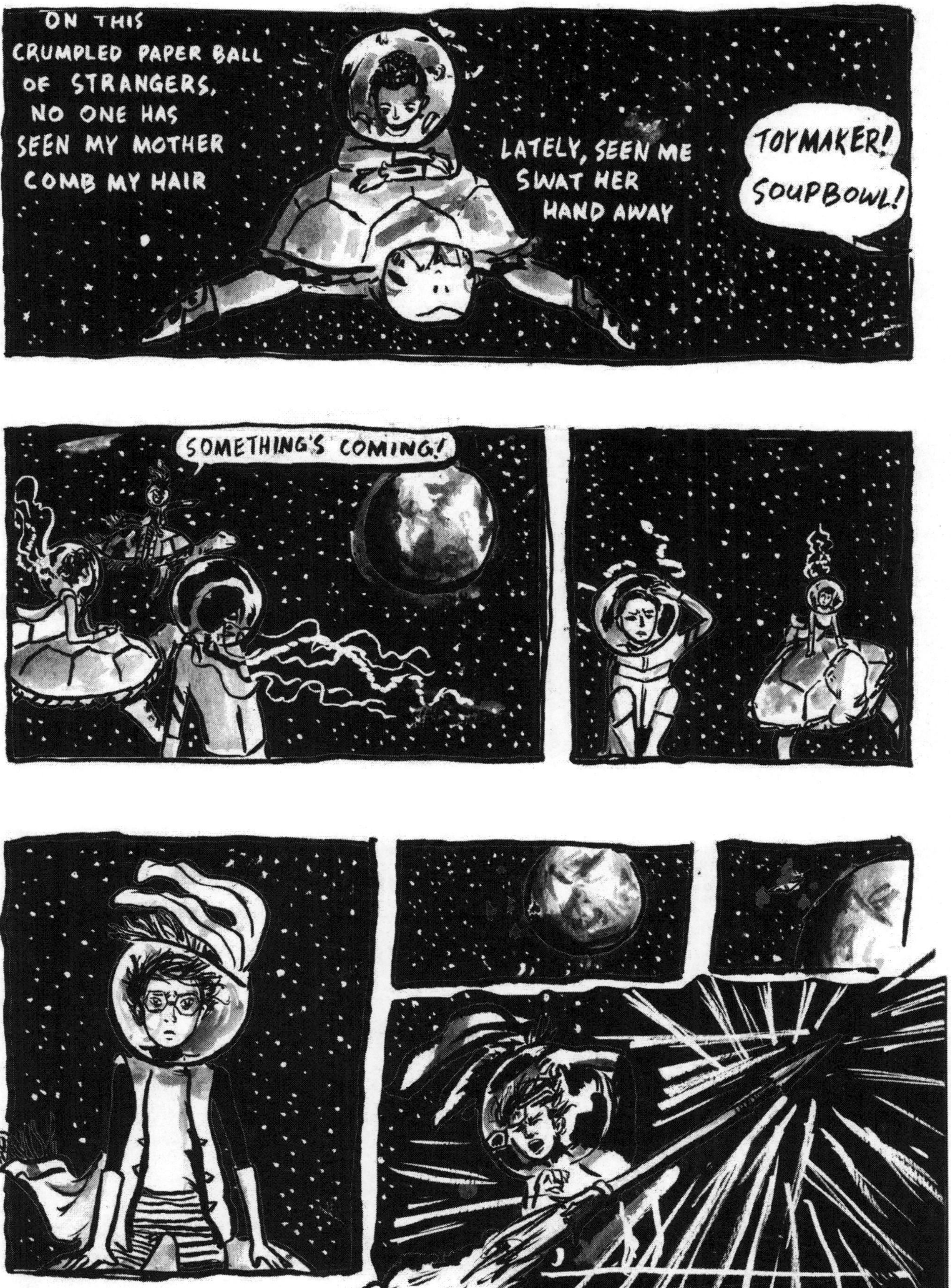
ON THIS CRUMPLED PAPER BALL OF STRANGERS, NO ONE HAS SEEN MY MOTHER COMB MY HAIR
LATELY, SEEN ME SWAT HER HAND AWAY
TOYMAKER! SOUPBOWL!
SOMETHING'S COMING!

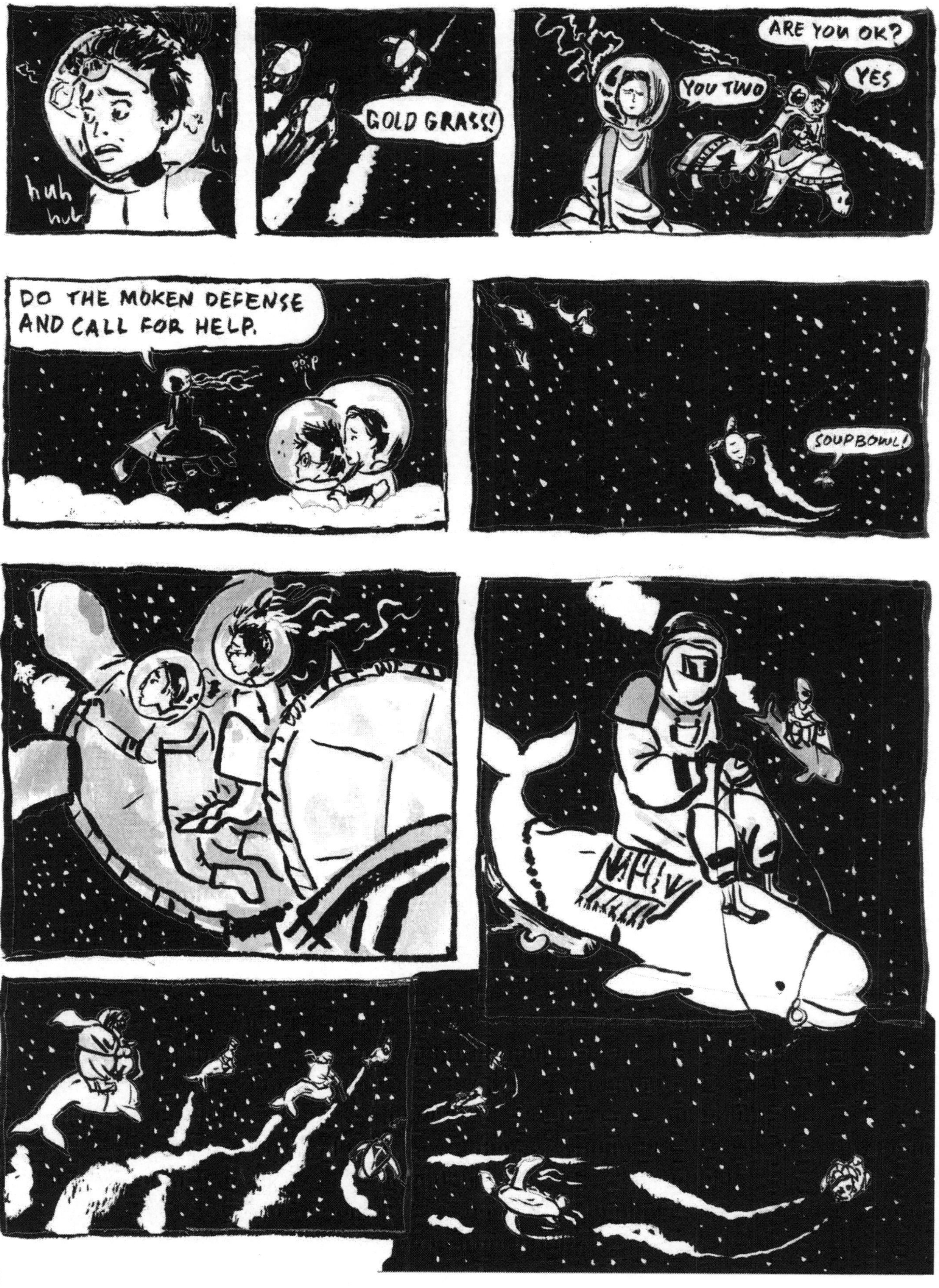
huh
huh
GOLD GRASS!
ARE YOU OK?
YOU TWO
YES
DO THE MOKEN DEFENSE
AND CALL FOR HELP.
POP
SOUPBOWL!

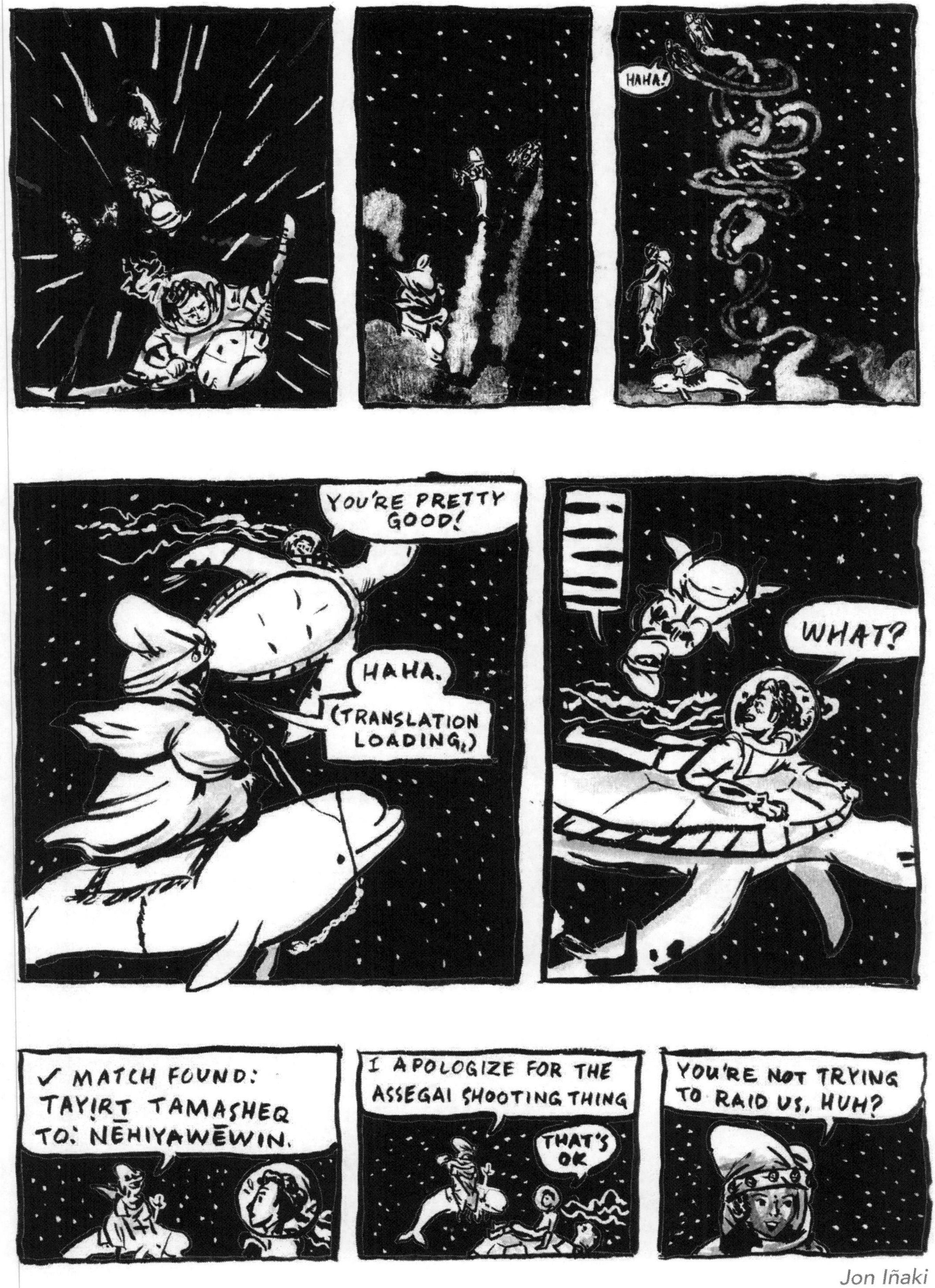
HAHA!
YOU'RE PRETTY GOOD!
HAHA.
(TRANSLATION LOADING..)
WHAT?
✓ MATCH FOUND: TAYIRT TAMASHEQ TO: NĒHIYAWĒWIN.
I APOLOGIZE FOR THE ASSEGAI SHOOTING THING
THAT'S OK
YOU'RE NOT TRYING TO RAID US, HUH?

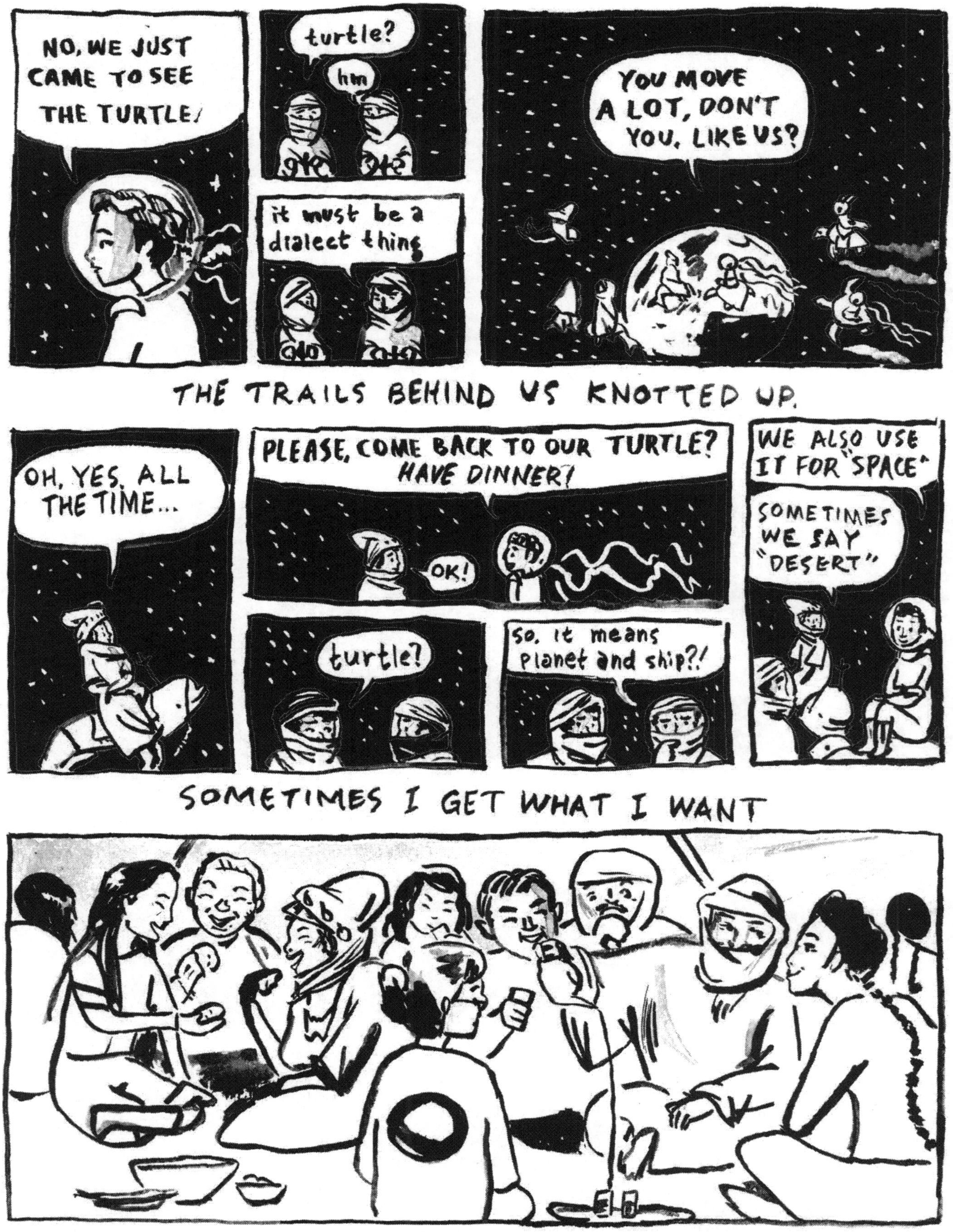
NO, WE JUST CAME TO SEE THE TURTLE!
turtle?
hm
it must be a dialect thing
YOU MOVE A LOT, DON'T YOU, LIKE US?
THE TRAILS BEHIND US KNOTTED UP.
OH, YES, ALL THE TIME...
PLEASE, COME BACK TO OUR TURTLE? HAVE DINNER!
OK!
turtle?
so, it means planet and ship?!
WE ALSO USE IT FOR "SPACE"
SOMETIMES WE SAY "DESERT"
SOMETIMES I GET WHAT I WANT
DELIVERED BY SOMETHING UNDER MY FEET.

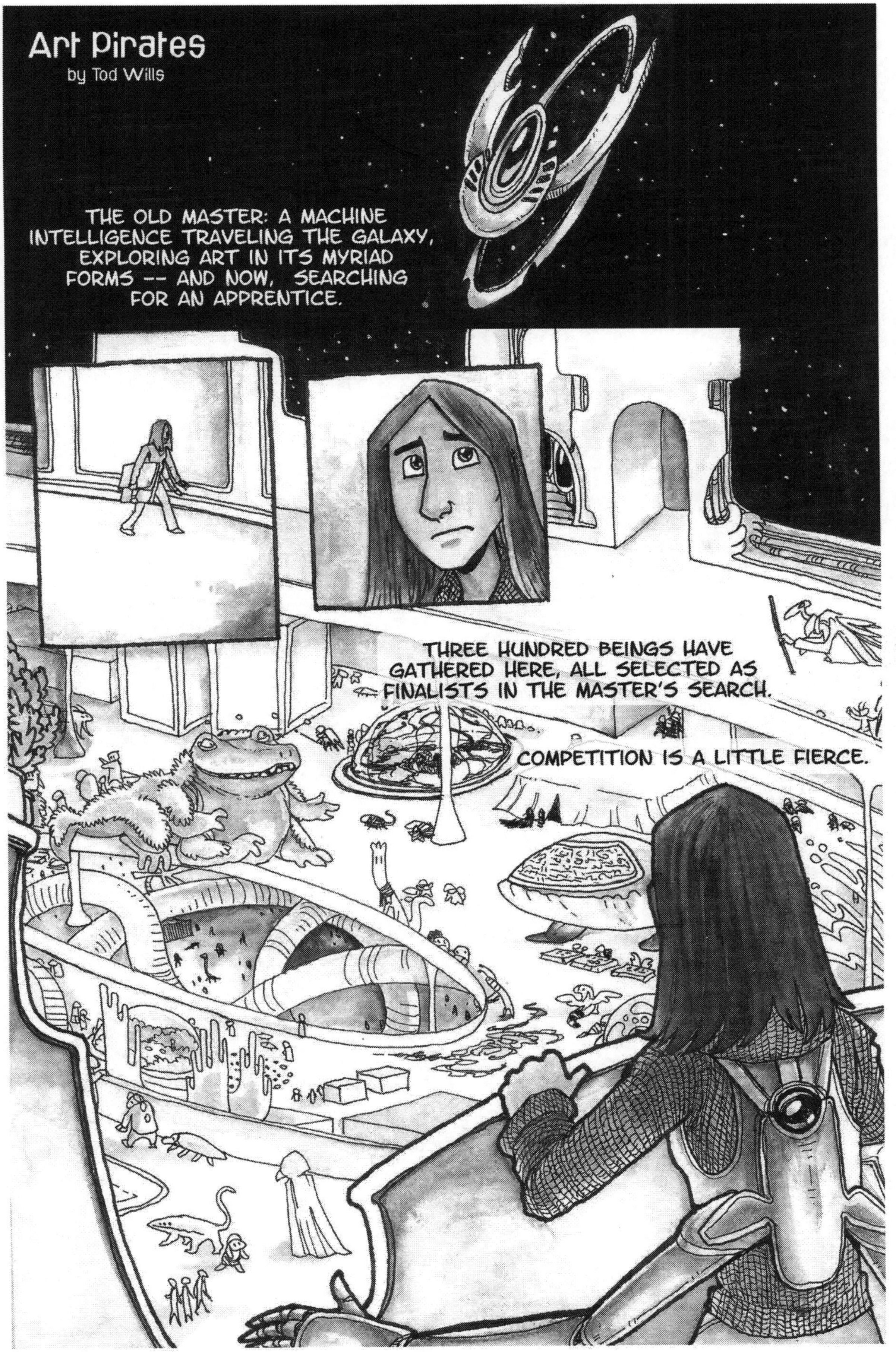
Art Pirates
by Tod Wills
THE OLD MASTER: A MACHINE INTELLIGENCE TRAVELING THE GALAXY, EXPLORING ART IN ITS MYRIAD FORMS -- AND NOW, SEARCHING FOR AN APPRENTICE.
THREE HUNDRED BEINGS HAVE GATHERED HERE, ALL SELECTED AS FINALISTS IN THE MASTER'S SEARCH.
COMPETITION IS A LITTLE FIERCE.

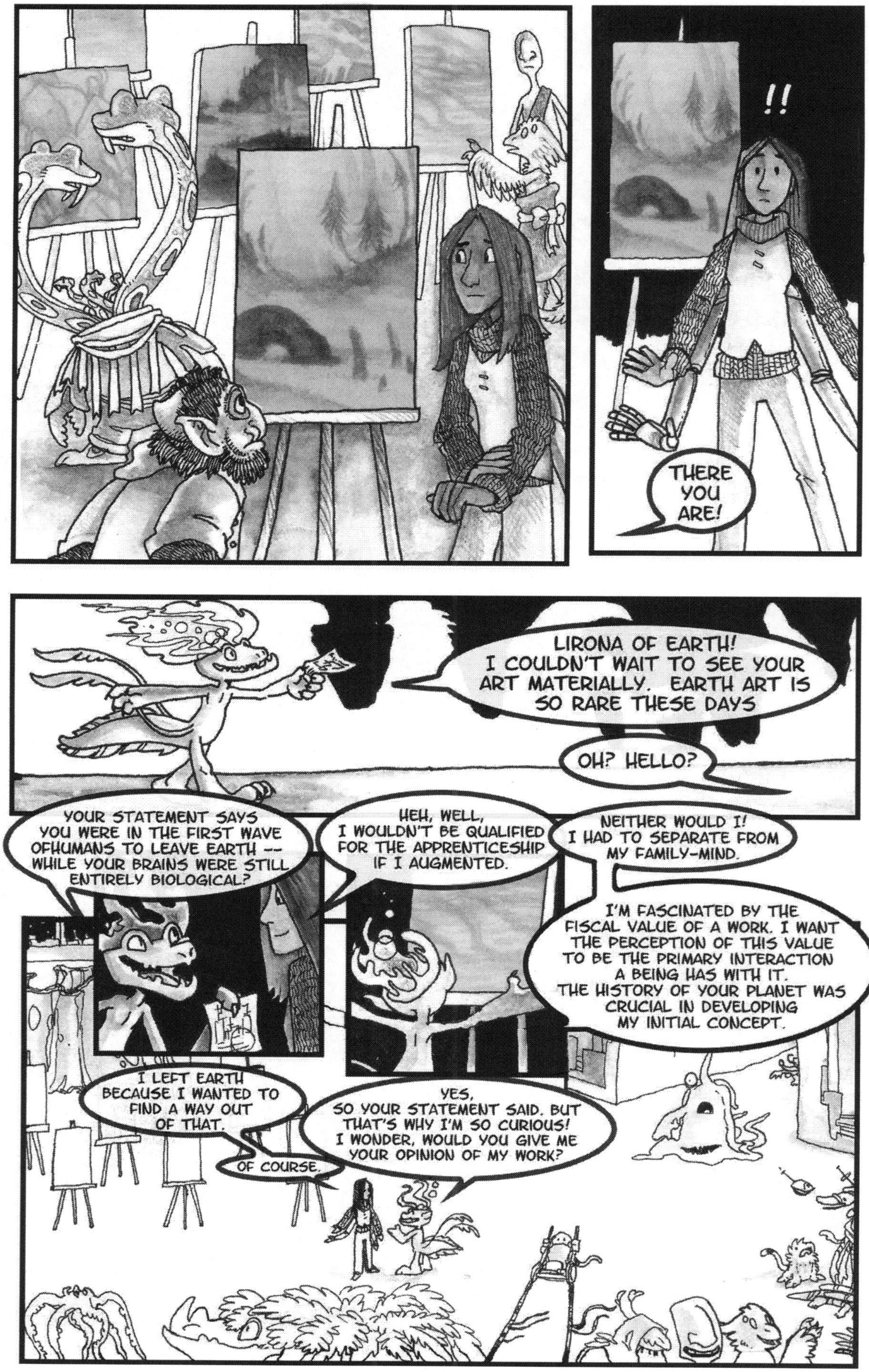
!!
THERE YOU ARE!
LIRONA OF EARTH! I COULDN'T WAIT TO SEE YOUR ART MATERIALLY. EARTH ART IS SO RARE THESE DAYS
OH? HELLO?
YOUR STATEMENT SAYS YOU WERE IN THE FIRST WAVE OFHUMANS TO LEAVE EARTH -- WHILE YOUR BRAINS WERE STILL ENTIRELY BIOLOGICAL?
HEH, WELL, I WOULDN'T BE QUALIFIED FOR THE APPRENTICESHIP IF I AUGMENTED.
NEITHER WOULD I! I HAD TO SEPARATE FROM MY FAMILY-MIND.
I'M FASCINATED BY THE FISCAL VALUE OF A WORK. I WANT THE PERCEPTION OF THIS VALUE TO BE THE PRIMARY INTERACTION A BEING HAS WITH IT. THE HISTORY OF YOUR PLANET WAS CRUCIAL IN DEVELOPING MY INITIAL CONCEPT.
I LEFT EARTH BECAUSE I WANTED TO FIND A WAY OUT OF THAT.
YES, SO YOUR STATEMENT SAID. BUT THAT'S WHY I'M SO CURIOUS! I WONDER, WOULD YOU GIVE ME YOUR OPINION OF MY WORK?
OF COURSE.

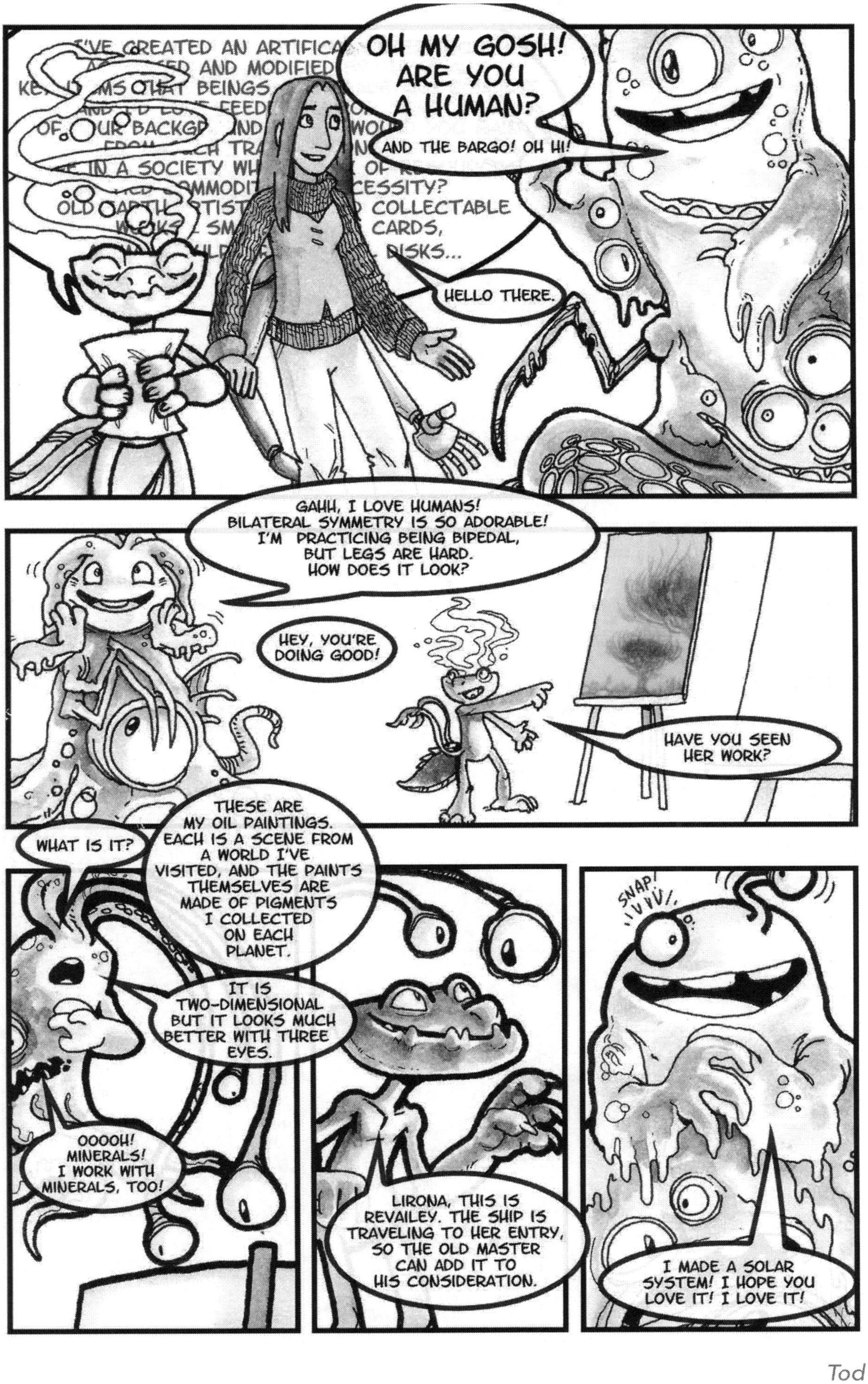
OH MY GOSH! ARE YOU A HUMAN?
AND THE BARGO! OH HI!
HELLO THERE.
GAHH, I LOVE HUMANS! BILATERAL SYMMETRY IS SO ADORABLE! I'M PRACTICING BEING BIPEDAL, BUT LEGS ARE HARD. HOW DOES IT LOOK?
HEY, YOU'RE DOING GOOD!
HAVE YOU SEEN HER WORK?
WHAT IS IT?
THESE ARE MY OIL PAINTINGS. EACH IS A SCENE FROM A WORLD I'VE VISITED, AND THE PAINTS THEMSELVES ARE MADE OF PIGMENTS I COLLECTED ON EACH PLANET.
IT IS TWO-DIMENSIONAL BUT IT LOOKS MUCH BETTER WITH THREE EYES.
OOOOH! MINERALS! I WORK WITH MINERALS, TOO!
LIRONA, THIS IS REVAILEY. THE SHIP IS TRAVELING TO HER ENTRY, SO THE OLD MASTER CAN ADD IT TO HIS CONSIDERATION.
SNAP!
I MADE A SOLAR SYSTEM! I HOPE YOU LOVE IT! I LOVE IT!

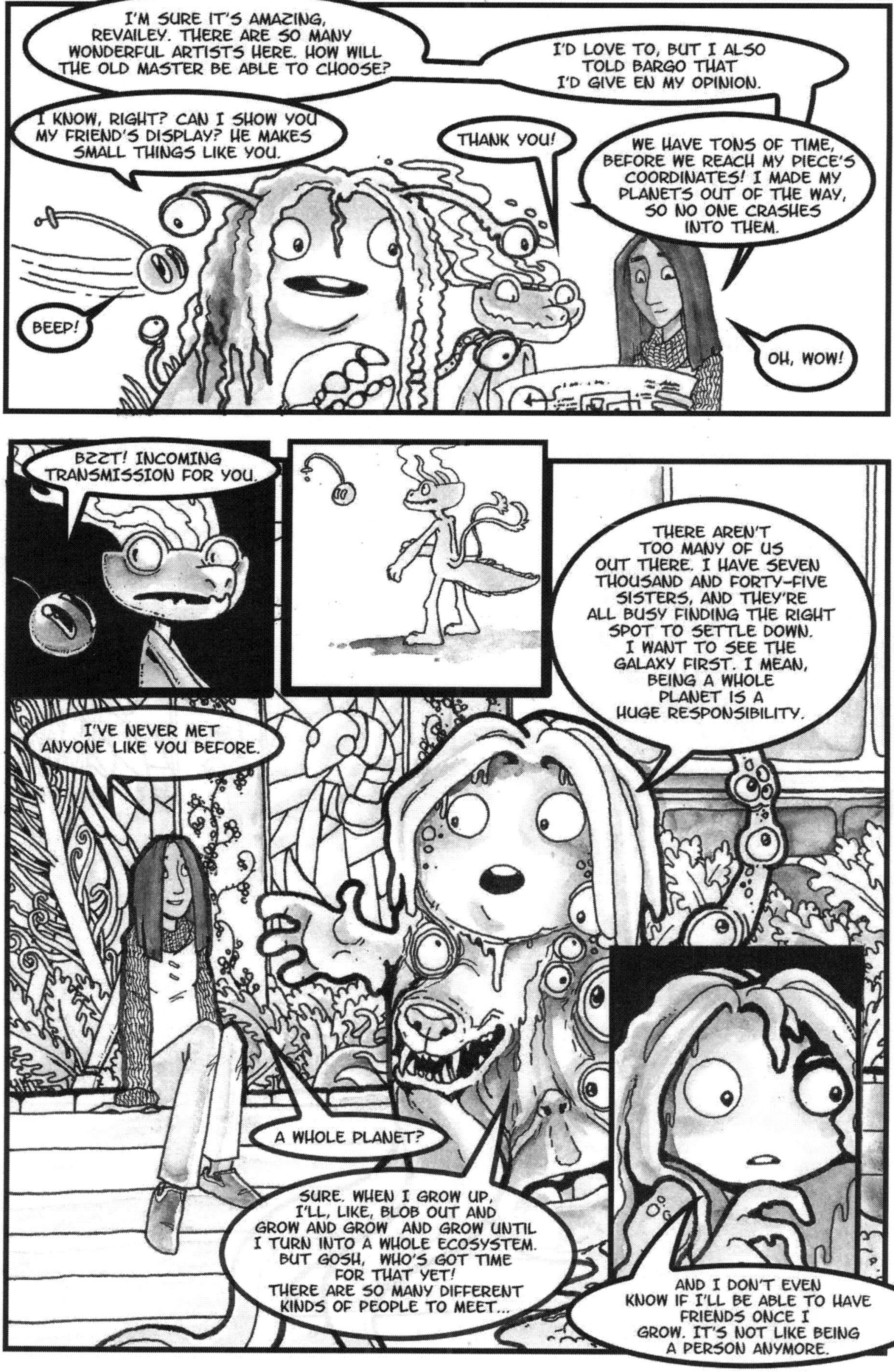
I'M SURE IT'S AMAZING, REVAILEY. THERE ARE SO MANY WONDERFUL ARTISTS HERE. HOW WILL THE OLD MASTER BE ABLE TO CHOOSE?
I'D LOVE TO, BUT I ALSO TOLD BARGO THAT I'D GIVE EN MY OPINION.
I KNOW, RIGHT? CAN I SHOW YOU MY FRIEND'S DISPLAY? HE MAKES SMALL THINGS LIKE YOU.
THANK YOU!
WE HAVE TONS OF TIME, BEFORE WE REACH MY PIECE'S COORDINATES! I MADE MY PLANETS OUT OF THE WAY, SO NO ONE CRASHES INTO THEM.
BEEP!
OH, WOW!
BZZT! INCOMING TRANSMISSION FOR YOU.
THERE AREN'T TOO MANY OF US OUT THERE. I HAVE SEVEN THOUSAND AND FORTY-FIVE SISTERS, AND THEY'RE ALL BUSY FINDING THE RIGHT SPOT TO SETTLE DOWN. I WANT TO SEE THE GALAXY FIRST. I MEAN, BEING A WHOLE PLANET IS A HUGE RESPONSIBILITY.
I'VE NEVER MET ANYONE LIKE YOU BEFORE.
A WHOLE PLANET?
SURE. WHEN I GROW UP, I'LL, LIKE, BLOB OUT AND GROW AND GROW AND GROW UNTIL I TURN INTO A WHOLE ECOSYSTEM. BUT GOSH, WHO'S GOT TIME FOR THAT YET! THERE ARE SO MANY DIFFERENT KINDS OF PEOPLE TO MEET...
AND I DON'T EVEN KNOW IF I'LL BE ABLE TO HAVE FRIENDS ONCE I GROW. IT'S NOT LIKE BEING A PERSON ANYMORE.

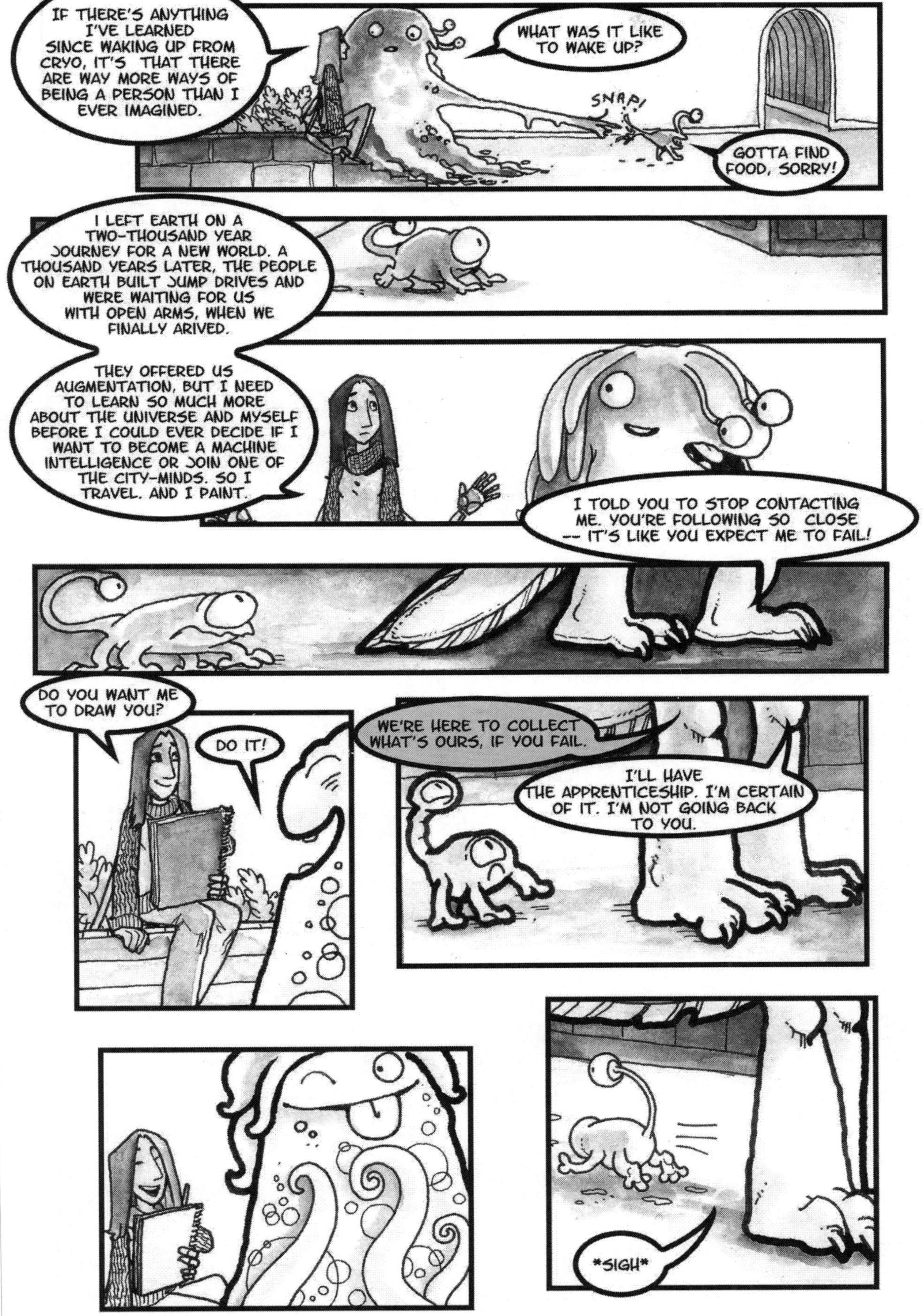
IF THERE'S ANYTHING I'VE LEARNED SINCE WAKING UP FROM CRYO, IT'S THAT THERE ARE WAY MORE WAYS OF BEING A PERSON THAN I EVER IMAGINED.
WHAT WAS IT LIKE TO WAKE UP?
SNAP!
GOTTA FIND FOOD, SORRY!
I LEFT EARTH ON A TWO-THOUSAND YEAR JOURNEY FOR A NEW WORLD. A THOUSAND YEARS LATER, THE PEOPLE ON EARTH BUILT JUMP DRIVES AND WERE WAITING FOR US WITH OPEN ARMS, WHEN WE FINALLY ARIVED.
THEY OFFERED US AUGMENTATION, BUT I NEED TO LEARN SO MUCH MORE ABOUT THE UNIVERSE AND MYSELF BEFORE I COULD EVER DECIDE IF I WANT TO BECOME A MACHINE INTELLIGENCE OR JOIN ONE OF THE CITY-MINDS. SO I TRAVEL. AND I PAINT.
I TOLD YOU TO STOP CONTACTING ME. YOU'RE FOLLOWING SO CLOSE -- IT'S LIKE YOU EXPECT ME TO FAIL!
DO YOU WANT ME TO DRAW YOU?
DO IT!
WE'RE HERE TO COLLECT WHAT'S OURS, IF YOU FAIL.
I'LL HAVE THE APPRENTICESHIP. I'M CERTAIN OF IT. I'M NOT GOING BACK TO YOU.
SIGH

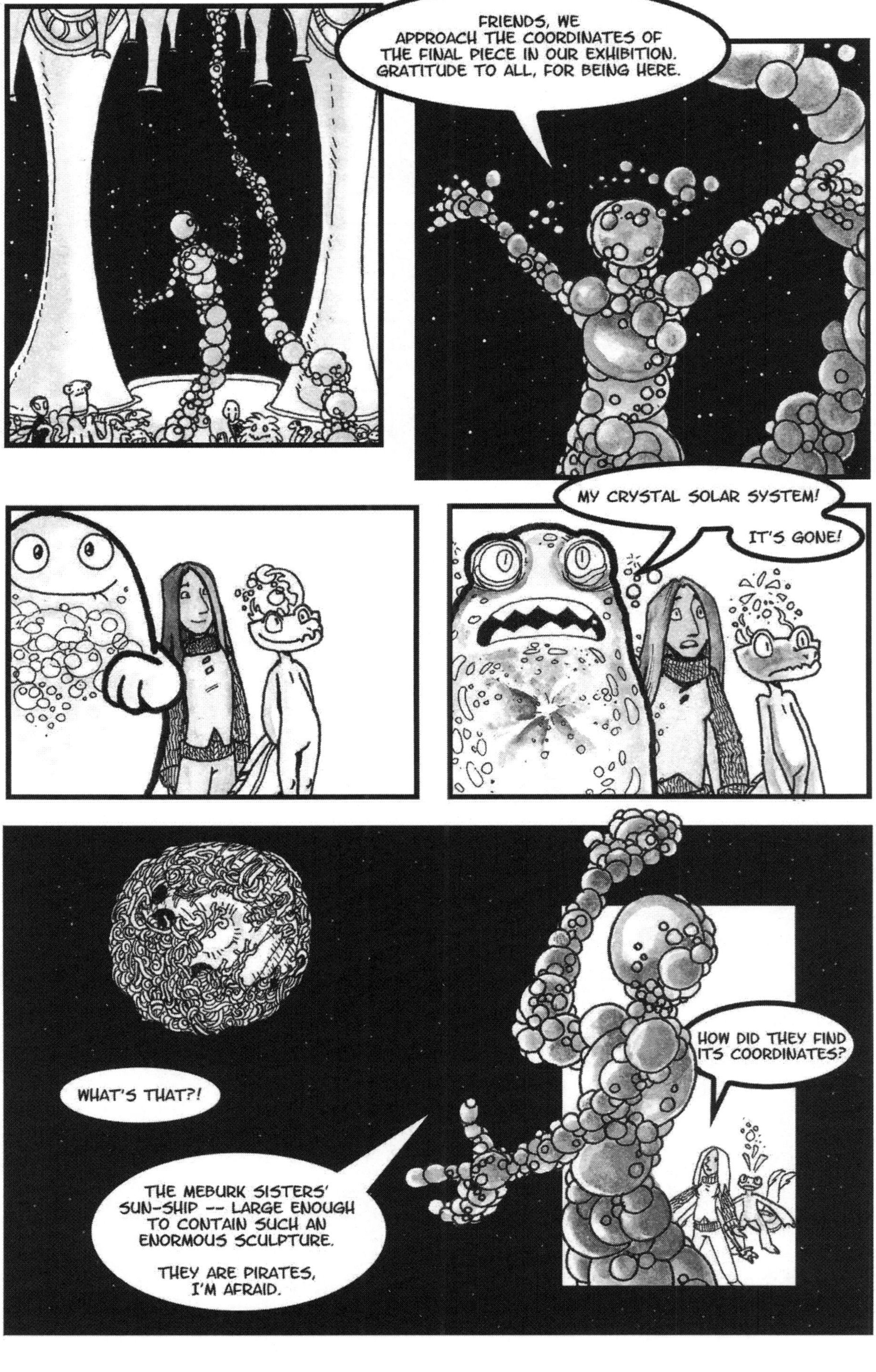
FRIENDS, WE APPROACH THE COORDINATES OF THE FINAL PIECE IN OUR EXHIBITION. GRATITUDE TO ALL, FOR BEING HERE.
MY CRYSTAL SOLAR SYSTEM!
IT'S GONE!
WHAT'S THAT?!
THE MEBURK SISTERS' SUN-SHIP -- LARGE ENOUGH TO CONTAIN SUCH AN ENORMOUS SCULPTURE.
THEY ARE PIRATES, I'M AFRAID.
HOW DID THEY FIND ITS COORDINATES?

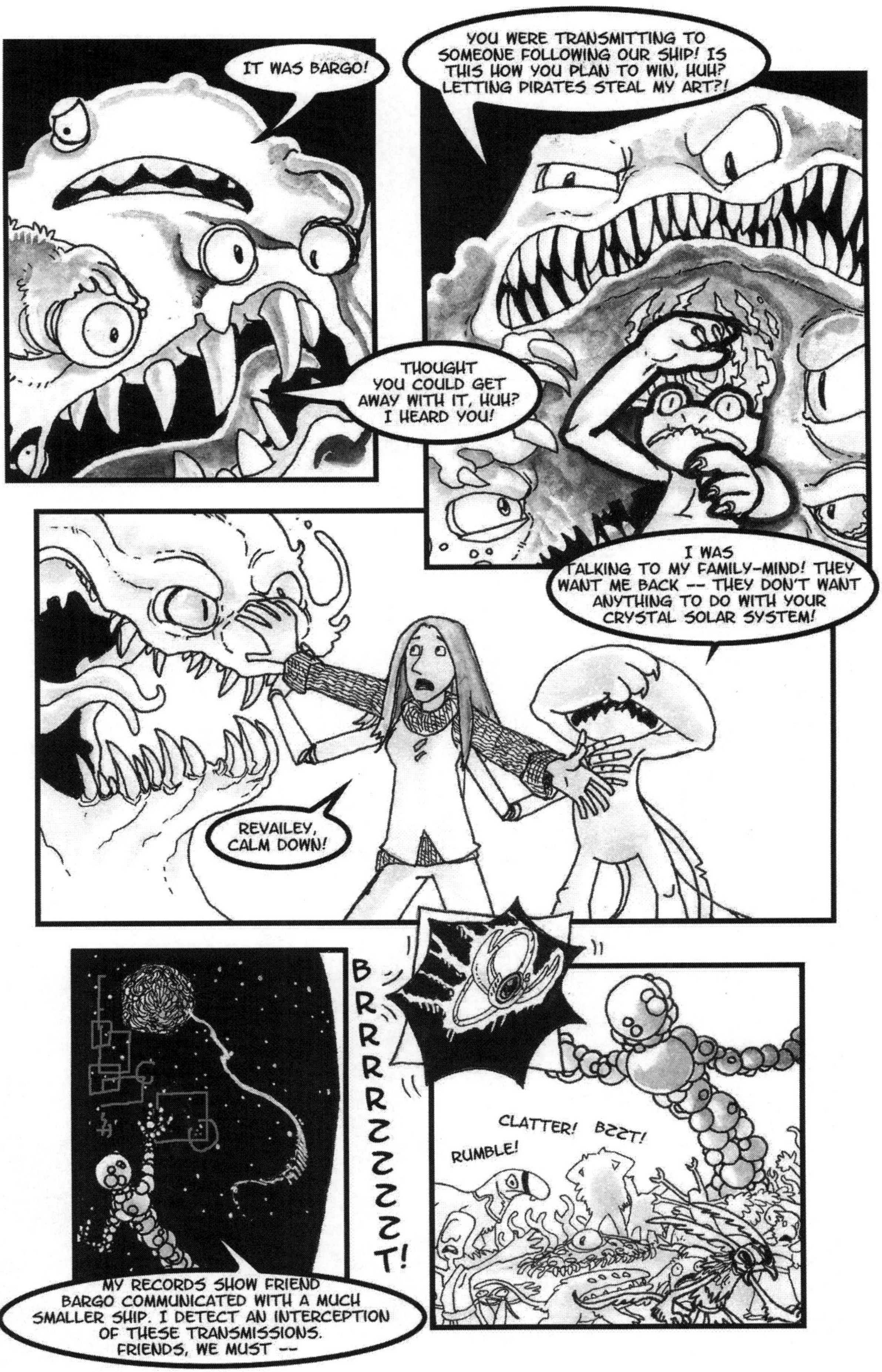
IT WAS BARGO!
YOU WERE TRANSMITTING TO SOMEONE FOLLOWING OUR SHIP! IS THIS HOW YOU PLAN TO WIN, HUH? LETTING PIRATES STEAL MY ART?!
THOUGHT YOU COULD GET AWAY WITH IT, HUH? I HEARD YOU!
I WAS TALKING TO MY FAMILY-MIND! THEY WANT ME BACK -- THEY DON'T WANT ANYTHING TO DO WITH YOUR CRYSTAL SOLAR SYSTEM!
REVAILEY, CALM DOWN!
BRRRRZZZZT!
MY RECORDS SHOW FRIEND BARGO COMMUNICATED WITH A MUCH SMALLER SHIP. I DETECT AN INTERCEPTION OF THESE TRANSMISSIONS. FRIENDS, WE MUST --
CLATTER! BZZT!
RUMBLE!

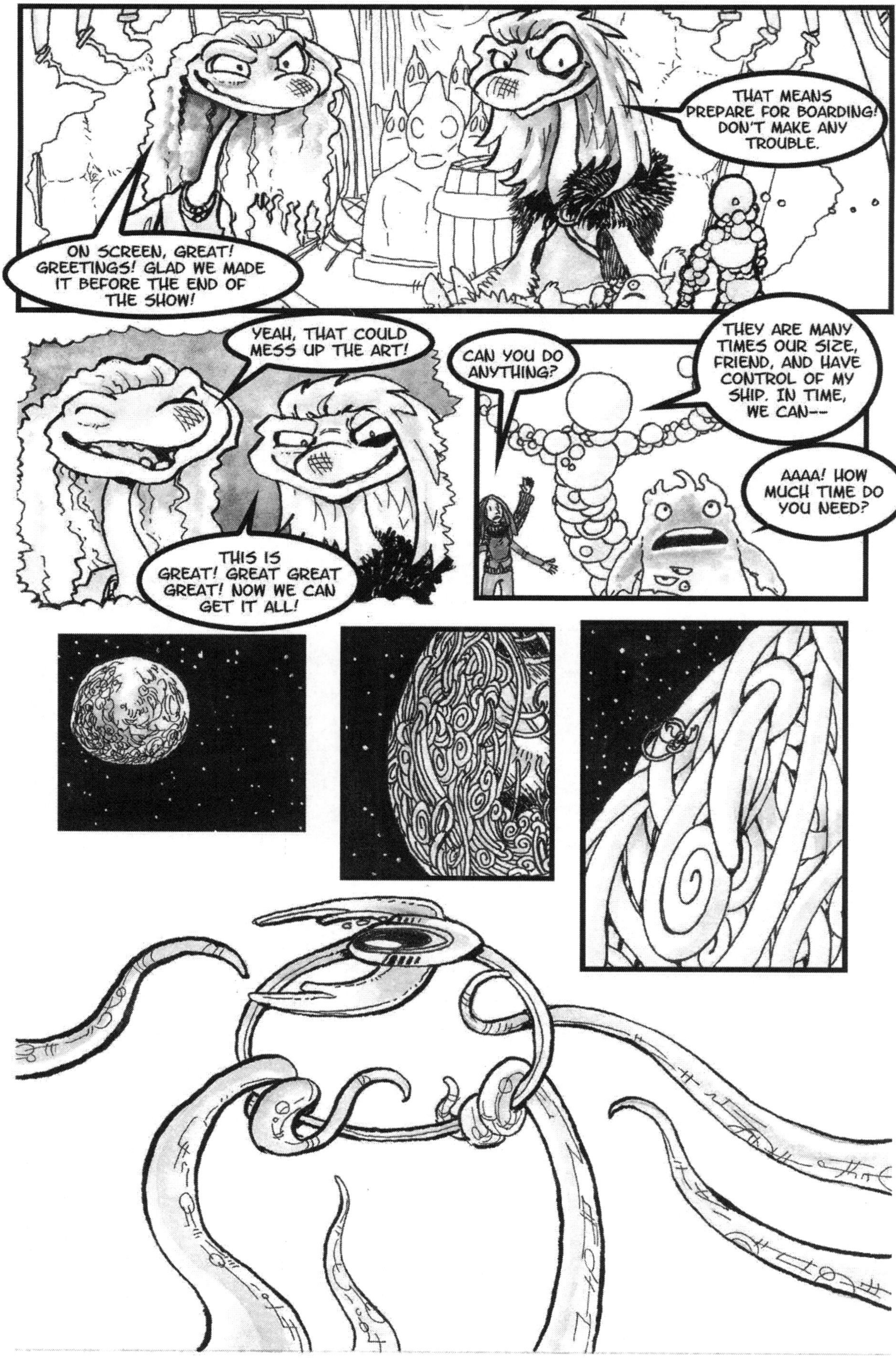
ON SCREEN, GREAT! GREETINGS! GLAD WE MADE IT BEFORE THE END OF THE SHOW!
THAT MEANS PREPARE FOR BOARDING! DON'T MAKE ANY TROUBLE.
YEAH, THAT COULD MESS UP THE ART!
THIS IS GREAT! GREAT GREAT GREAT! NOW WE CAN GET IT ALL!
CAN YOU DO ANYTHING?
THEY ARE MANY TIMES OUR SIZE, FRIEND, AND HAVE CONTROL OF MY SHIP. IN TIME, WE CAN--
AAAA! HOW MUCH TIME DO YOU NEED?

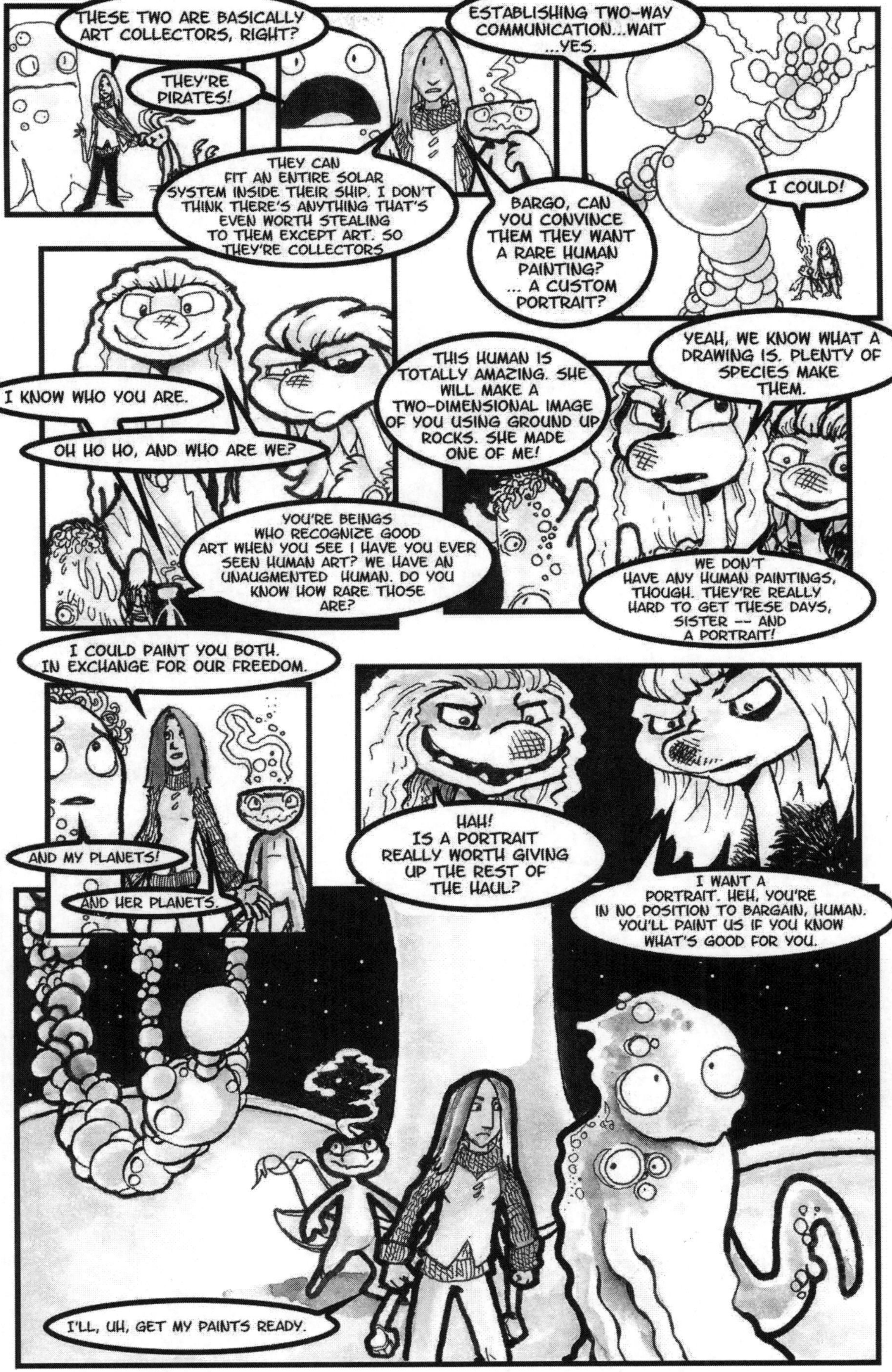
THESE TWO ARE BASICALLY ART COLLECTORS, RIGHT?
THEY'RE PIRATES!
THEY CAN FIT AN ENTIRE SOLAR SYSTEM INSIDE THEIR SHIP. I DON'T THINK THERE'S ANYTHING THAT'S EVEN WORTH STEALING TO THEM EXCEPT ART. SO THEY'RE COLLECTORS
ESTABLISHING TWO-WAY COMMUNICATION...WAIT ...YES.
BARGO, CAN YOU CONVINCE THEM THEY WANT A RARE HUMAN PAINTING? ... A CUSTOM PORTRAIT?
I COULD!
I KNOW WHO YOU ARE.
OH HO HO, AND WHO ARE WE?
YOU'RE BEINGS WHO RECOGNIZE GOOD ART WHEN YOU SEE I HAVE YOU EVER SEEN HUMAN ART? WE HAVE AN UNAUGMENTED HUMAN. DO YOU KNOW HOW RARE THOSE ARE?
THIS HUMAN IS TOTALLY AMAZING. SHE WILL MAKE A TWO-DIMENSIONAL IMAGE OF YOU USING GROUND UP ROCKS. SHE MADE ONE OF ME!
YEAH, WE KNOW WHAT A DRAWING IS. PLENTY OF SPECIES MAKE THEM.
WE DON'T HAVE ANY HUMAN PAINTINGS, THOUGH. THEY'RE REALLY HARD TO GET THESE DAYS, SISTER -- AND A PORTRAIT!
I COULD PAINT YOU BOTH. IN EXCHANGE FOR OUR FREEDOM.
AND MY PLANETS!
AND HER PLANETS.
HAH! IS A PORTRAIT REALLY WORTH GIVING UP THE REST OF THE HAUL?
I WANT A PORTRAIT. HEH, YOU'RE IN NO POSITION TO BARGAIN, HUMAN. YOU'LL PAINT US IF YOU KNOW WHAT'S GOOD FOR YOU.
I'LL, UH, GET MY PAINTS READY.

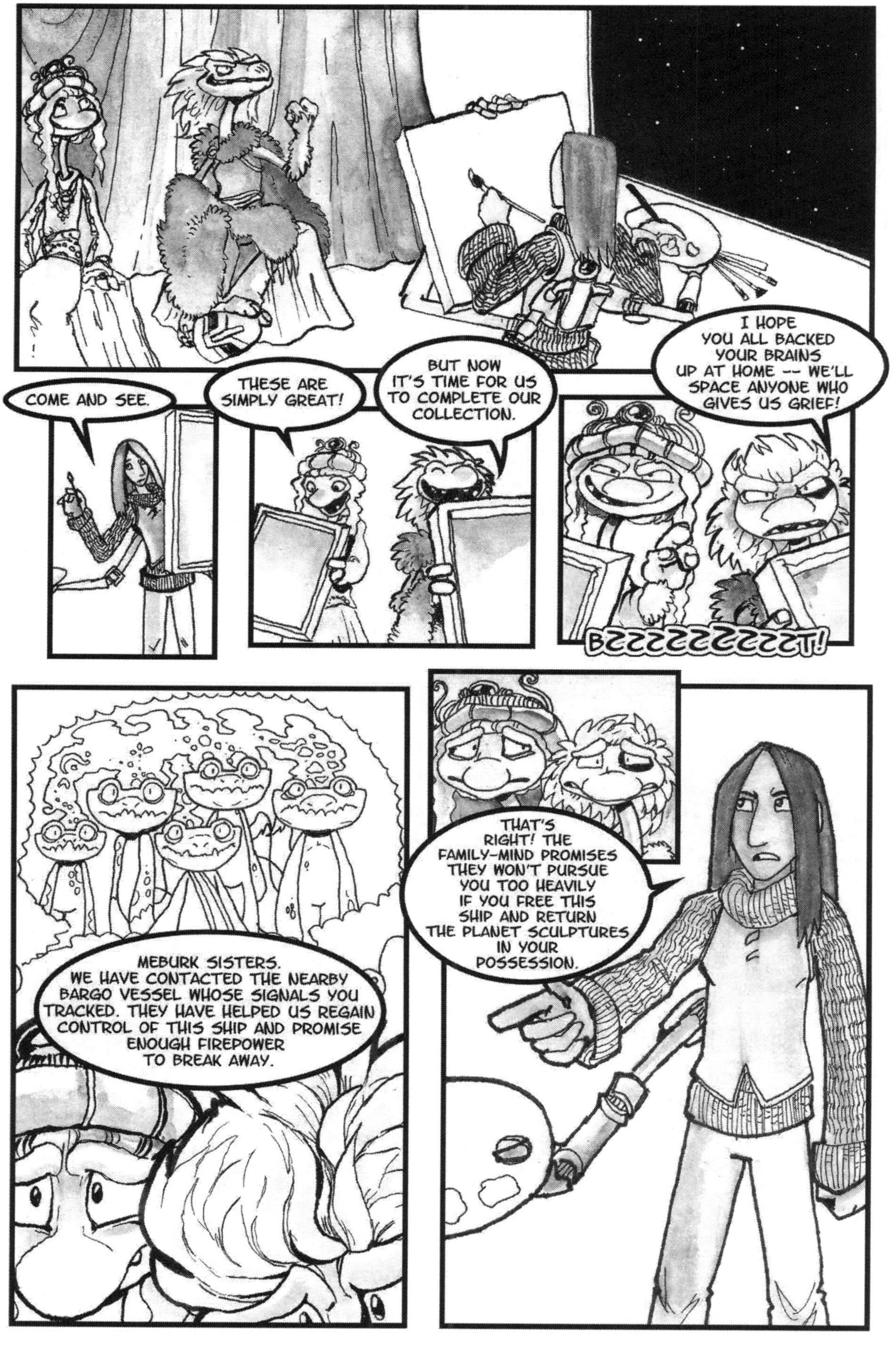
COME AND SEE.
THESE ARE SIMPLY GREAT!
BUT NOW IT'S TIME FOR US TO COMPLETE OUR COLLECTION.
I HOPE YOU ALL BACKED YOUR BRAINS UP AT HOME -- WE'LL SPACE ANYONE WHO GIVES US GRIEF!
BZZZZZZZZZZT!
MEBURK SISTERS. WE HAVE CONTACTED THE NEARBY BARGO VESSEL WHOSE SIGNALS YOU TRACKED. THEY HAVE HELPED US REGAIN CONTROL OF THIS SHIP AND PROMISE ENOUGH FIREPOWER TO BREAK AWAY.
THAT'S RIGHT! THE FAMILY-MIND PROMISES THEY WON'T PURSUE YOU TOO HEAVILY IF YOU FREE THIS SHIP AND RETURN THE PLANET SCULPTURES IN YOUR POSSESSION.

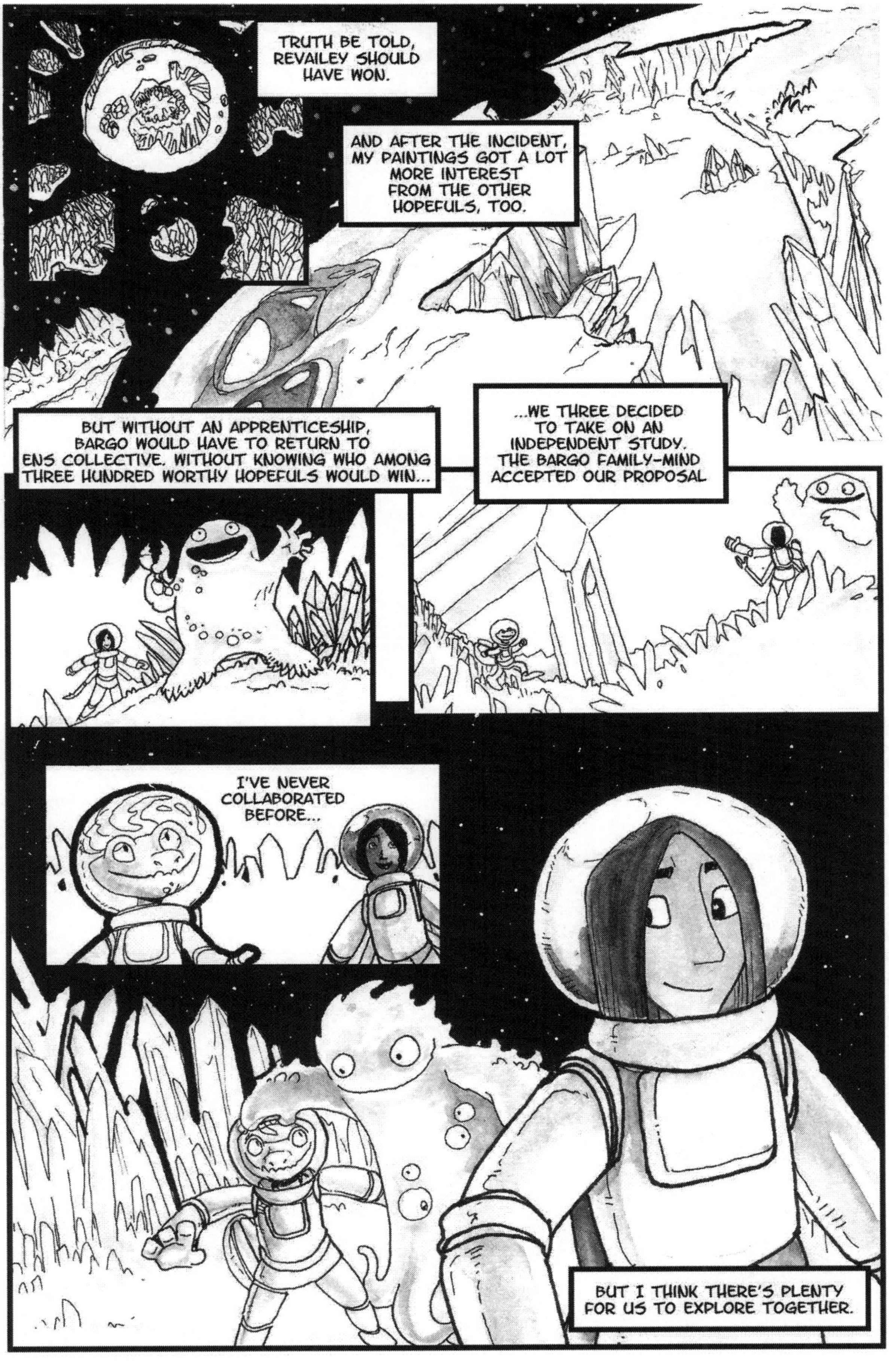
TRUTH BE TOLD, REVAILEY SHOULD HAVE WON.
AND AFTER THE INCIDENT, MY PAINTINGS GOT A LOT MORE INTEREST FROM THE OTHER HOPEFULS, TOO.
BUT WITHOUT AN APPRENTICESHIP, BARGO WOULD HAVE TO RETURN TO ENS COLLECTIVE. WITHOUT KNOWING WHO AMONG THREE HUNDRED WORTHY HOPEFULS WOULD WIN...
...WE THREE DECIDED TO TAKE ON AN INDEPENDENT STUDY. THE BARGO FAMILY-MIND ACCEPTED OUR PROPOSAL
I'VE NEVER COLLABORATED BEFORE...
BUT I THINK THERE'S PLENTY FOR US TO EXPLORE TOGETHER.

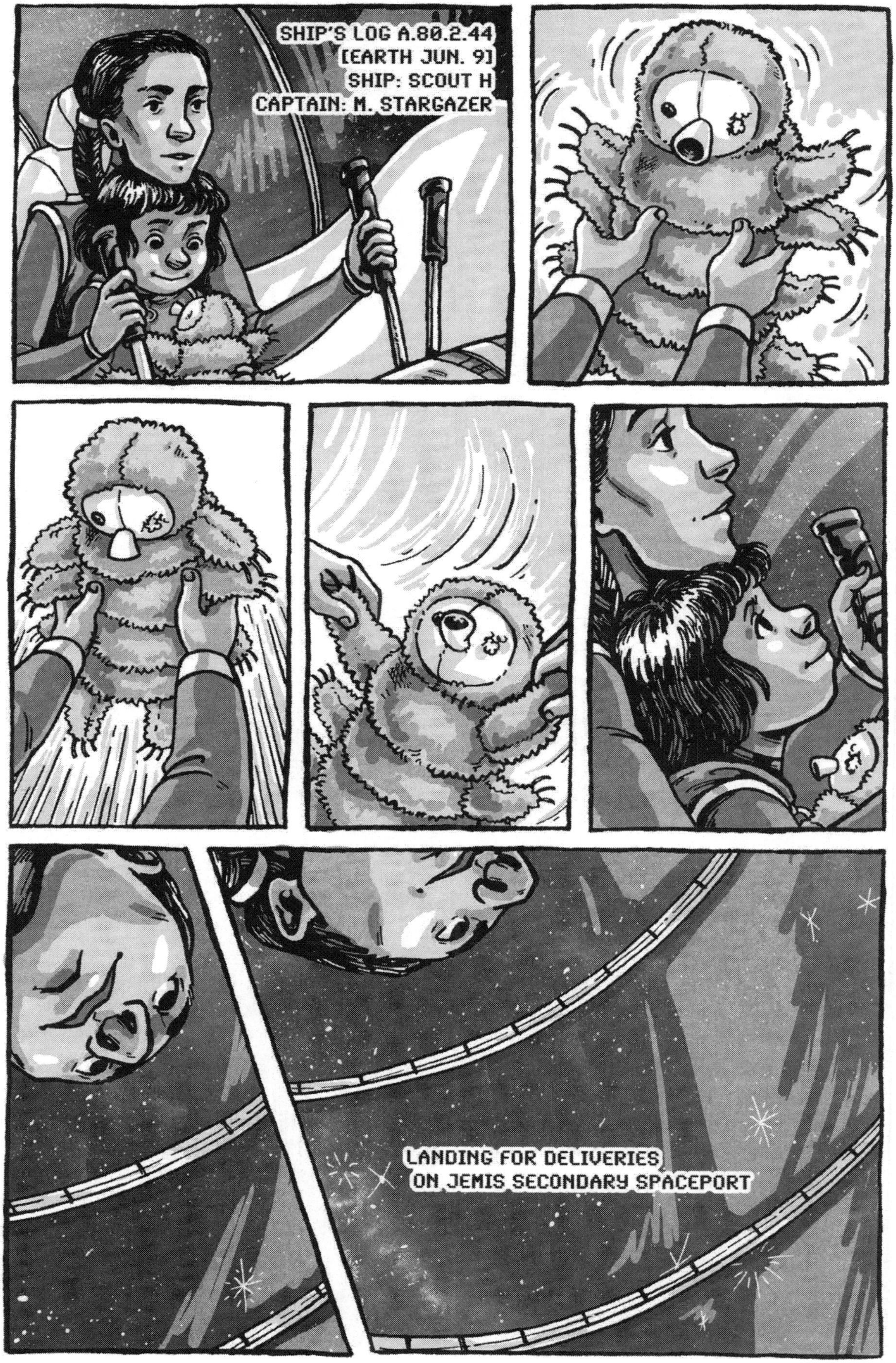
SHIP'S LOG A.80.2.44
[EARTH JUN. 9]
SHIP: SCOUT H
CAPTAIN: M. STARGAZER
LANDING FOR DELIVERIES
ON JEMIS SECONDARY SPACEPORT

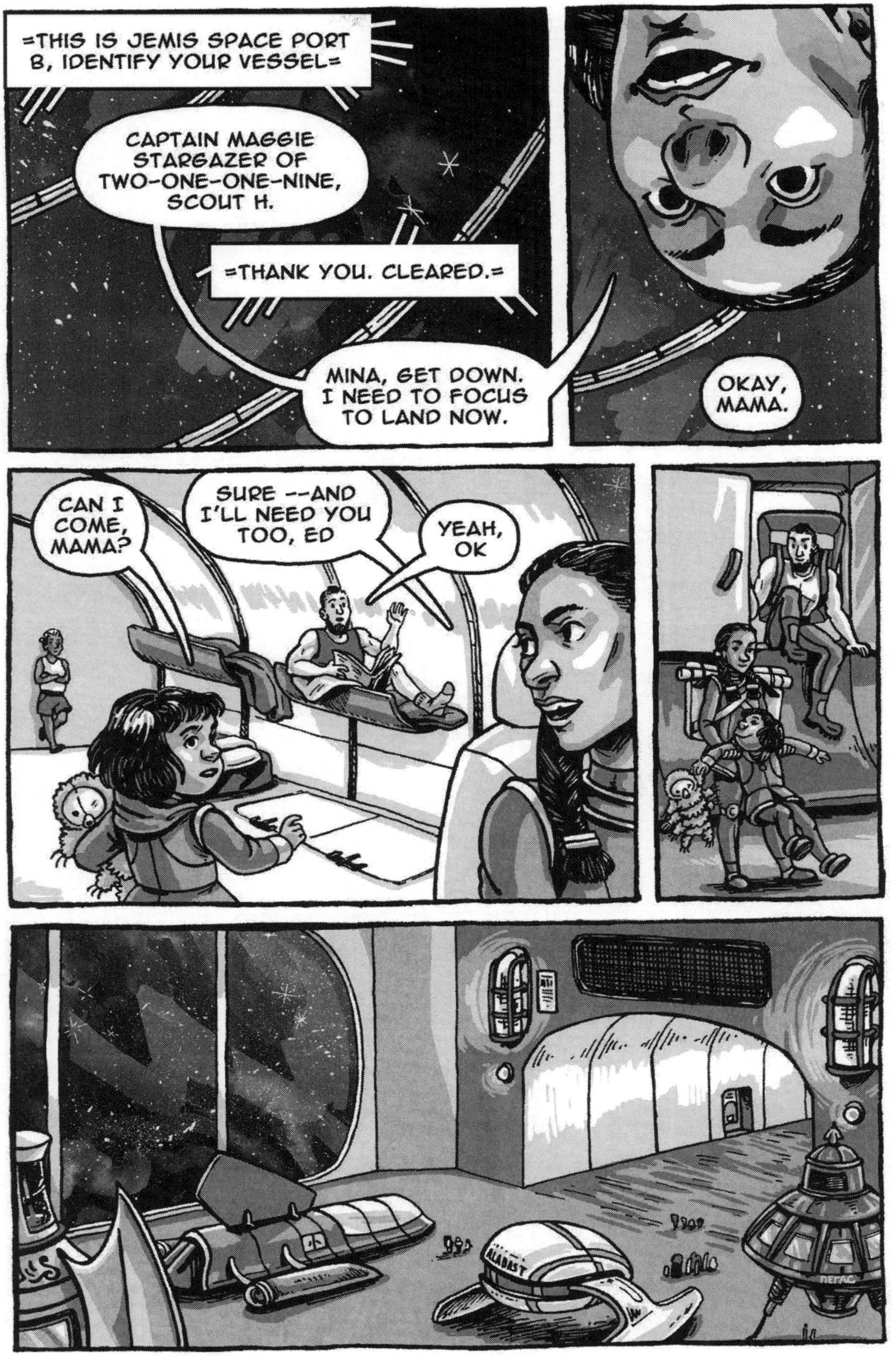
=THIS IS JEMIS SPACE PORT B, IDENTIFY YOUR VESSEL=
CAPTAIN MAGGIE STARGAZER OF TWO-ONE-ONE-NINE, SCOUT H.
=THANK YOU. CLEARED.=
MINA, GET DOWN. I NEED TO FOCUS TO LAND NOW.
OKAY, MAMA.
CAN I COME, MAMA?
SURE --AND I'LL NEED YOU TOO, ED
YEAH, OK

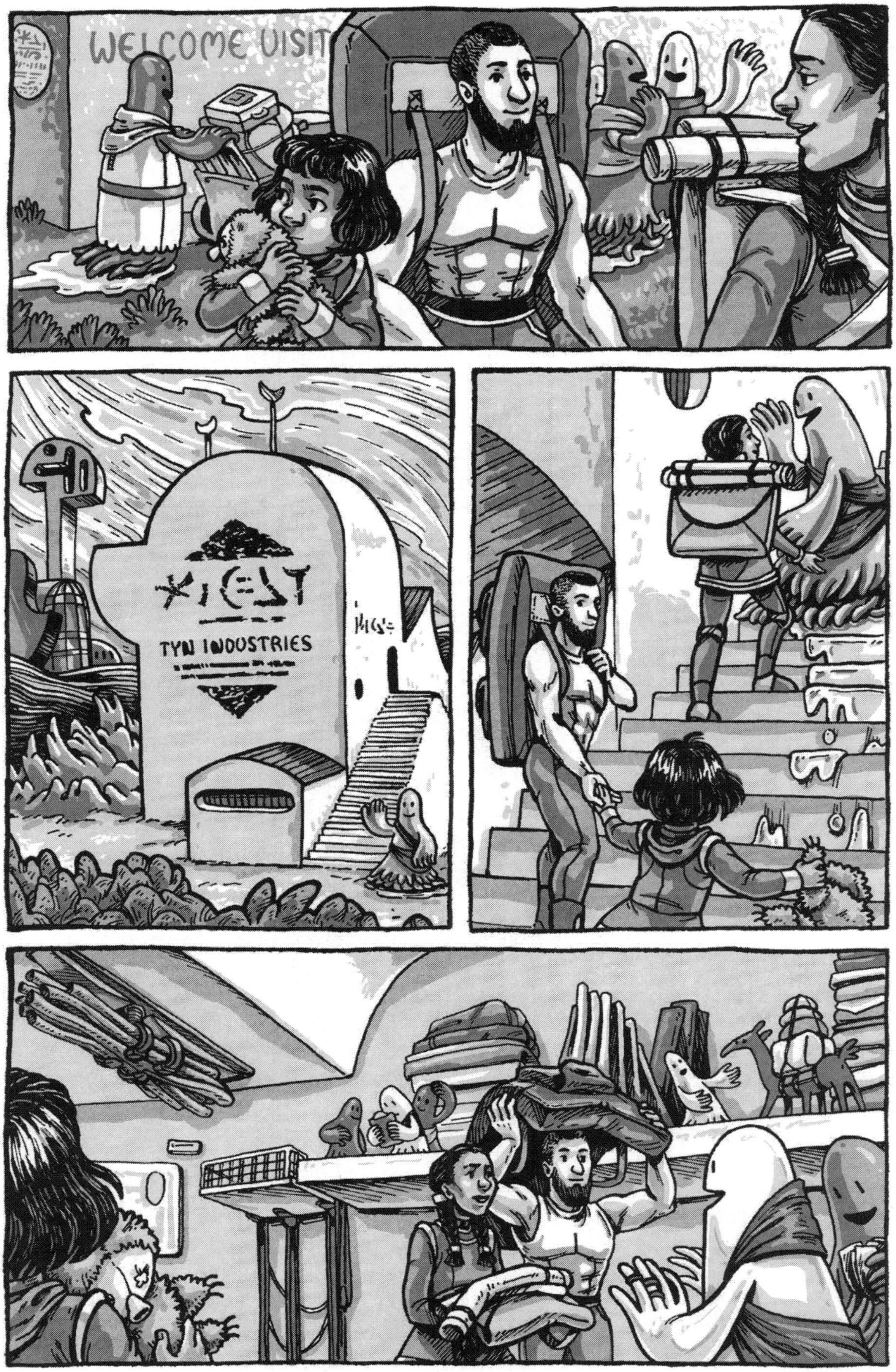
WELCOME VISIT
TYN INDUSTRIES

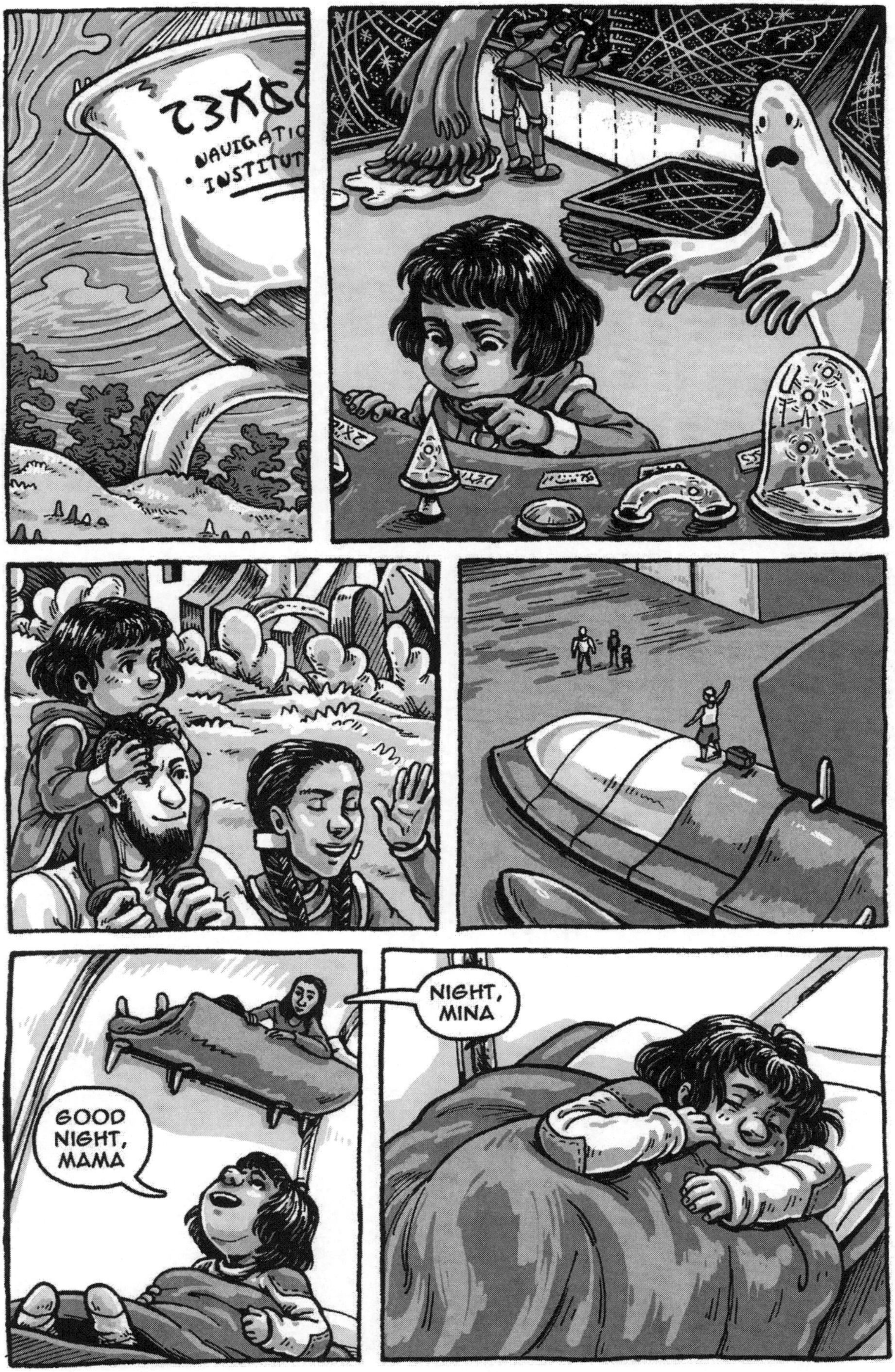
NAVIGATIO
INSTITUT
NIGHT, MINA
GOOD NIGHT, MAMA

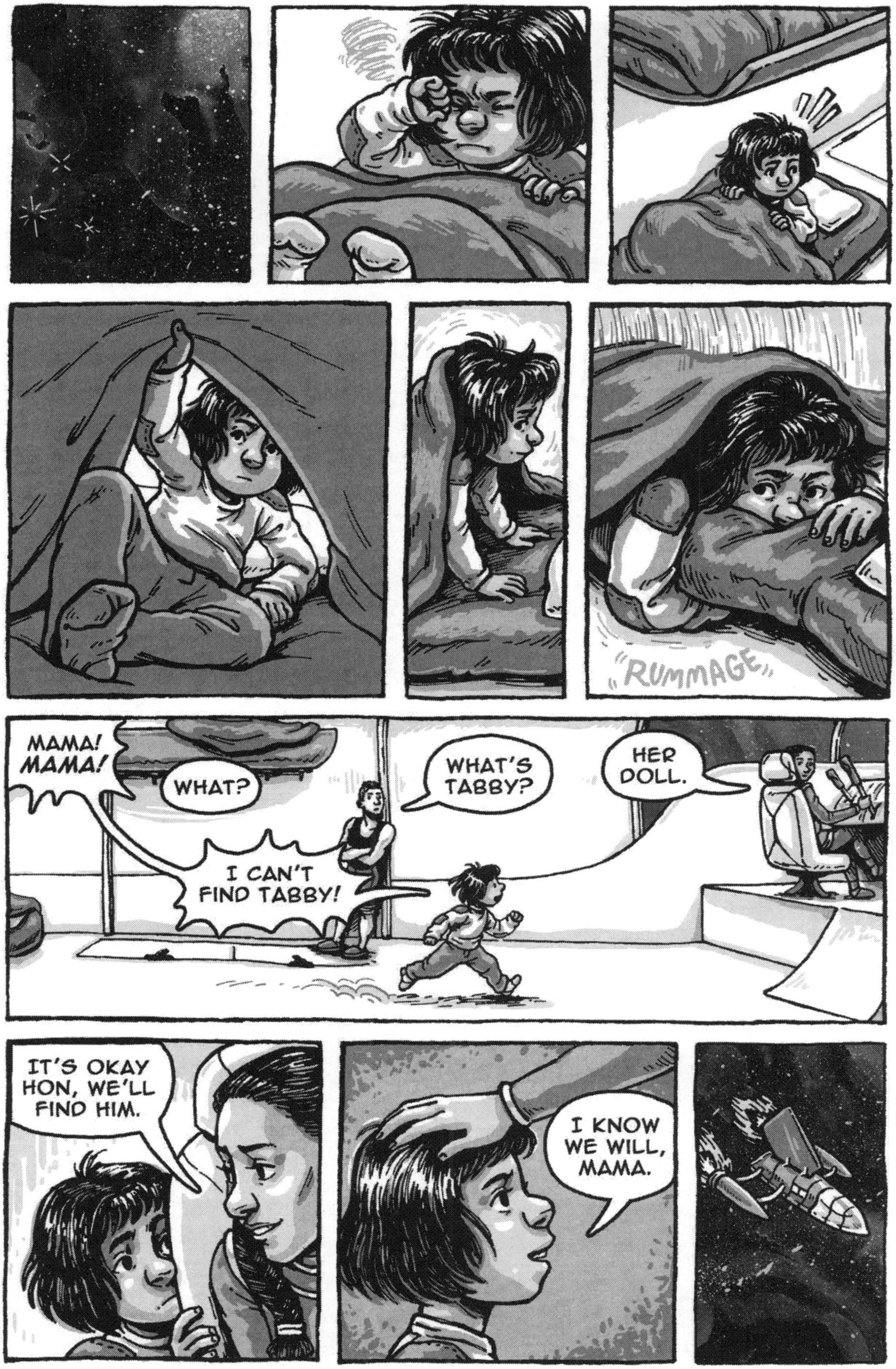
RUMMAGE
MAMA! MAMA!
WHAT?
WHAT'S TABBY?
HER DOLL.
I CAN'T FIND TABBY!
IT'S OKAY HON, WE'LL FIND HIM.
I KNOW WE WILL, MAMA.

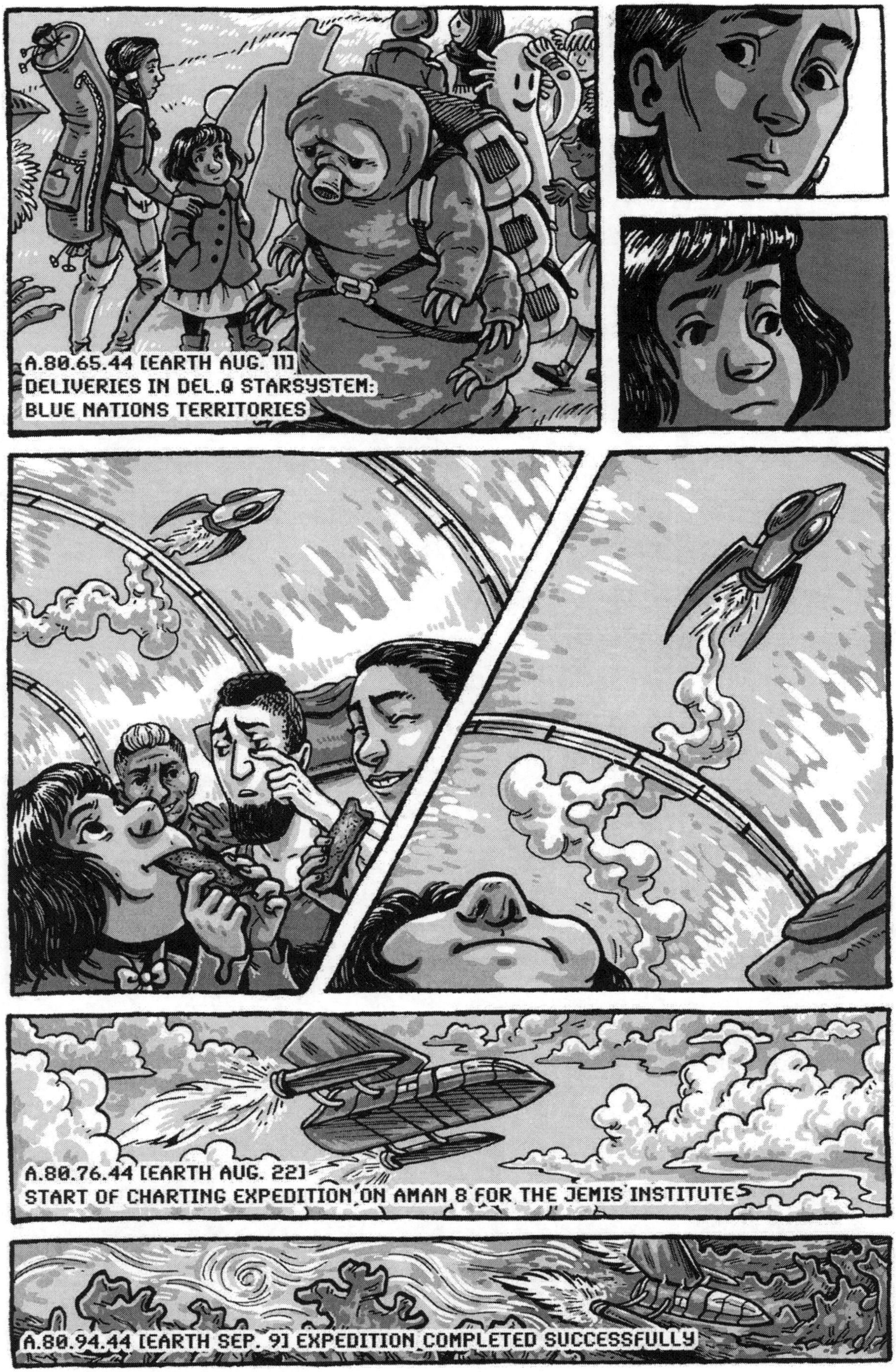
A.80.65.44 [EARTH AUG. 11]
DELIVERIES IN DEL.Q STARSYSTEM:
BLUE NATIONS TERRITORIES
A.80.76.44 [EARTH AUG. 22]
START OF CHARTING EXPEDITION ON AMAN 8 FOR THE JEMIS INSTITUTE
A.80.94.44 [EARTH SEP. 9] EXPEDITION COMPLETED SUCCESSFULLY

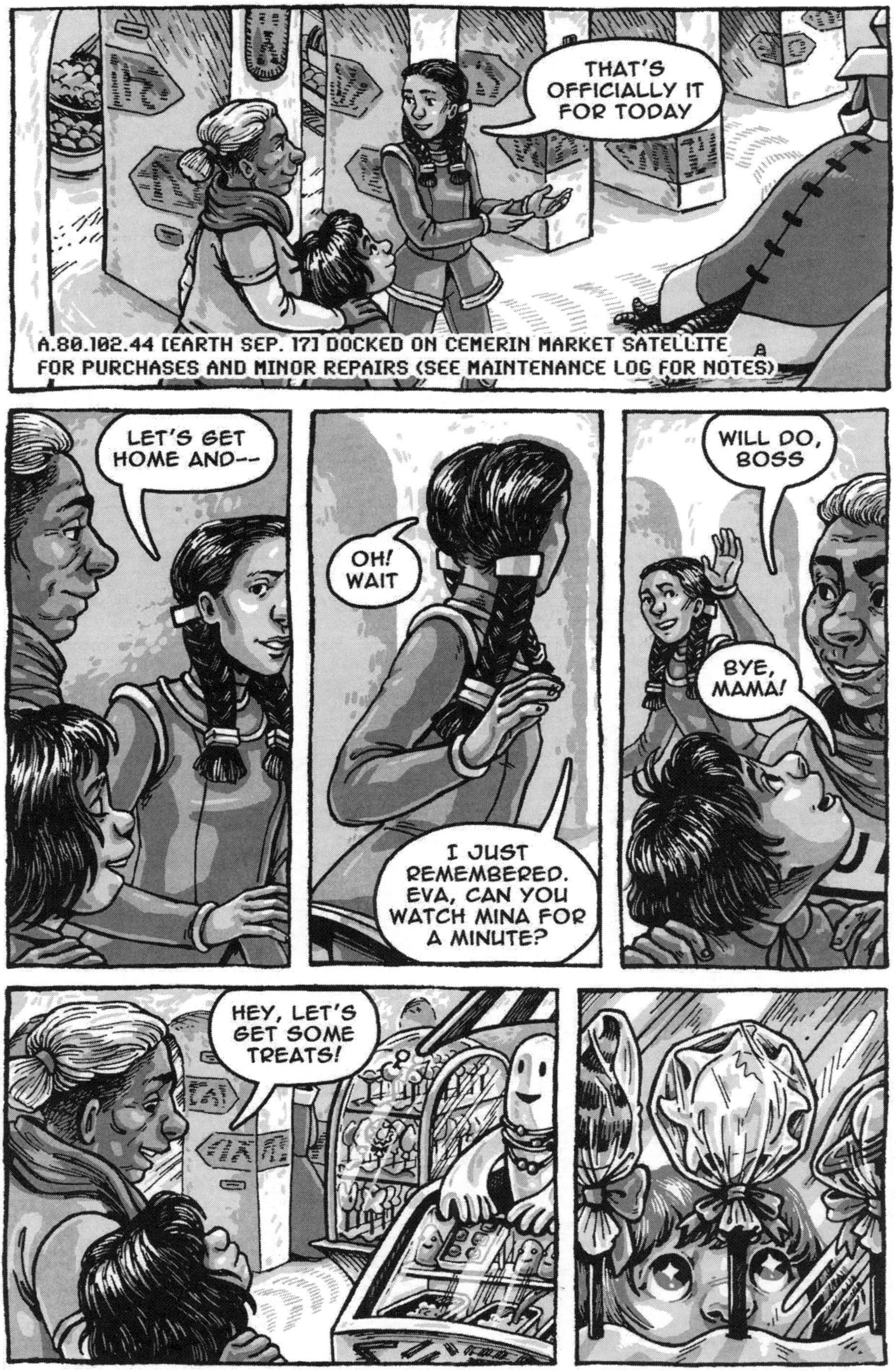
THAT'S OFFICIALLY IT FOR TODAY
A.80.102.44 [EARTH SEP. 17] DOCKED ON CEMERIN MARKET SATELLITE FOR PURCHASES AND MINOR REPAIRS (SEE MAINTENANCE LOG FOR NOTES)
LET'S GET HOME AND--
OH! WAIT
I JUST REMEMBERED. EVA, CAN YOU WATCH MINA FOR A MINUTE?
WILL DO, BOSS
BYE, MAMA!
HEY, LET'S GET SOME TREATS!

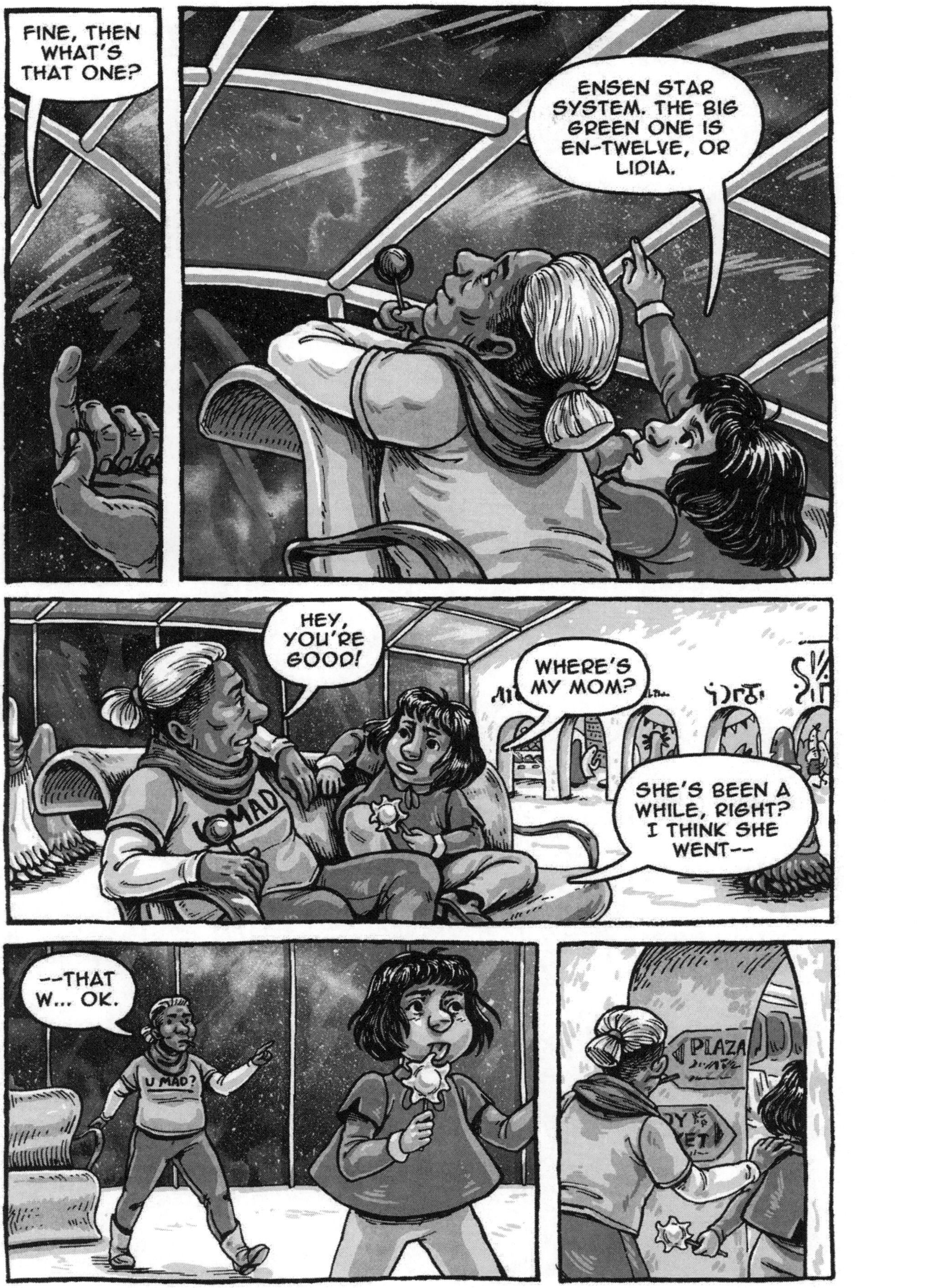
FINE, THEN WHAT'S THAT ONE?
ENSEN STAR SYSTEM. THE BIG GREEN ONE IS EN-TWELVE, OR LIDIA.
HEY, YOU'RE GOOD!
WHERE'S MY MOM?
SHE'S BEEN A WHILE, RIGHT? I THINK SHE WENT--
U MAD
--THAT W... OK.
U MAD?
PLAZA

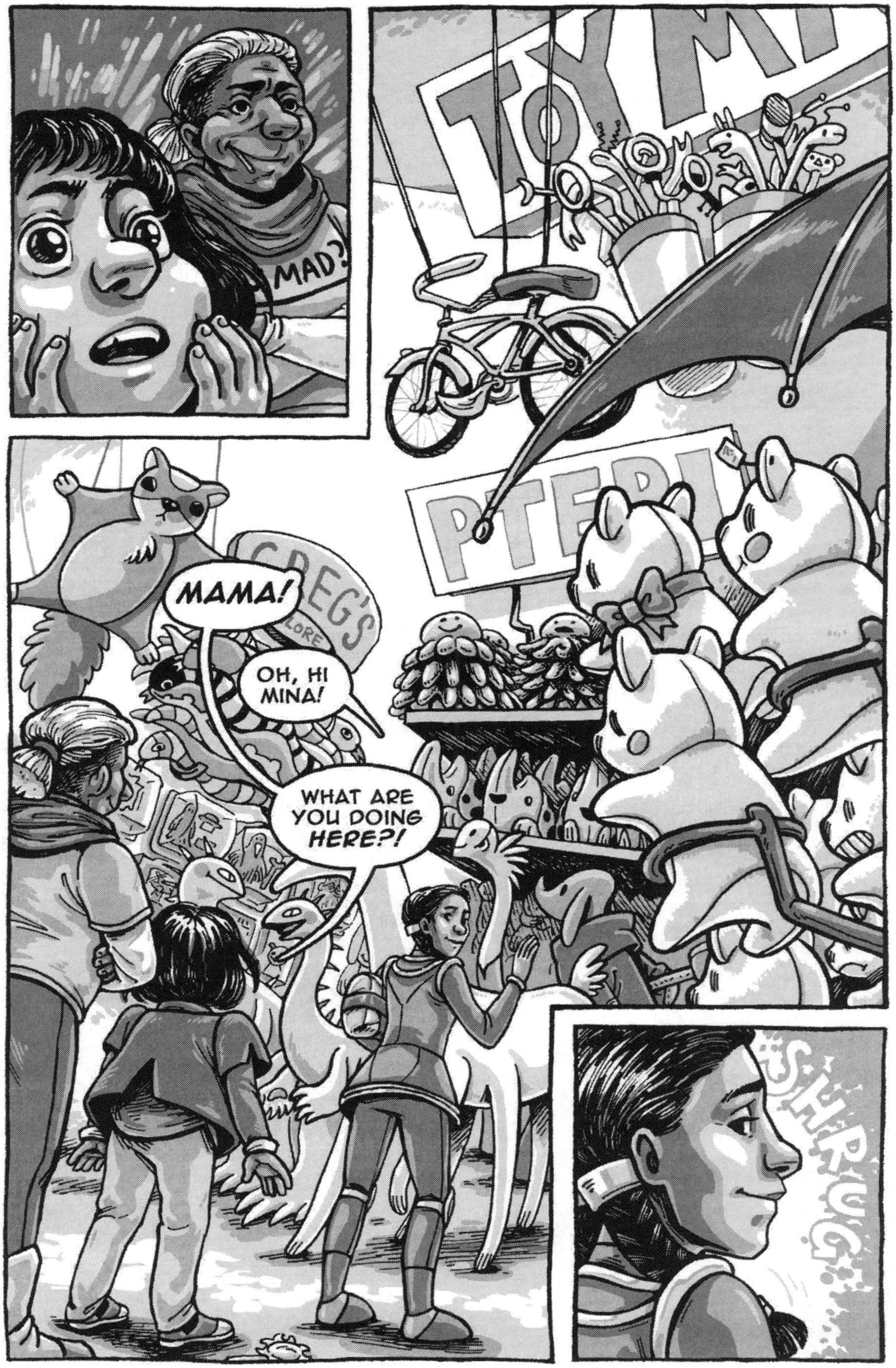
MAMA!
OH, HI MINA!
GREG'S
WHAT ARE YOU DOING HERE?!
SHRUG

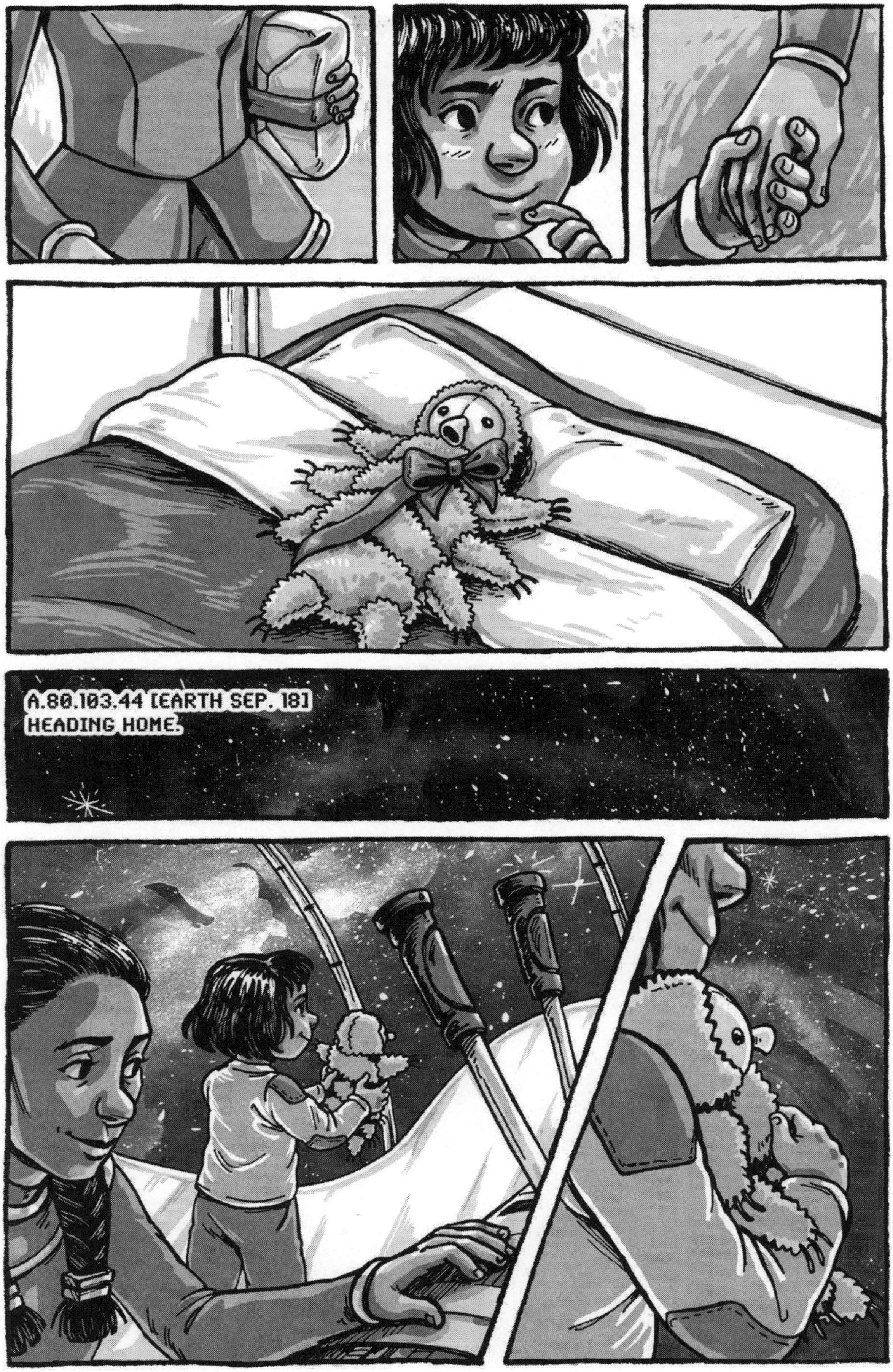
A.80.103.44 [EARTH SEP. 18]
HEADING HOME.

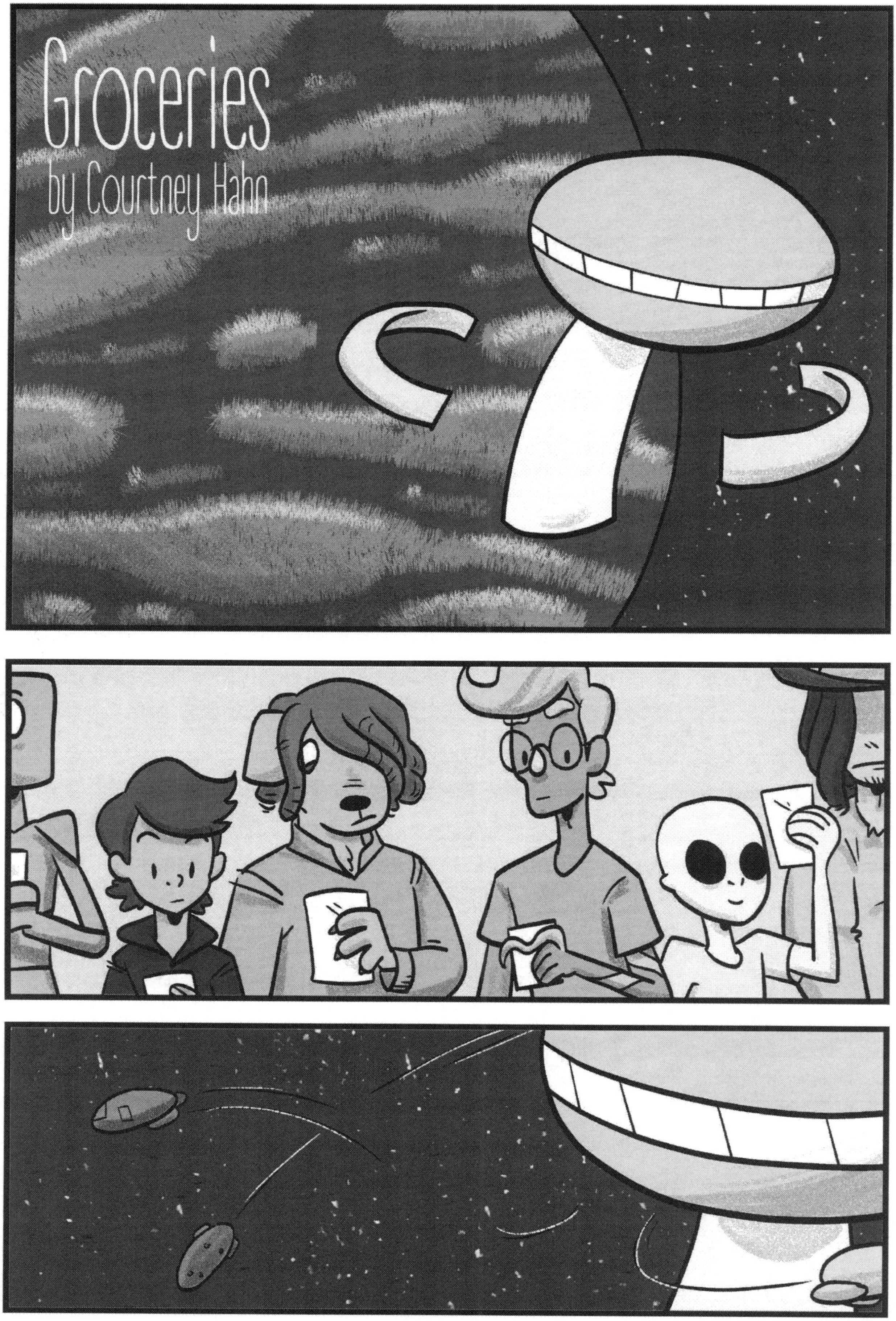
Groceries
by Courtney Hahn

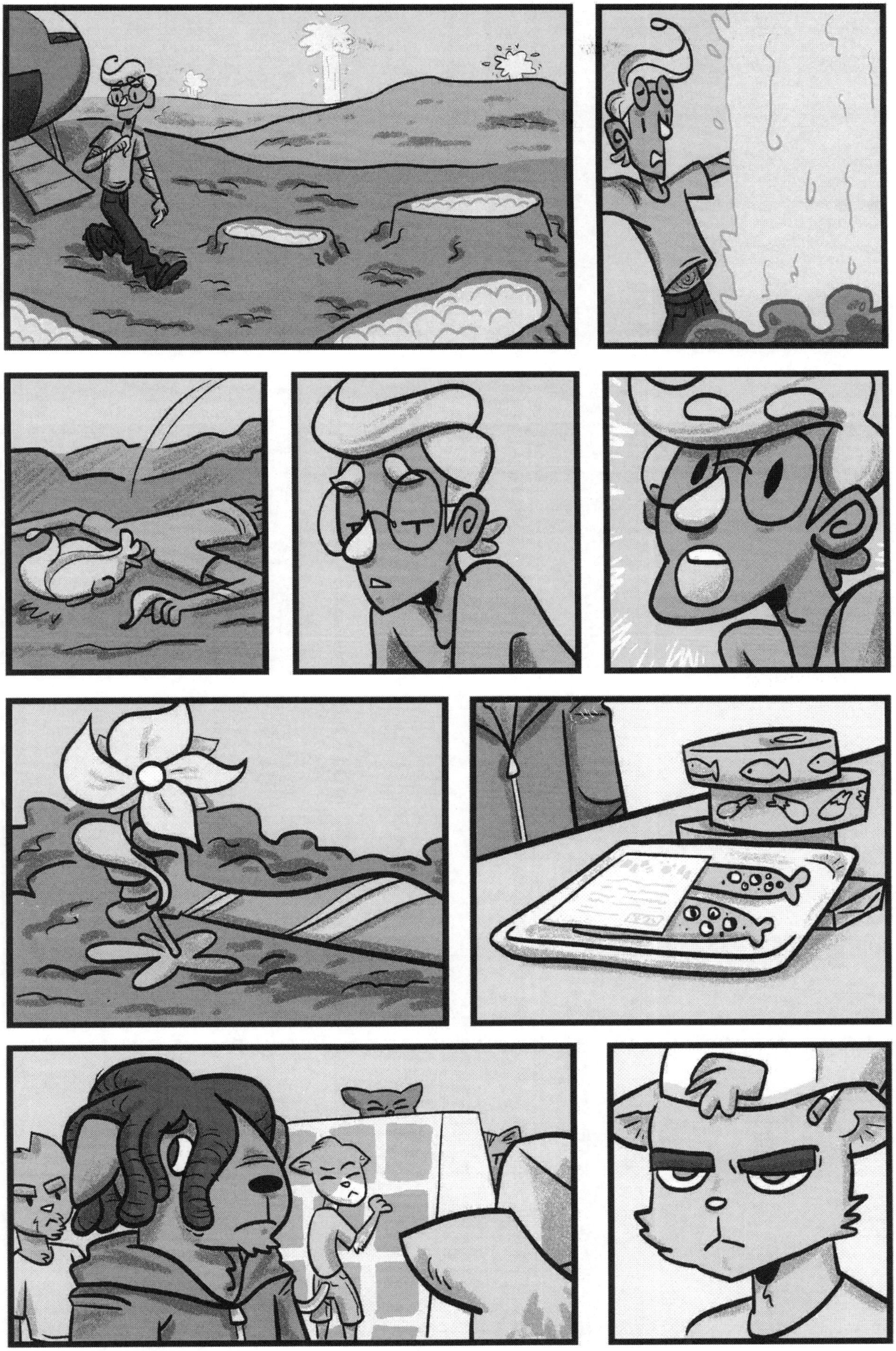

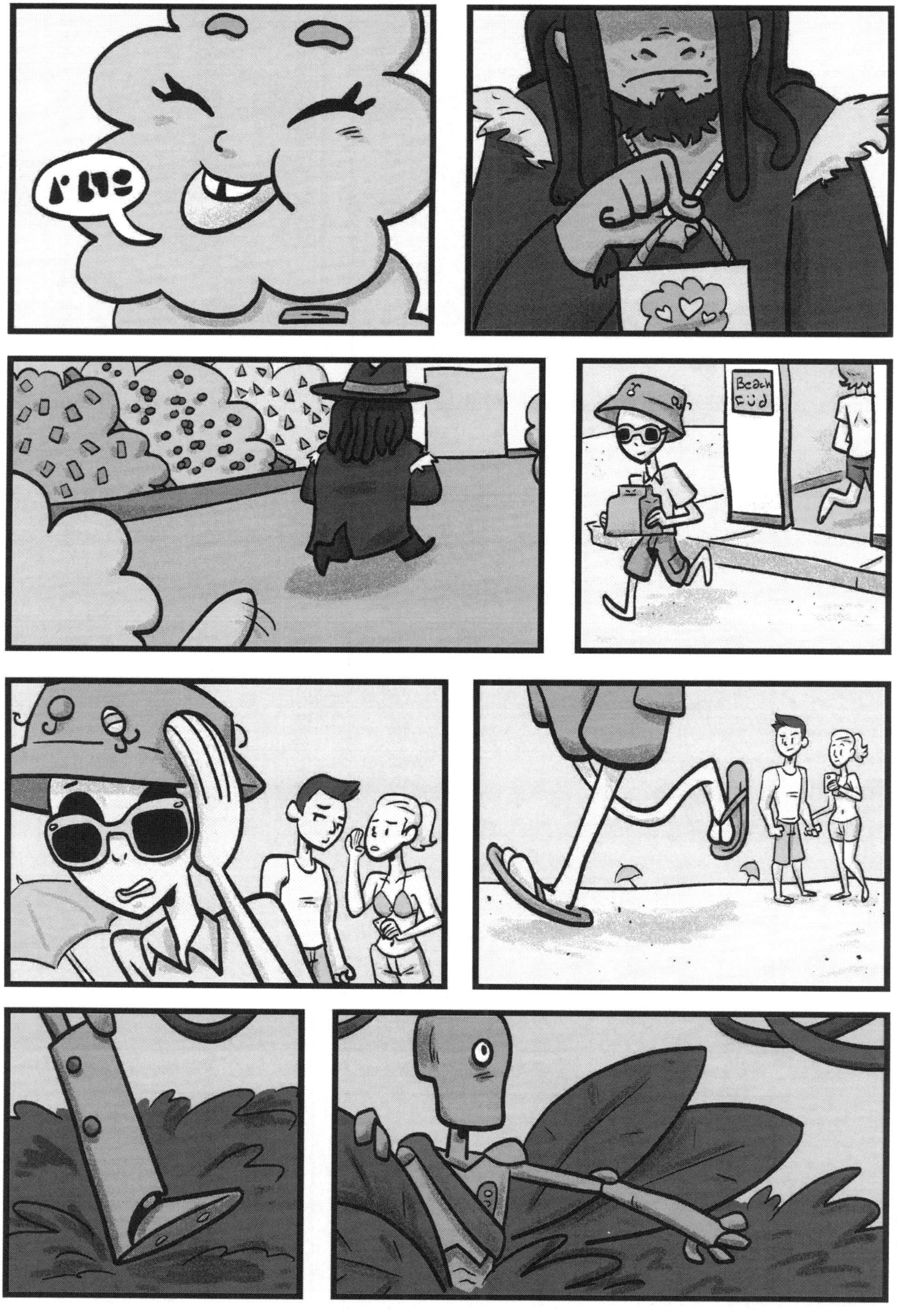
Beach

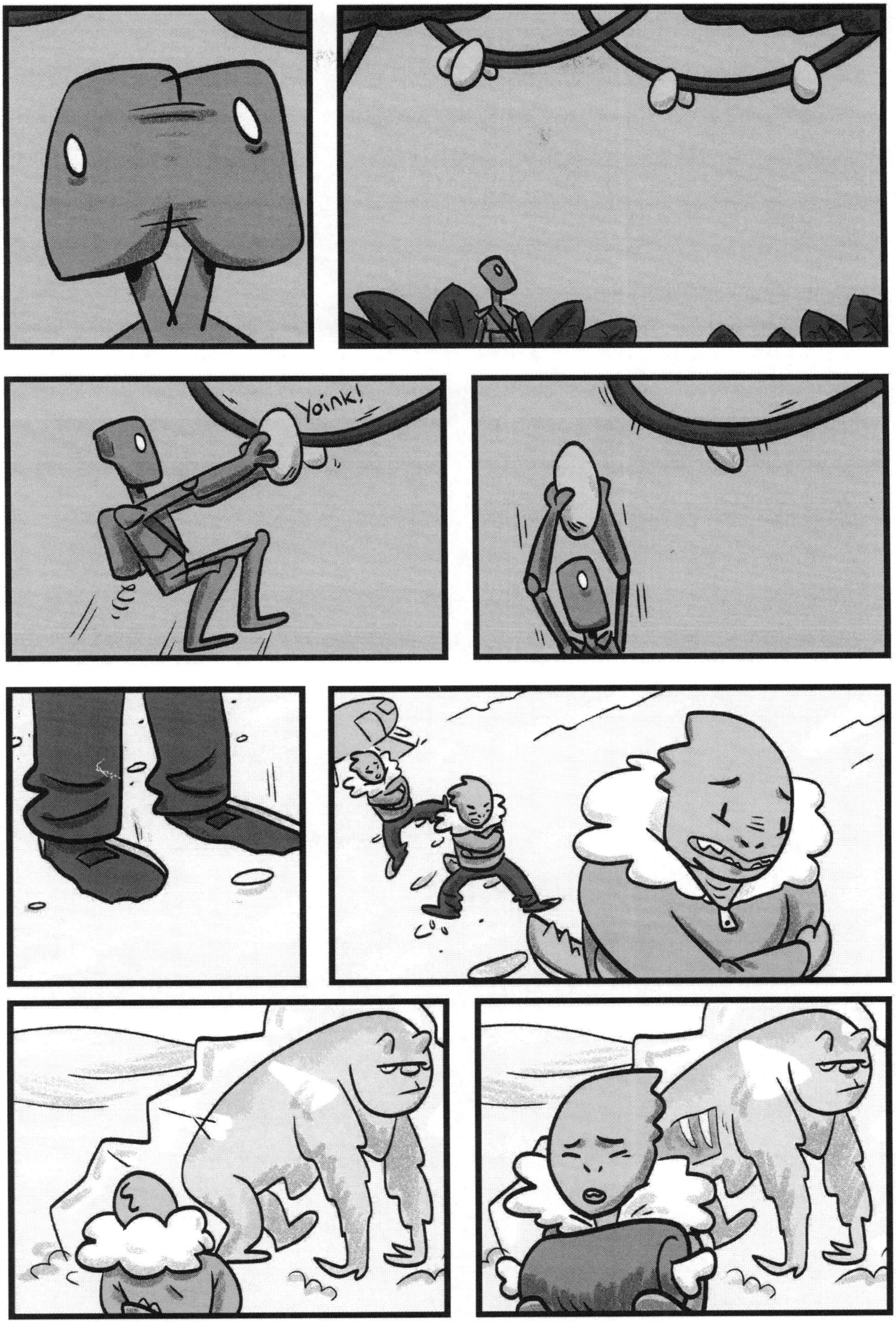
Yoink!

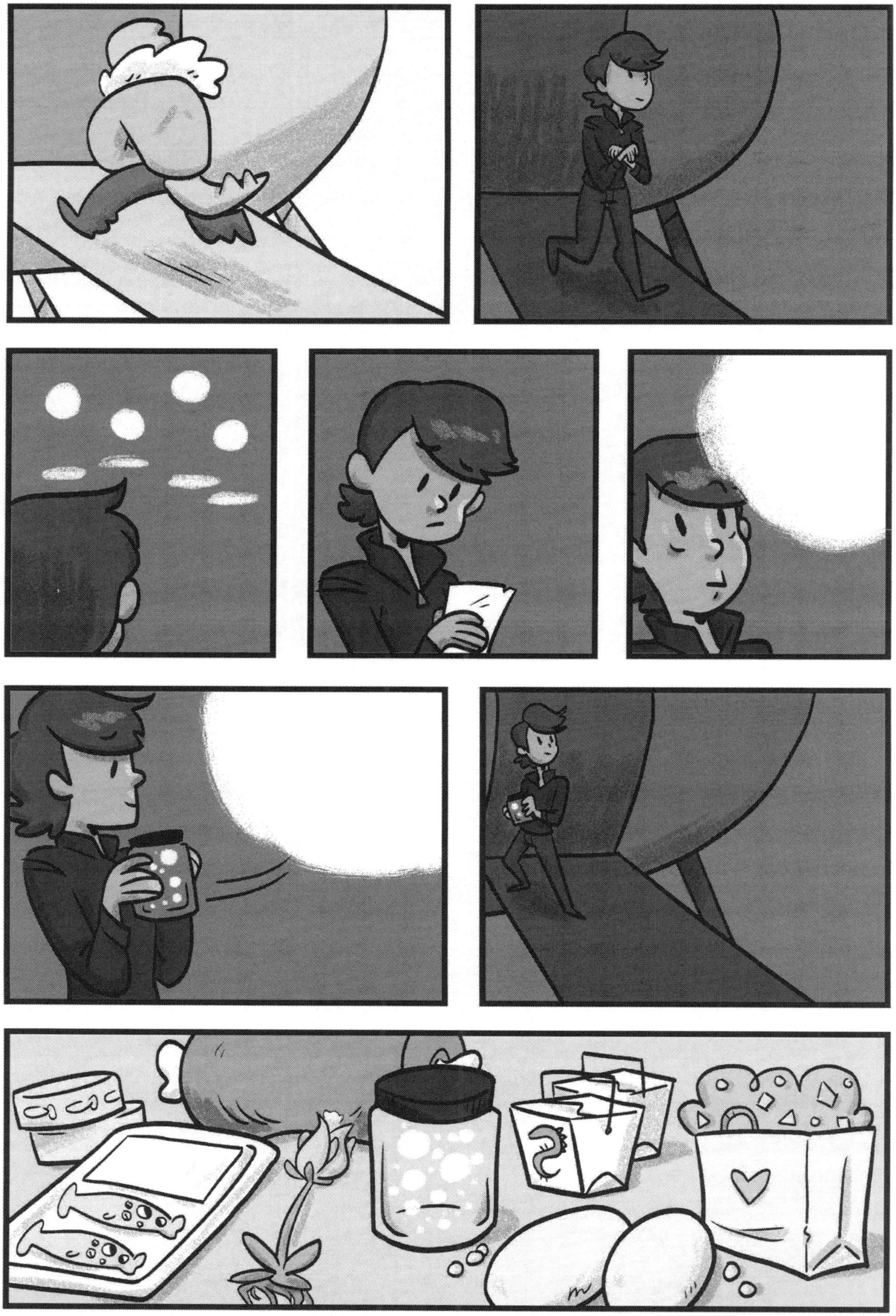

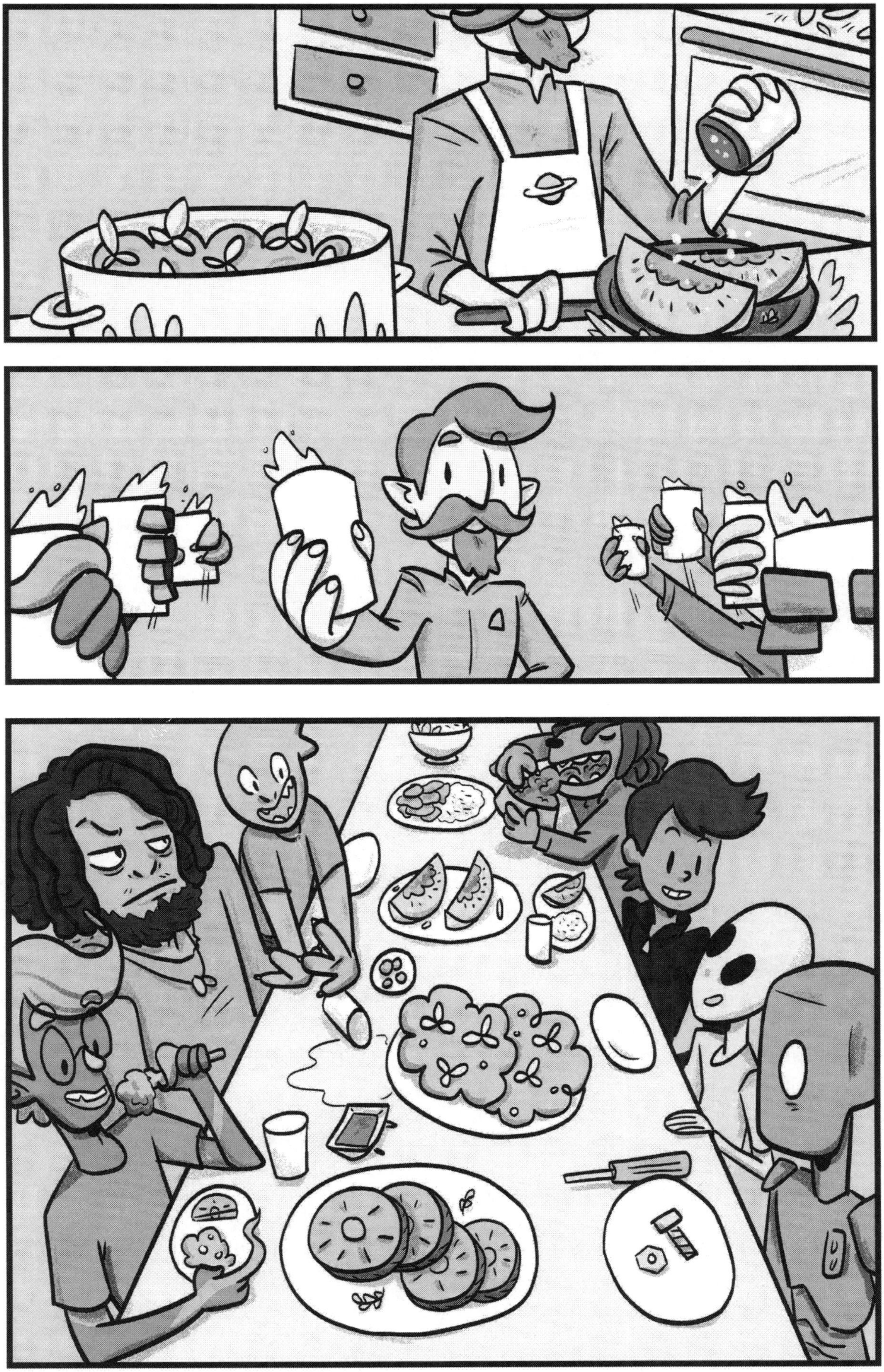

Starflowers

Samantha Rich

Kesha guides Dani's hands over the control board, showing her how to turn and tweak the sail to keep their craft skittering along over the solar winds.

"You see?" She keeps her voice light and soothing, never letting herself slip into a lecture. Her niece is an eager learner, happy beyond words to be able to venture out with Kesha and gather spectra to keep their systems humming along, but nothing shuts a child's ears and mind like being given orders. Guidance and direction, never instruction. Or at least that's Kesha's belief.

"You make the sail into a cup," Dani says, her voice nearly certain. "But a cup at an angle, so it only holds so much, and the rest spills out."

"That's a wonderful way to see it." Kesha squeezes Dani's shoulder. "Now you try it on your own. Turn us toward that blue field over there, see?"

Blue is the color arbitrarily assigned to a certain energy signature on the datascreens in the gathercraft. Kesha has been a gatherer for long enough that she dreams in the colors and shapes of radiation fields, filtered through tech and presented on screens. If she really looked out on the energy streaming through space from the sun, she would only see stretches of empty space encircling the grand nuclear drama of the living star. Of course, if she really looked out on that, she would go blind. Dani's hands are cautious on the controls, but she does well, tacking the craft against a stream of energy to move them near the current of another energy frequency that the screens designate as blue.

"Do you remember what I showed you last time?" Kesha reaches over Dani's shoulder and touches the control that brings the craft to a relative halt, the sail angled to hold them in stasis between two streams of energy that balance each other's push to zero.

"About how to collect?" Dani hesitates and turns to the far right screen, waving her hand to activate its sensors and bring it on line. The screen extends from the control bank, moving easily to place itself above Dani's lap, at the easiest angle for her to work from.

"Yes." Kesha cues her seat to move her over next to her niece, where she can again see the screen over Dani's shoulder. "Go on, show me as best you can. You can't mess anything up out here, it's all good and stable today."

Strictly speaking, that's a lie; a living star is never stable, it's constant nuclear hellfire and destruction. But in space and education, everything is relative. They are relatively safe enough for Dani to work the collector without fear.

She concentrates hard as she brings up the correct tools, her lower lip caught between her teeth. Kesha twists her fingers together to keep from reaching out and showing Dani an easier way to access what she needs; there's a shortcut to the process she's following, a quick double-tap that skips four steps, but today is for building Dani's confidence, not flaunting her own experience at this task.

"Okay," Dani says finally, when she has the collection grid showing and has activated the freehand menu. "Now I just draw?"

"Right." Kesha relaxes her fingers, giving Dani a quick pat on the arm to reinforce her praise. "Trace out how you want the collector to move."

Just like the last time, Dani works in flower patterns, drawing lopsided petals and curled leaves across the screen. Kesha watches, imagining the collectors that extend from the craft into open space, tuned to draw in the energy frequencies designated blue and channel them to charge the corresponding batteries in the gathercraft's hull. After blue, they'll move on to gathering shades of cinnamon and coral, today, and then sail back to the docking station. Three shades of collection is the limit of Dani's attention span, and in honesty, Kesha can't blame her. Days when she goes for five or six collections are trying, even if she puts on music or a reading to fill the silence.

Dani keeps drawing flowers, the details varying while the concept stays the same. Three petals on one, six on another, though the most typical design she reverts to holds five.

When Kesha is collecting, she draws spirals and abstract shapes, letting her mind wander freely rather than trying to capture the energy in an image. It makes no difference; the energy is gathered exactly the same through disciplined shapes or flowing. She knows of one collector who creates astonishing, detailed linework portraits of everyone he knows, combining the work of a day into multicolored, multilayered likenesses. She knows of another who places his palms flat over the screen and gathers in great flat washes of pressure, and deletes every image as soon as that shade is done. Every approach works the same in the way that counts: bringing energy back to their homes to keep their systems alive.

"Can I help move the batteries today, too?" Dani asks, tracing out a third identical flower in a row.

"Not today." Kesha thinks ahead to the docking station, to the panel crews who will be patiently waiting to remove the battery segments of the gathercraft's hull and send them planetside for distribution. It's fiddly work that requirescareful hands. They'll need a slow day and a patient crew on duty to let Dani help with it.

She opens her personal device and makes a note to catch Daryn soon; he's always willing to make a little extra time to show a youngster how to carry out the craft. If Dani expresses interest in mechanics as well as gathering, Kesha will put in a word to send her out with Daryn's crew to try it out for a day.

"Soon?" Dani presses, and Kesha makes a vague sound of acknowledgment, glancing over the messages that have come in while she was supervising Dani's steering. One from her brother asking how Dani is doing, one from Arielle reminding her not to be late for dinner with the Representative tonight, one notice that the choir is beginning double practices next week. Typical all around.

"It's done," Dani says, pulling her hands back from the screen. Kesha snaps her personal closed and checks the readings along the left edge; the blue battery segment is topped out.

"Good job," she says, giving Dani a quick smile. "Remember how to close it out?"

Dani's forehead creases slightly. "Show me again? I think I remember but I don't want to mess it up."

"Okay." Kesha taps out the first two commands, then waits, raising her eyebrows at her niece. Dani hesitates a second, then finishes the sequence flawlessly. "See, you did remember."Dani grins and touches the command sigil again. "Can I save my image?"

"Sure." Kesha in general subscribes to the school of the images being as ephemeral as the energy, and letting them go at the end of each shade, but she doesn't see any reason to impose that on Dani. And her flowers are lovely. "Save it to the remote backup and then let's move on to the next shade. We want to finish three today and I've got to have you home by eighteen hundred so I'm home for dinner."

"Or Arielle will be mad." Dani's grin shifts to a smirk. "And you don't want THAT."

"You're right, I don't." Arielle in a temper was as much a work of art as anything Kesha drew while gathering, but dangerous art, more like capturing a solar flare than the tepid energy fields they were working today. "So let's keep moving."

Dani squares her shoulders and moves back to the navigation panel. "Remind me?"

"Breaking a stationary position," Kesha intones, watching Dani's hands move deftly over the controls. She already has more confidence than she did half an hour ago. It's an amazing thing to see. "Tip the sail to break the balance of the solar winds, then find another stream that takes us where we're going…"

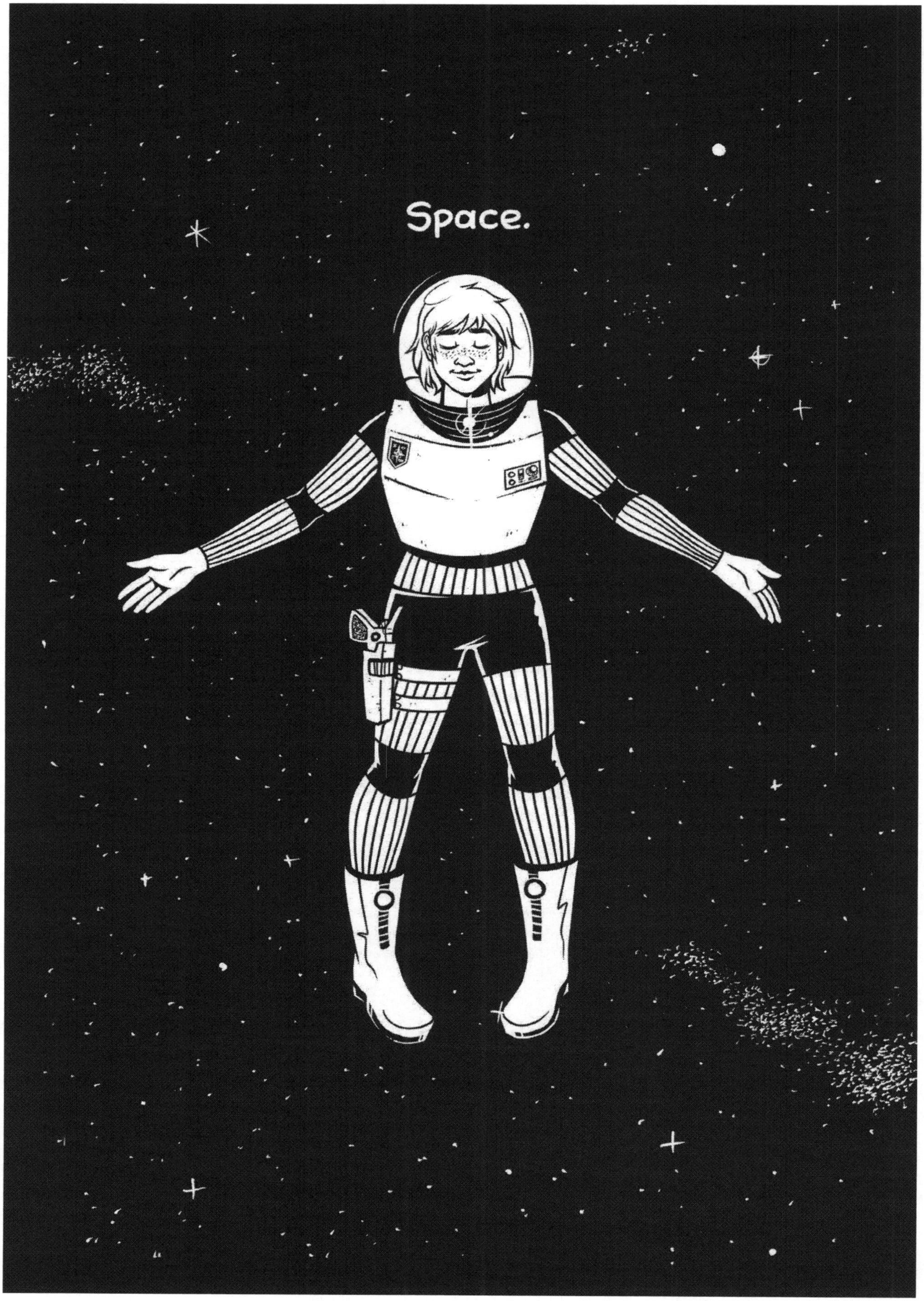
Space.

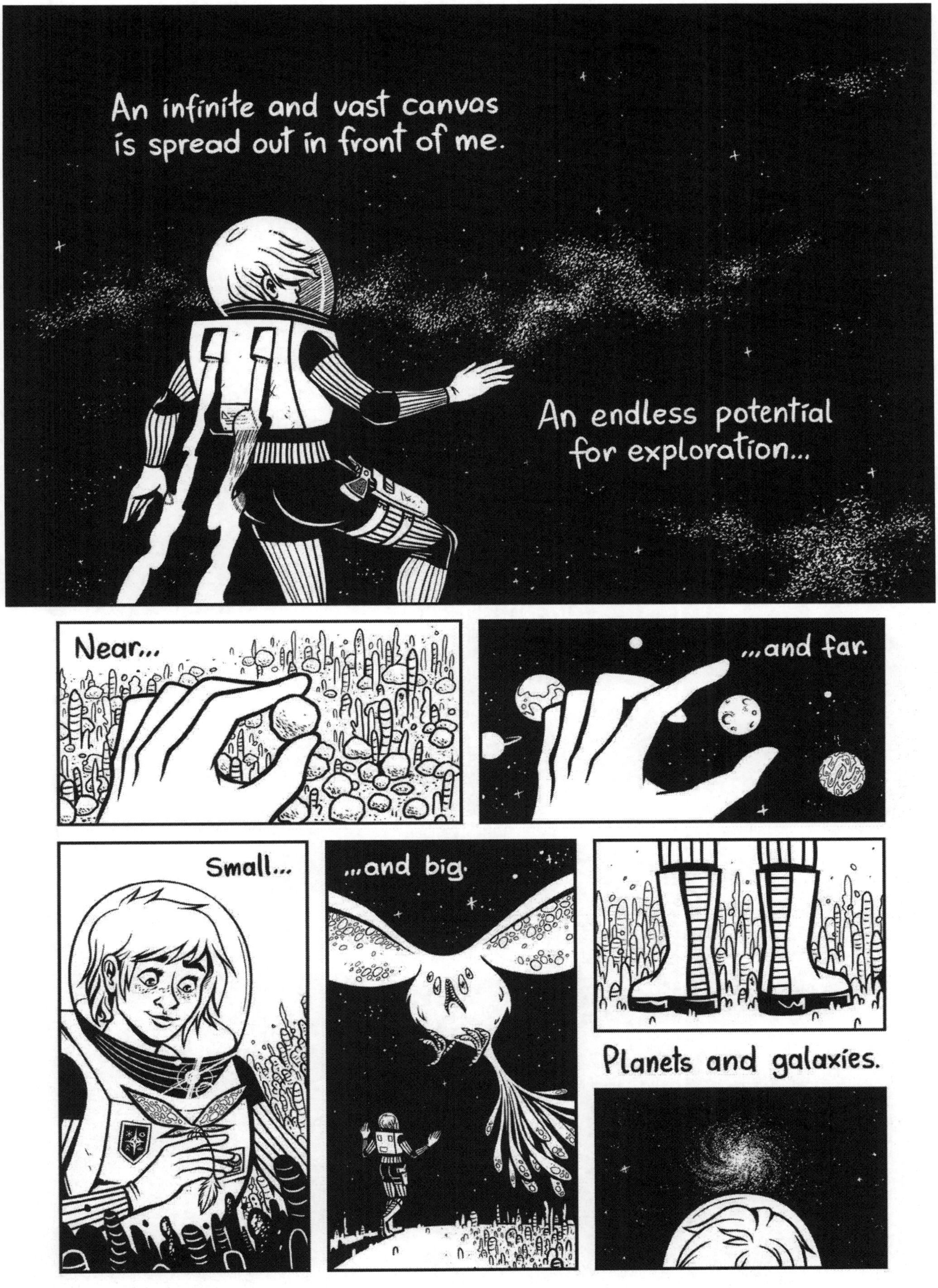
An infinite and vast canvas is spread out in front of me.
An endless potential for exploration...
Near...
...and far.
Small...
...and big.
Planets and galaxies.

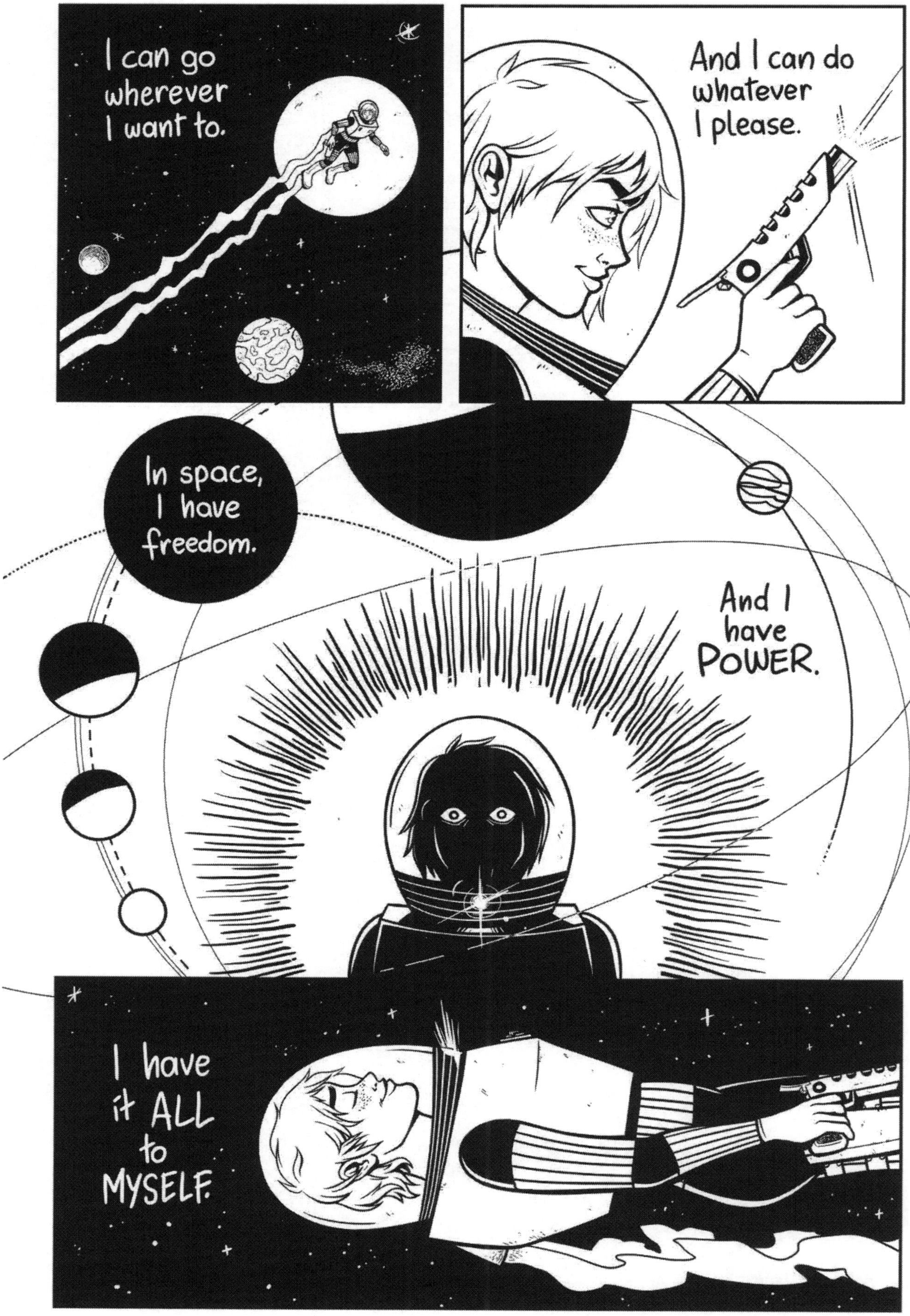
I can go wherever I want to.
And I can do whatever I please.
In space, I have freedom.
And I have POWER.
I have it ALL to MYSELF.

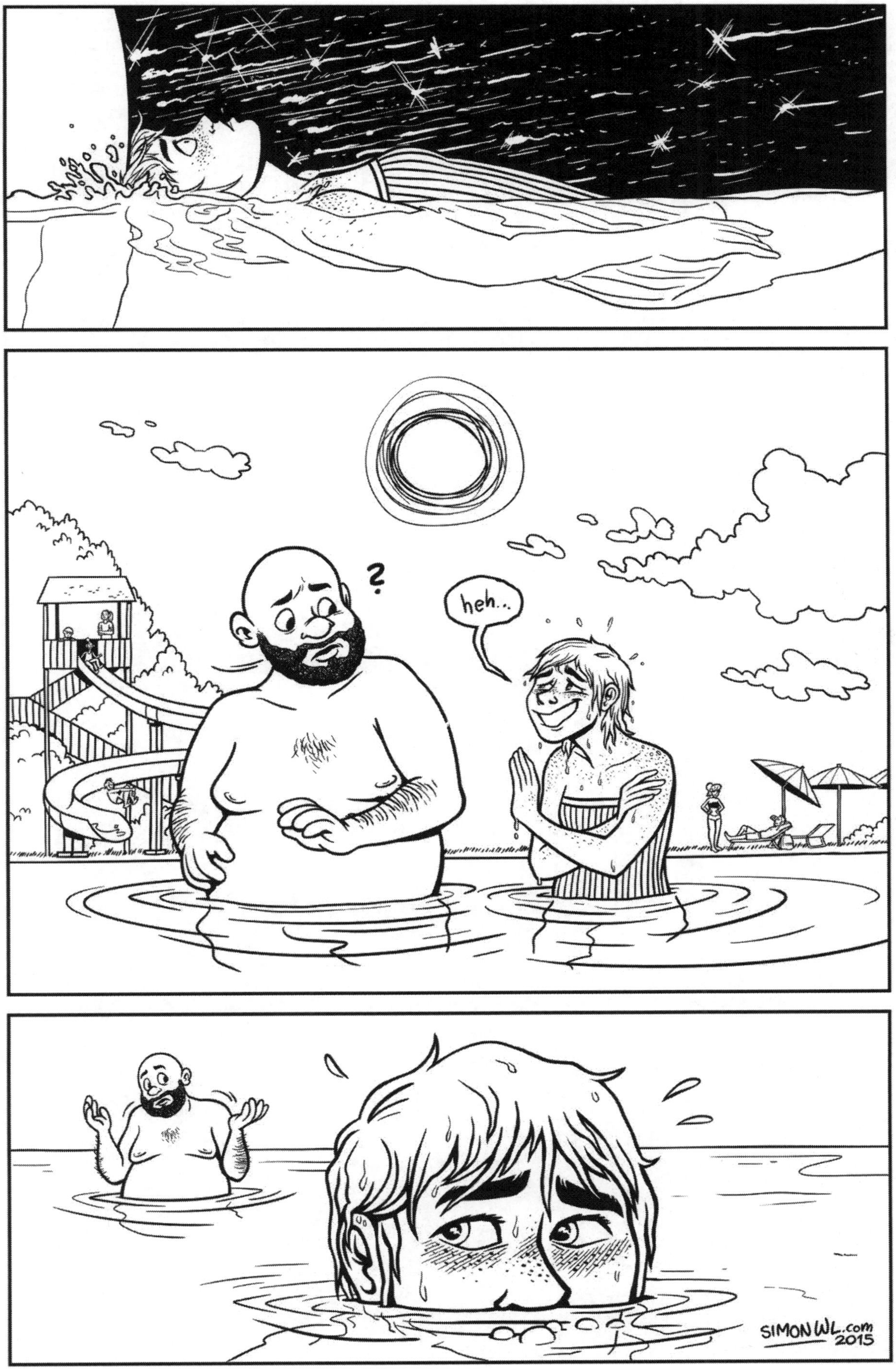
?
heh...
SIMONWL.com 2015

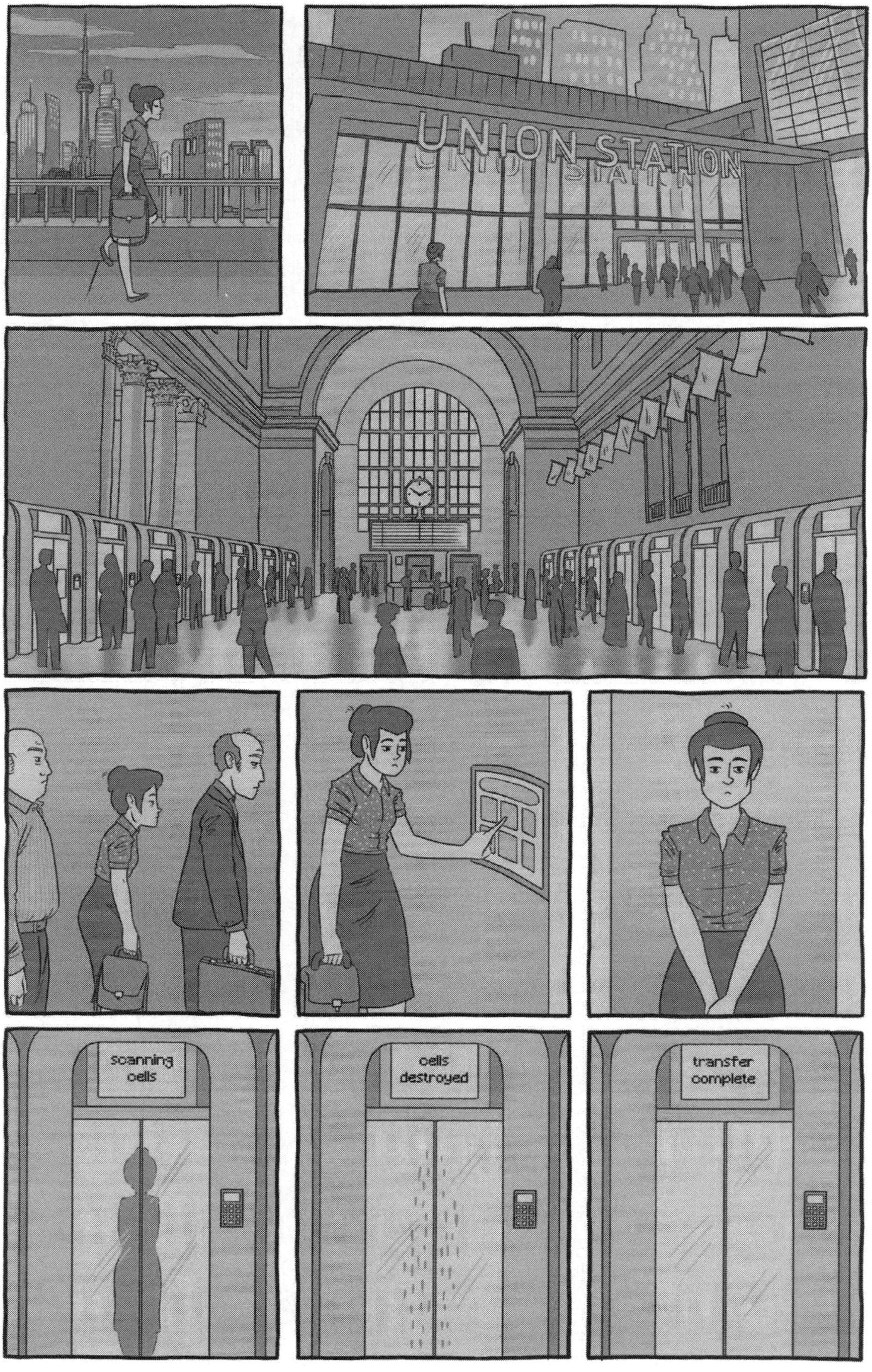
UNION STATION
scanning cells
cells destroyed
transfer complete

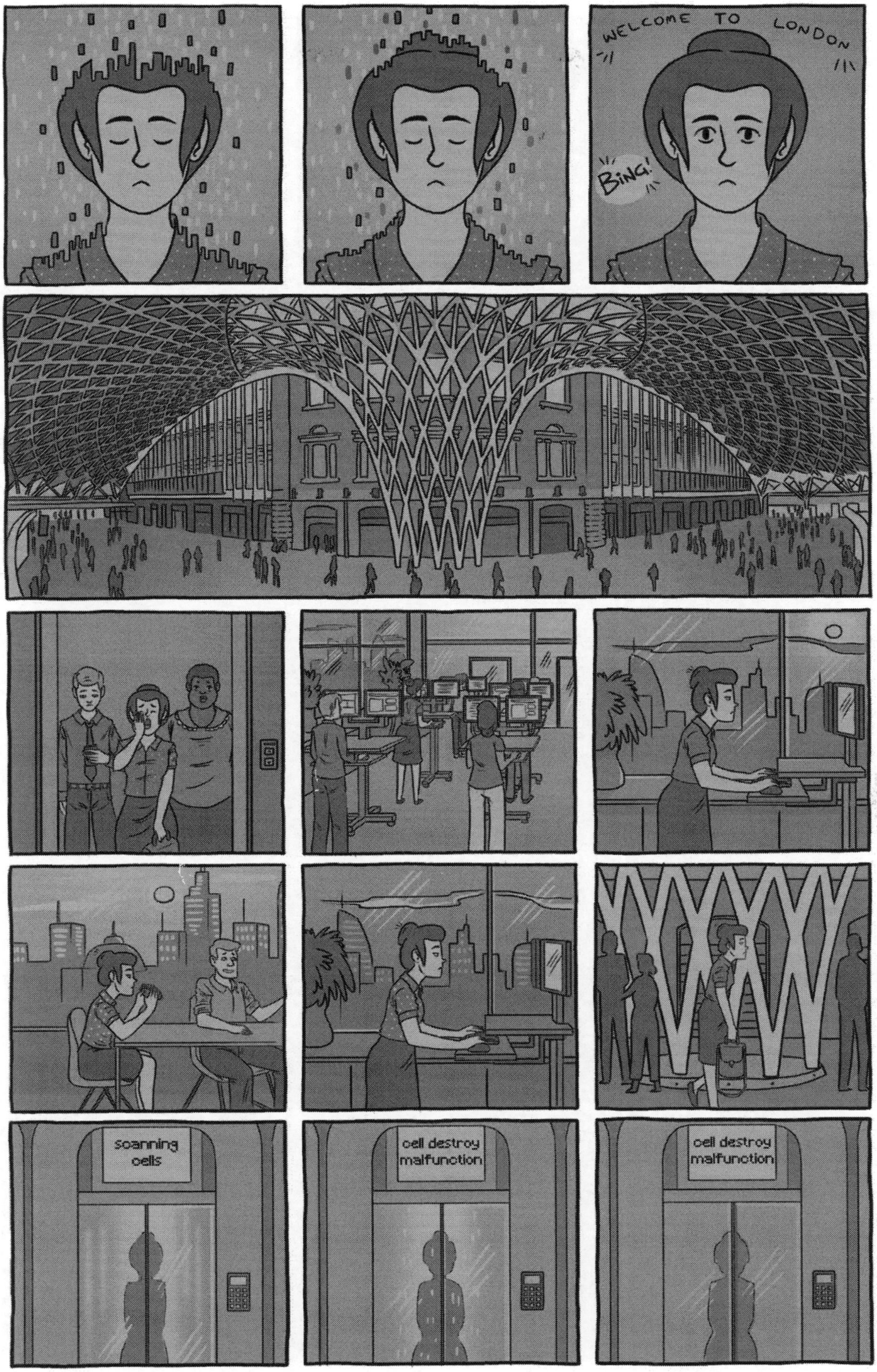
WELCOME TO LONDON
BING!
scanning cells
cell destroy malfunction
cell destroy malfunction

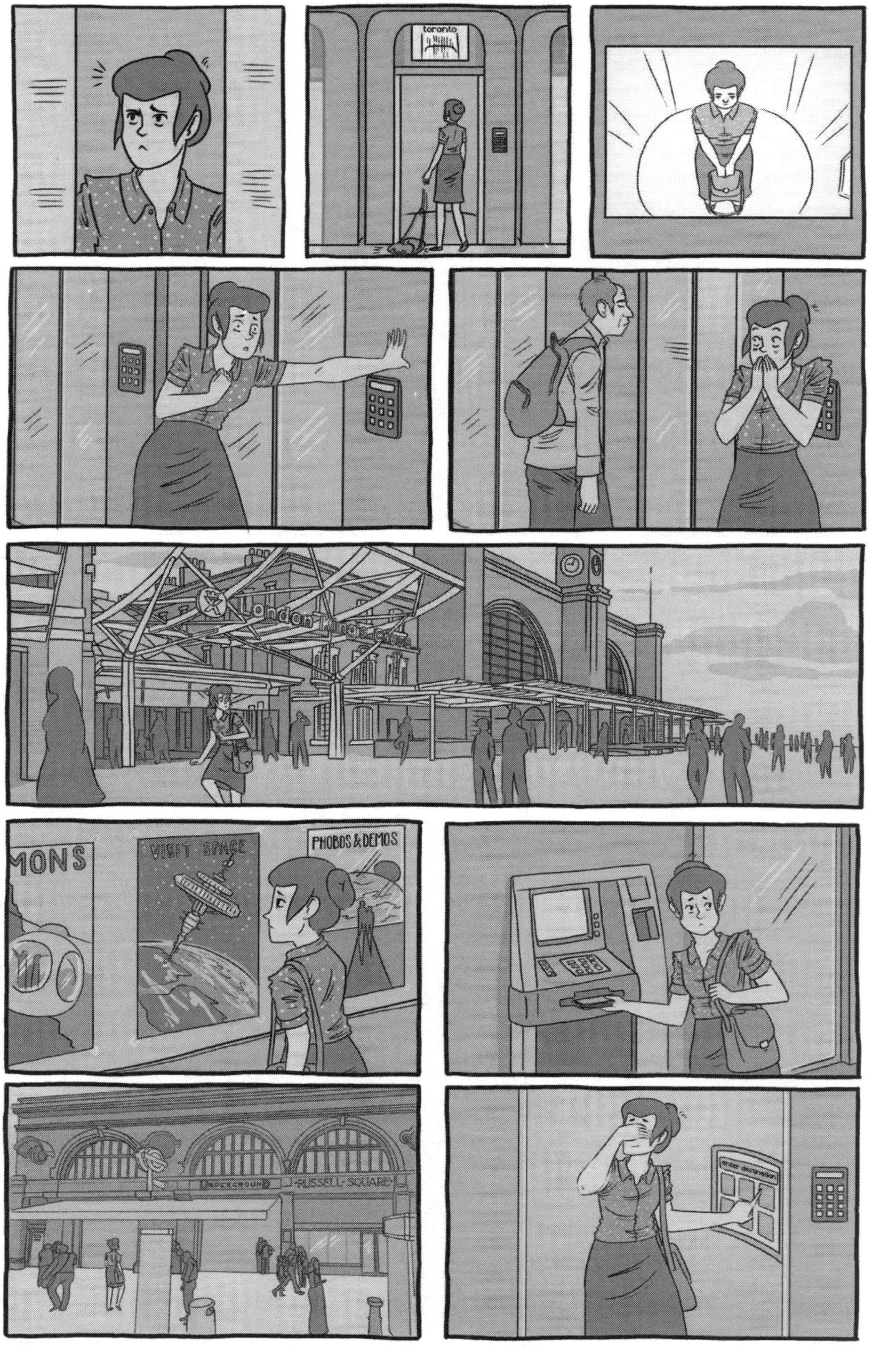
toronto
London Kings Cross
MONS
VISIT SPACE
PHOBOS & DEMOS
UNDERGROUND
RUSSELL SQUARE

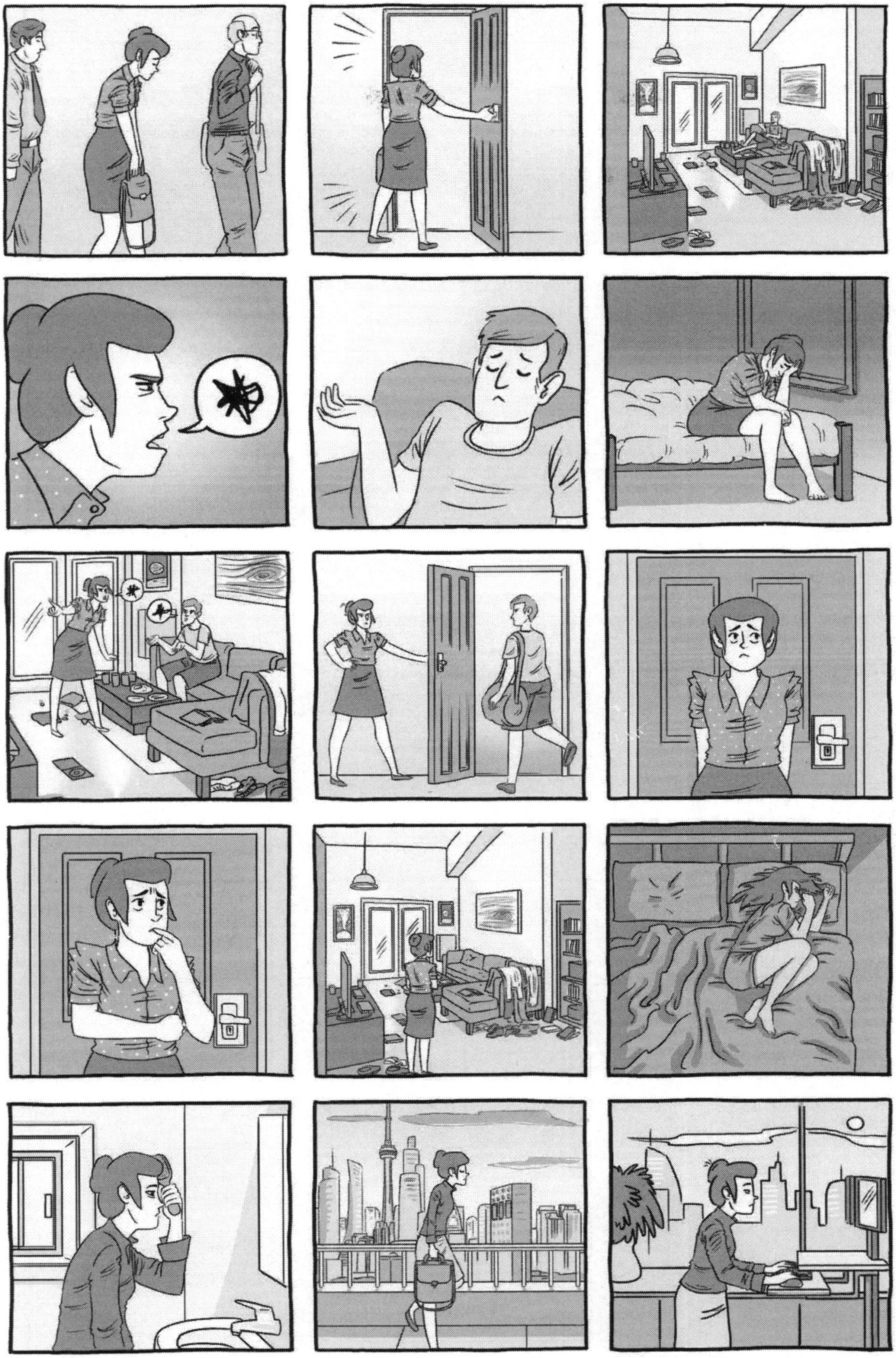

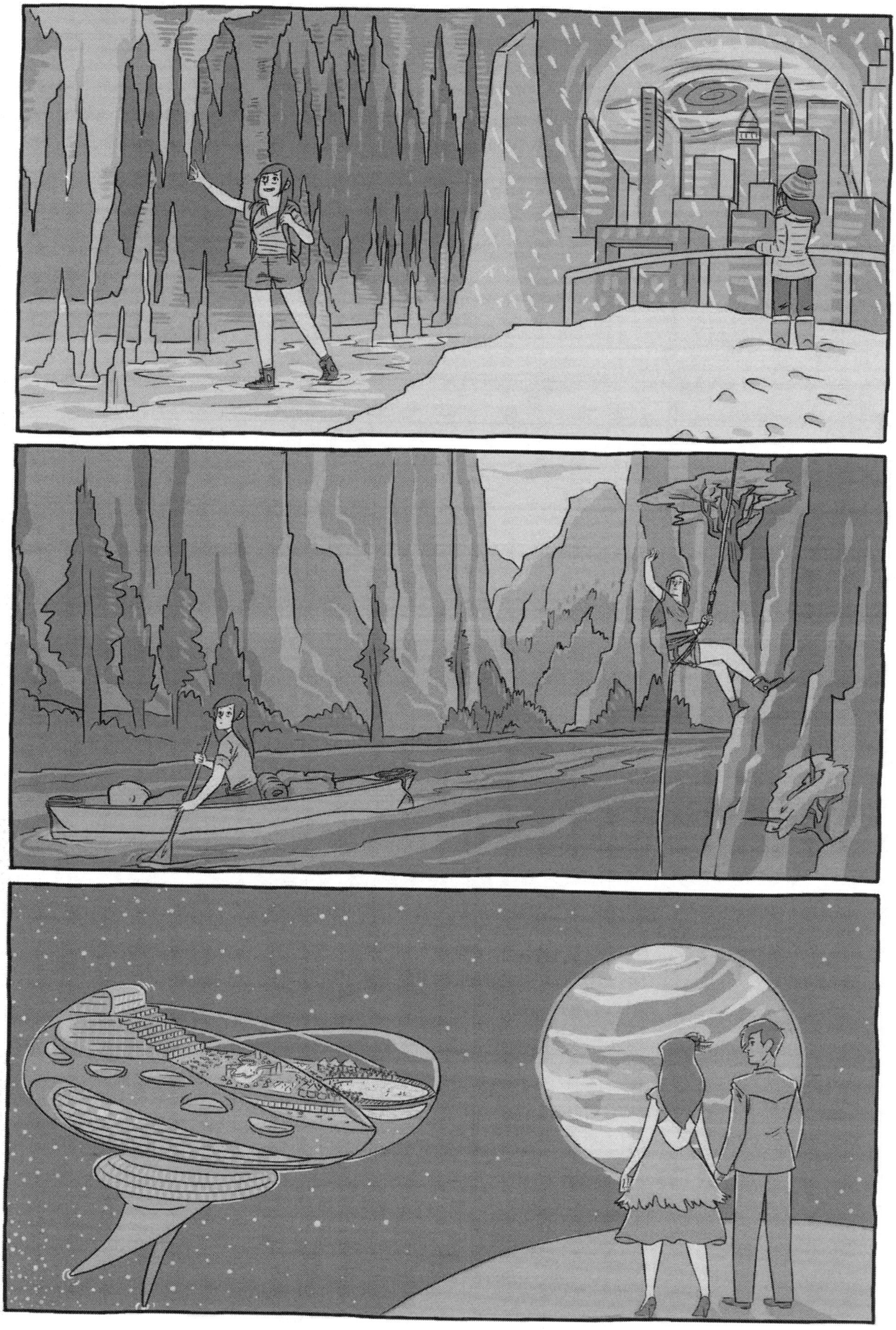

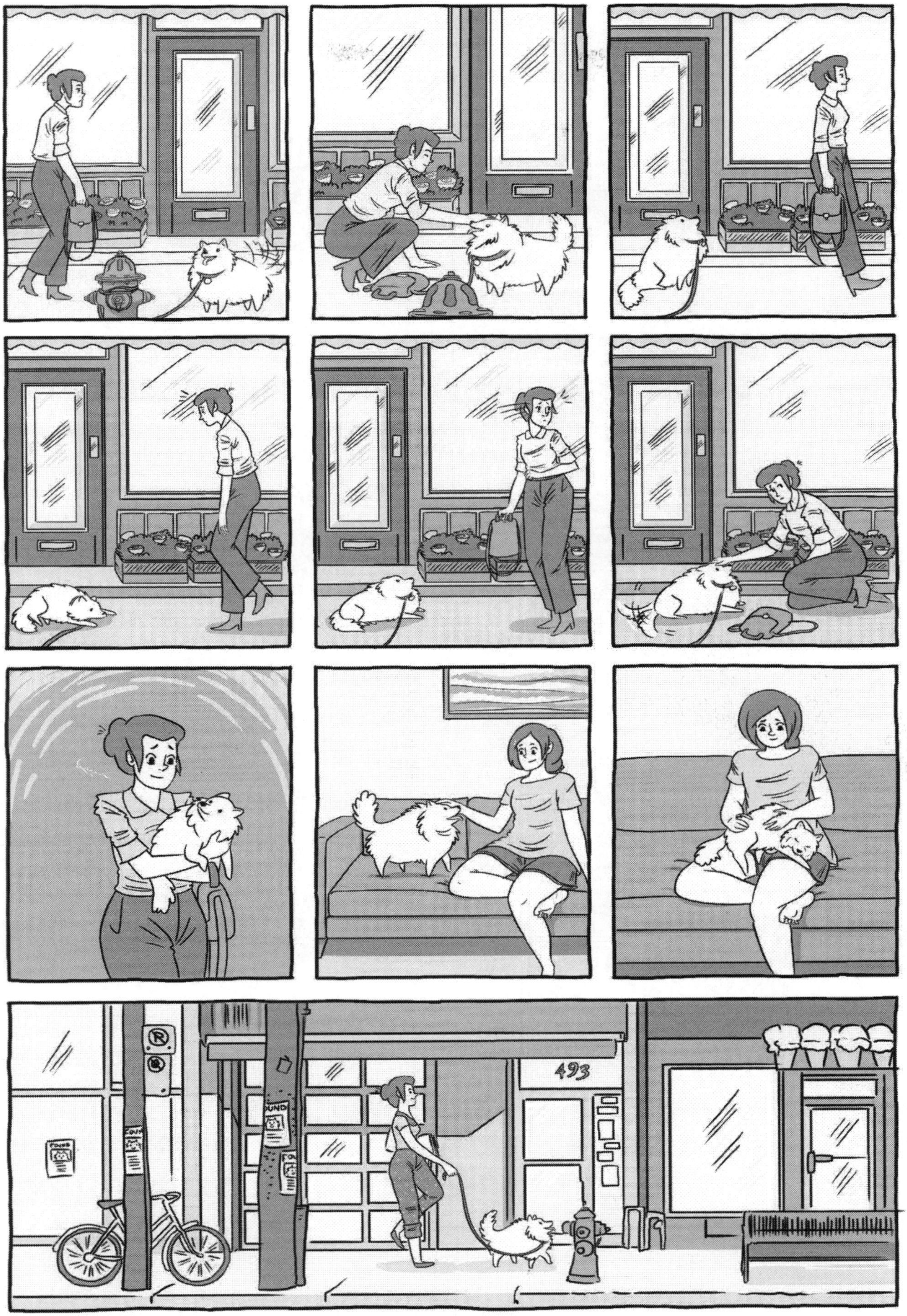
493

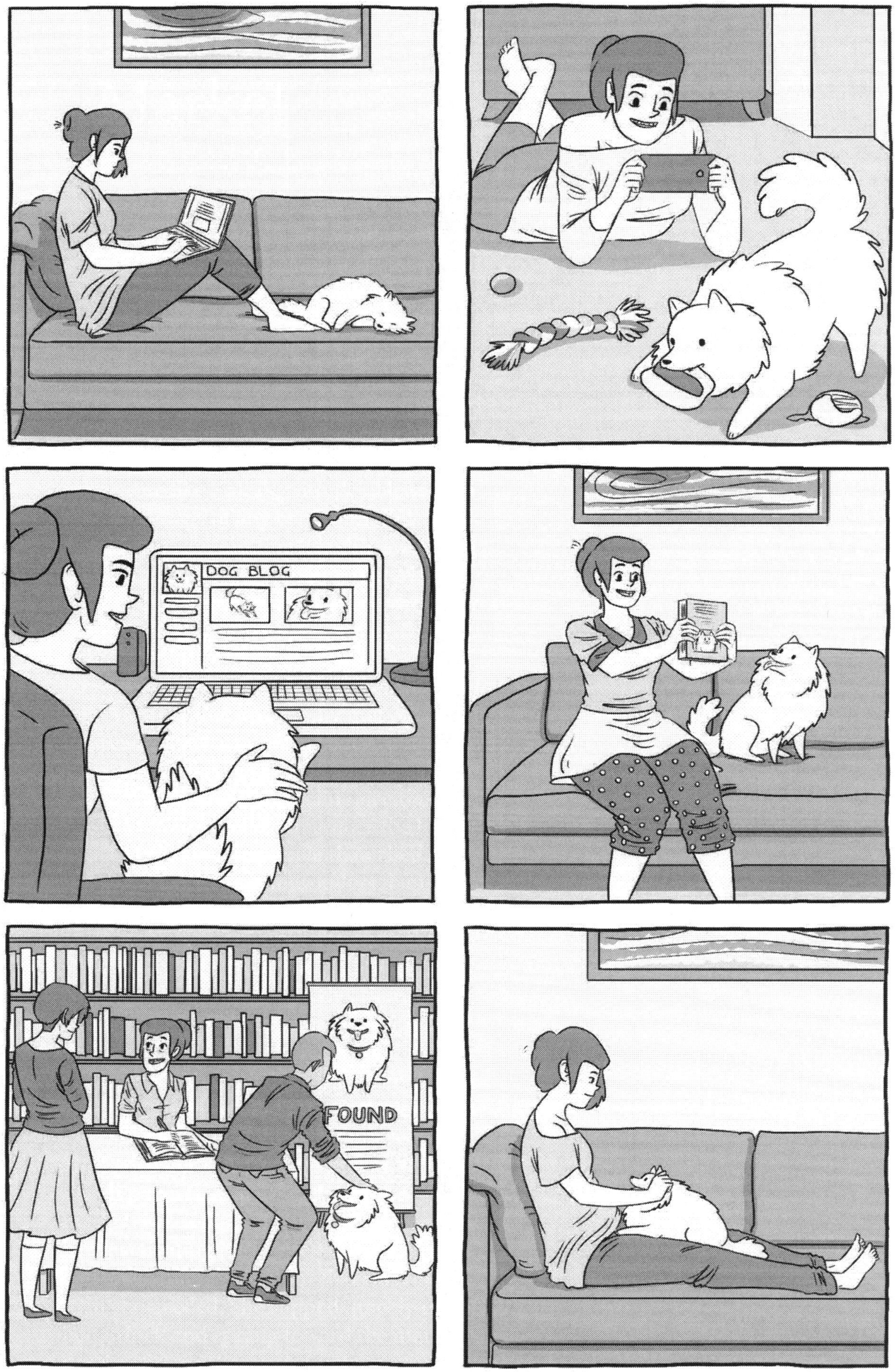
DOG BLOG
FOUND

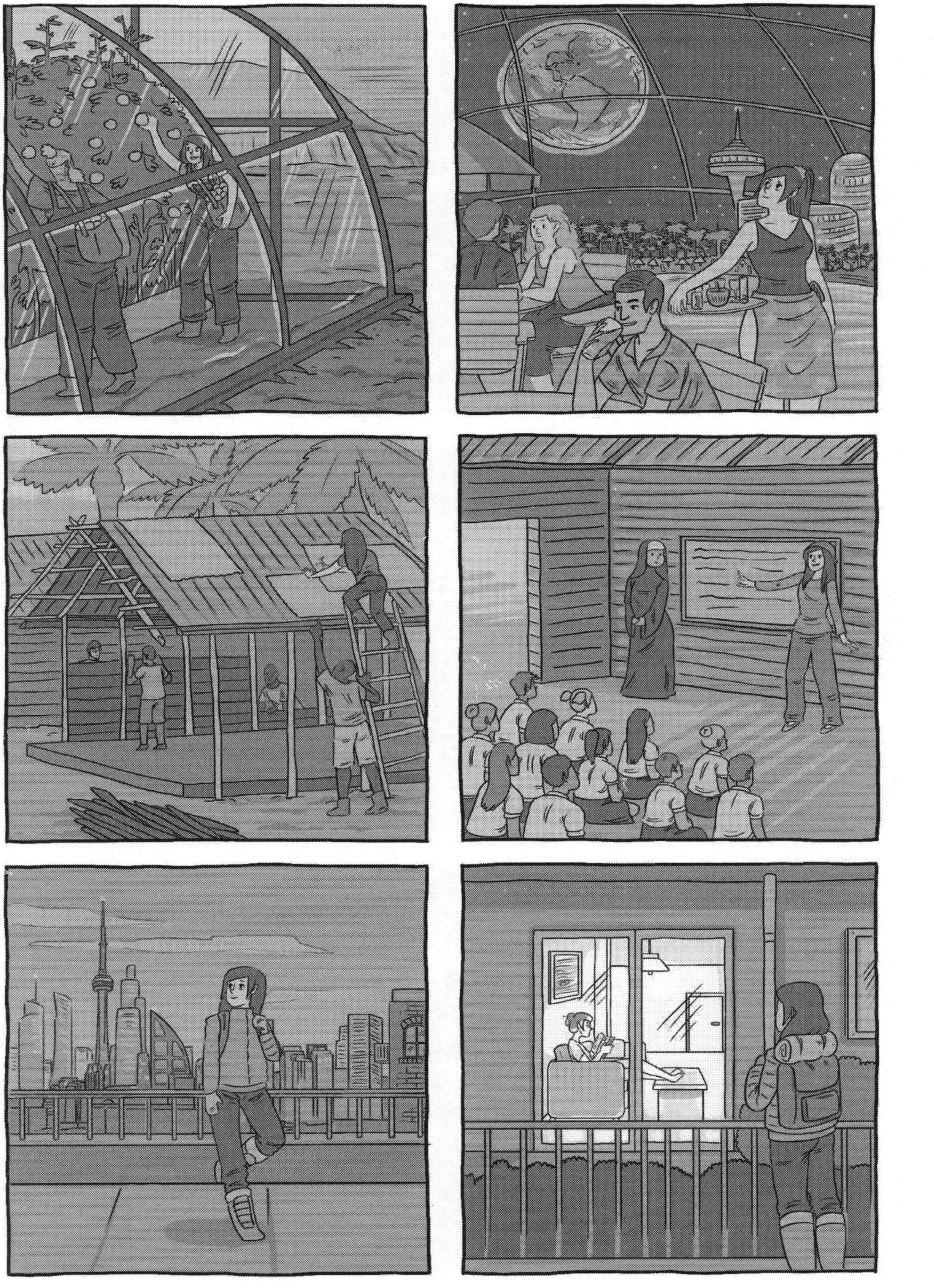

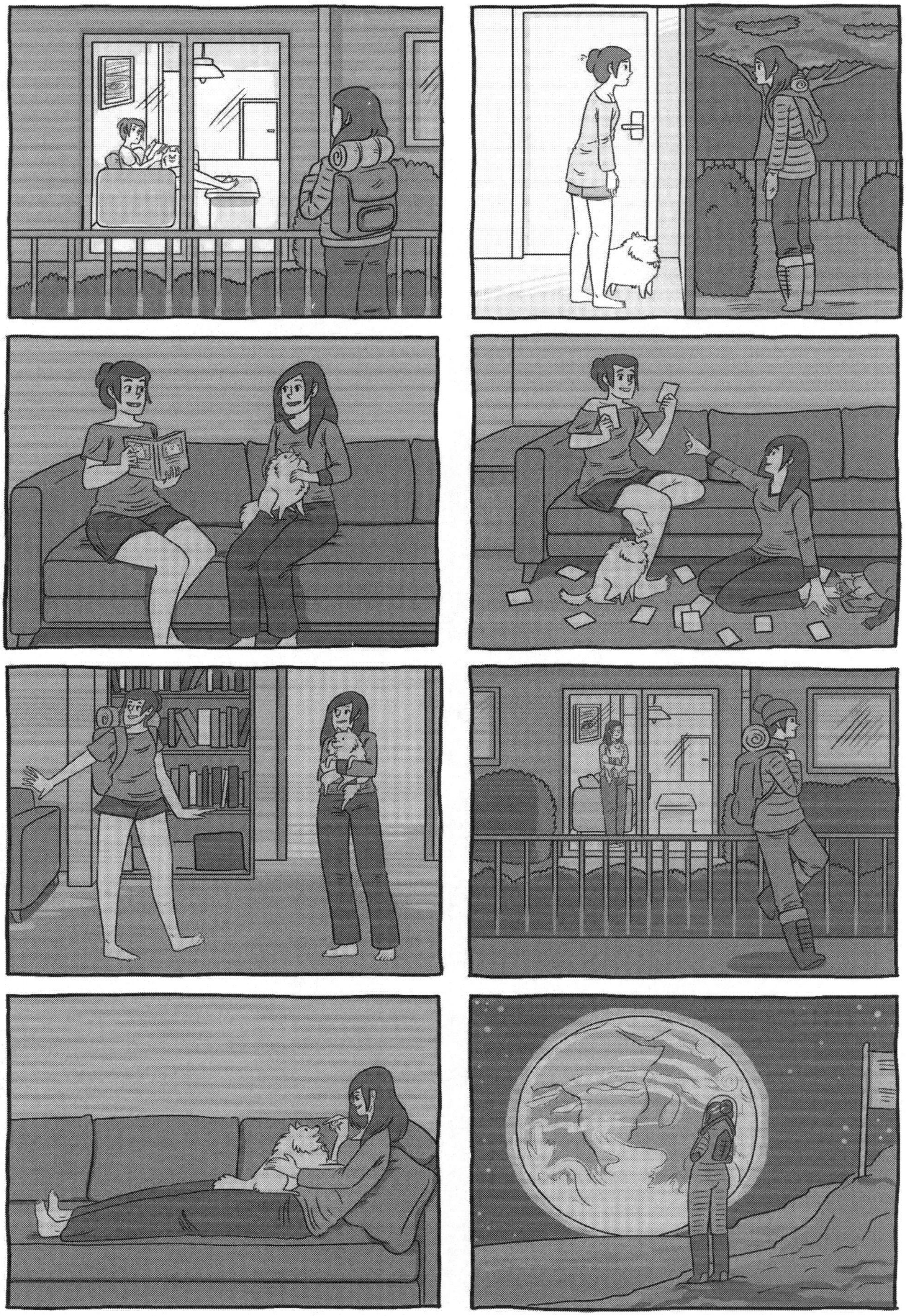

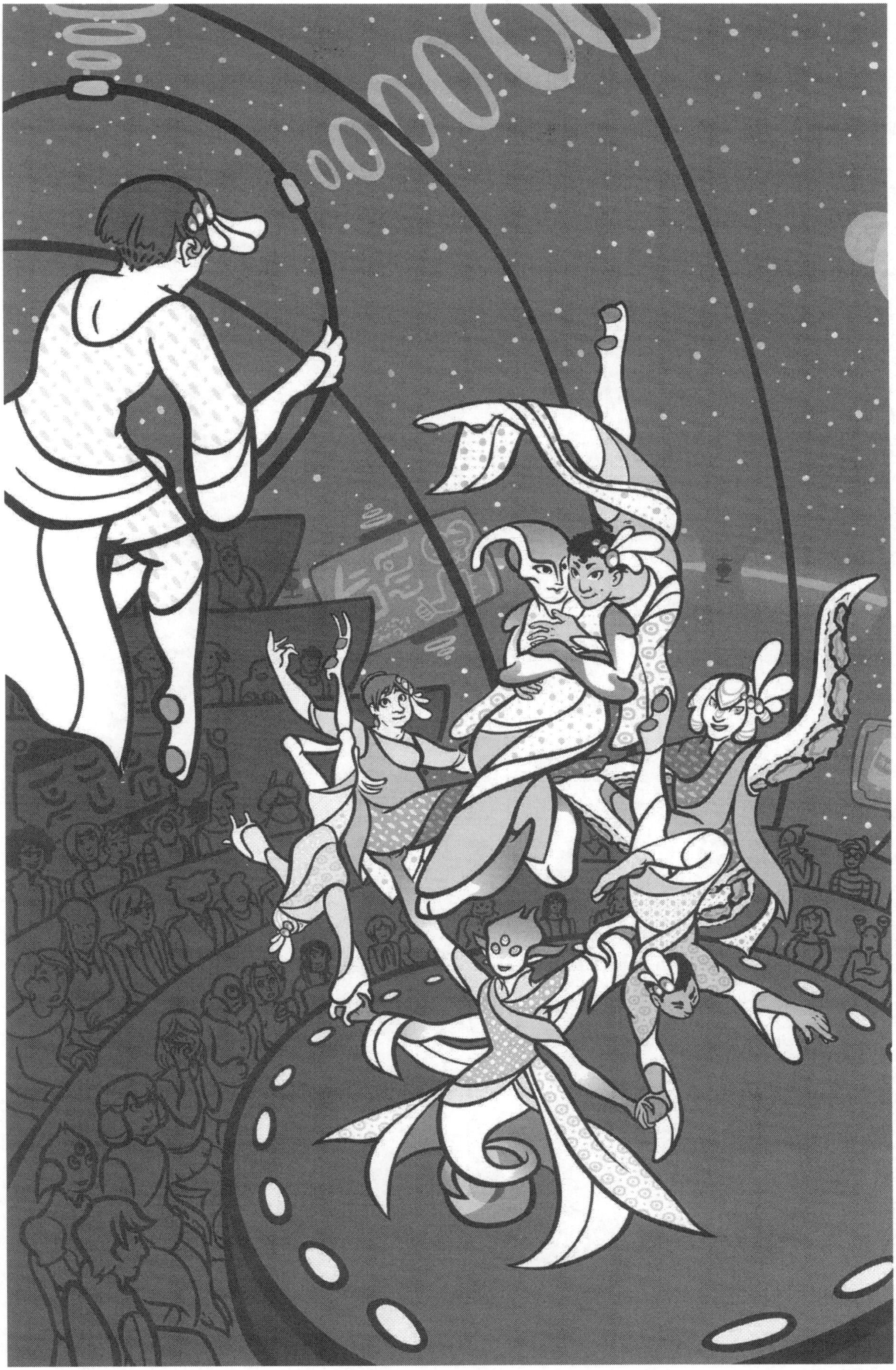

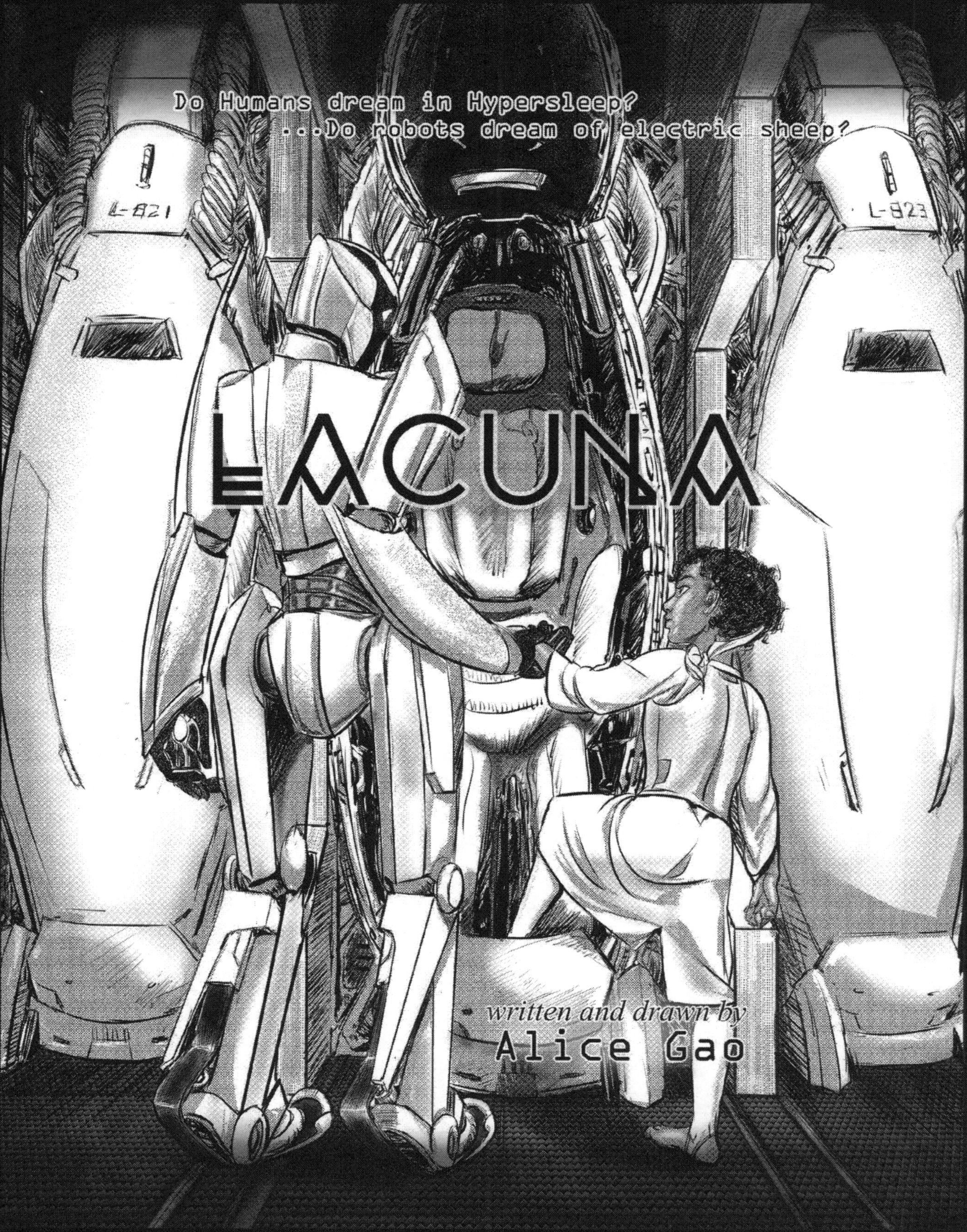
Do Humans dream in Hypersleep?
...Do robots dream of electric sheep?
L-821
L-823
LACUNA
written and drawn by
Alice Gao

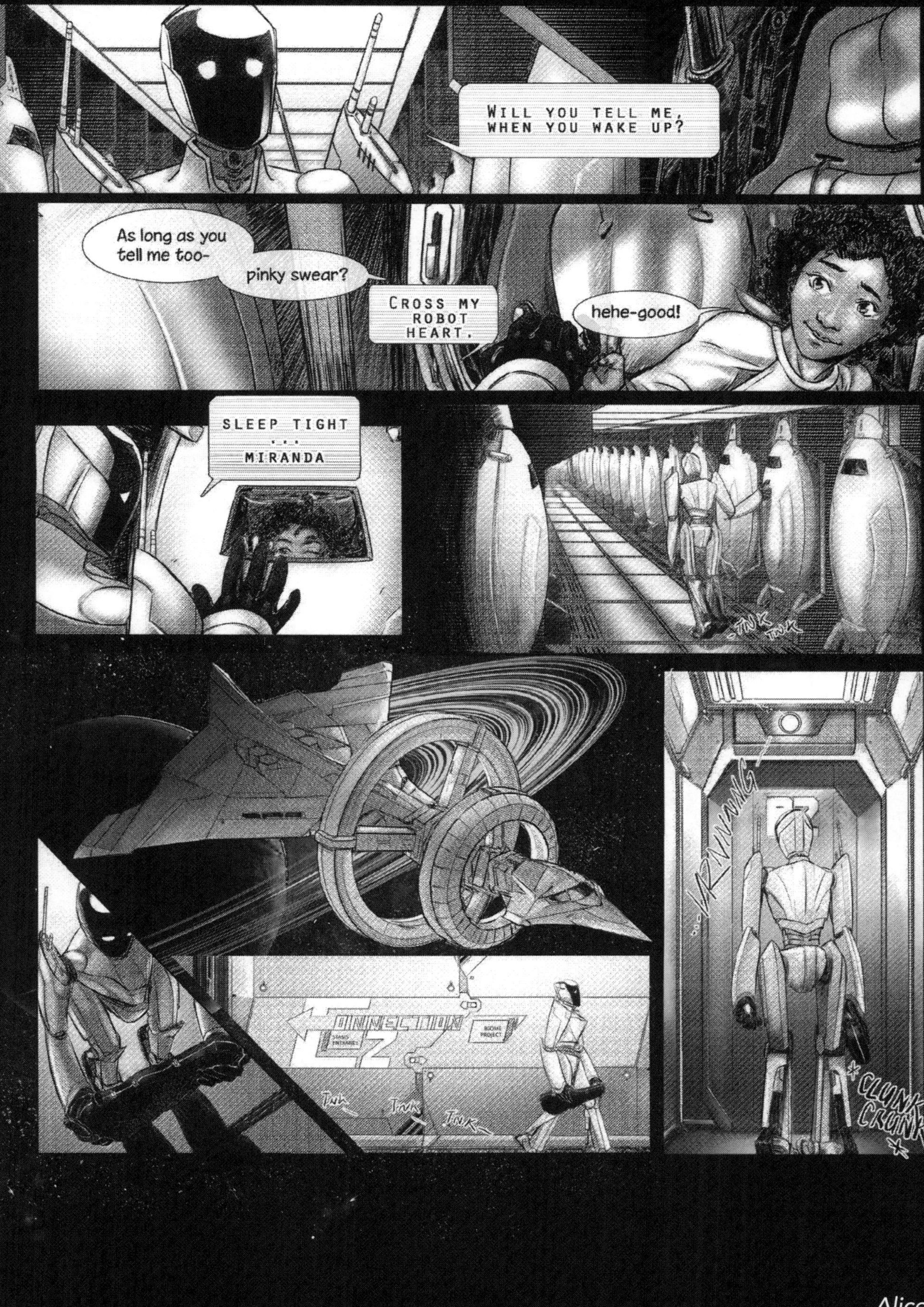
WILL YOU TELL ME, WHEN YOU WAKE UP?
As long as you tell me too-
pinky swear?
CROSS MY ROBOT HEART.
hehe-good!
SLEEP TIGHT ... MIRANDA
TNK TNK
CONNECTION C2
STASIS ENTRANCE
BIOME PROJECT
TNK
TNK
TNK
VRNNNNG
CLUNK CRUNK

Alice Gao

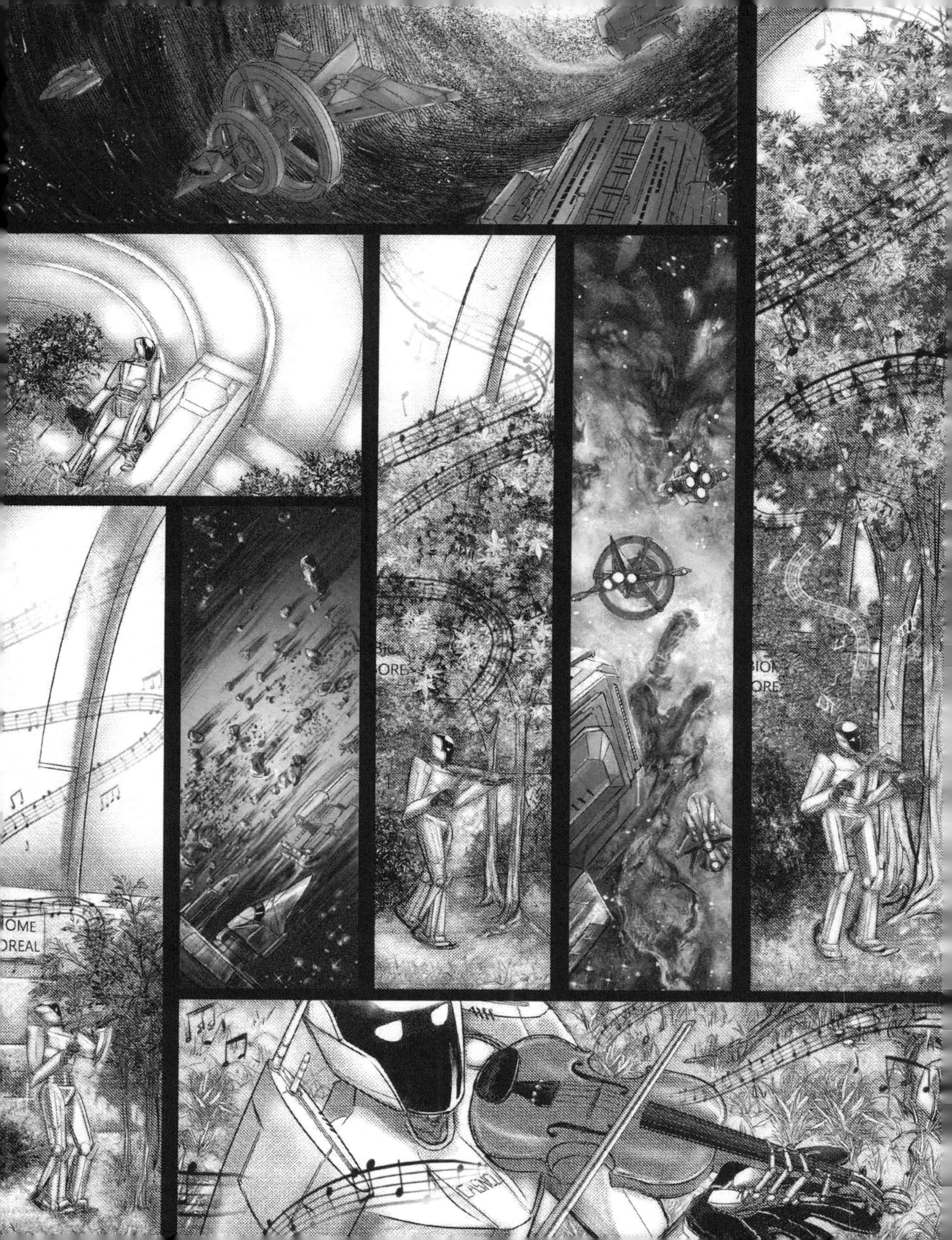
OME
OREAL

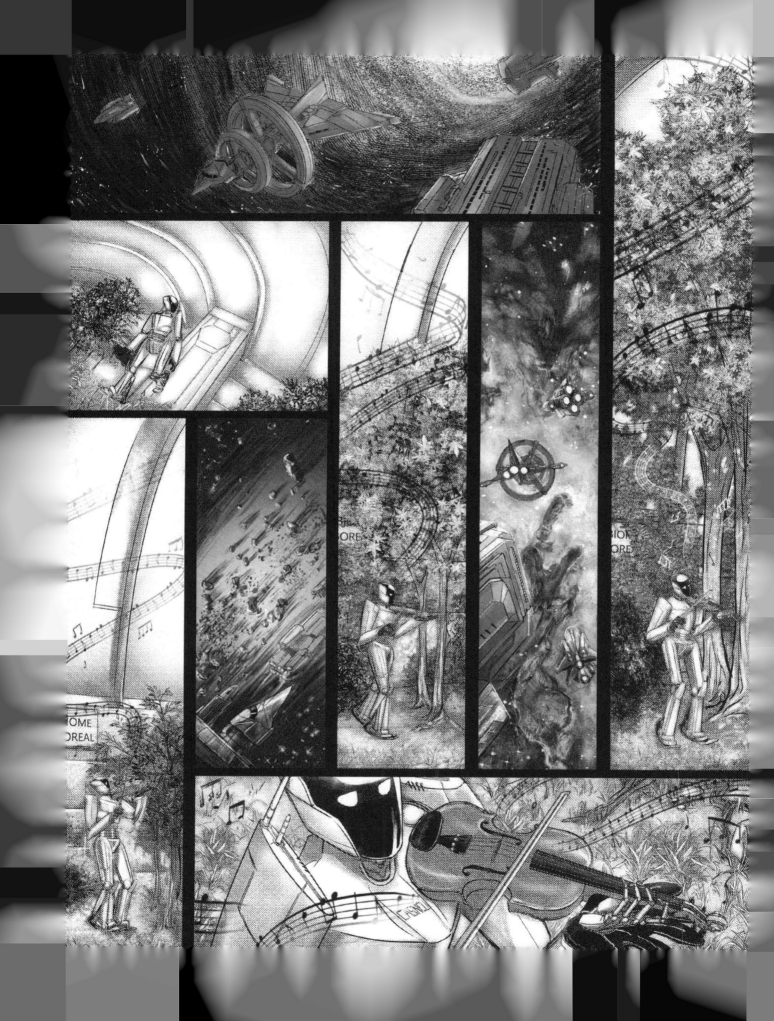

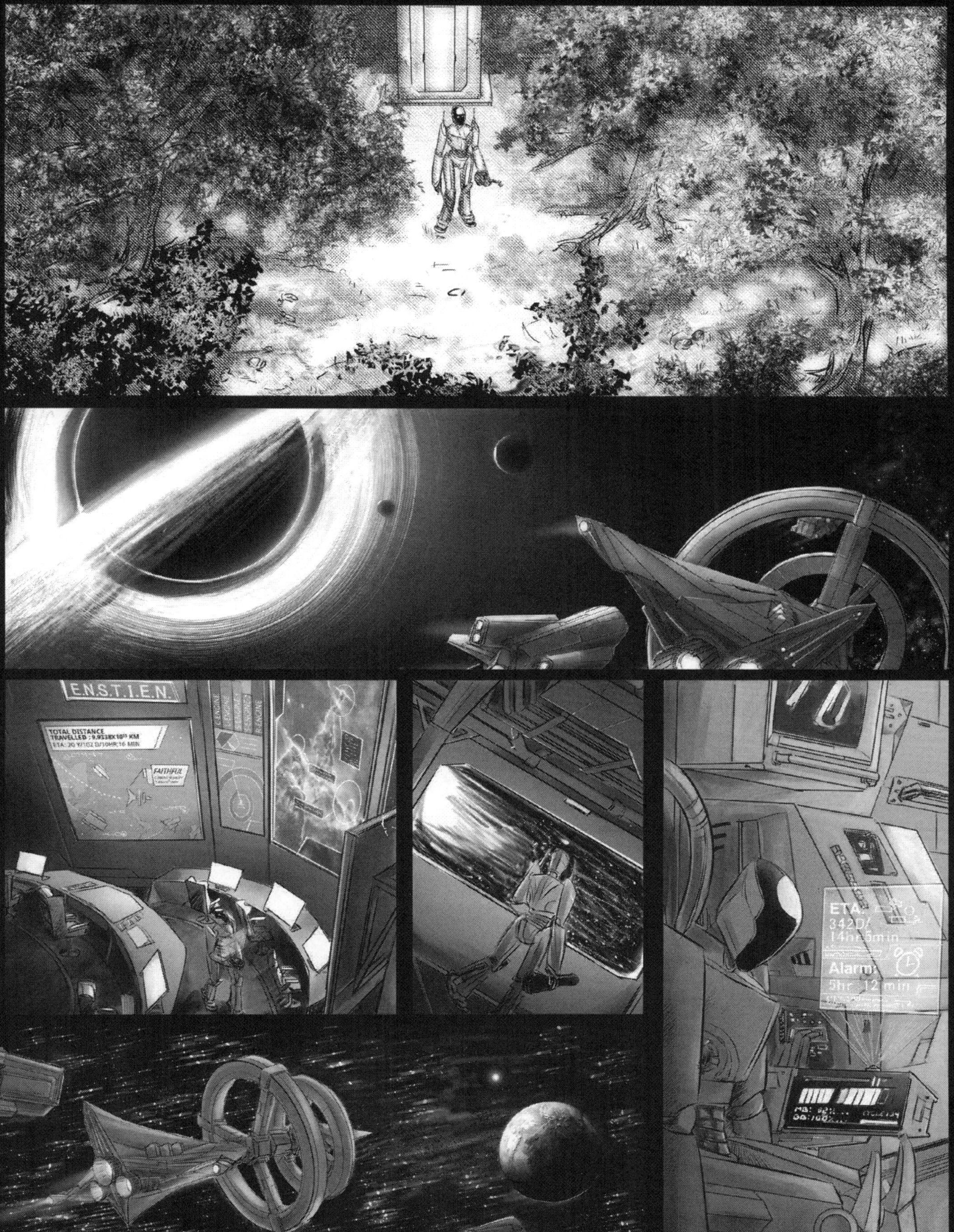

E.N.S.T.I.E.N.
TOTAL DISTANCE
FAITHFUL
ETA:
342D/
Alarm:
5hr 12 min

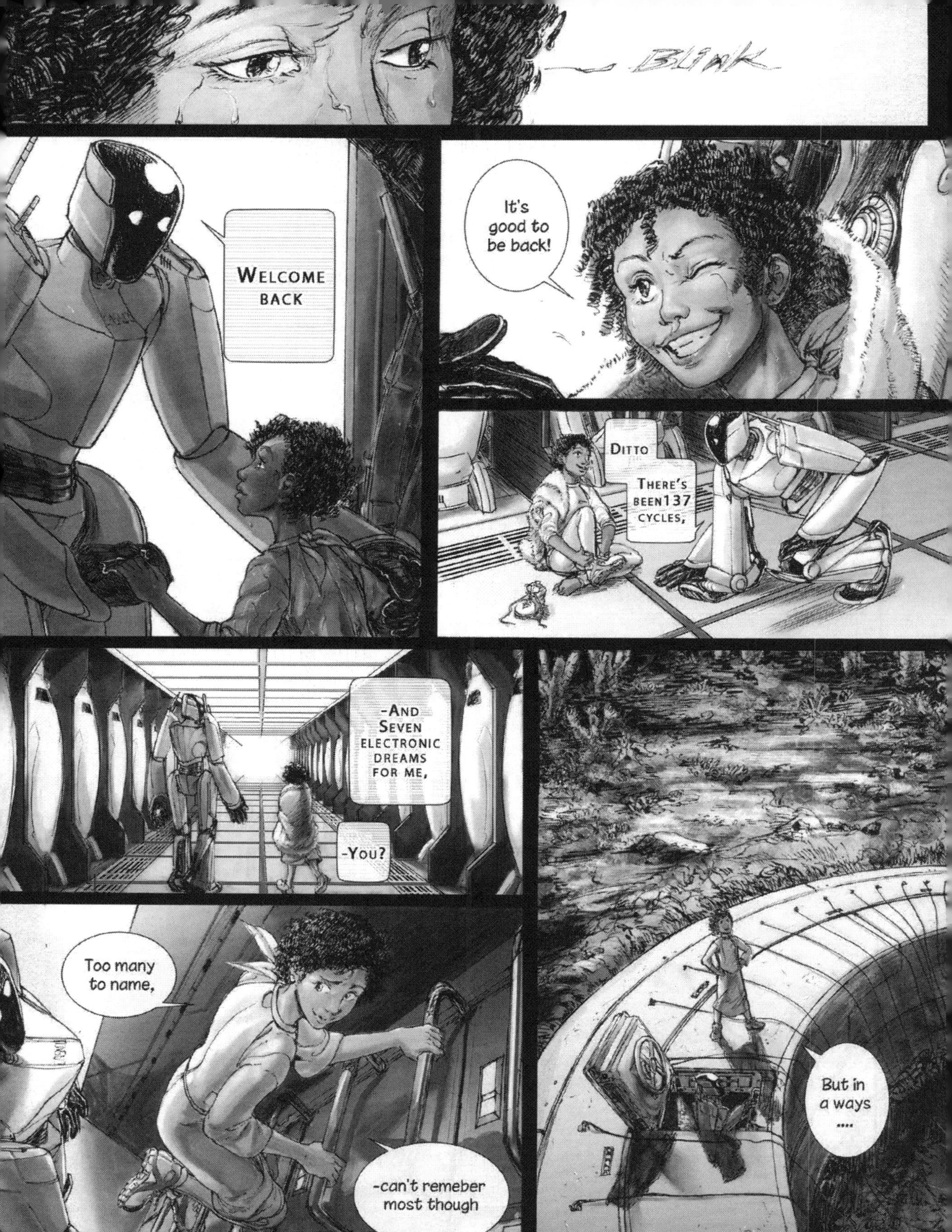
BLINK
WELCOME BACK
It's good to be back!
DITTO
THERE'S BEEN137 CYCLES,
-AND SEVEN ELECTRONIC DREAMS FOR ME,
-YOU?
Too many to name,
-can't remeber most though
But in a ways
....

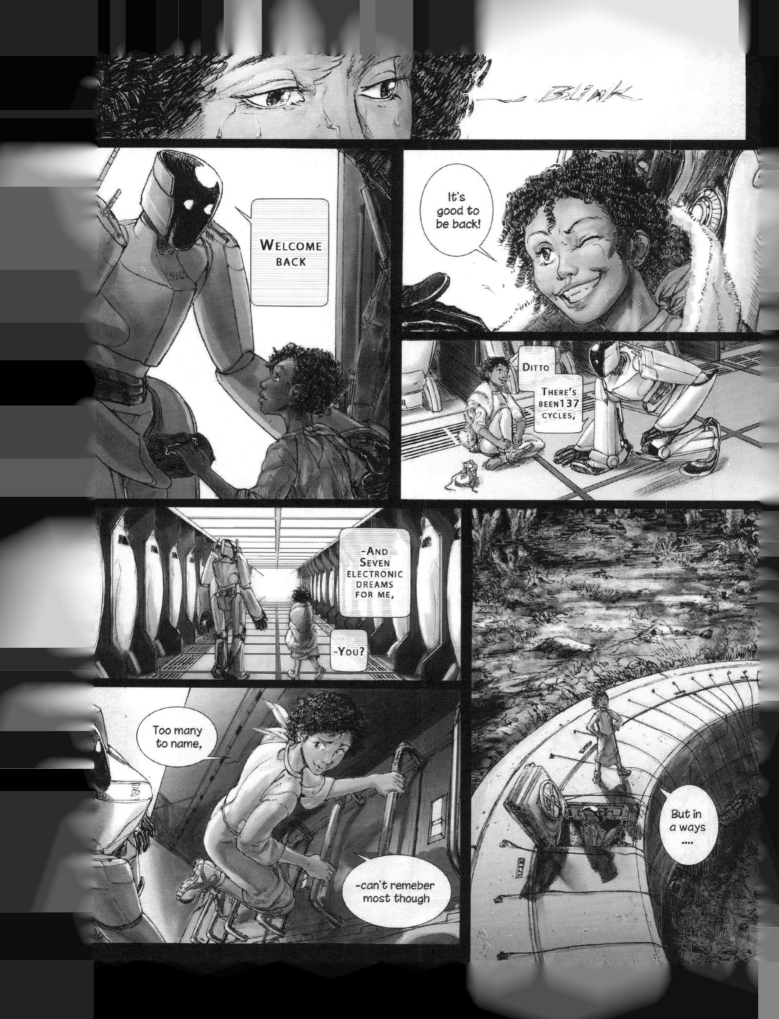

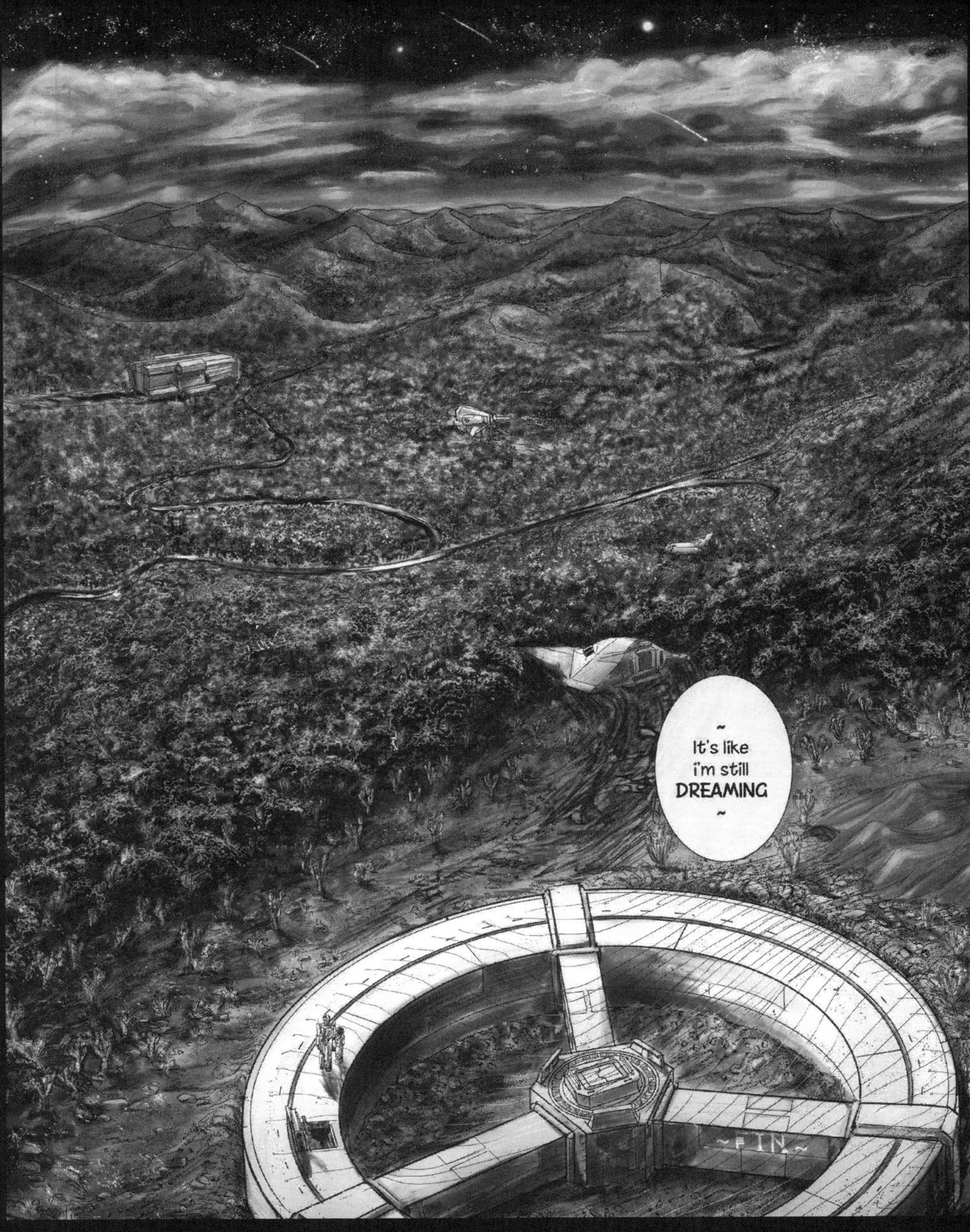
~ It's like i'm still DREAMING ~
~FIN~

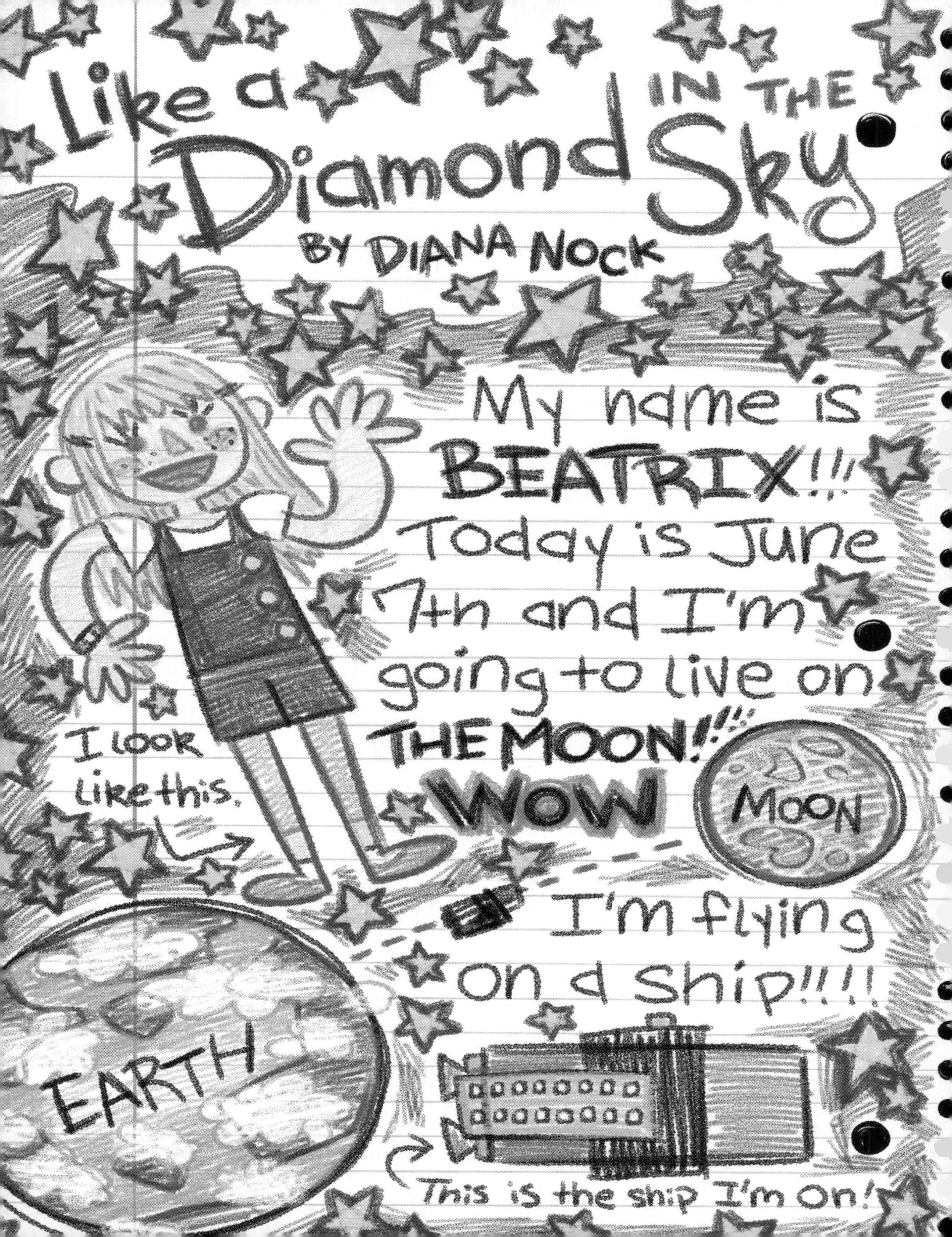
Like a Diamond in the Sky
BY DIANA NOCK
My name is BEATRIX!!!
Today is June 7th and I'm going to live on THE MOON!!!
WOW
MOON
I look like this.
I'm flying on a ship!!!!
EARTH
This is the ship I'm on!

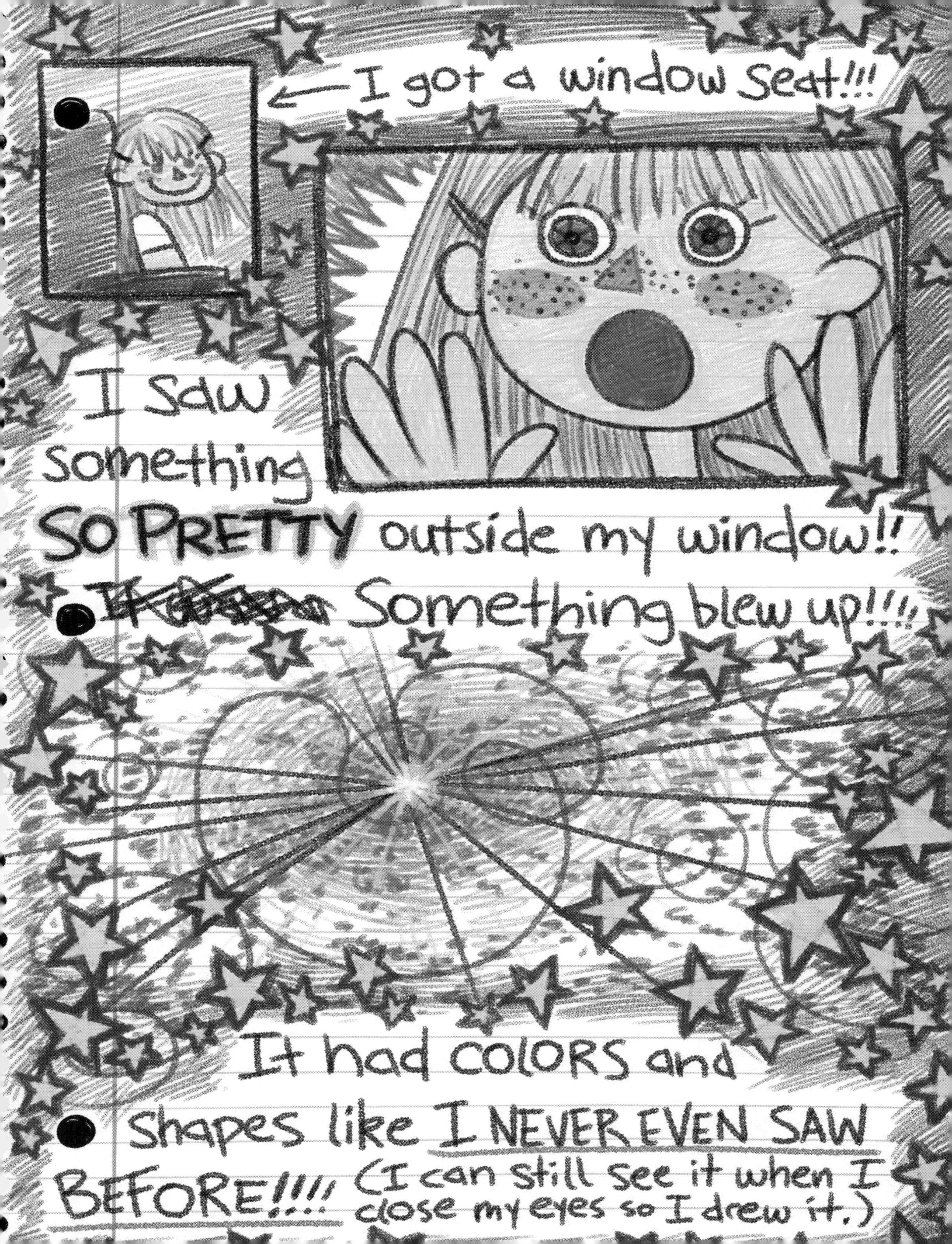
I got a window seat!!!
I saw something SO PRETTY outside my window!!
Something blew up!!!!
It had COLORS and shapes like I NEVER EVEN SAW BEFORE!!!!
(I can still see it when I close my eyes so I drew it.)

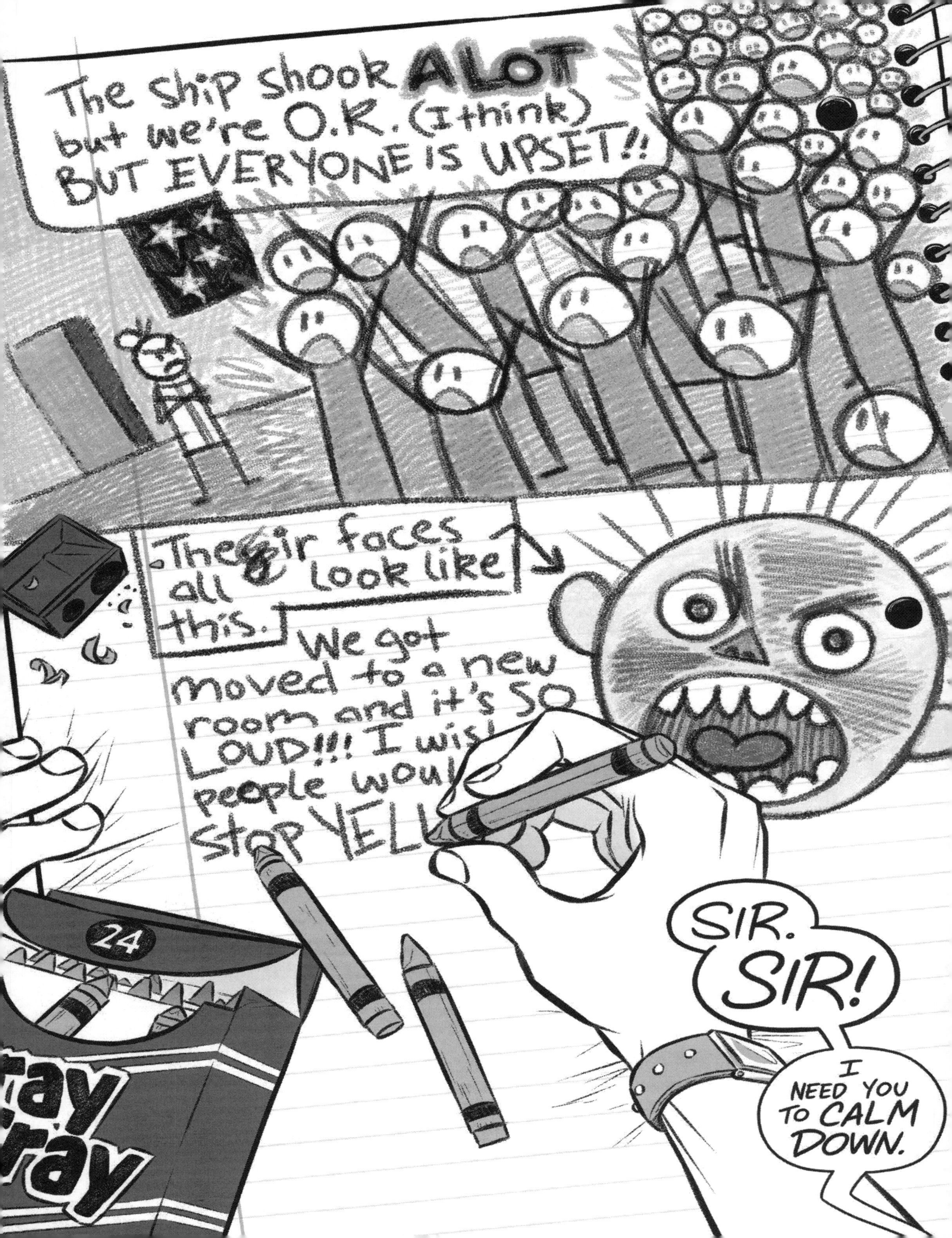
The ship shook A LOT but we're O.K. (I think) BUT EVERYONE IS UPSET!!
Their faces all look like this.
We got moved to a new room and it's SO LOUD!!! I wis
people woul
STOP YELL
24
SIR. SIR!
I NEED YOU TO CALM DOWN.

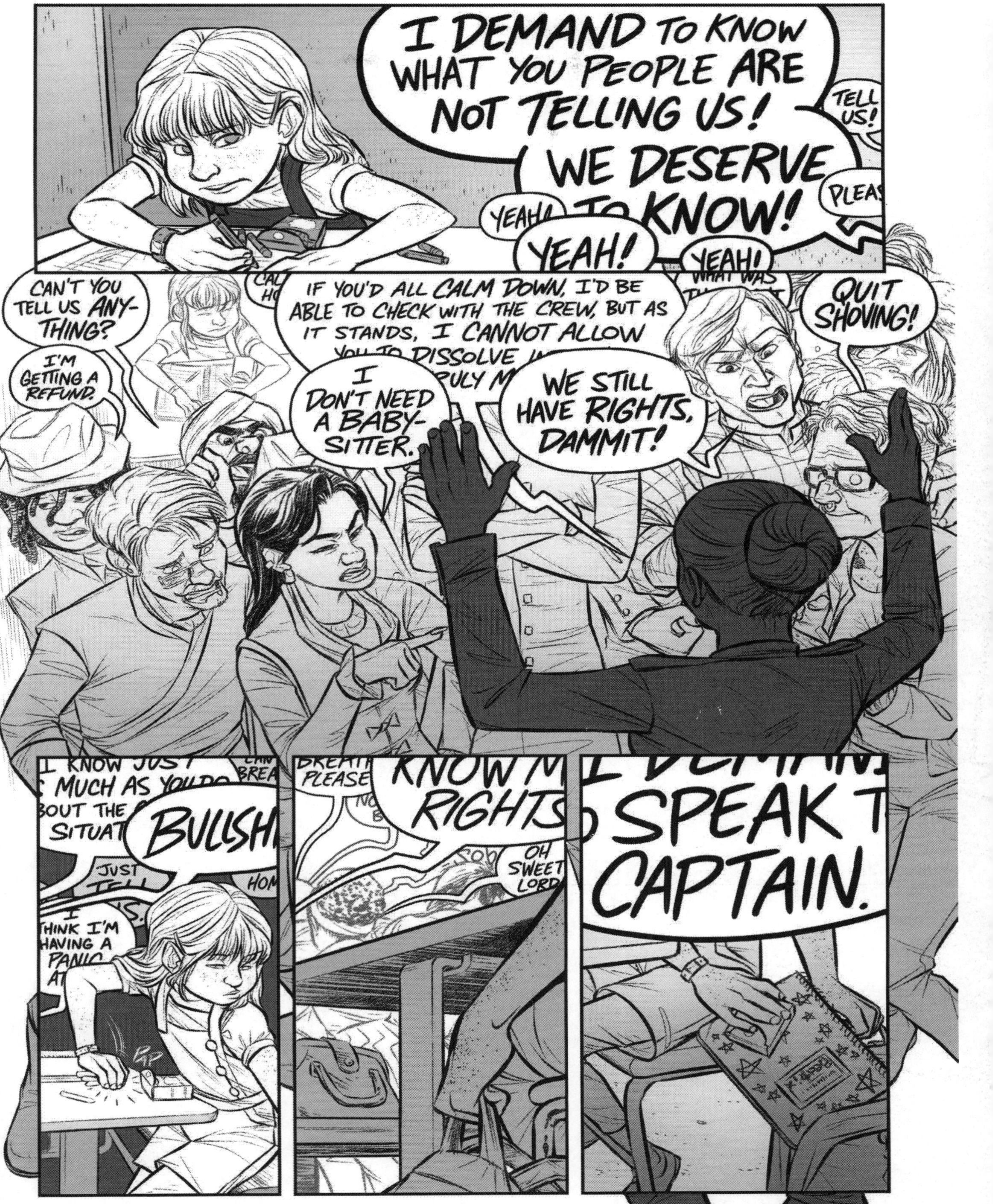
I DEMAND TO KNOW WHAT YOU PEOPLE ARE NOT TELLING US!
TELL US!
WE DESERVE TO KNOW!
YEAH!
YEAH!
YEAH!
CAN'T YOU TELL US ANYTHING?
I'M GETTING A REFUND.
IF YOU'D ALL CALM DOWN, I'D BE ABLE TO CHECK WITH THE CREW, BUT AS IT STANDS, I CANNOT ALLOW
QUIT SHOVING!
I DON'T NEED A BABY-SITTER.
WE STILL HAVE RIGHTS, DAMMIT!
SITUAT
JUST
THINK I'M HAVING A
PLEASE
RIGHTS
OH SWEET LORD
SPEAK
CAPTAIN.

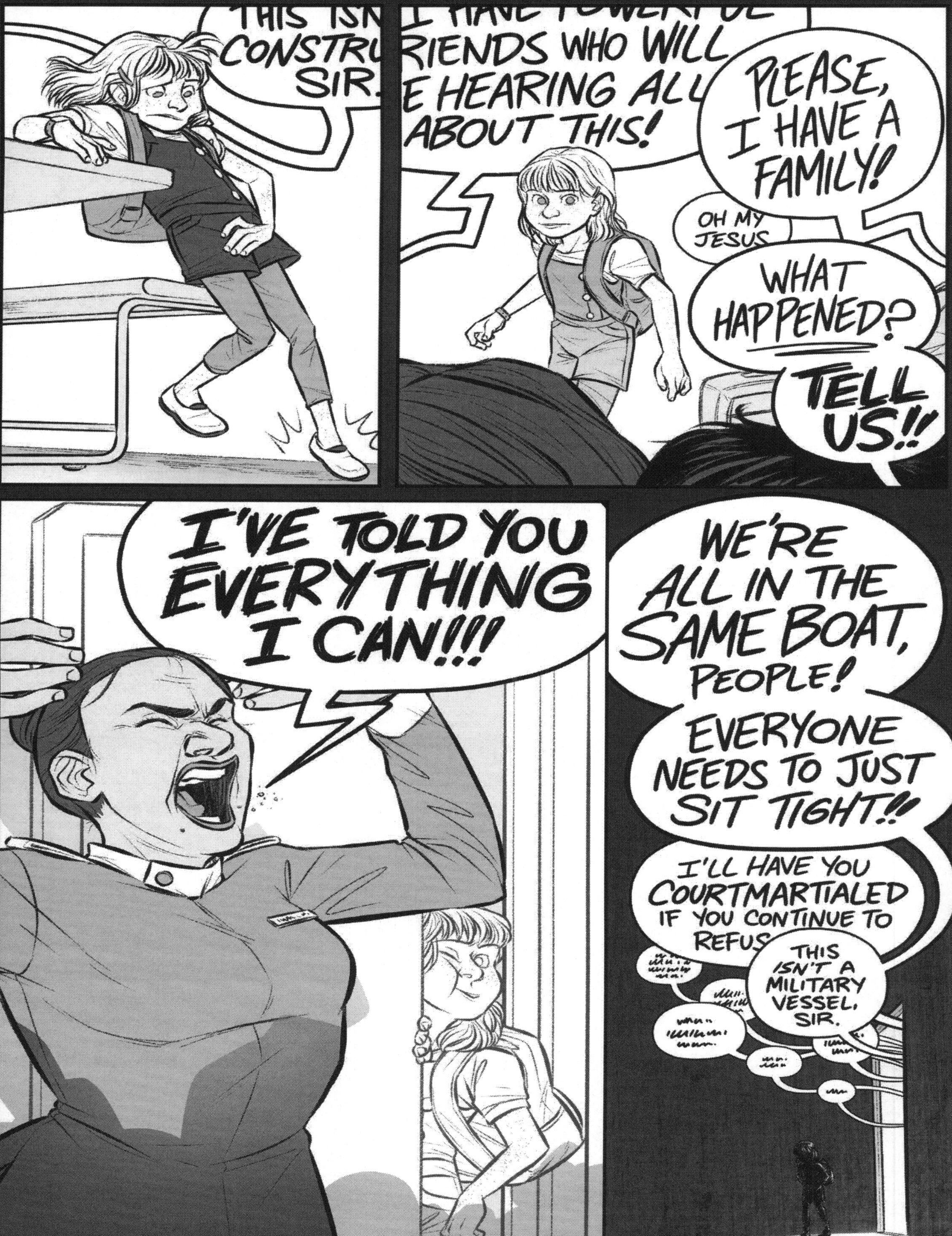
THIS ISN
CONSTRU
SIR.
RIENDS WHO WILL
E HEARING ALL
ABOUT THIS!
PLEASE, I HAVE A FAMILY!
OH MY JESUS
WHAT HAPPENED?
TELL US!!
I'VE TOLD YOU EVERYTHING I CAN!!!
WE'RE ALL IN THE SAME BOAT, PEOPLE!
EVERYONE NEEDS TO JUST SIT TIGHT!!
I'LL HAVE YOU COURTMARTIALED IF YOU CONTINUE TO REFUS
THIS ISN'T A MILITARY VESSEL, SIR.

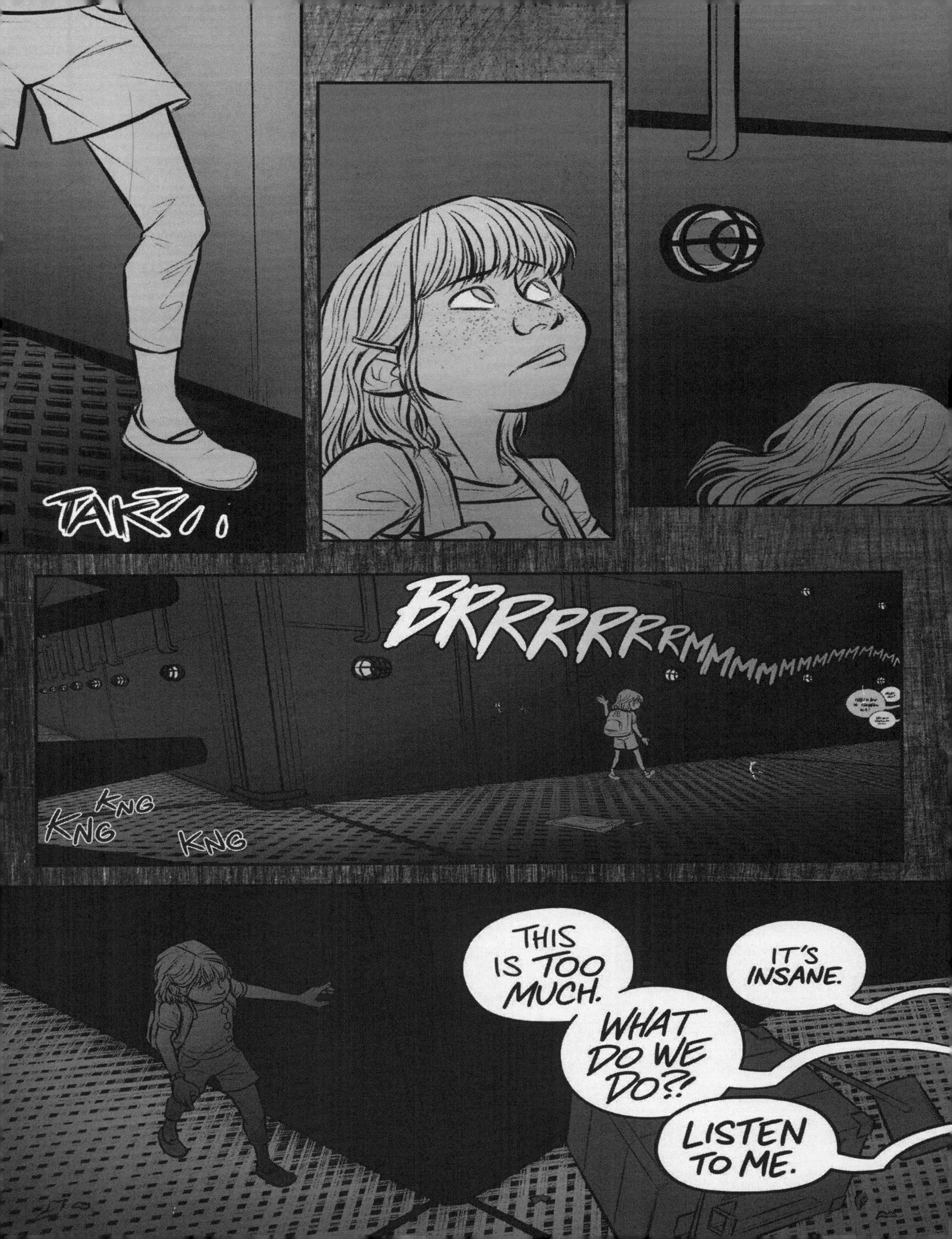
TAK! . .
BRRRRRRRMMMMMMMMMMMMM
KNG
KNG
KNG
THIS IS TOO MUCH.
IT'S INSANE.
WHAT DO WE DO?!
LISTEN TO ME.

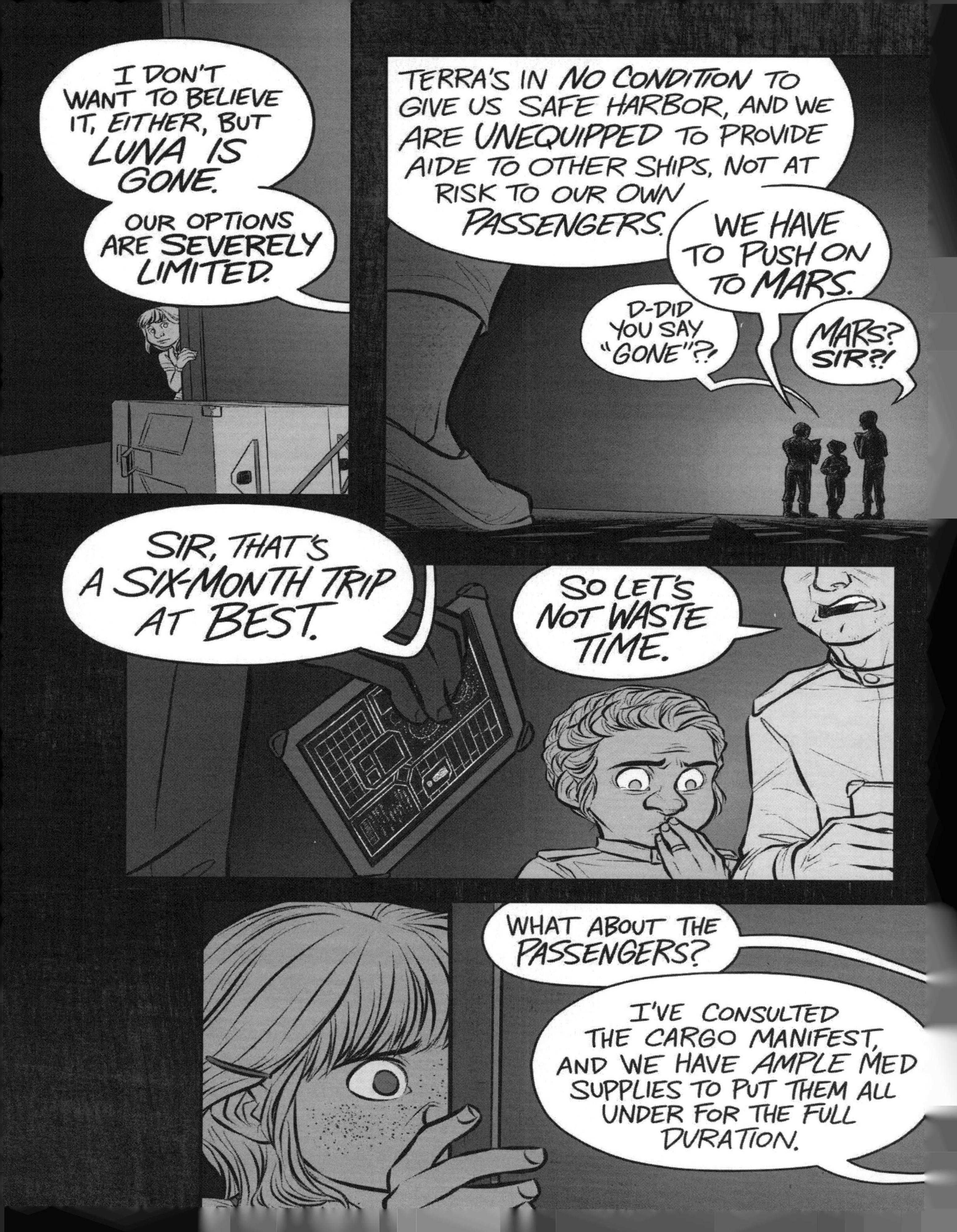
I DON'T WANT TO BELIEVE IT, EITHER, BUT LUNA IS GONE.
OUR OPTIONS ARE SEVERELY LIMITED.
TERRA'S IN NO CONDITION TO GIVE US SAFE HARBOR, AND WE ARE UNEQUIPPED TO PROVIDE AIDE TO OTHER SHIPS, NOT AT RISK TO OUR OWN PASSENGERS.
WE HAVE TO PUSH ON TO MARS.
D-DID YOU SAY "GONE"?!
MARS? SIR?!
SIR, THAT'S A SIX-MONTH TRIP AT BEST.
SO LET'S NOT WASTE TIME.
WHAT ABOUT THE PASSENGERS?
I'VE CONSULTED THE CARGO MANIFEST, AND WE HAVE AMPLE MED SUPPLIES TO PUT THEM ALL UNDER FOR THE FULL DURATION.

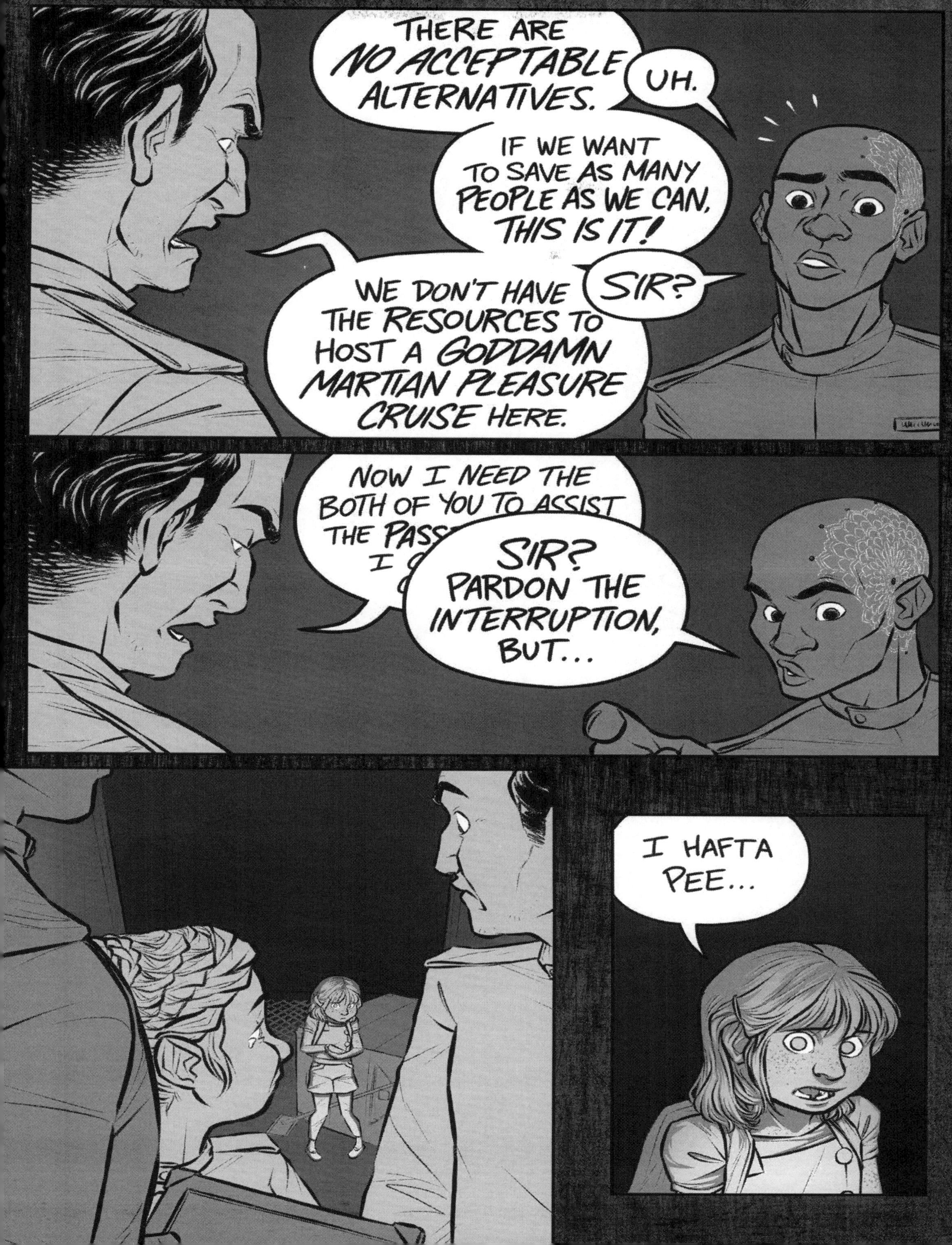
THERE ARE NO ACCEPTABLE ALTERNATIVES.
UH.
IF WE WANT TO SAVE AS MANY PEOPLE AS WE CAN, THIS IS IT!
WE DON'T HAVE THE RESOURCES TO HOST A GODDAMN MARTIAN PLEASURE CRUISE HERE.
SIR?
NOW I NEED THE BOTH OF YOU TO ASSIST THE
SIR? PARDON THE INTERRUPTION, BUT...
I HAFTA PEE...

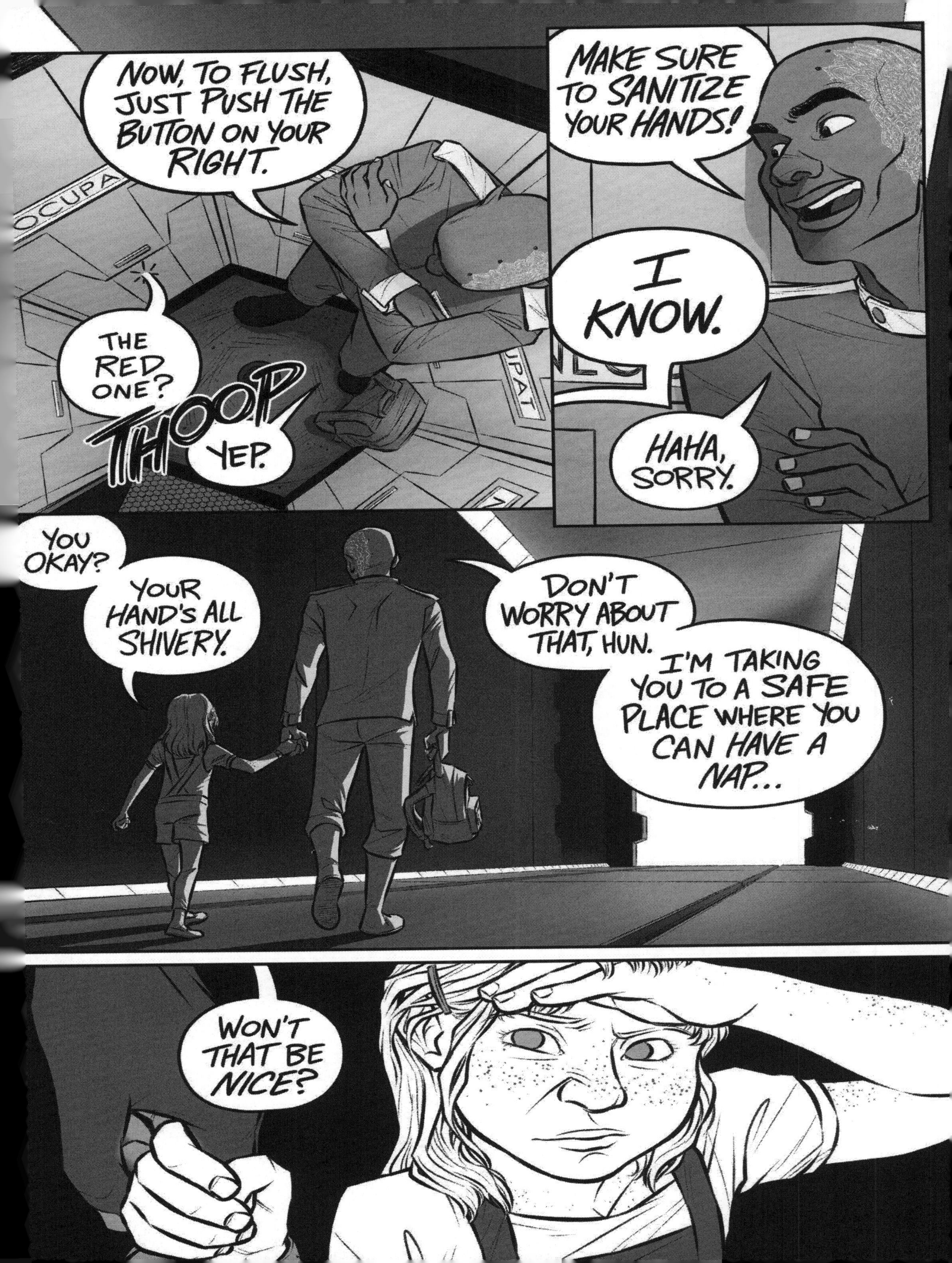
NOW, TO FLUSH, JUST PUSH THE BUTTON ON YOUR RIGHT.
THE RED ONE?
THOOP
YEP.
MAKE SURE TO SANITIZE YOUR HANDS!
I KNOW.
HAHA, SORRY.
YOU OKAY?
YOUR HAND'S ALL SHIVERY.
DON'T WORRY ABOUT THAT, HUN.
I'M TAKING YOU TO A SAFE PLACE WHERE YOU CAN HAVE A NAP...
WON'T THAT BE NICE?

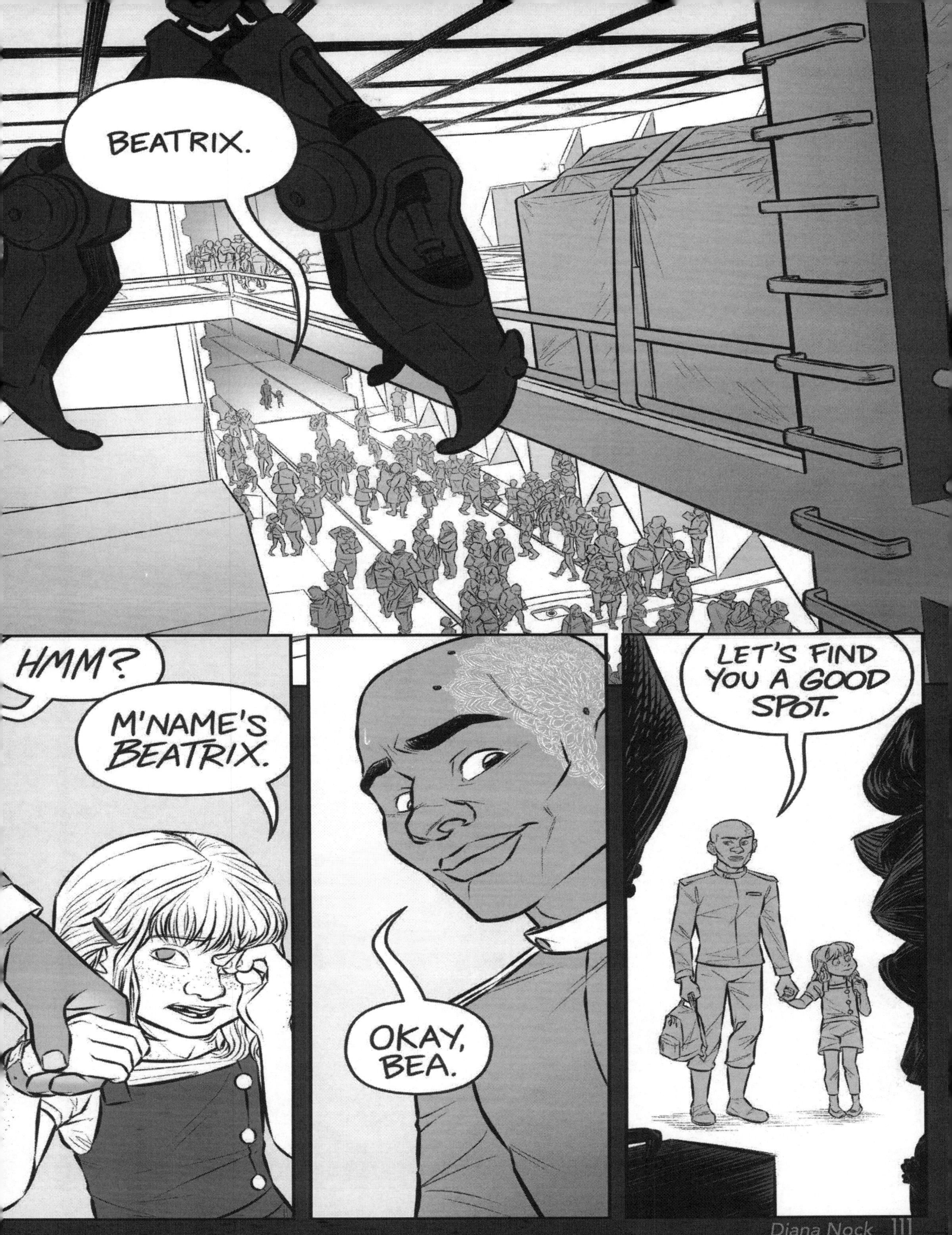
BEATRIX.
HMM?
M'NAME'S BEATRIX.
OKAY, BEA.
LET'S FIND YOU A GOOD SPOT.

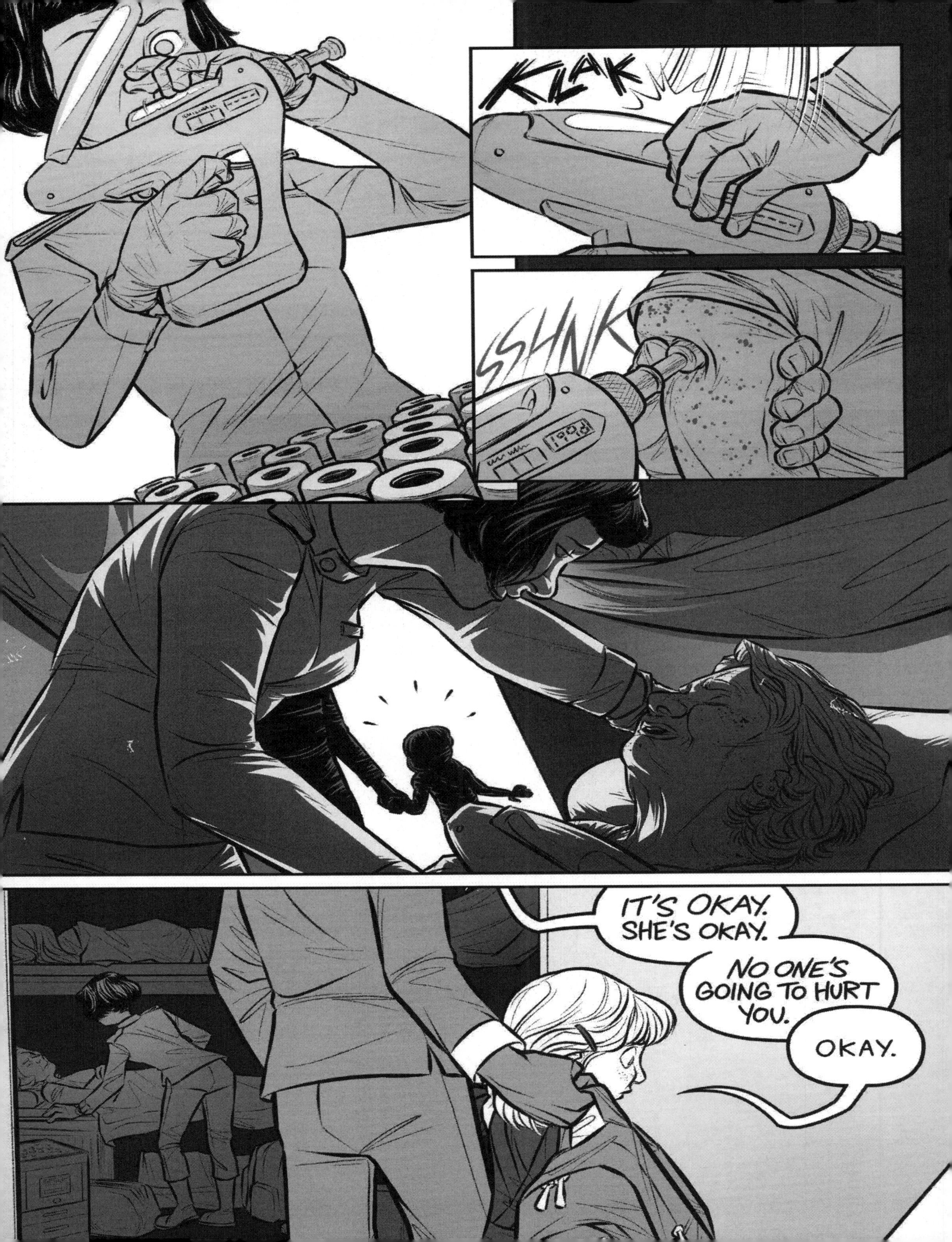
KLAK
SSHNK
IT'S OKAY.
SHE'S OKAY.
NO ONE'S GOING TO HURT YOU.
OKAY.

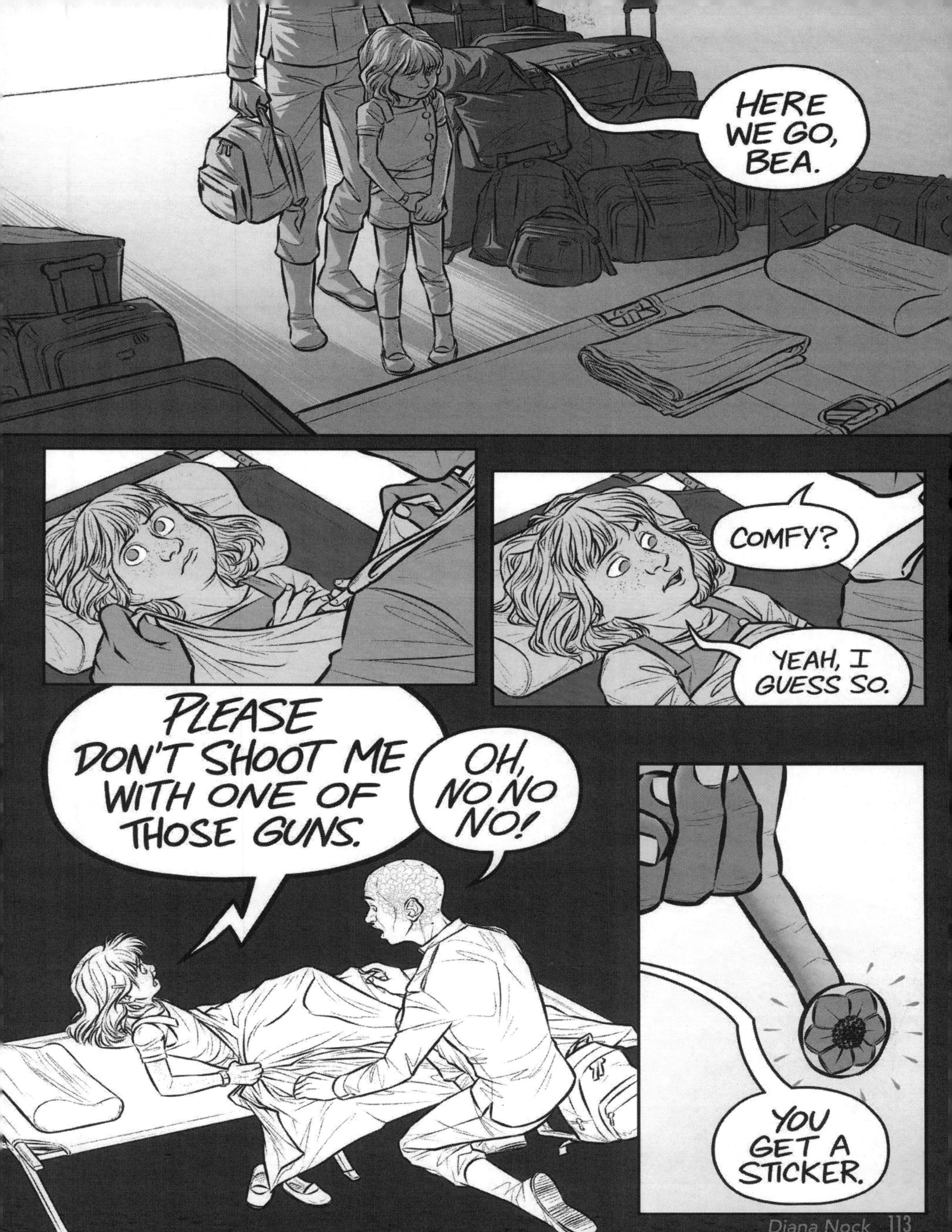
HERE WE GO, BEA.
COMFY?
YEAH, I GUESS SO.
PLEASE DON'T SHOOT ME WITH ONE OF THOSE GUNS.
OH, NO NO NO!
YOU GET A STICKER.

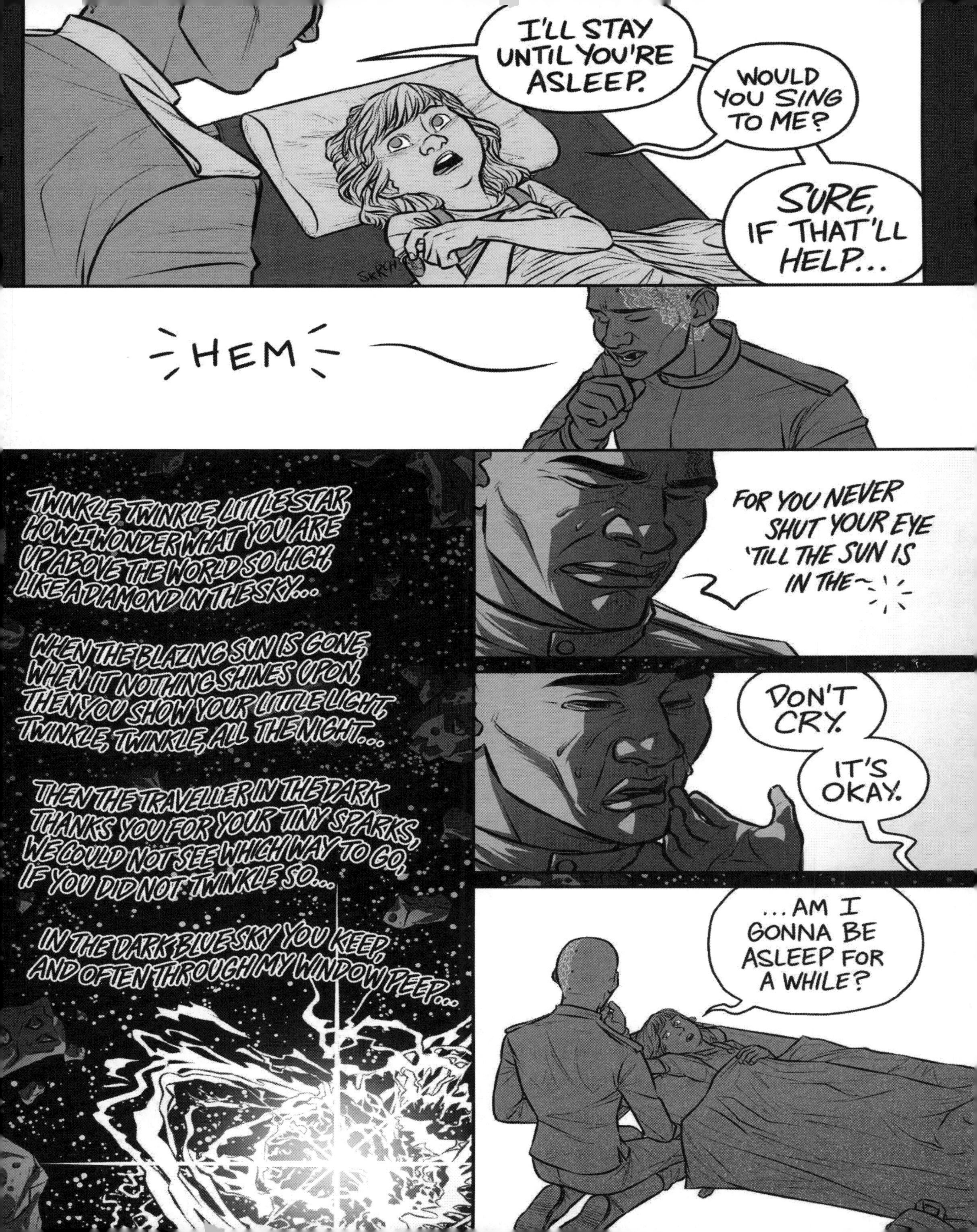
I'LL STAY UNTIL YOU'RE ASLEEP.
WOULD YOU SING TO ME?
SURE, IF THAT'LL HELP...
HEM
TWINKLE, TWINKLE, LITTLE STAR, HOW I WONDER WHAT YOU ARE UP ABOVE THE WORLD SO HIGH, LIKE A DIAMOND IN THE SKY...
WHEN THE BLAZING SUN IS GONE, WHEN IT NOTHING SHINES UPON, THEN YOU SHOW YOUR LITTLE LIGHT, TWINKLE, TWINKLE, ALL THE NIGHT...
THEN THE TRAVELLER IN THE DARK THANKS YOU FOR YOUR TINY SPARKS, WE COULD NOT SEE WHICH WAY TO GO, IF YOU DID NOT TWINKLE SO...
IN THE DARK BLUE SKY YOU KEEP, AND OFTEN THROUGH MY WINDOW PEEP...
FOR YOU NEVER SHUT YOUR EYE 'TILL THE SUN IS IN THE~
DON'T CRY.
IT'S OKAY.
...AM I GONNA BE ASLEEP FOR A WHILE?

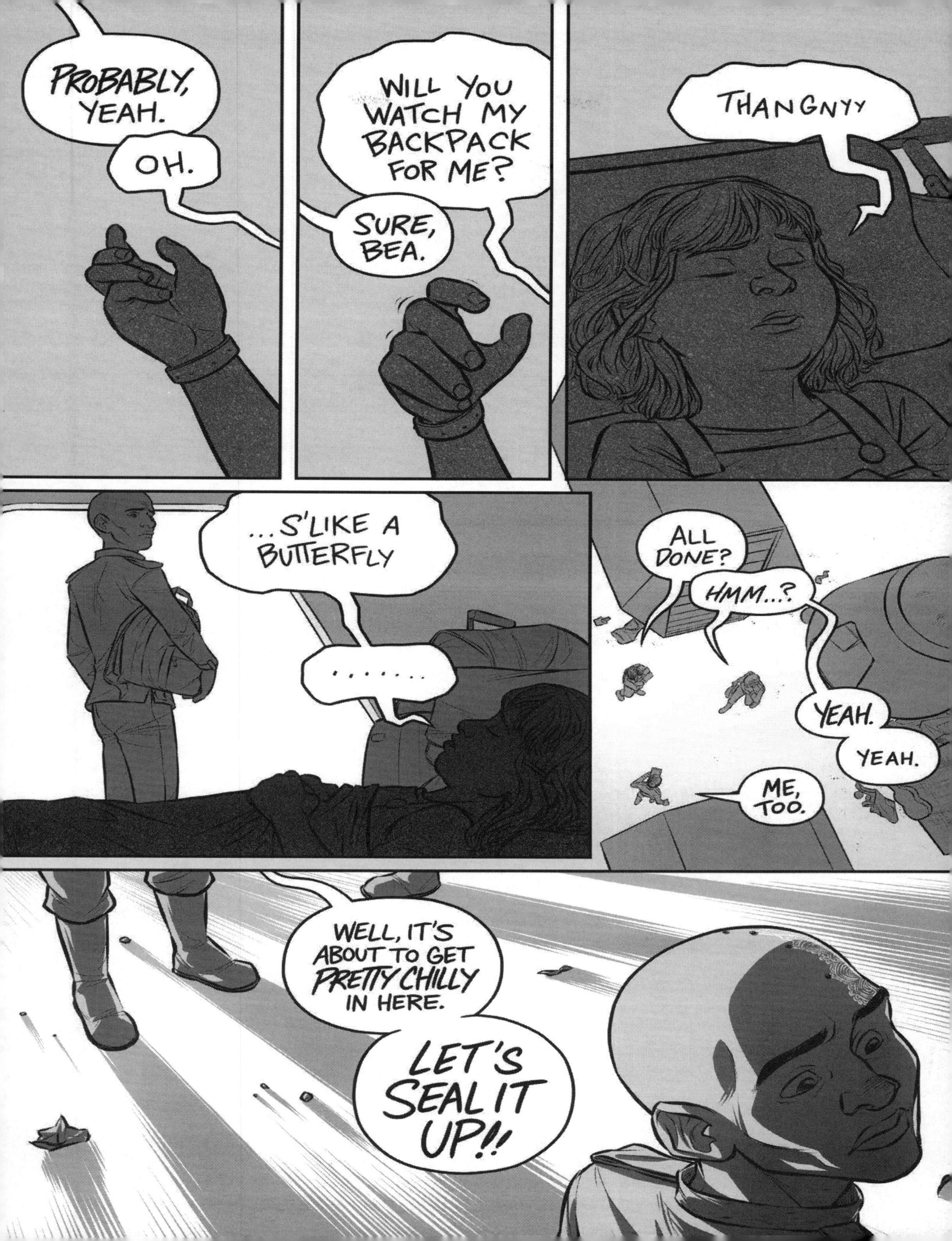
PROBABLY, YEAH.
OH.
WILL YOU WATCH MY BACKPACK FOR ME?
SURE, BEA.
THANGNYY
...S'LIKE A BUTTERFLY
....
ALL DONE?
HMM...?
YEAH.
YEAH.
ME, TOO.
WELL, IT'S ABOUT TO GET PRETTY CHILLY IN HERE.
LET'S SEAL IT UP!!

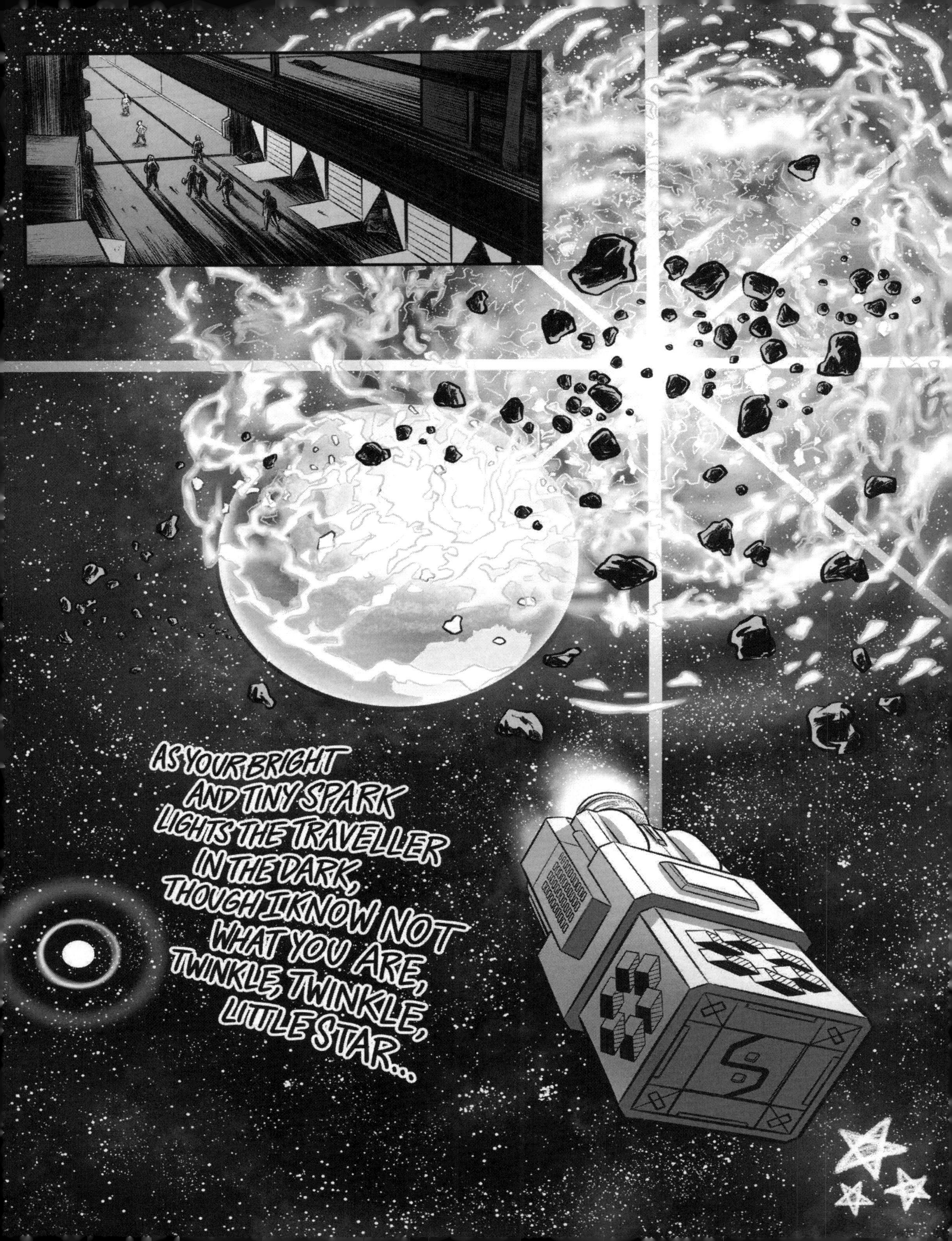
AS YOUR BRIGHT AND TINY SPARK LIGHTS THE TRAVELLER IN THE DARK, THOUGH I KNOW NOT WHAT YOU ARE, TWINKLE, TWINKLE, LITTLE STAR...

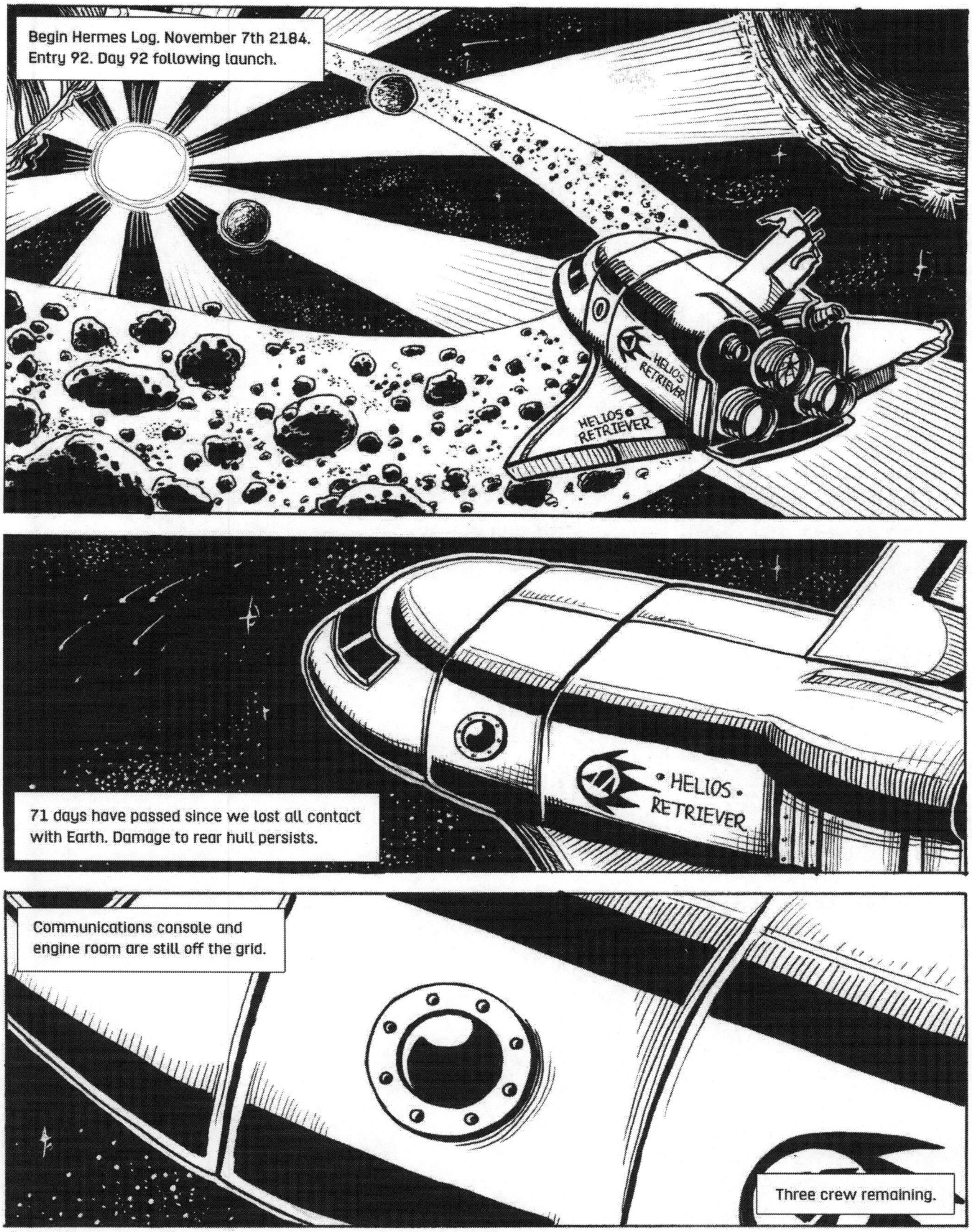
Begin Hermes Log. November 7th 2184. Entry 92. Day 92 following launch.
HELIOS RETRIEVER
HELIOS RETRIEVER
HELIOS RETRIEVER
71 days have passed since we lost all contact with Earth. Damage to rear hull persists.
Communications console and engine room are still off the grid.
Three crew remaining.

We have food to sustain us for a further two weeks. Suggested rationing has not been properly enforced.

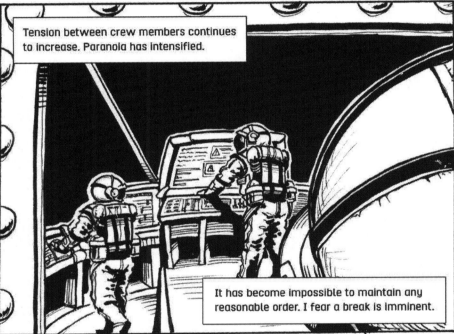

Tension between crew members continues to increase. Paranoia has intensified.

It has become impossible to maintain any reasonable order. I fear a break is imminent.

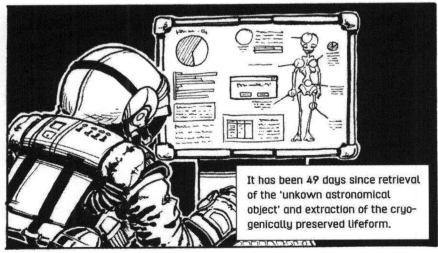

It has been 49 days since retrieval of the 'unkown astronomical object' and extraction of the cryo-genically preserved lifeform.

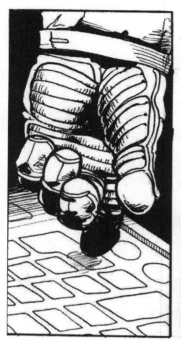

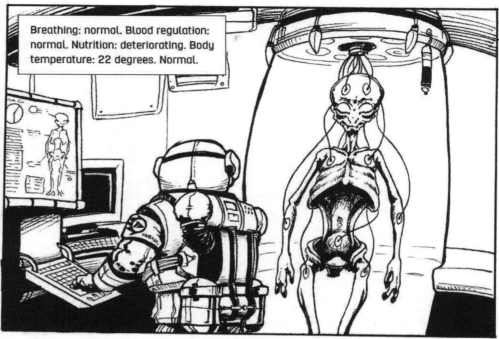

Breathing: normal. Blood regulation: normal. Nutrition: deteriorating. Body temperature: 22 degrees. Normal.

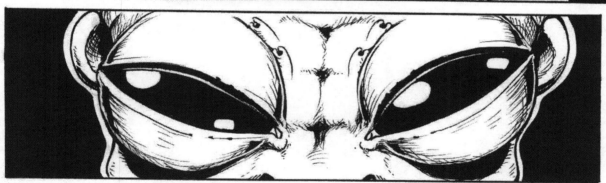

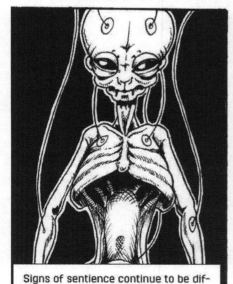

Signs of sentience continue to be difficult to monitor. It seems to lack the ability, or will, to move its limbs.

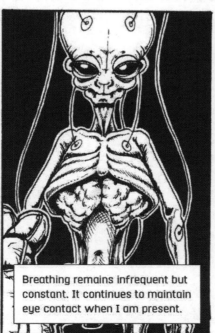

Breathing remains infrequent but constant. It continues to maintain eye contact when I am present.

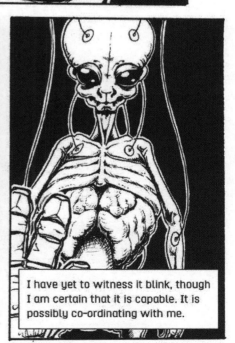

I have yet to witness it blink, though I am certain that it is capable. It is possibly co-ordinating with me.

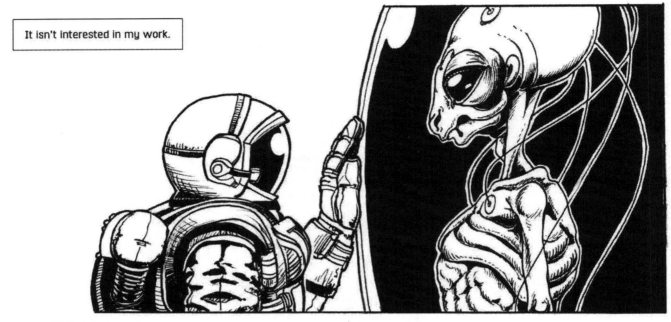

It isn't interested in my work.

It just watches me with those unblinking eyes.

It's trying to tell me something. I know. But it doesn't know how.

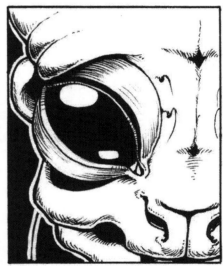

Is it asking for my help?

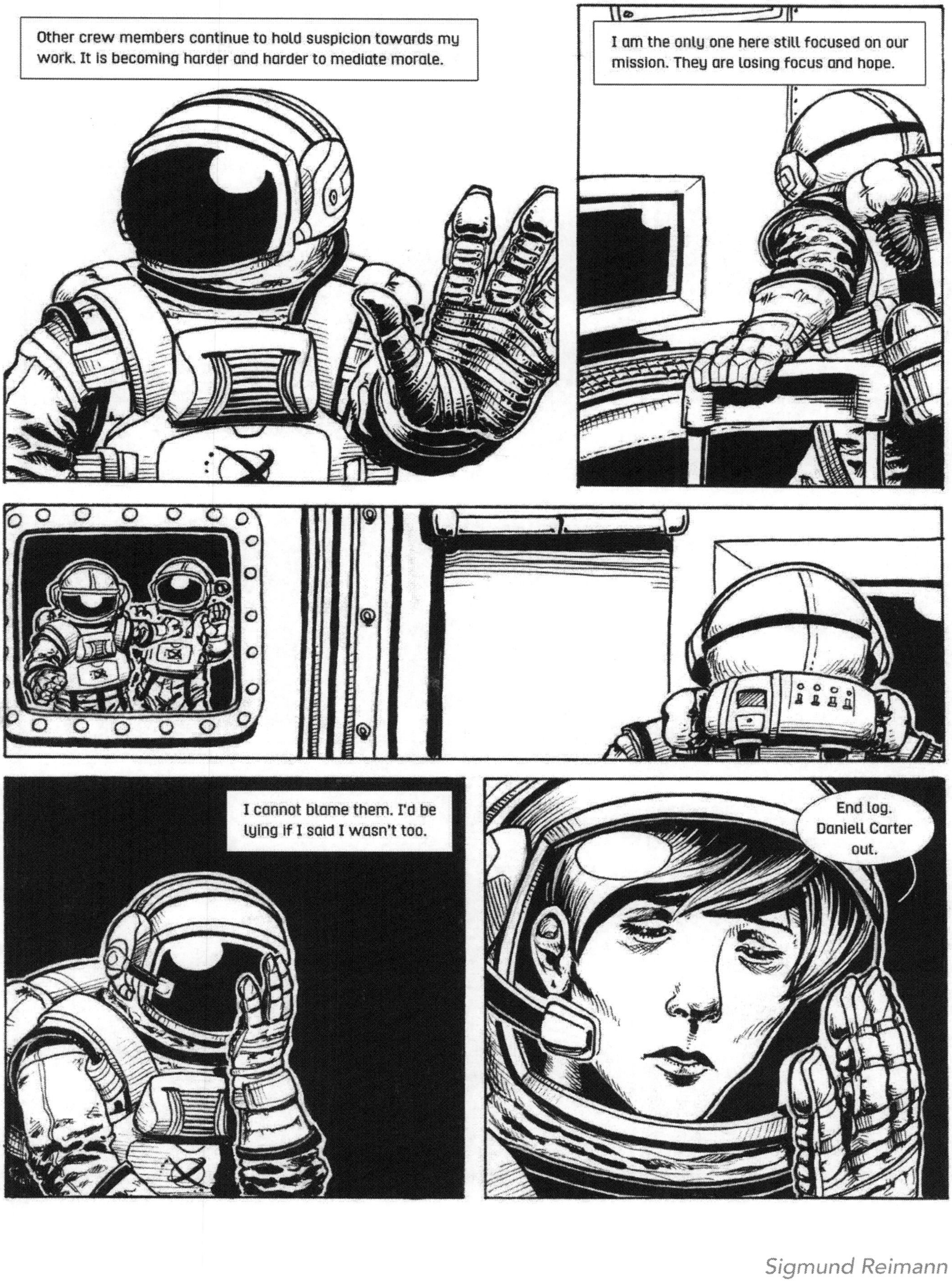
Other crew members continue to hold suspicion towards my work. It is becoming harder and harder to mediate morale.
I am the only one here still focused on our mission. They are losing focus and hope.
I cannot blame them. I'd be lying if I said I wasn't too.
End log. Daniell Carter out.

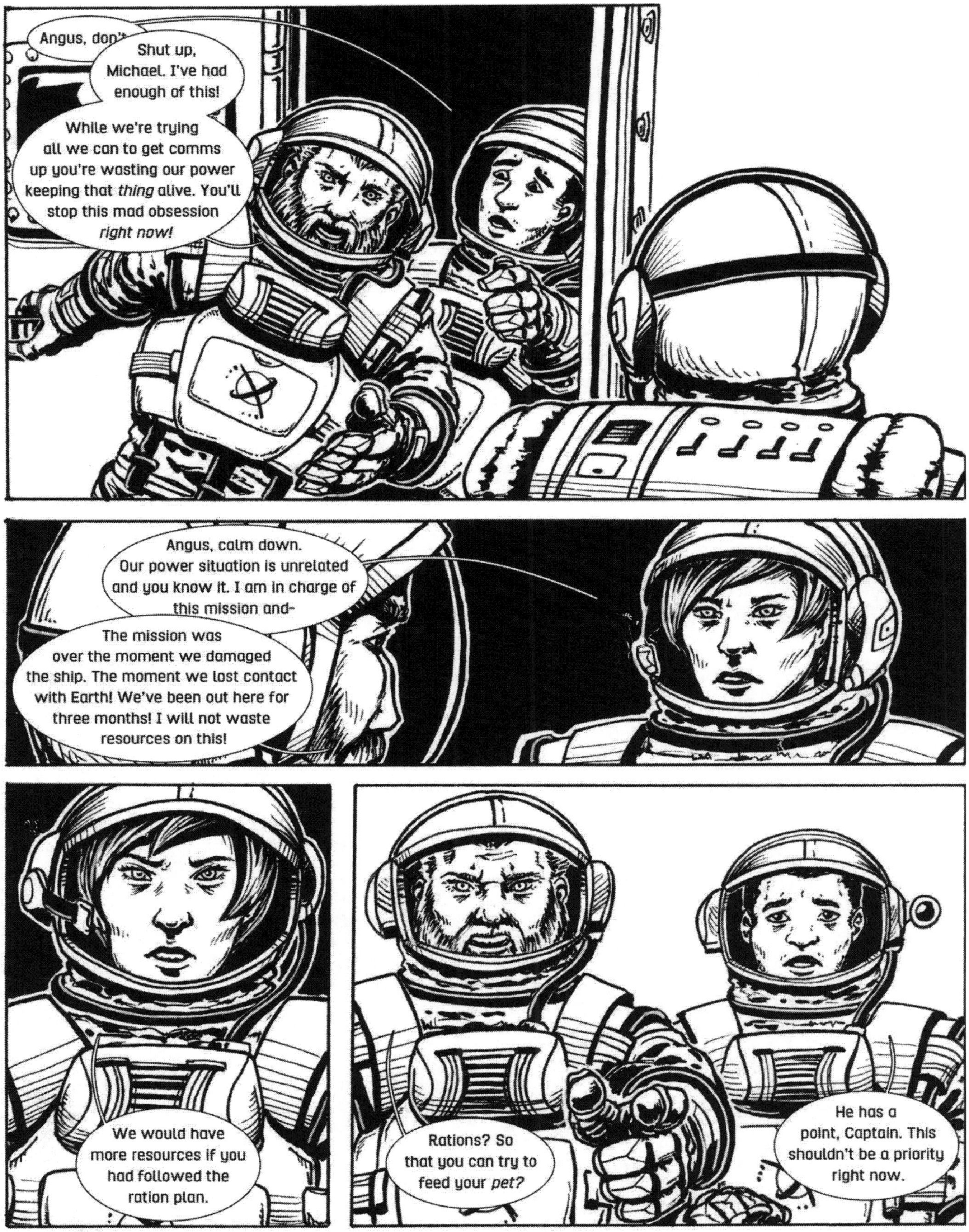
Angus, don't
Shut up, Michael. I've had enough of this!
While we're trying all we can to get comms up you're wasting our power keeping that *thing* alive. You'll stop this mad obsession *right now!*
Angus, calm down. Our power situation is unrelated and you know it. I am in charge of this mission and–
The mission was over the moment we damaged the ship. The moment we lost contact with Earth! We've been out here for three months! I will not waste resources on this!
We would have more resources if you had followed the ration plan.
Rations? So that you can try to feed your *pet?*
He has a point, Captain. This shouldn't be a priority right now.

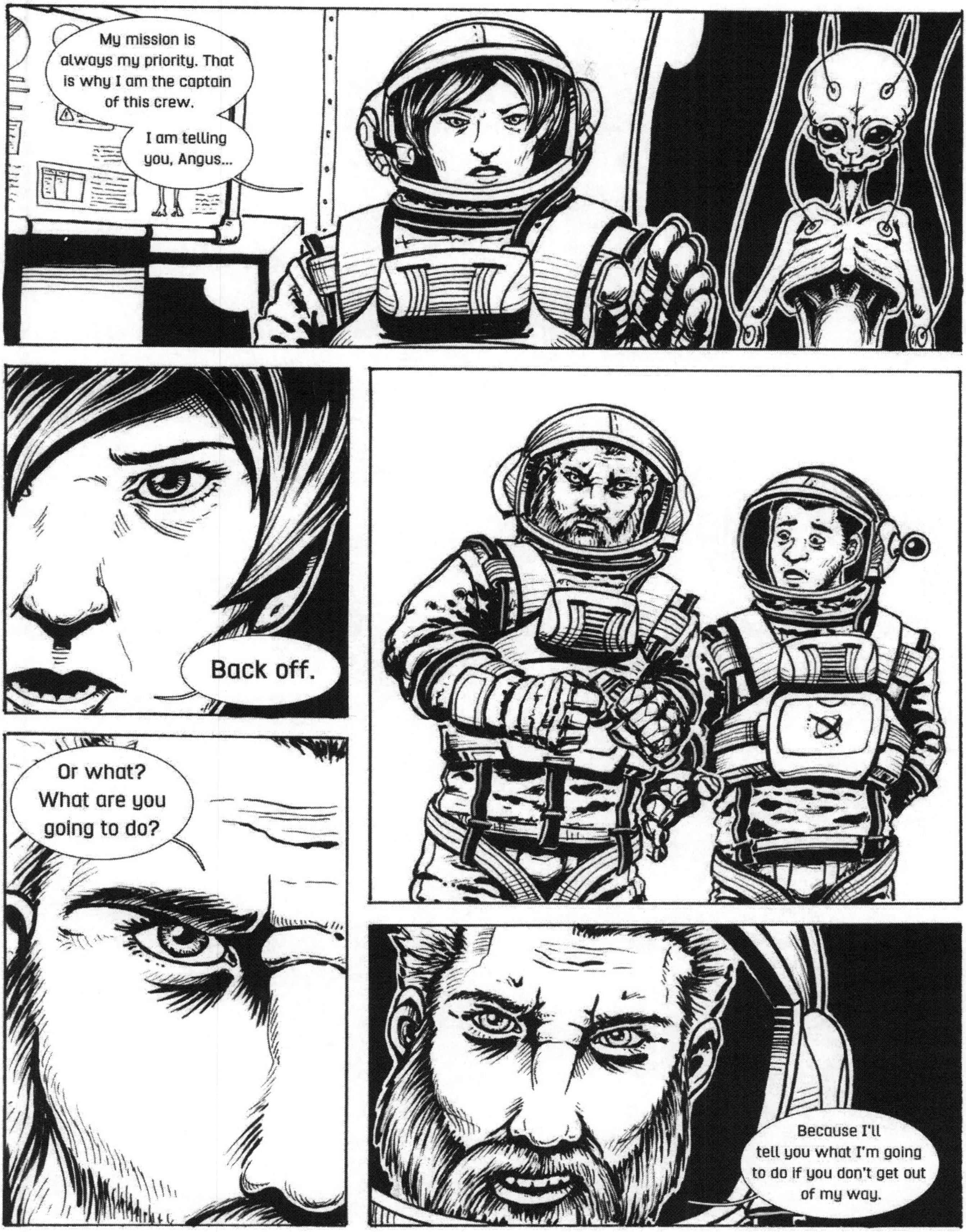
My mission is always my priority. That is why I am the captain of this crew.
I am telling you, Angus...
Back off.
Or what? What are you going to do?
Because I'll tell you what I'm going to do if you don't get out of my way.

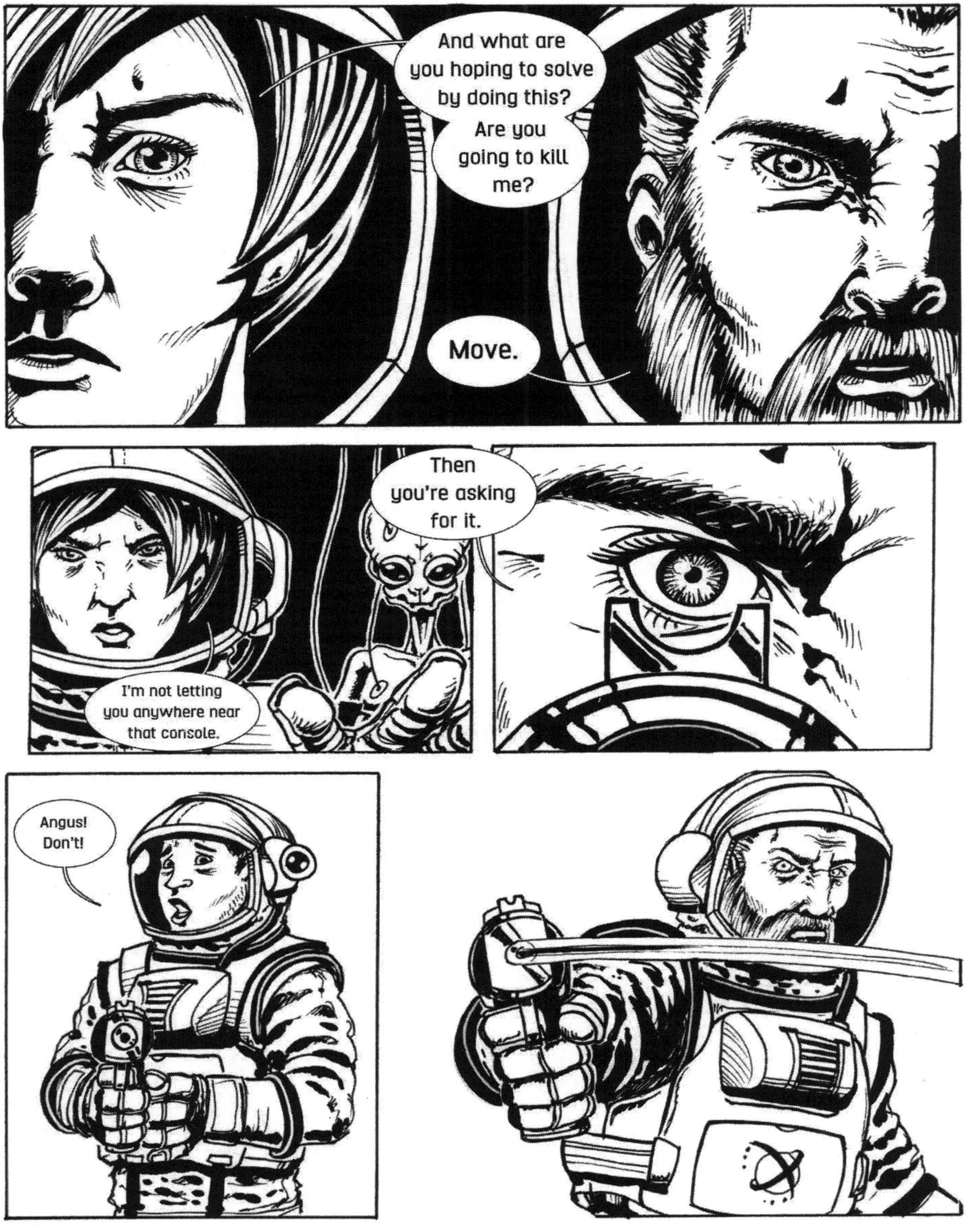
And what are you hoping to solve by doing this?
Are you going to kill me?
Move.
I'm not letting you anywhere near that console.
Then you're asking for it.
Angus! Don't!

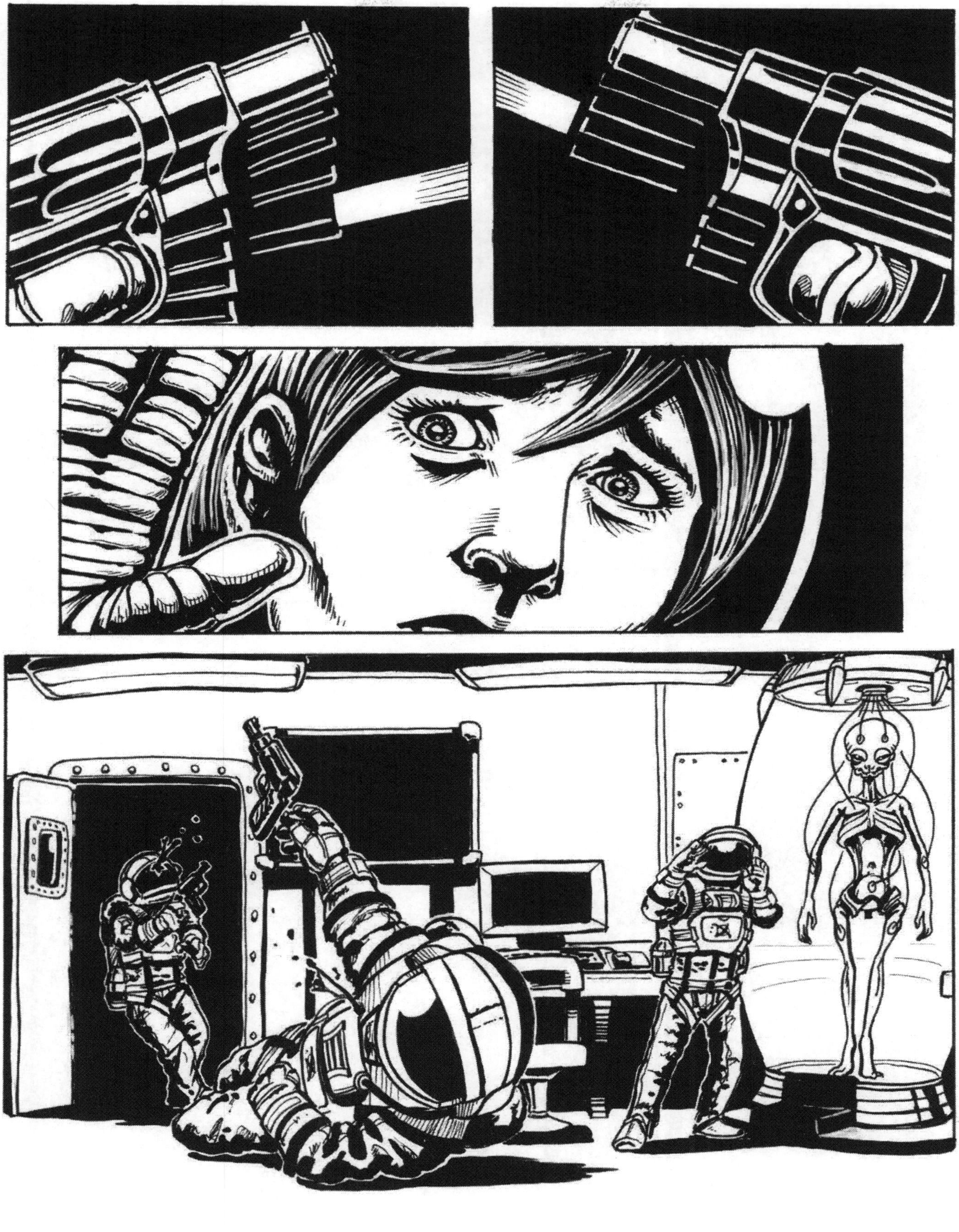

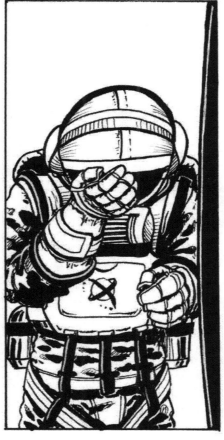

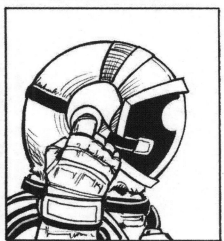

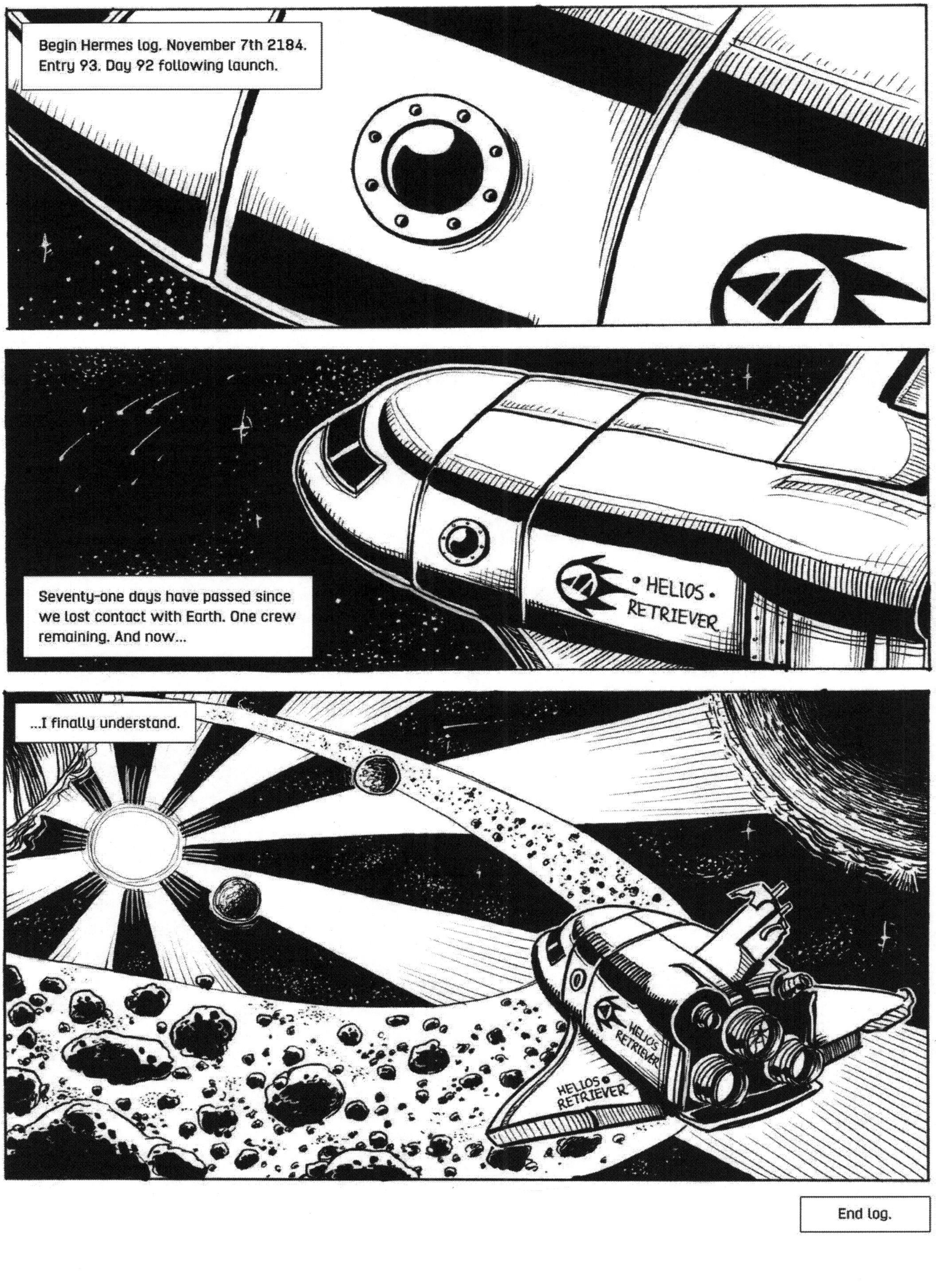
Begin Hermes log. November 7th 2184. Entry 93. Day 92 following launch.
Seventy-one days have passed since we lost contact with Earth. One crew remaining. And now...
HELIOS RETRIEVER
...I finally understand.
HELIOS RETRIEVER
HELIOS RETRIEVER
End log.

The Sailors' Market

TS Porter

The solar winds drew sailors in from every corner of the system, in ships of all kinds, and Kalea's was one of them. There were ships dwarfed by solar sails many thousand times their size, designed to navigate the edges of the solar system where there was almost no light to drive them. There were ships with sharp blunt wings to flirt with how close to the sun they could fly. Most of the ships were more like Kalea's, with flexible sails to take advantage of any condition. Kalea tacked against the sun, sending her ship swooping in on her final approach to the Great Market.

There were markets everywhere, some more permanent than others. Anywhere two sailors met out in the big empty inevitably served as a point of trade, but there was only one Great Market and it only met once every ten years. It was assembled out of a thousand ships into a many-pointed star and would be disassembled to sail off again once the market was over. Kalea could remember the last Great Market, more people than she'd ever imagined existed, more wonders than she'd been able to take in. She'd hidden behind her mother the first day, until she met other children to befriend.

Kalea was no child this time. She'd worked long and hard to earn a ship of her very own. She was as accomplished a sailor as any you'd meet. She'd made more than one speed run between the solar factories on the interior out to the cold dark of the edges. She furled her sails and coasted in, tethering her ship to a free space in the edge of the market. Kalea flipped her hood up over her head, activating it as a pressure suit. It only had a few minutes' air, but that was more than she needed. She slipped quickly out of her airlock and sprang toward the market – floating free in the empty.

No planet-bound human would do this. They were sad, stumpy things; Kalea met them sometimes. They were afraid of the empty, of the sun, of everything it seemed. They could not read their positions with a glance at the stars and the feel of the sun in their sails – if their graceless ships bothered to have sails at all. They lived tethered to their gravity wells and tethered themselves obsessively to anything they could when they had to leave their ships. They could not judge a short leap from one ship to another, when any sailing child could do it before they were weaned.

Kalea's fingers caught on the edge of the Great Market and she crawled toward the nearest airlock, falling into line with others doing so. There was not a single face without a smile. She could see the wonder on the faces of children to match her memory though they weren't even inside yet.

She was not the only one who had to pause on the other side of the airlock. Kalea remembered the Great Market, but the lights and the sound and the people still caught her off guard. No sailor was ever truly alone – the empty was full of clicked radio conversations to listen to or join – but that was different from having people physically present.

There were stalls set up in every direction. Barkers clicked out sales pitches for different sail makes and materials, for decorative and functional air-cleaning plants, for new tailored pressure suits and beautiful jewelry, handed out samples of different food or fiber algae and yeast strains.

Kalea wanted to see it all, and she would, but that wasn't why she was really here. She laughed aloud as she launched herself, twisting her body through empty spaces as she raced toward the center. She was involved in a few mild collisions, inevitable with so many people, but no one was angry in the celebration of the Great Market. They caught themselves, untangled, and kept on their own ways.

The center of the star was open in all directions, with no selling stalls, more space than Kalea had ever seen anywhere other than the endless empty. It was full of people, but she caught sight of her goal all the way across it.

Lani was already waiting. She had grown up so much since they met at their first Great Market. Her suit must have been purchased new here – it was designed with an extra wrap of brightly decorated green and yellow fabric tethered to the outside of her ankles to make a soft flowing skirt. It wrapped neatly up her torso, covering only one shoulder and arm. It was impractical, but Lani in it was the most beautiful person Kalea had ever seen. Her skin gleamed, sun-blessed as black as the empty, and the ends of her tightly curled brown hair were faded to gold. She smiled, big and wide with that perfect little gap between her front teeth, when her eyes finally found Kalea.

They both launched themselves into the space, reaching for each other. Their hands caught each others, Kalea's long brown fingers intertwining with Lani's black. They tumbled slowly together, knees briefly colliding before they hooked together like any two people talking who didn't want to drift apart. Kalea didn't have any words, though. Not now that they were finally together. They'd become inseparable in the few days of their first Great Market, the best friend either of them had ever had. Their families frequented different sailing routes, but there hadn't been a day since then Lani and Kalea hadn't sent each other messages clicking back and forth through the empty. It was different to see Lani, though.

"I'm so, so happy to see you," Lani whispered, just for Kalea. Her family spoke with a different accent, used different words than Kalea's, but they could understand each other easily enough. Some people spoke differently enough they could only understand each other in common radio clicks. Lani released Kalea's hands and hesitantly wrapped her arms around her shoulders instead, so their foreheads could rest together. Kalea's own hands found Lani's hips, warm beneath her palms.

They'd been friends as children, but they were not children anymore. The messages they clicked back and forth had been different in

recent years, sweet with hope and promises. There was no one else either of them was nearly as close to. There was no one else Kalea wanted to sail in convoy with – or combine ships to sail catamaran together and always be within reach. They had agreed to make no final decisions until they met again in person.

There was nothing Kalea couldn't tell Lani in radio clicks, but here in person her throat was frozen. Everything seemed too intimate to be said in words, or maybe words too crude a language to say them in.

Kalea clicked instead, light on the end of her tongue in imitation of a radio signal. "My Lani."

"My Kalea," Lani clicked back, laughing slightly. Those familiar sounds, softened in her mouth, were the sweetest thing Kalea had ever heard.

"I have my own ship, a good ship." Kalea finally found her voice. "I can sail near and far the sun, fast as any sailor, trading anywhere I go. Sail with me?" She'd worked so hard and so long to be good enough to make the offer. She could provide in a partnership.

"Of course." Lani's deep brown eyes smiled into Kalea's. "My ship is sound and my plants sell everywhere I go, we'll be so strong together. But first let's see the Great Market. They built a botanical garden in here. Imagine, a library of all the plants you can grow! Come see it with me."

Lani unhooked her knee from Kalea's, holding her hand to tow her along as she launched them both toward it. Kalea was caught off guard, tugged along helplessly for a moment before she laughed and caught a piece of wall to pull them along quicker through the crowds. She was more than happy to see all the gardens and stalls Lani wanted. Kalea could browse the entire market with her heart full and content.

She already had what she came for.

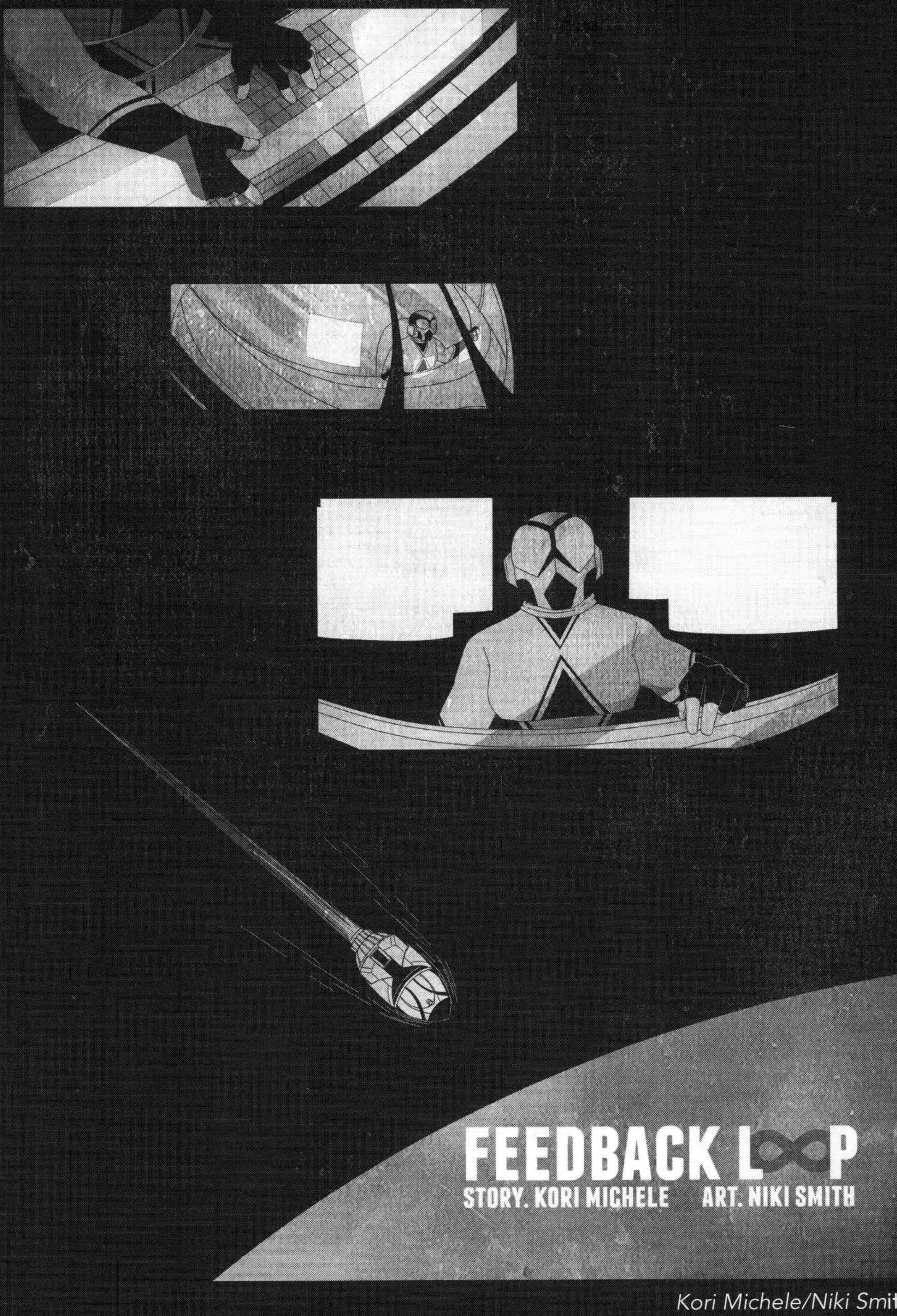
FEEDBACK L∞P
STORY. KORI MICHELE ART. NIKI SMITH

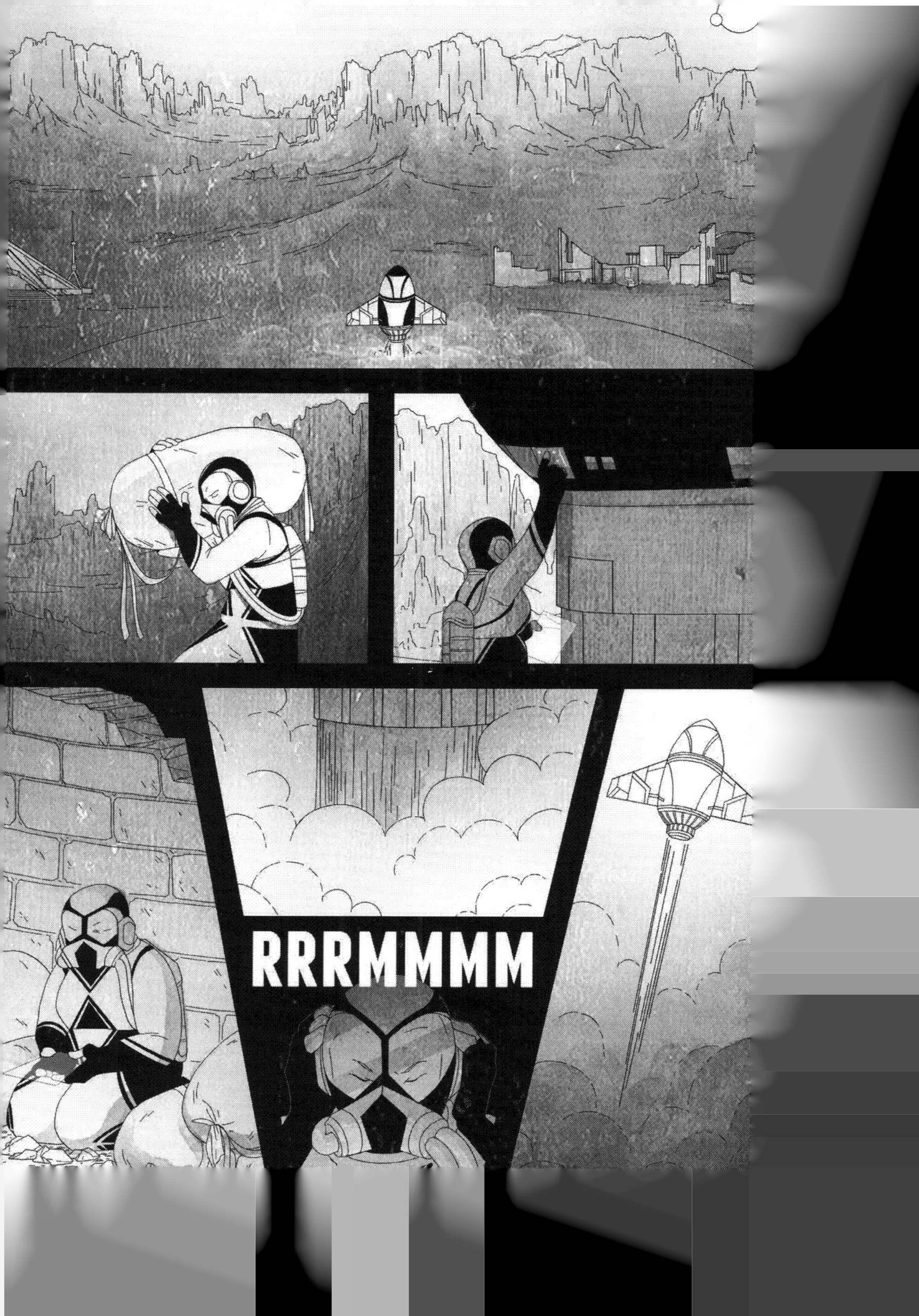
RRRMMMM

PHOENIX, ALPHA 1012
VACATED 9092
ABANDONED PROPERTIES
FOR SALE

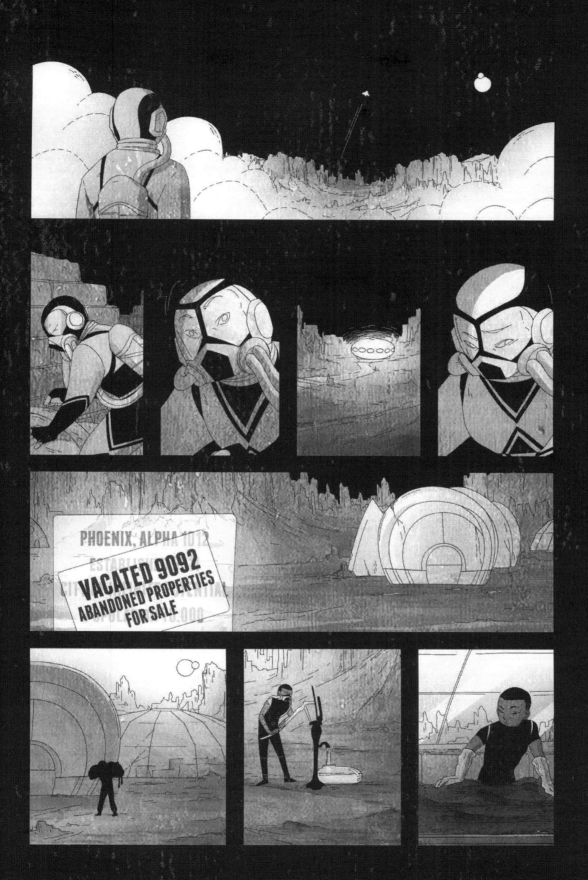

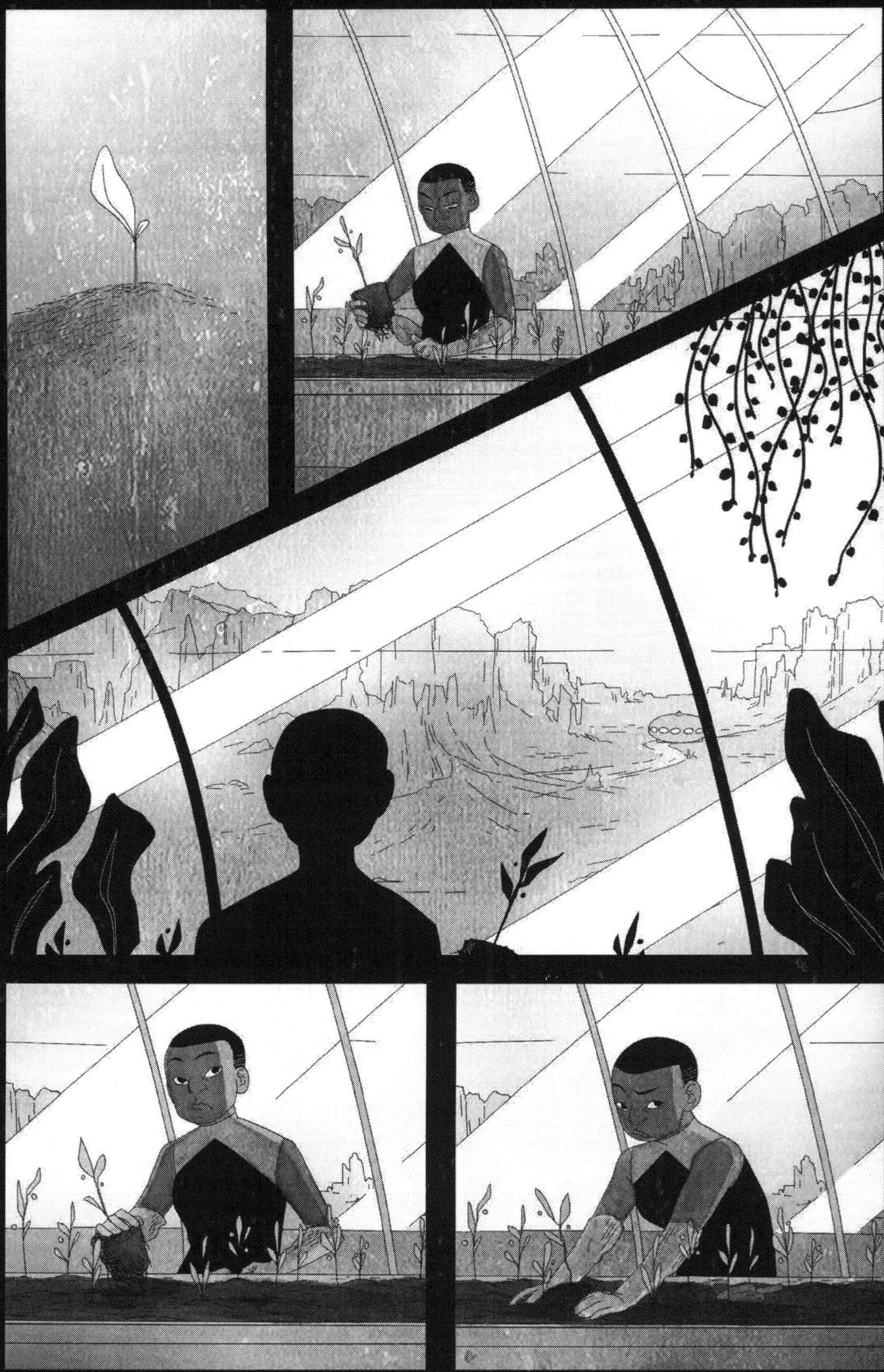

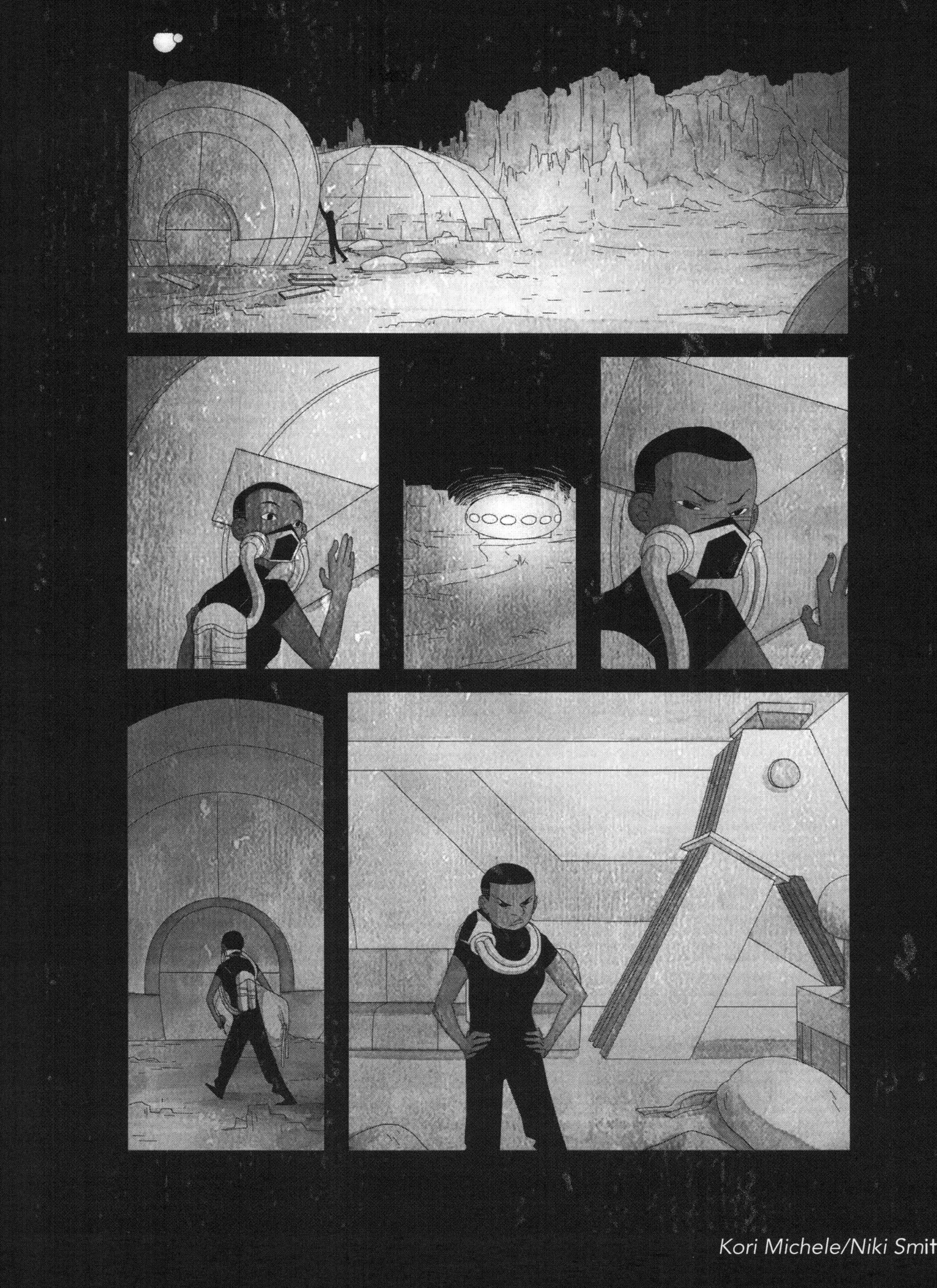

Kori Michele/Niki Smit

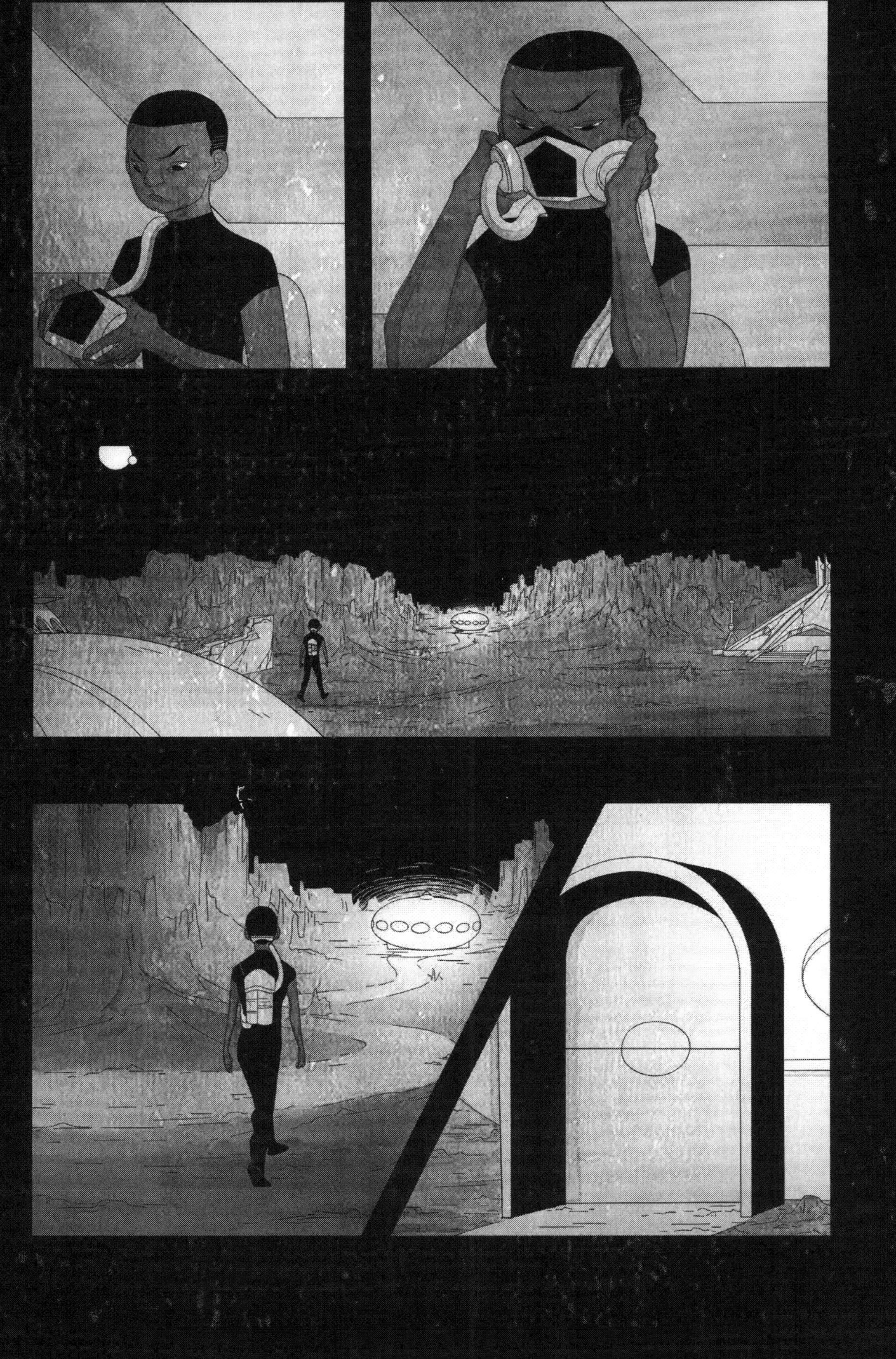

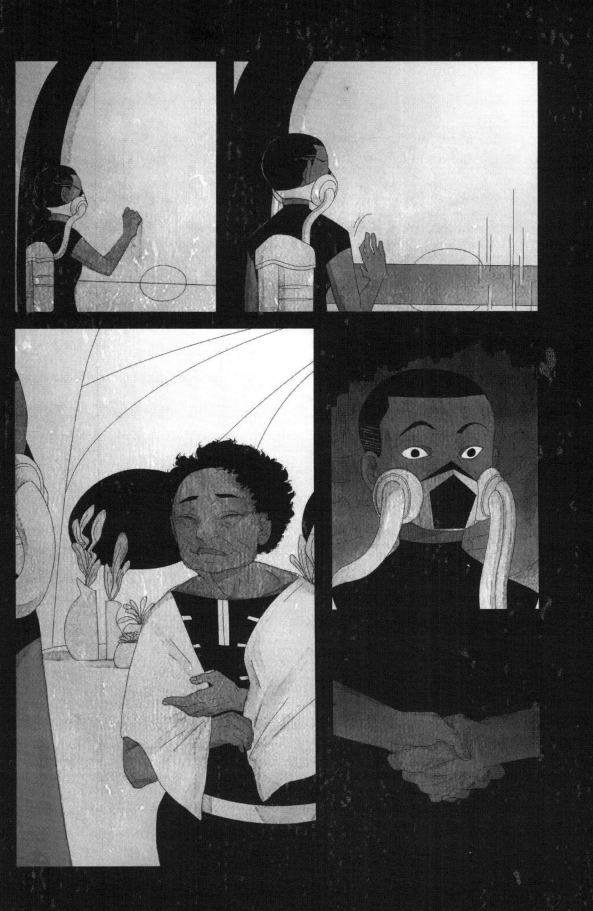

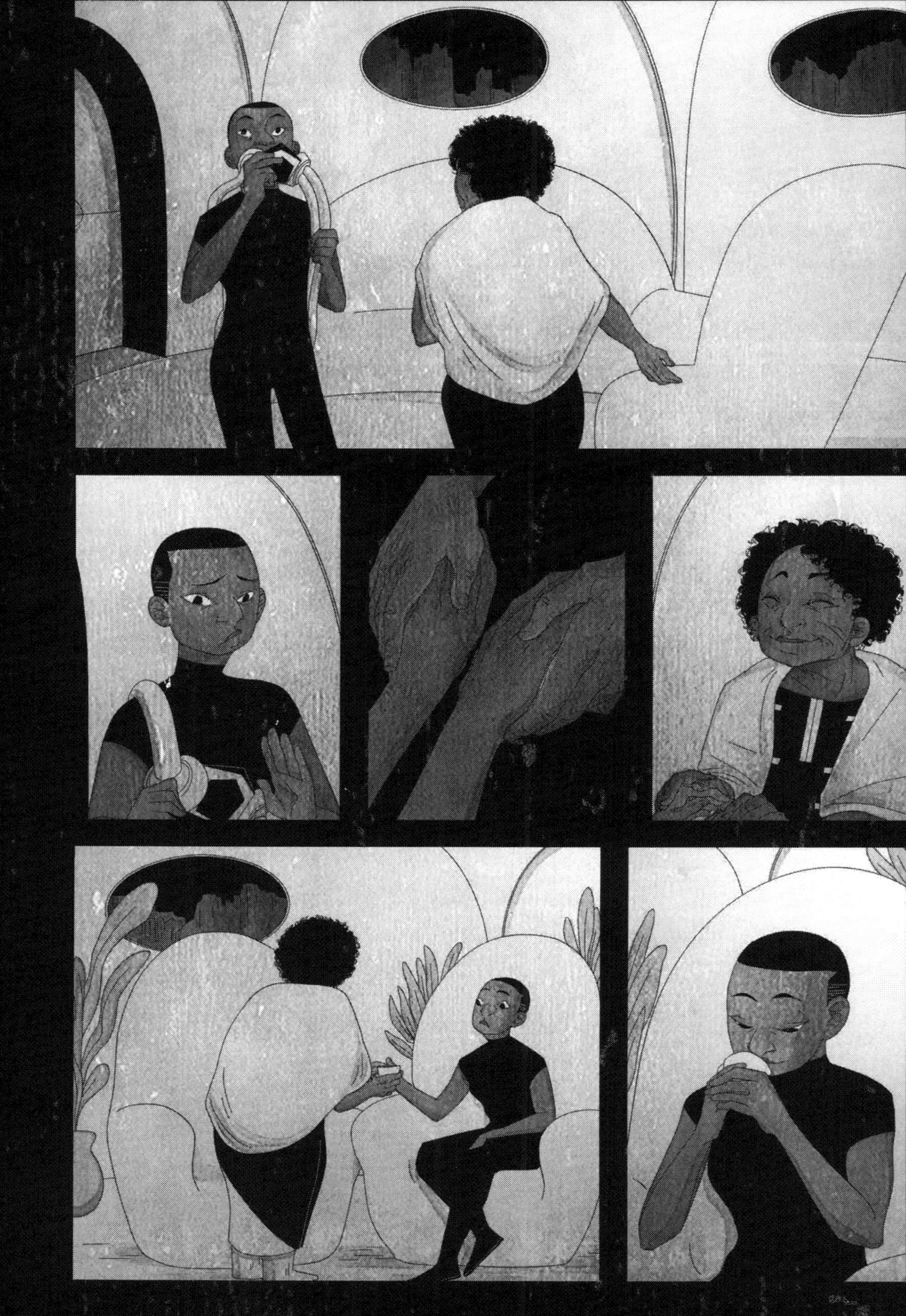

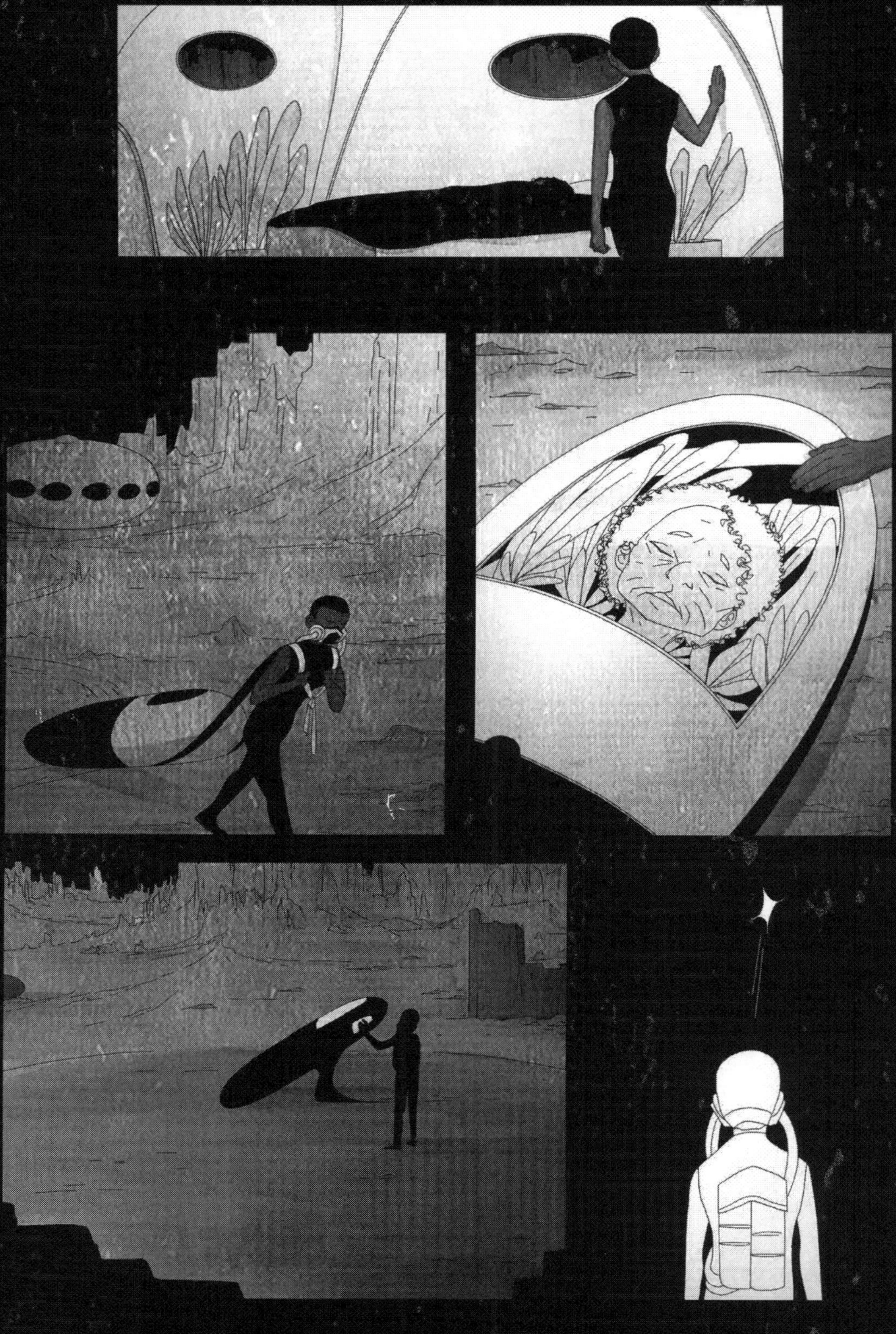

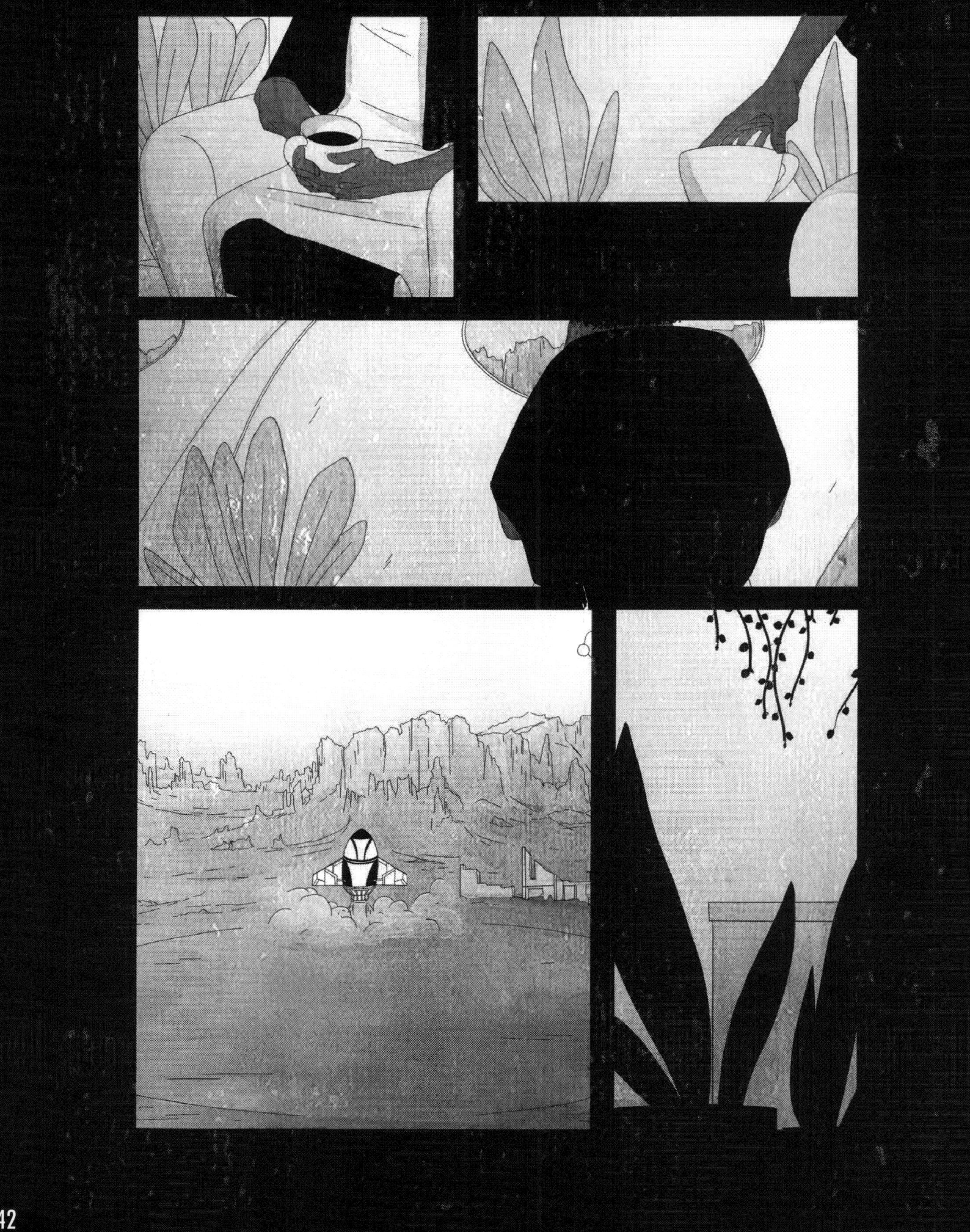

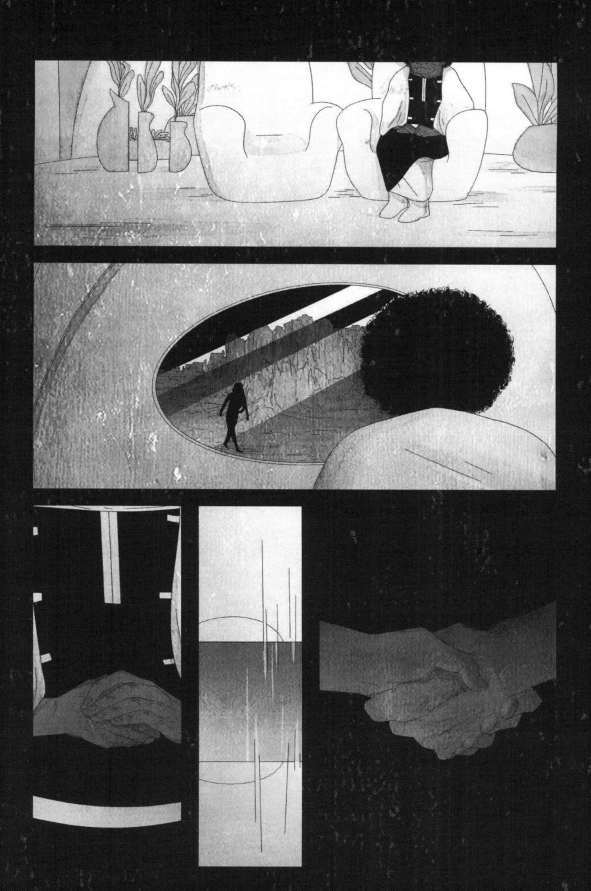

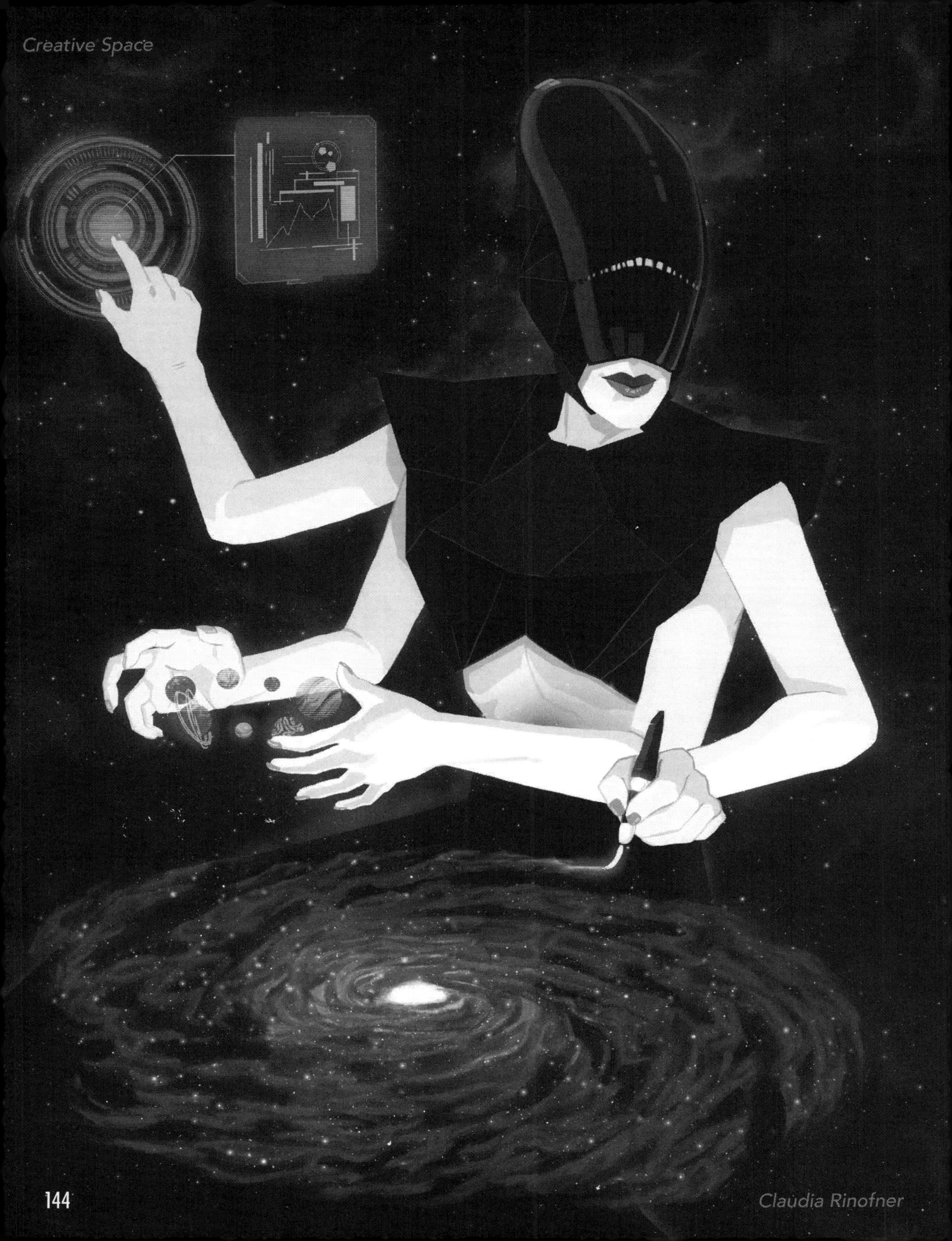

Claudia Rinofner

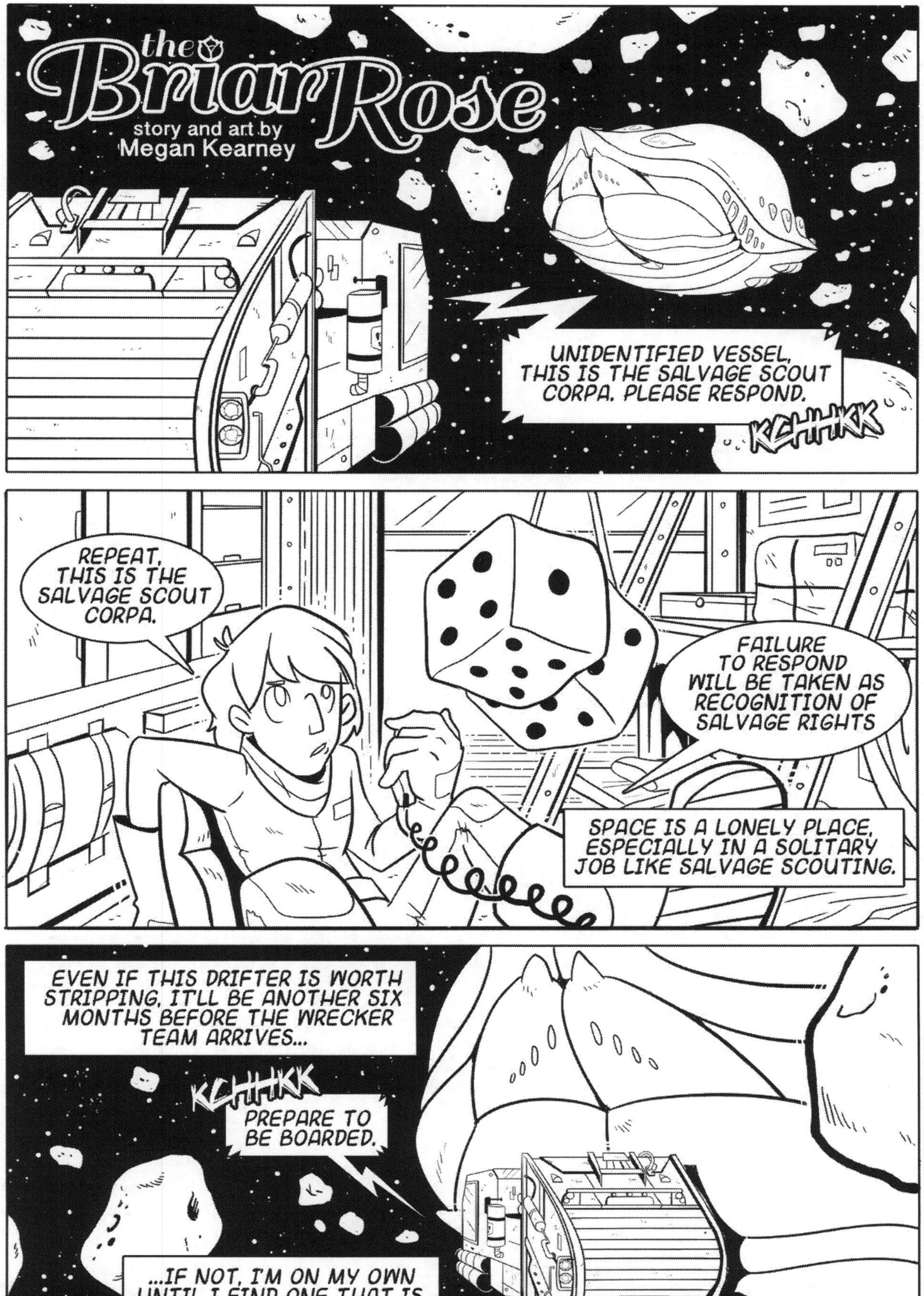
the Briar Rose
story and art by
Megan Kearney
UNIDENTIFIED VESSEL, THIS IS THE SALVAGE SCOUT CORPA. PLEASE RESPOND.
KCHHKK
REPEAT, THIS IS THE SALVAGE SCOUT CORPA.
FAILURE TO RESPOND WILL BE TAKEN AS RECOGNITION OF SALVAGE RIGHTS
SPACE IS A LONELY PLACE, ESPECIALLY IN A SOLITARY JOB LIKE SALVAGE SCOUTING.
EVEN IF THIS DRIFTER IS WORTH STRIPPING, IT'LL BE ANOTHER SIX MONTHS BEFORE THE WRECKER TEAM ARRIVES...
KCHHKK
PREPARE TO BE BOARDED.
...IF NOT, I'M ON MY OWN UNTIL I FIND ONE THAT IS.

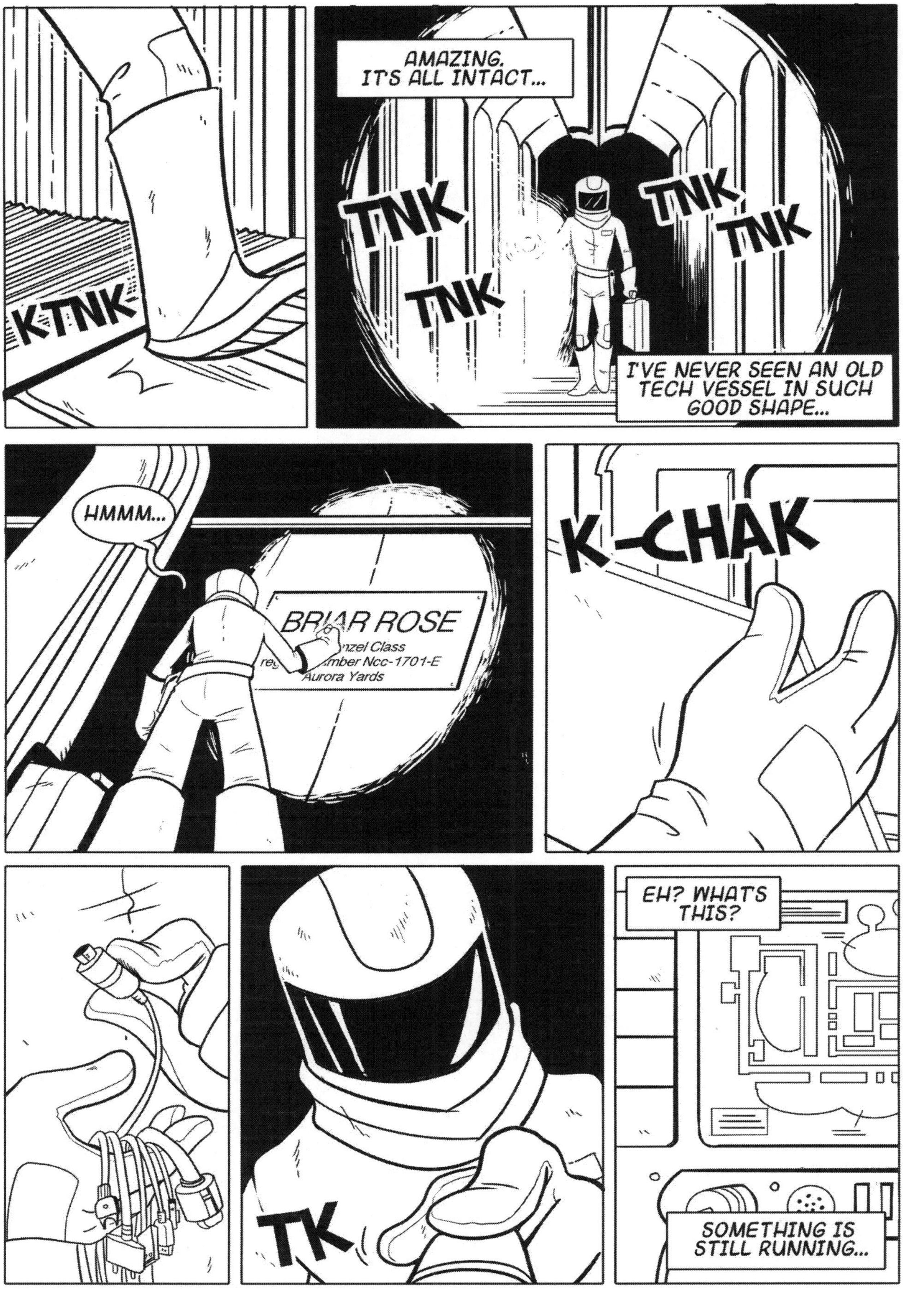
KTNK
AMAZING. IT'S ALL INTACT...
TNK
TNK
TNK
TNK
I'VE NEVER SEEN AN OLD TECH VESSEL IN SUCH GOOD SHAPE...
HMMM...
BRIAR ROSE
Aurora Yards
K-CHAK
TK
EH? WHAT'S THIS?
SOMETHING IS STILL RUNNING...

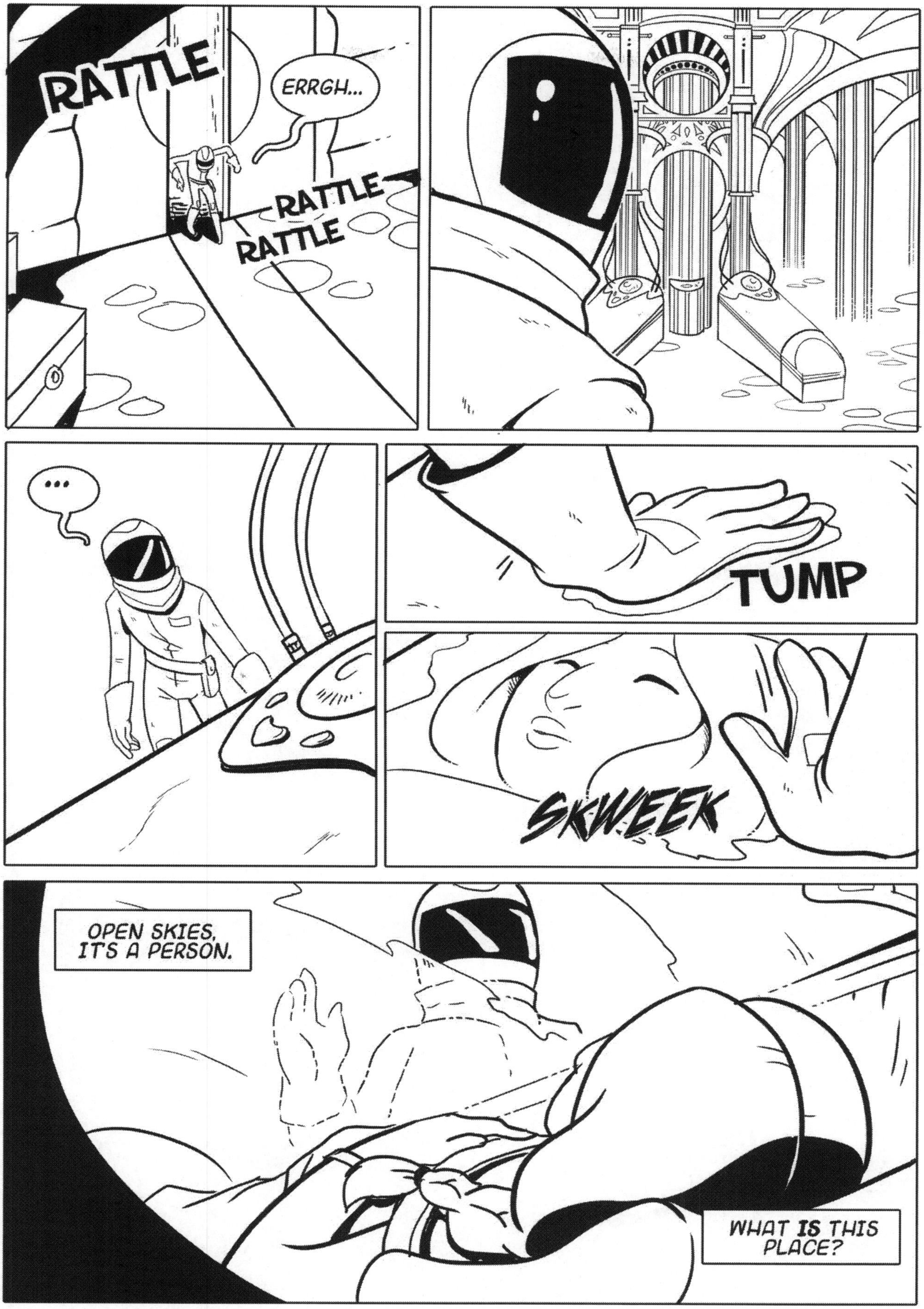
RATTLE
ERRGH...
RATTLE
RATTLE
...
TUMP
SKWEEK
OPEN SKIES, IT'S A PERSON.
WHAT IS THIS PLACE?

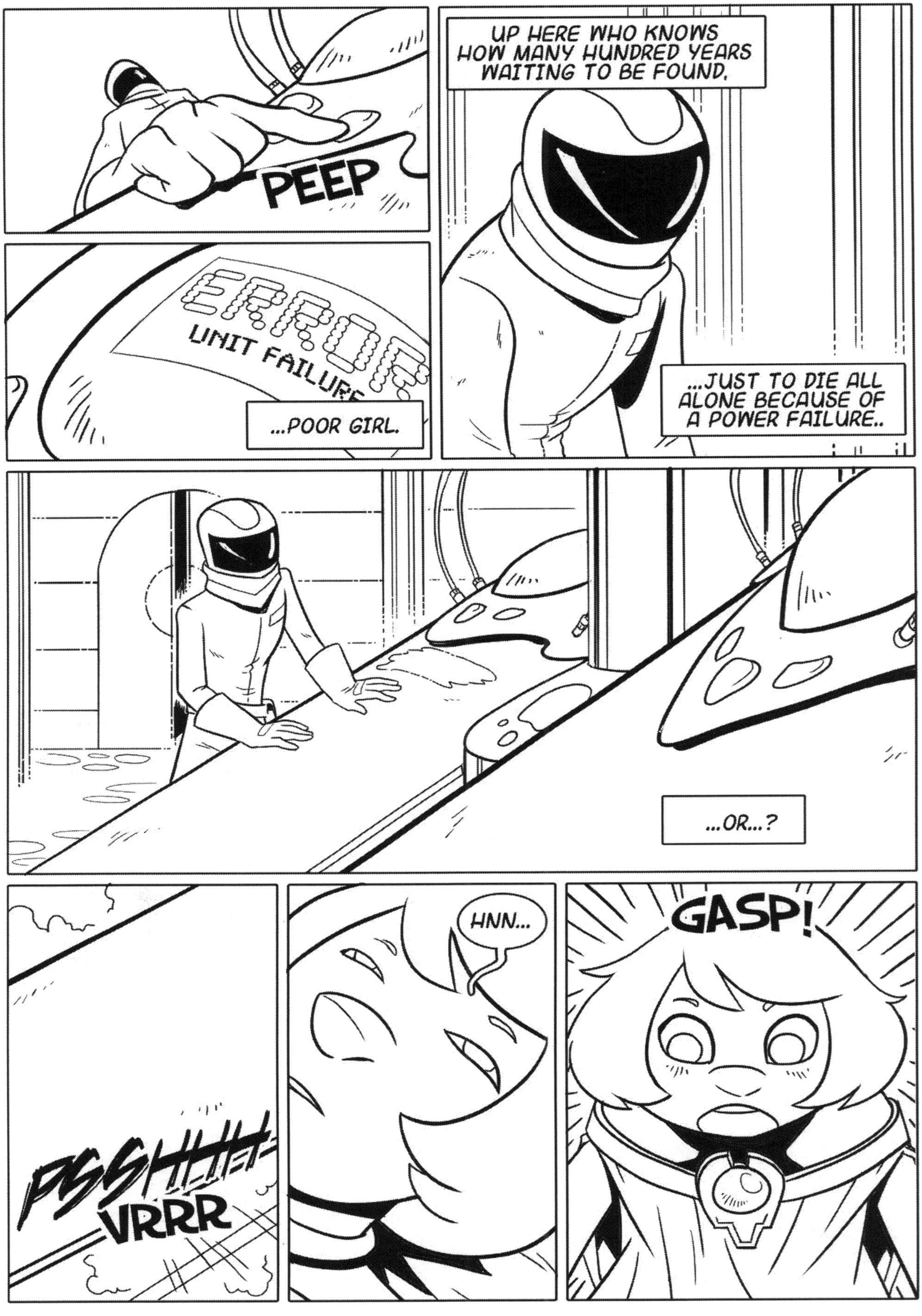
PEEP
UP HERE WHO KNOWS HOW MANY HUNDRED YEARS WAITING TO BE FOUND.
ERROR
UNIT FAILURE
...POOR GIRL.
...JUST TO DIE ALL ALONE BECAUSE OF A POWER FAILURE..
...OR...?
PSSHHH
VRRR
HNN...
GASP!

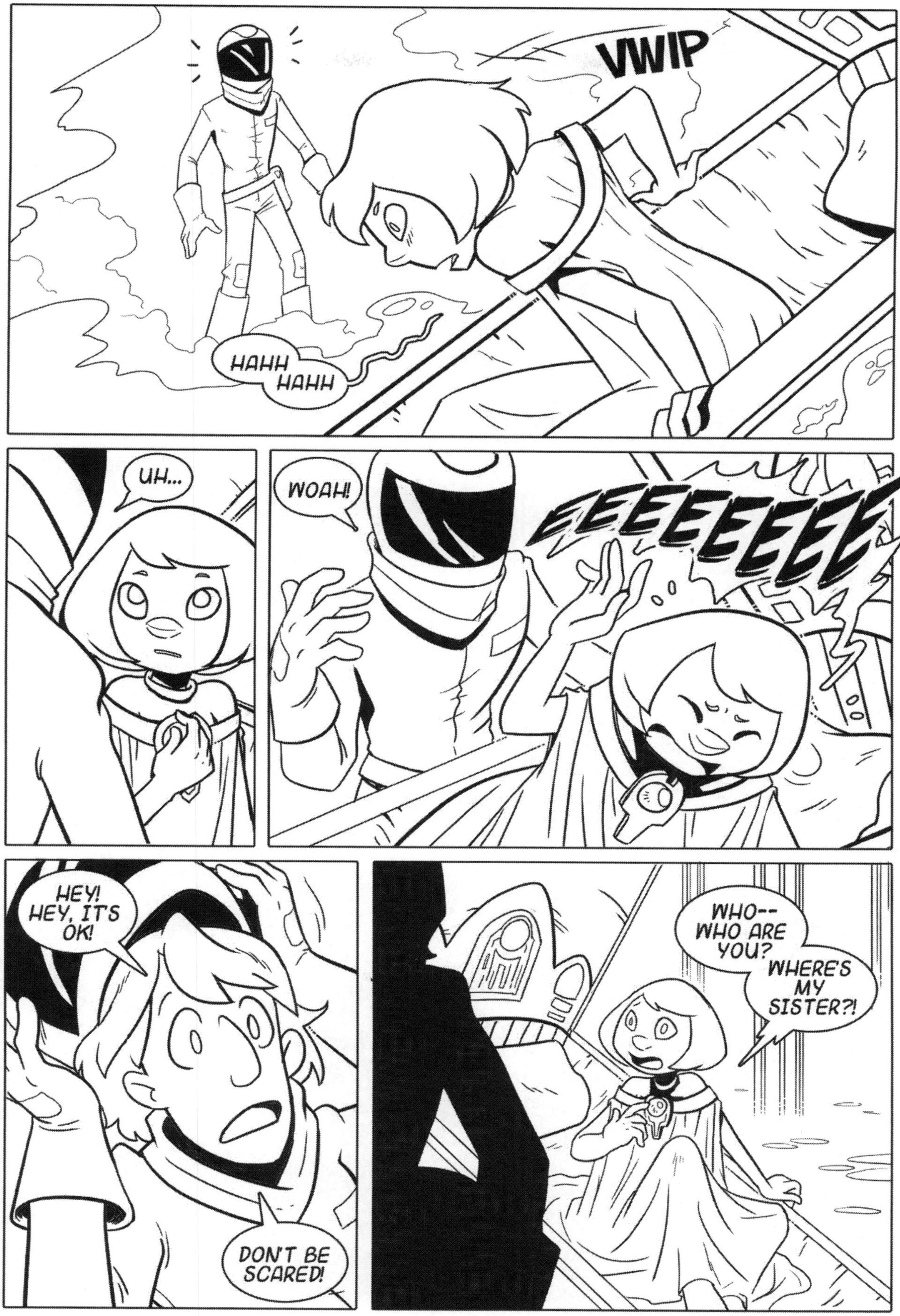
VWIP
HAHH HAHH
UH...
WOAH!
EEEEEEEE
HEY! HEY, IT'S OK!
DON'T BE SCARED!
WHO-- WHO ARE YOU?
WHERE'S MY SISTER?!

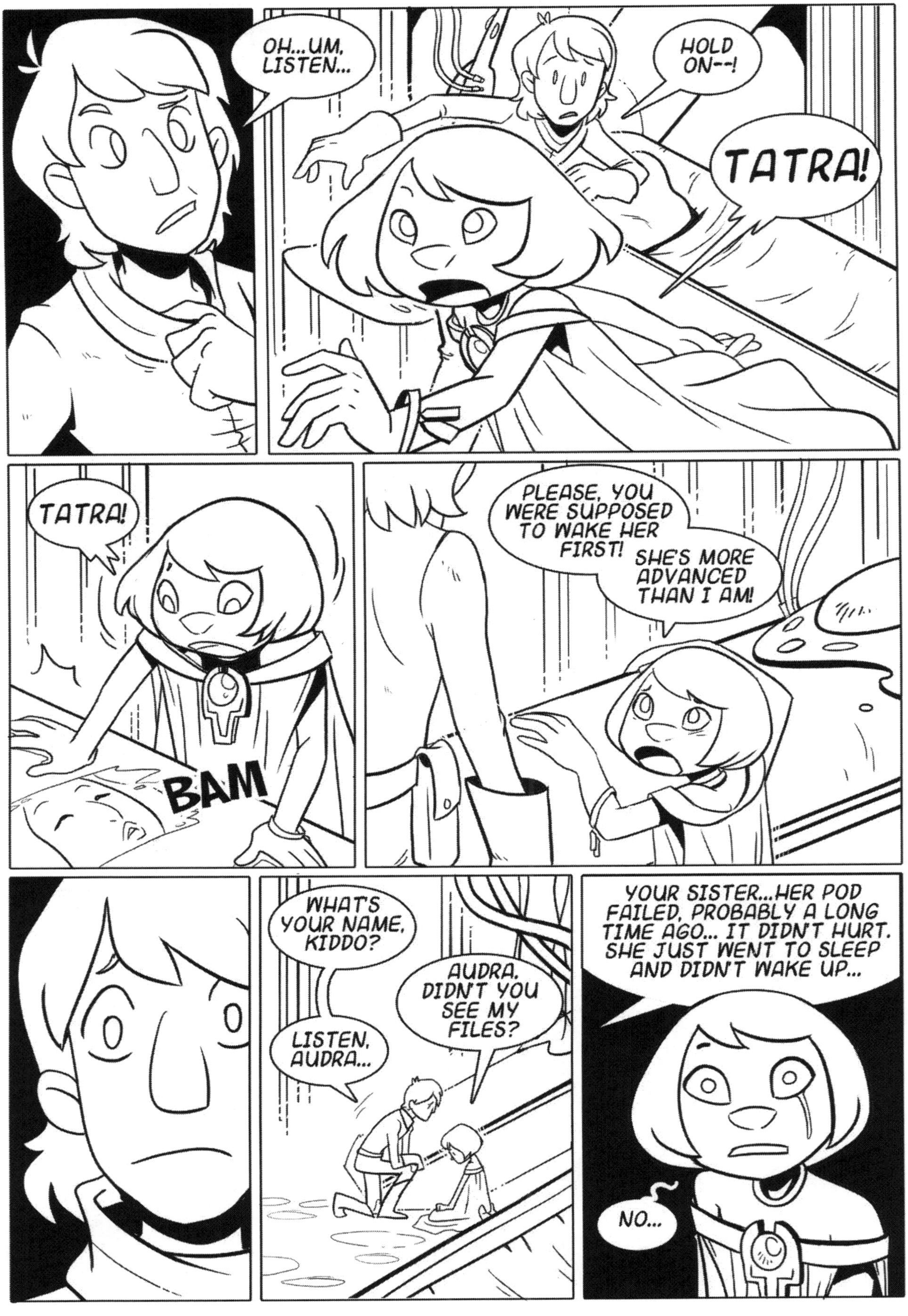
OH...UM, LISTEN...
HOLD ON--!
TATRA!
TATRA!
BAM
PLEASE, YOU WERE SUPPOSED TO WAKE HER FIRST!
SHE'S MORE ADVANCED THAN I AM!
WHAT'S YOUR NAME, KIDDO?
AUDRA. DIDN'T YOU SEE MY FILES?
LISTEN, AUDRA...
YOUR SISTER...HER POD FAILED, PROBABLY A LONG TIME AGO... IT DIDN'T HURT. SHE JUST WENT TO SLEEP AND DIDN'T WAKE UP...
NO...

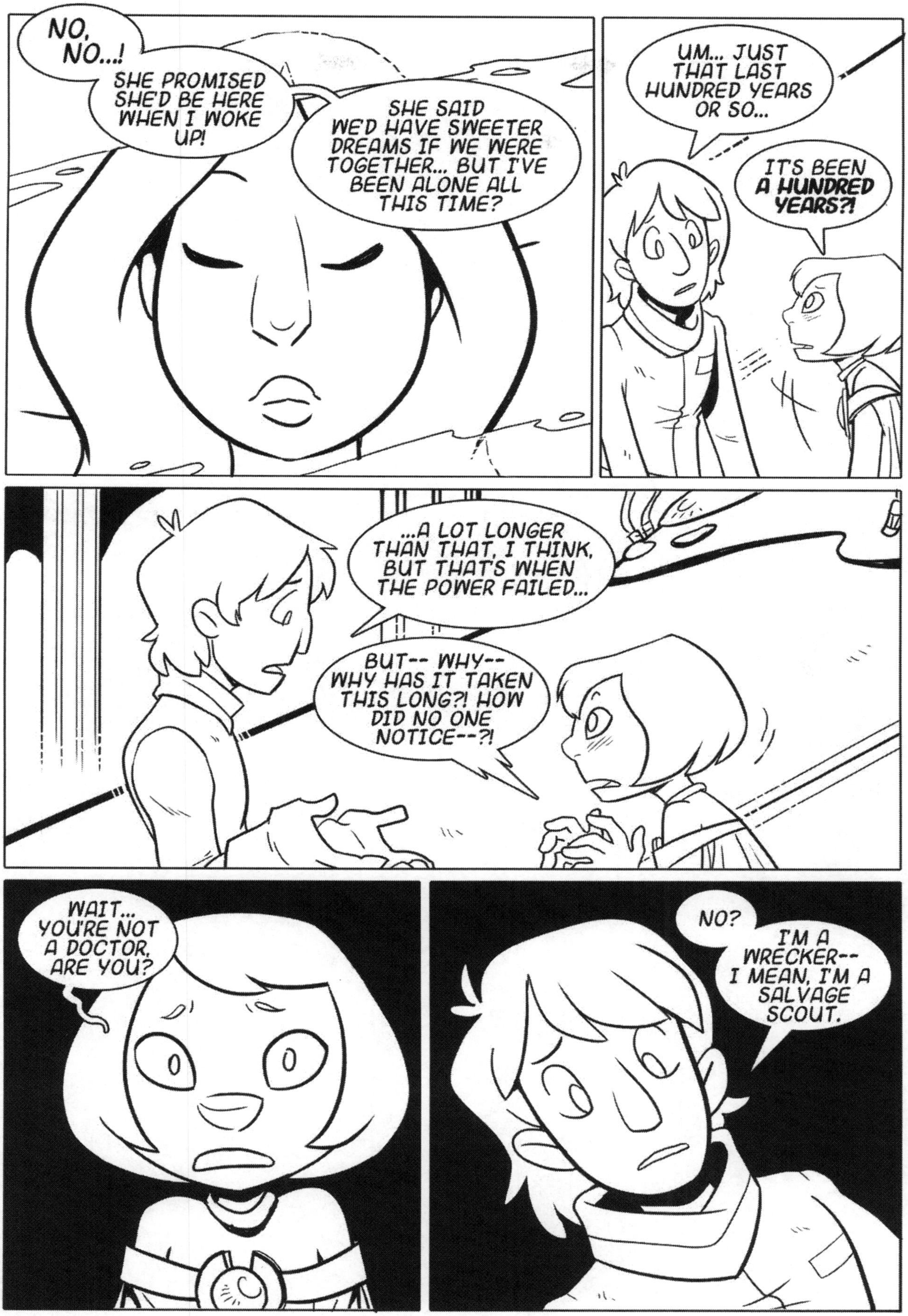

NO, NO...!
SHE PROMISED SHE'D BE HERE WHEN I WOKE UP!
SHE SAID WE'D HAVE SWEETER DREAMS IF WE WERE TOGETHER... BUT I'VE BEEN ALONE ALL THIS TIME?
UM... JUST THAT LAST HUNDRED YEARS OR SO...
IT'S BEEN **A HUNDRED YEARS?!**
...A LOT LONGER THAN THAT, I THINK, BUT THAT'S WHEN THE POWER FAILED...
BUT-- WHY-- WHY HAS IT TAKEN THIS LONG?! HOW DID NO ONE NOTICE--?!
WAIT... YOU'RE NOT A DOCTOR, ARE YOU?
NO?
I'M A WRECKER-- I MEAN, I'M A SALVAGE SCOUT.

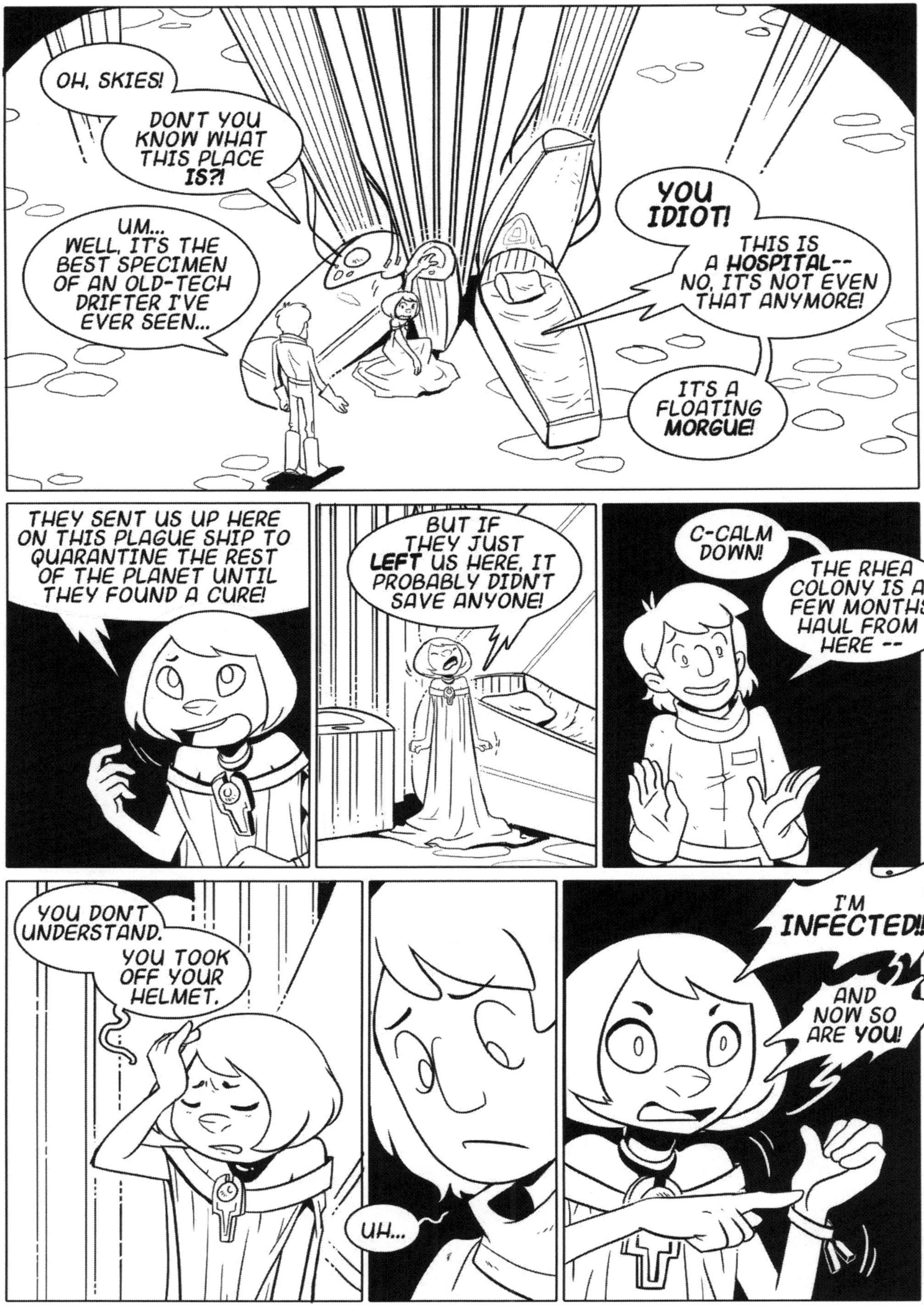
OH, SKIES!
DON'T YOU KNOW WHAT THIS PLACE IS?!
UM... WELL, IT'S THE BEST SPECIMEN OF AN OLD-TECH DRIFTER I'VE EVER SEEN...
YOU IDIOT!
THIS IS A HOSPITAL-- NO, IT'S NOT EVEN THAT ANYMORE!
IT'S A FLOATING MORGUE!
THEY SENT US UP HERE ON THIS PLAGUE SHIP TO QUARANTINE THE REST OF THE PLANET UNTIL THEY FOUND A CURE!
BUT IF THEY JUST LEFT US HERE, IT PROBABLY DIDN'T SAVE ANYONE!
C-CALM DOWN!
THE RHEA COLONY IS A FEW MONTHS HAUL FROM HERE --
YOU DON'T UNDERSTAND.
YOU TOOK OFF YOUR HELMET.
UH...
I'M INFECTED!!
AND NOW SO ARE YOU!

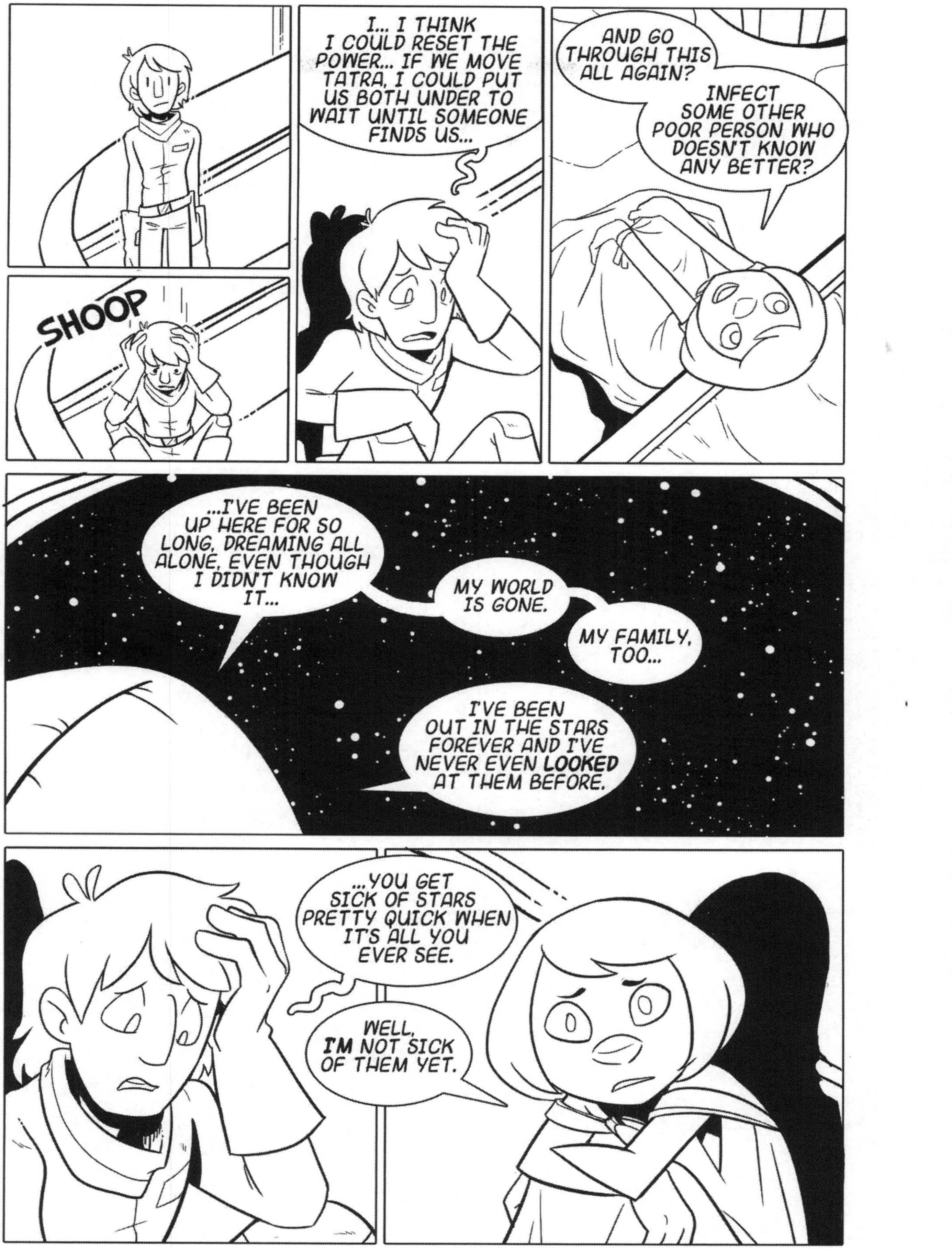
SHOOP
I... I THINK I COULD RESET THE POWER... IF WE MOVE TATRA, I COULD PUT US BOTH UNDER TO WAIT UNTIL SOMEONE FINDS US...
AND GO THROUGH THIS ALL AGAIN?
INFECT SOME OTHER POOR PERSON WHO DOESN'T KNOW ANY BETTER?
...I'VE BEEN UP HERE FOR SO LONG, DREAMING ALL ALONE, EVEN THOUGH I DIDN'T KNOW IT...
MY WORLD IS GONE.
MY FAMILY, TOO...
I'VE BEEN OUT IN THE STARS FOREVER AND I'VE NEVER EVEN LOOKED AT THEM BEFORE.
...YOU GET SICK OF STARS PRETTY QUICK WHEN IT'S ALL YOU EVER SEE.
WELL, I'M NOT SICK OF THEM YET.

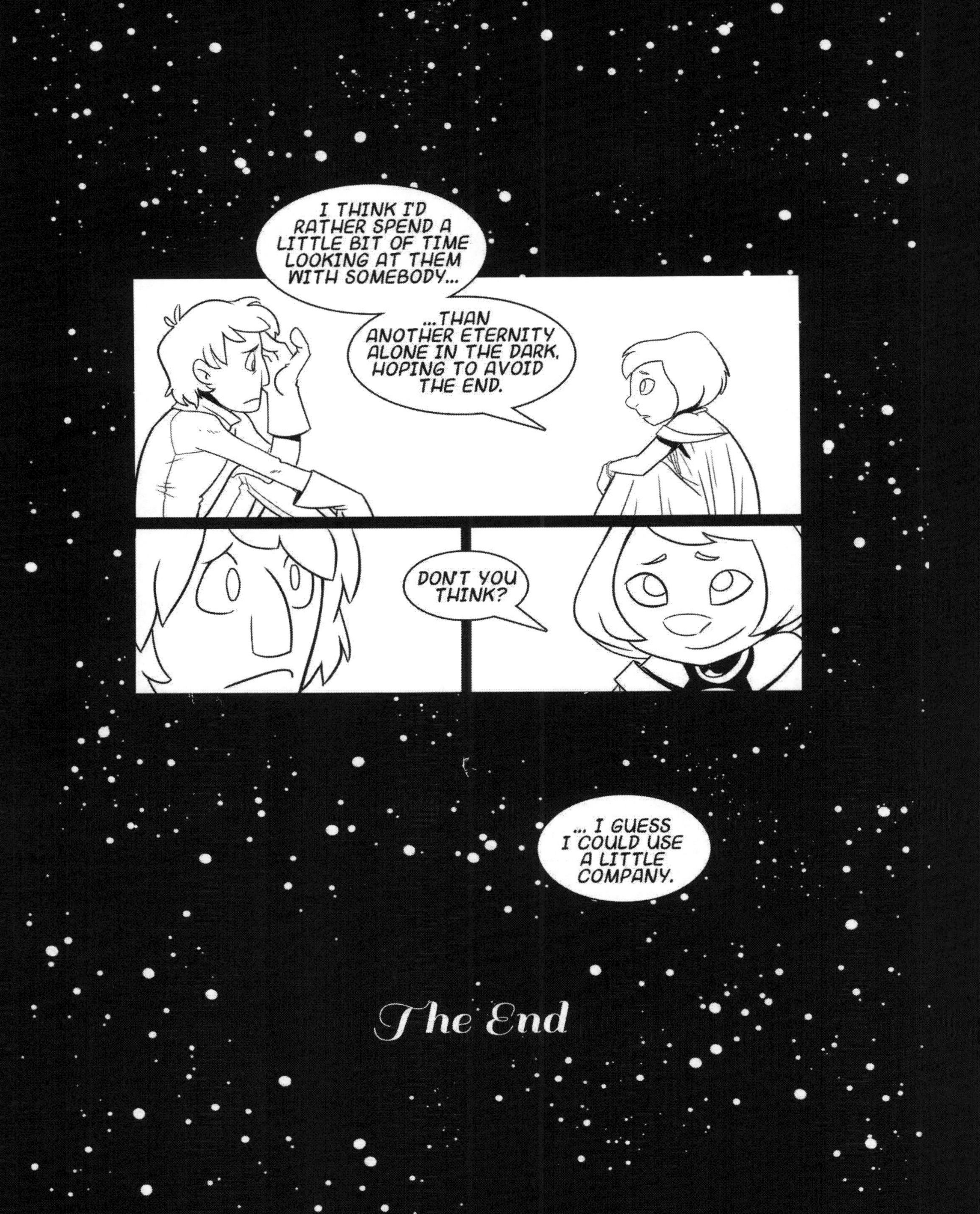
I THINK I'D RATHER SPEND A LITTLE BIT OF TIME LOOKING AT THEM WITH SOMEBODY...
...THAN ANOTHER ETERNITY ALONE IN THE DARK, HOPING TO AVOID THE END.
DON'T YOU THINK?
... I GUESS I COULD USE A LITTLE COMPANY.
The End

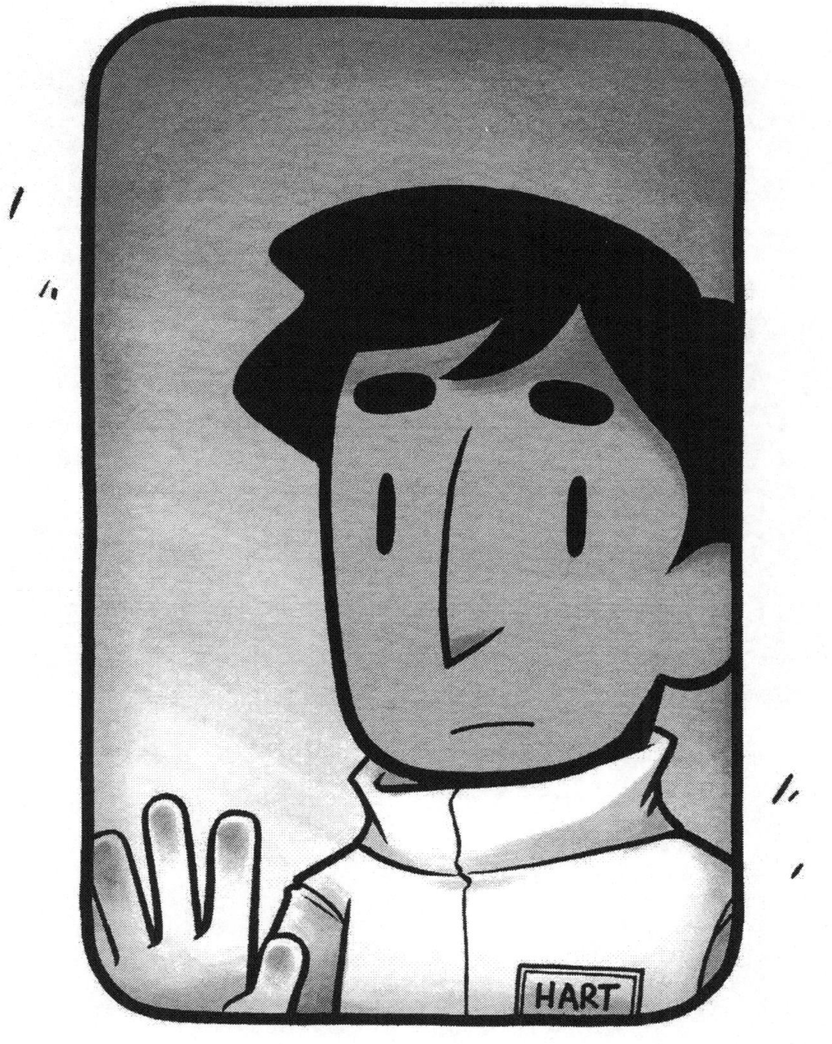
HART

I am a man of space.

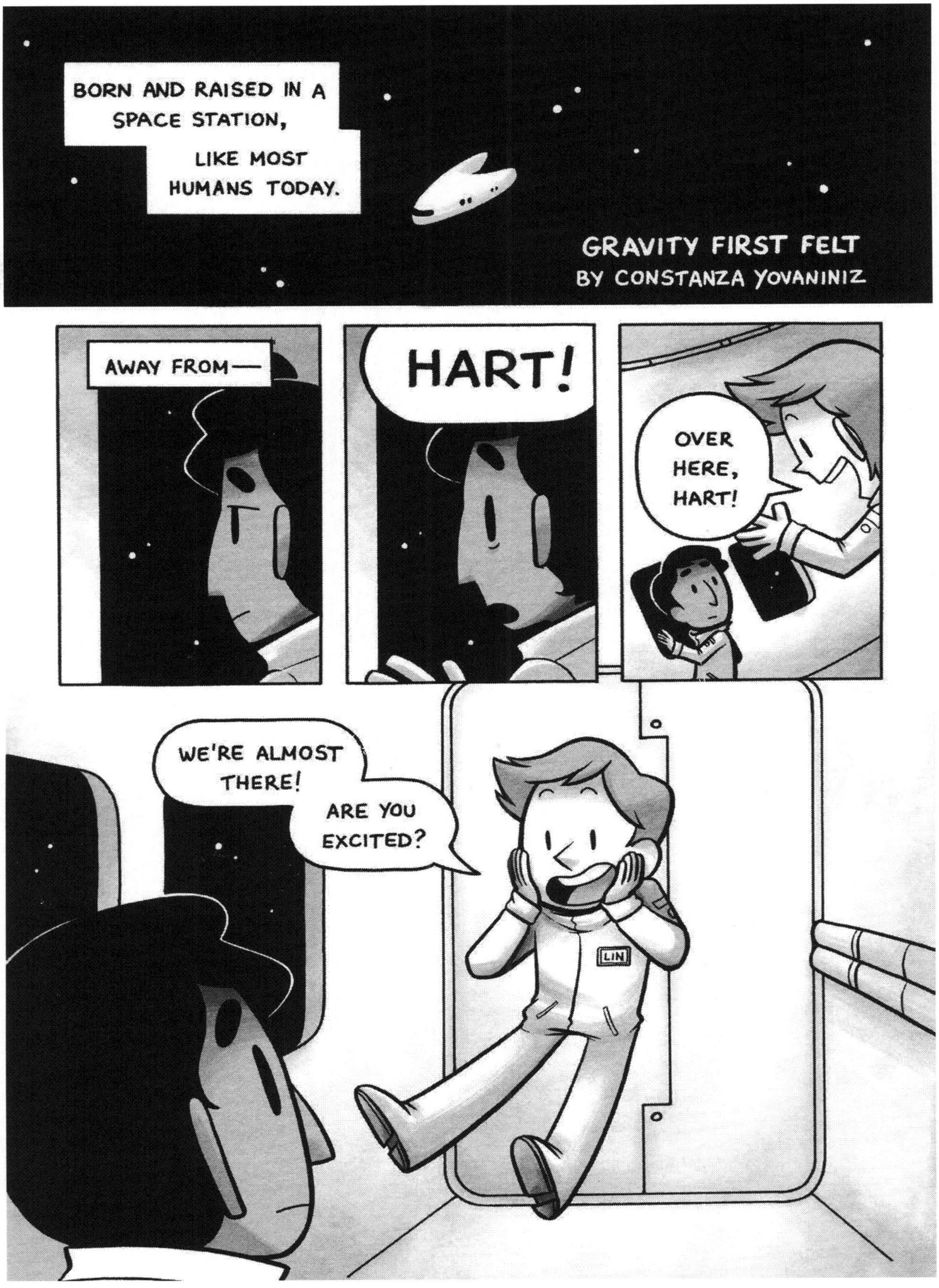
BORN AND RAISED IN A SPACE STATION,
LIKE MOST HUMANS TODAY.
GRAVITY FIRST FELT
BY CONSTANZA YOVANINIZ
AWAY FROM—
HART!
OVER HERE, HART!
WE'RE ALMOST THERE!
ARE YOU EXCITED?
LIN

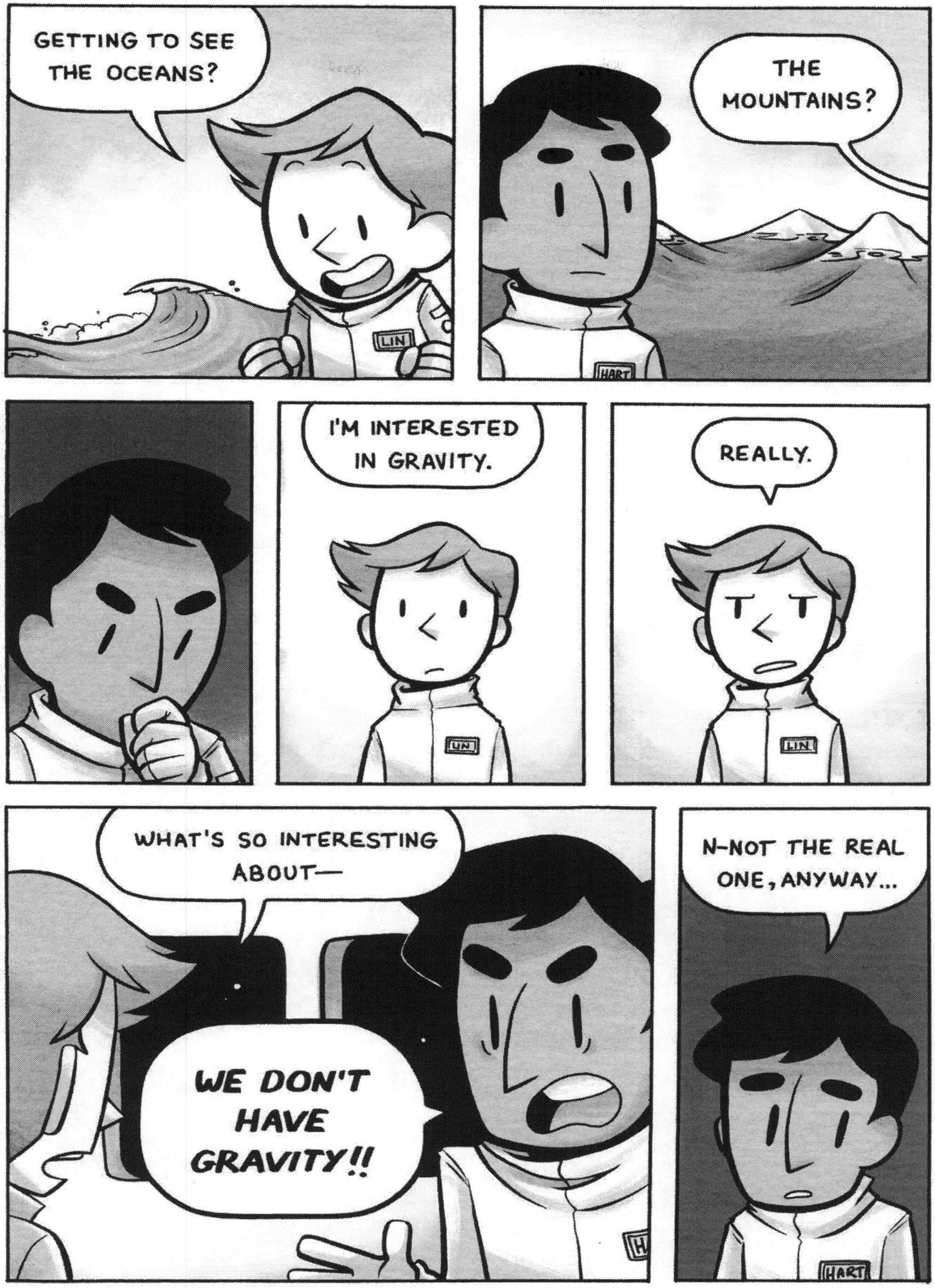
GETTING TO SEE THE OCEANS?
LIN
THE MOUNTAINS?
HART
I'M INTERESTED IN GRAVITY.
LIN
REALLY.
LIN
WHAT'S SO INTERESTING ABOUT—
WE DON'T HAVE GRAVITY!!
N-NOT THE REAL ONE, ANYWAY...
HART

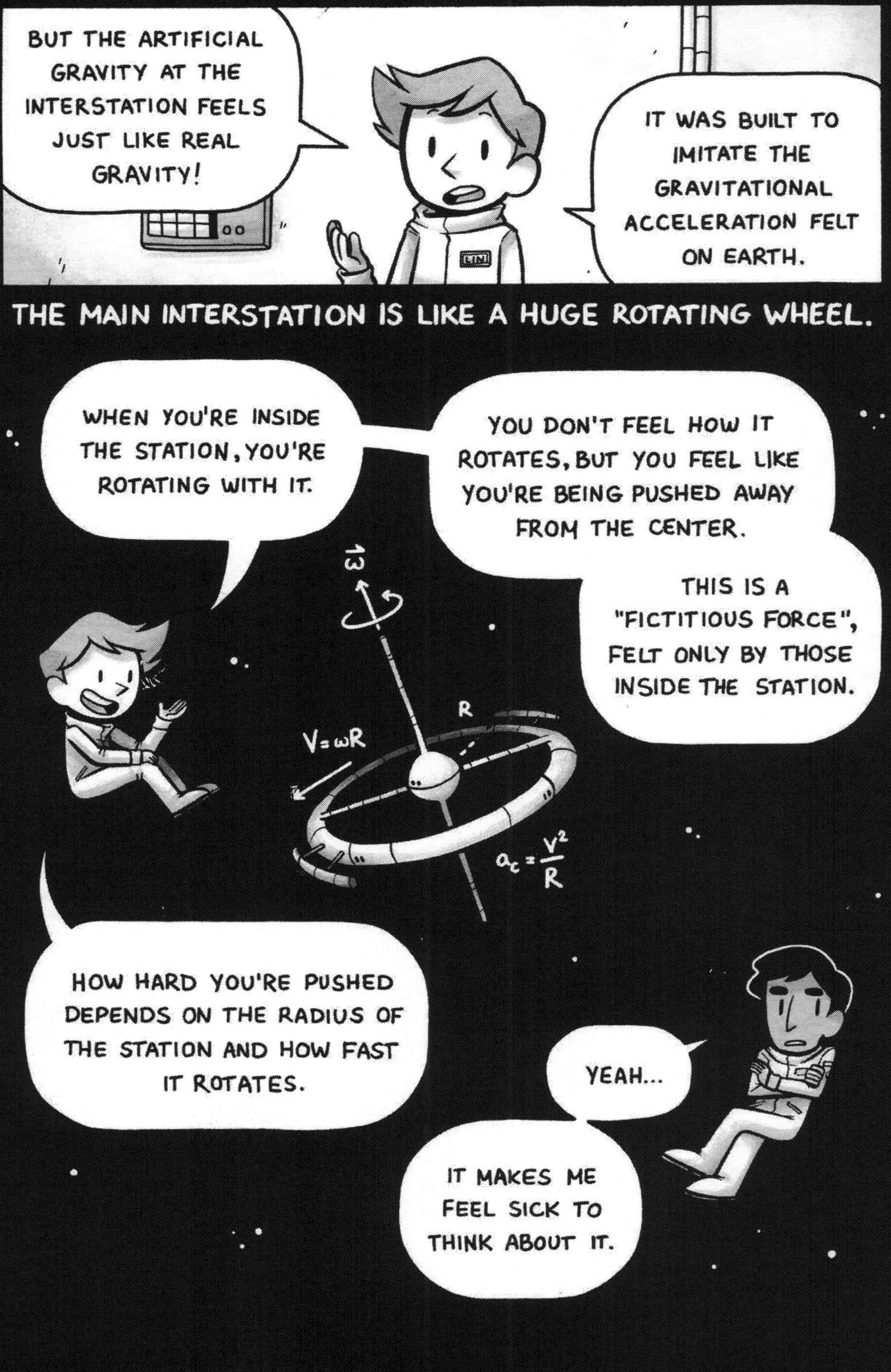
BUT THE ARTIFICIAL GRAVITY AT THE INTERSTATION FEELS JUST LIKE REAL GRAVITY!
IT WAS BUILT TO IMITATE THE GRAVITATIONAL ACCELERATION FELT ON EARTH.
THE MAIN INTERSTATION IS LIKE A HUGE ROTATING WHEEL.
WHEN YOU'RE INSIDE THE STATION, YOU'RE ROTATING WITH IT.
YOU DON'T FEEL HOW IT ROTATES, BUT YOU FEEL LIKE YOU'RE BEING PUSHED AWAY FROM THE CENTER.
THIS IS A "FICTITIOUS FORCE", FELT ONLY BY THOSE INSIDE THE STATION.
$\vec{\omega}$
R
$V = \omega R$
$a_c = \frac{V^2}{R}$
HOW HARD YOU'RE PUSHED DEPENDS ON THE RADIUS OF THE STATION AND HOW FAST IT ROTATES.
YEAH...
IT MAKES ME FEEL SICK TO THINK ABOUT IT.

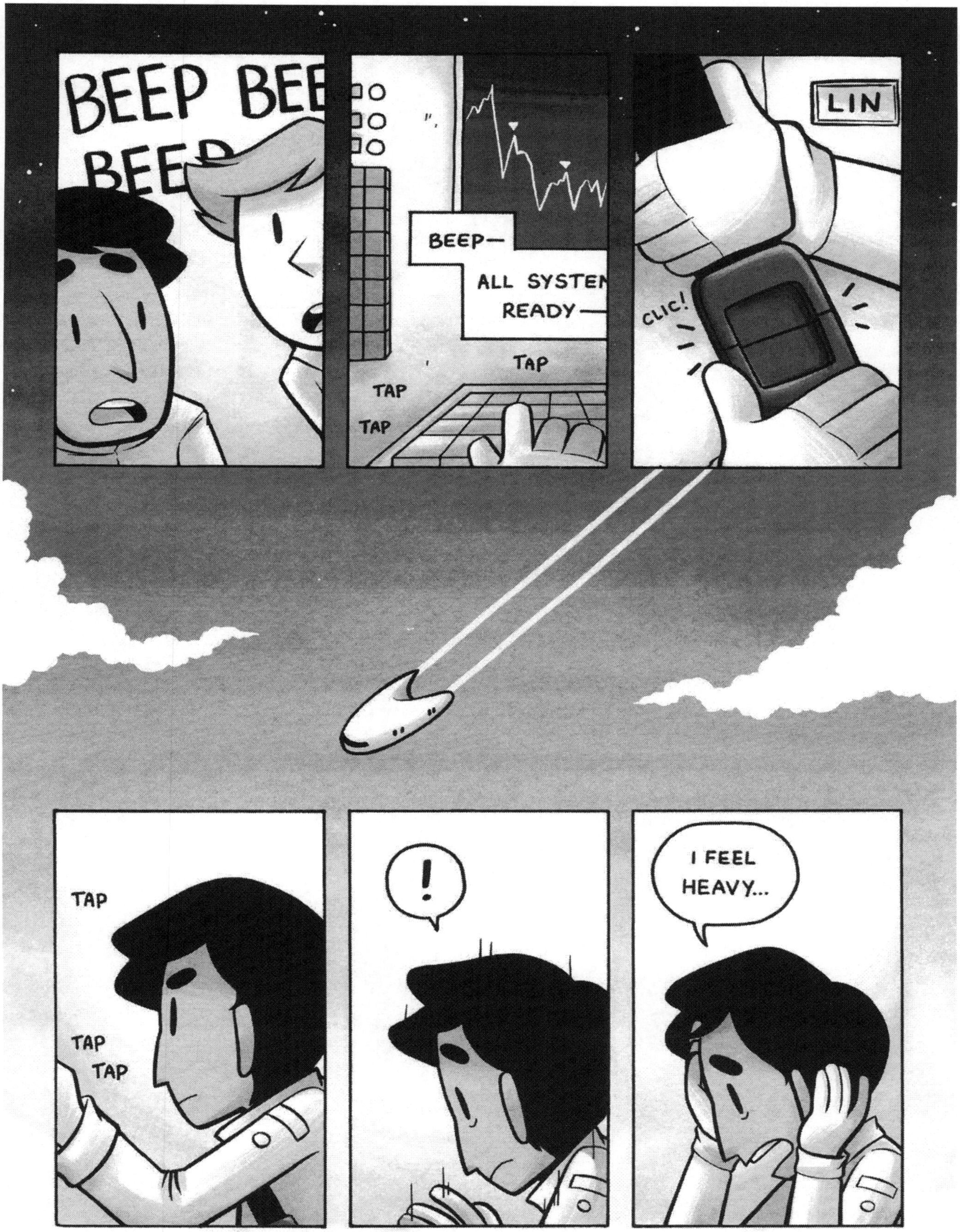

BEEP BEEP
BEEP
BEEP—
ALL SYSTEM
READY—
TAP
TAP
TAP
LIN
CLIC!
TAP
TAP
TAP
!
I FEEL HEAVY...

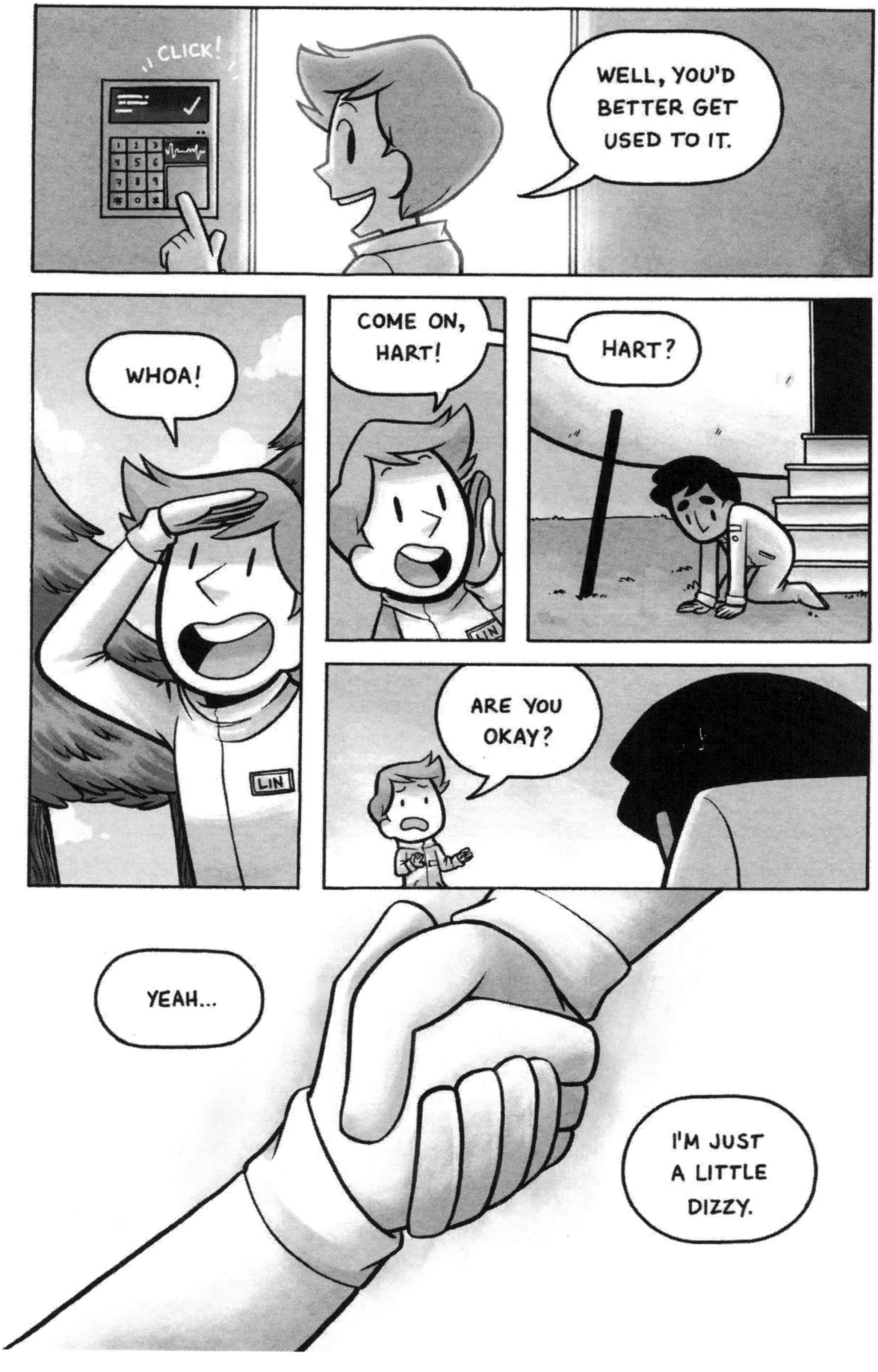
CLICK!
WELL, YOU'D BETTER GET USED TO IT.
WHOA!
COME ON, HART!
HART?
LIN
ARE YOU OKAY?
LIN
YEAH...
I'M JUST A LITTLE DIZZY.

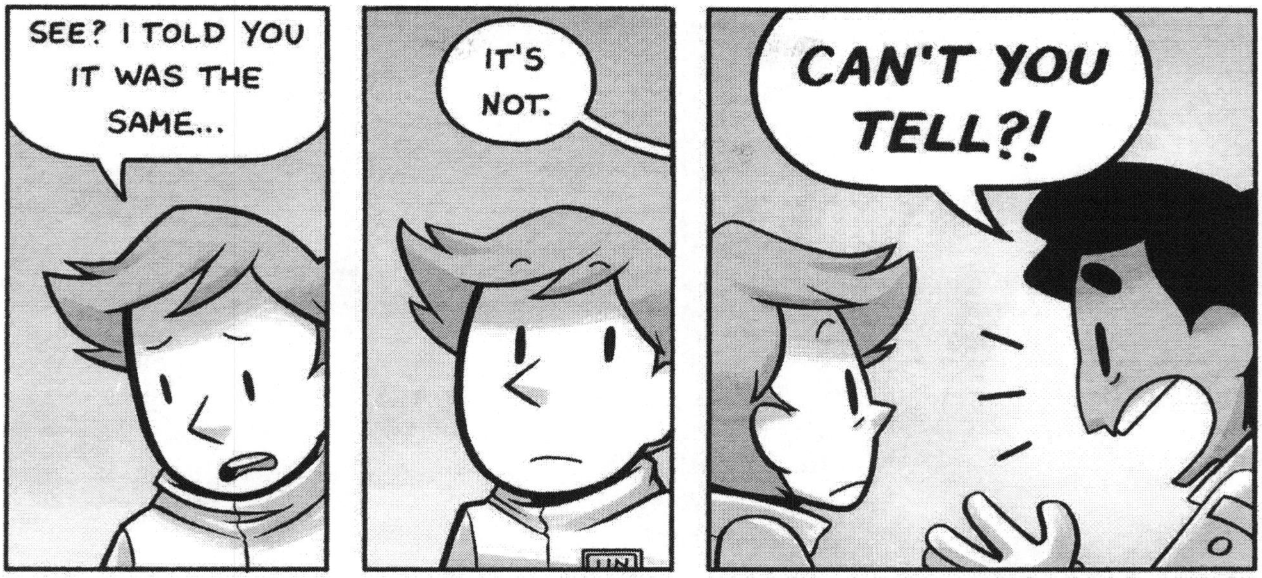
SEE? I TOLD YOU IT WAS THE SAME...
IT'S NOT.
CAN'T YOU TELL?!

THE "GRAVITY" AT THE INTERSTATION IS ARTIFICIAL,

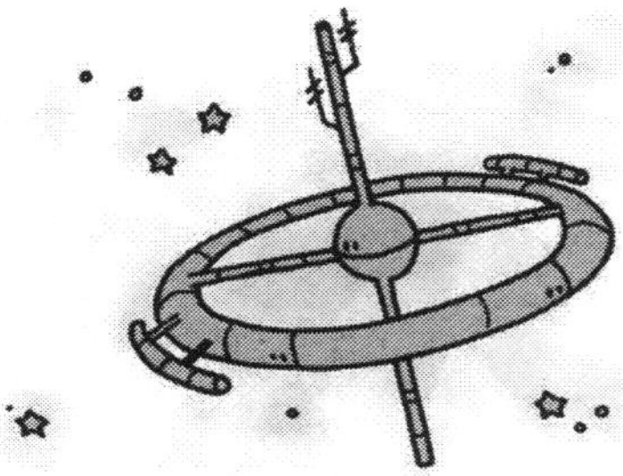

CREATED BY A FORCE THAT'S EVEN LABELED AS "FICTITIOUS"!!

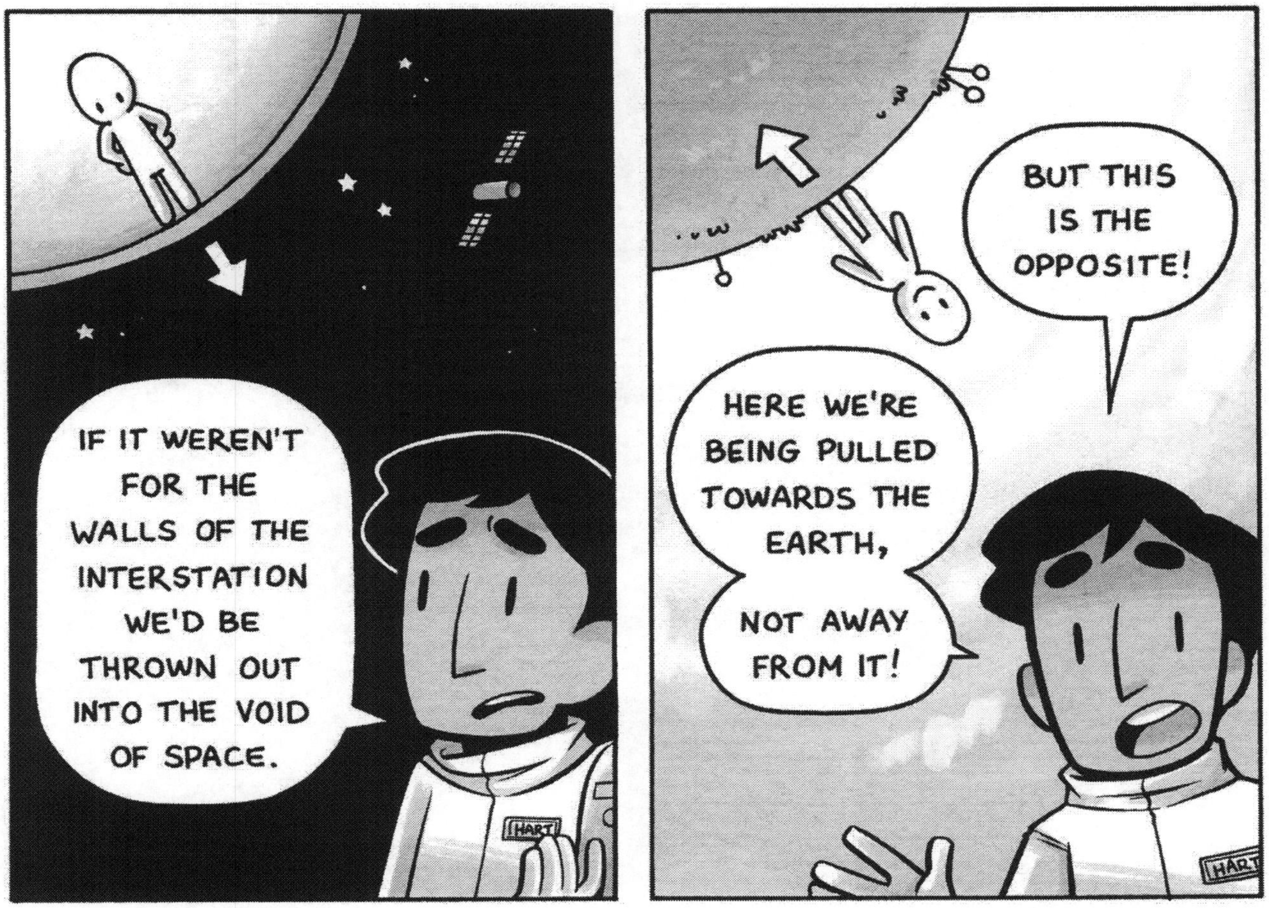
IF IT WEREN'T FOR THE WALLS OF THE INTERSTATION WE'D BE THROWN OUT INTO THE VOID OF SPACE.
HART
BUT THIS IS THE OPPOSITE!
HERE WE'RE BEING PULLED TOWARDS THE EARTH,
NOT AWAY FROM IT!
HART

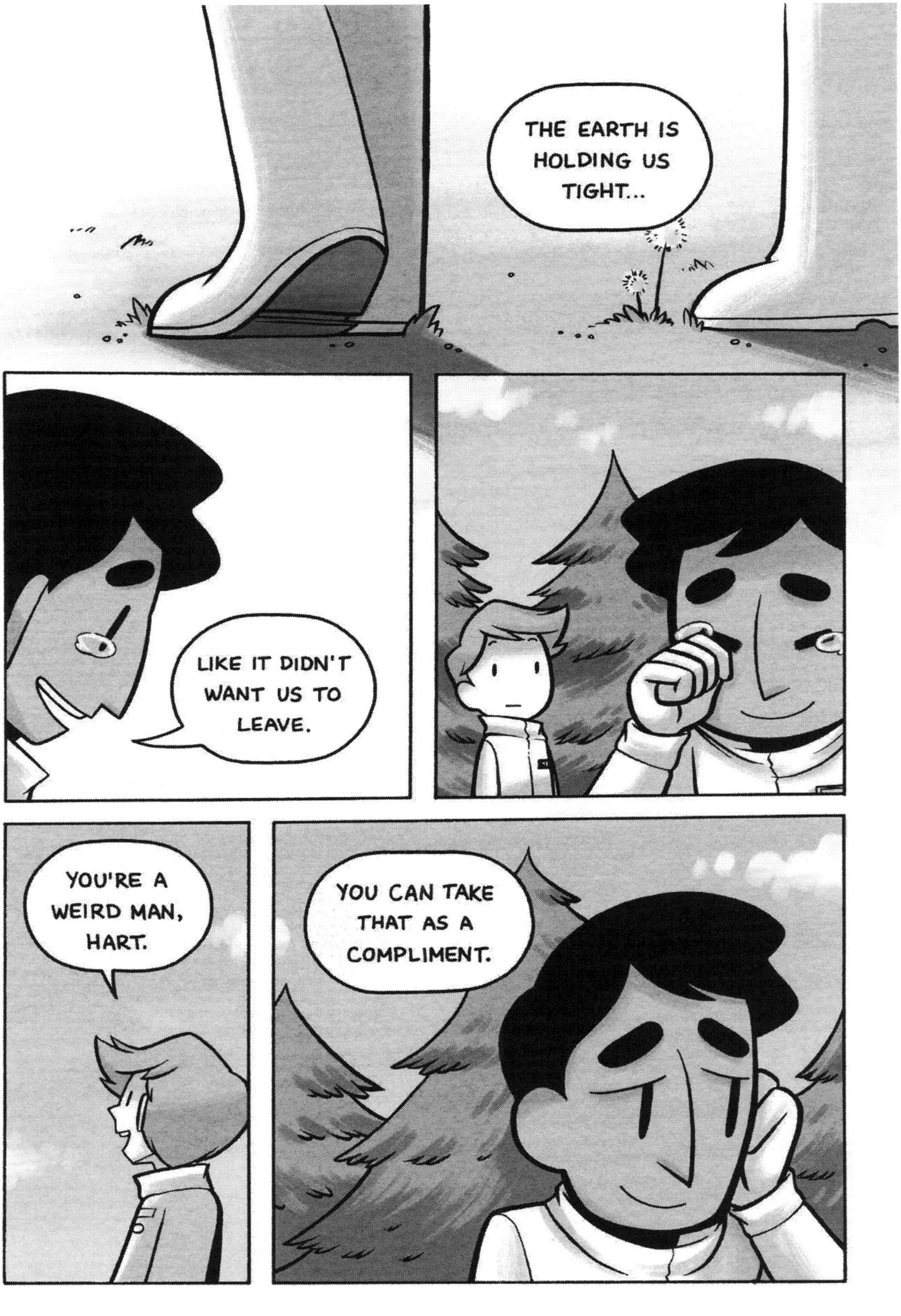
THE EARTH IS HOLDING US TIGHT...
LIKE IT DIDN'T WANT US TO LEAVE.
YOU'RE A WEIRD MAN, HART.
YOU CAN TAKE THAT AS A COMPLIMENT.

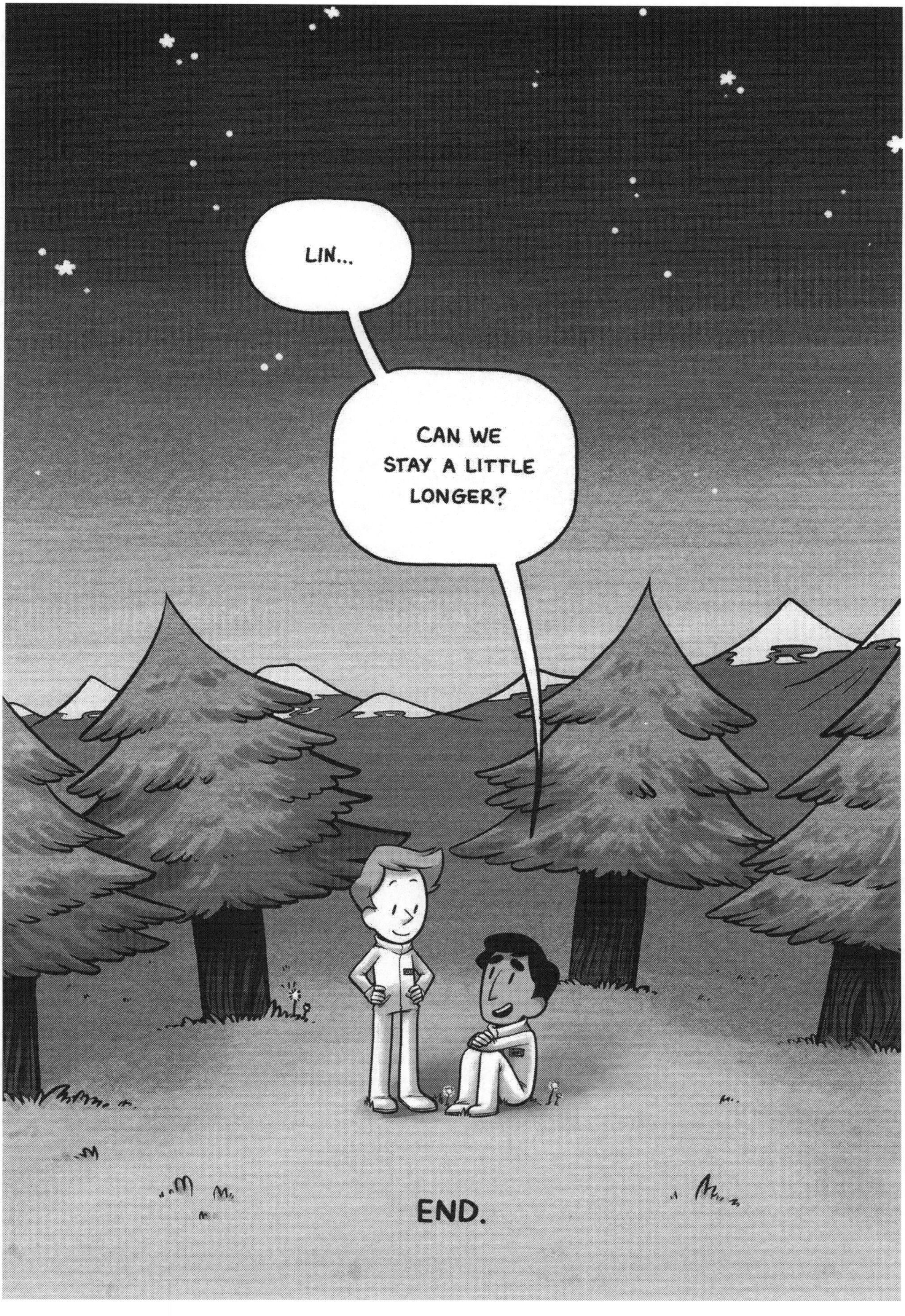
LIN...
CAN WE STAY A LITTLE LONGER?
END.

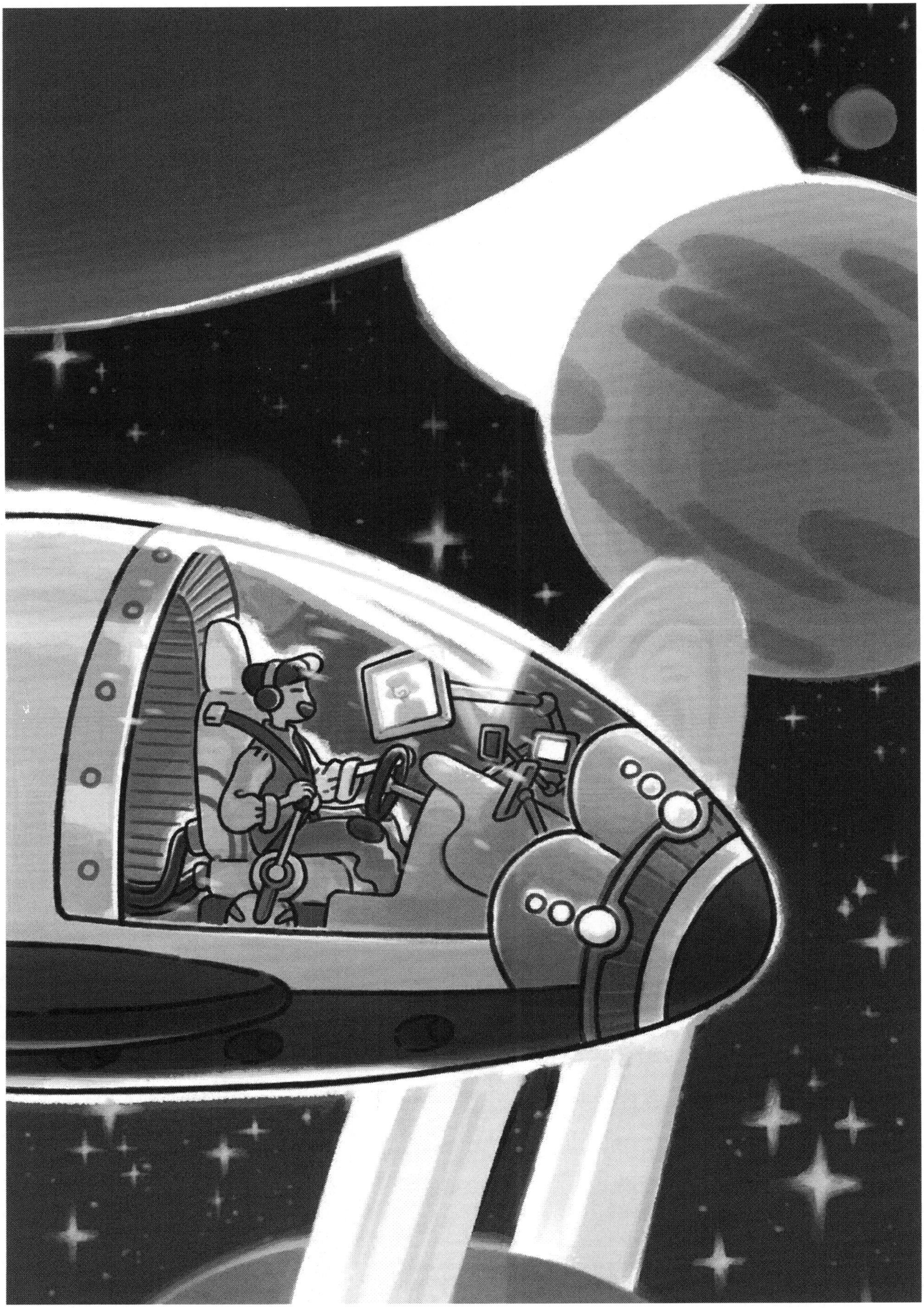

Elemei

The Fishbowl

S. Pace Smith

Audrey Carver was swimming in a sea of stars.

With her back to the space station and Earth hundreds of miles below, it was easy to imagine that both had let go of her, and she was light-years away. She could see Alpha Centauri straight ahead, somewhere the pull of any force in the solar system couldn't reach her.

"Fifty meters to maximum safe distance," an automated voice inside her helmet reminded her. The space station generated its own gravity well, intended primarily for the comfort of paying guests but useful for extravehicular activity; EVA technicians that strayed too far risked being lost in low Earth orbit.

Audrey breathed a sigh that fogged up her bubble helmet for a moment, and feathered her jetpack to turn around. Crystal Paradise looked back at her, a massive glass sphere hanging in front of the blue haze of Earth's horizon. A dozen tinier shapes floated around it, the other EVA techs from her shift inspecting the station's surface for debris; every guest aboard Crystal Paradise was paying for the view, and the techs ensured it remained flawless. It was her job to watch everything from afar, keeping the shuttles from knocking careless workers out of orbit, but the position had its perks.

Getting some distance from gawking civilians was one of them.

"Direct communication from Darwin -- "

"Accept. Hi, love."

The second was taking personal calls. Looking at the stars and talking to Merced made the Crystal Paradise contract almost bearable.

"Not too busy? I thought you might be on the clock..."

"Waiting for a late guest shuttle, so I have a few minutes." Audrey checked the display on the upper right of her helmet to confirm. "That poor pilot." She wondered if they'd run out of euphoria and mimosa straws yet; sober guests were rarely happy, especially in low gravity.

"I'm glad I caught you. I've got news."

"Good news?"

"I got a job offer... from the Interplanetary Exchange. How'd you like to go off-world with me?"

"Is it Venus?" Audrey knew this was coming. EVA technicians, especially licensed welders like her, could go anywhere, but Merced was a teacher. The Exchange only needed teachers where they had children -- like on Venus, Mars, or Ganymede.

"The school's on an orbital catfish farm." So, Venus. "But it would have us off-world the fastest... only six weeks."

Audrey's heart ached. It ached whenever she heard Merced's voice and she longed to hold her again; but now it ached for the prospect of holding her soon, and ached for the loss of Alpha Centauri. "If we leave Earth for that fishbowl, we lose our spot on the next Sagittarius mission -- "

" -- which has been delayed for five more years. By the time it happens, we'll be too old to go! Just... come home, baby." Audrey winced; Merced's voice was trembling. "I thought going up there would be good for you... I thought you'd see that Sagittarius is gone, and move past it."

Audrey turned her head to Earth, and the dozens of darker spinning spheres lower in orbit. They had their own gravity wells, too, accumulating millions of pieces of jagged debris: all that was left of the Borneo Space Elevator. The catastrophic collapse resulted in thousands of deaths, and put the next stage of interstellar exploration on hold indefinitely.

Crystal Paradise was originally built to wine and dine the mission's billionaire investors; but without a mission, the station became a luxury resort, and Audrey was stuck washing its windows.

"Audrey... will you at least think about it?"

The shuttle was on final approach, and the docking airlock prepared by adjusting its pressure -- venting vapor that gave off a fluorescent shimmer. That wasn't right.

"I have to take care of something. Sorry."

Merced was quiet, and Audrey winced again as she put her on hold; then she called command. "This is EVA Technician Carver, reporting a chemical leak in the docking airlock."

"Carver." She heard keys clicking on the other end of the line. "Our sensors aren't showing any leaks. Are you certain?"

She failed to bite back an incredulous laugh. "I don't know. What color do you think clean air is?"

There was another, longer pause; whoever was manning command's communications had muted her, probably to complain. What followed confirmed it: "Report to Personnel Airlock immediately. Your supervisor would like a word."

Audrey disconnected command before they could hear her swearing, and gave herself three seconds before she unmuted herself. "Sorry. Merced? You still there?"

"Direct communication lost; Darwin is out of range."

"Perfect."

* * * * *

Sharing space with the guests was something Audrey took pains to avoid, preferring the service elevators and restricted corridors that management encouraged the staff to use. None of them had felt the hardships that caused so many to volunteer for interplanetary and interstellar resetttlement; space had promised her an opportunity for a better life, but for the wealthy it was one more place to be tourists.

"Heaven help me," she sighed as she entered one of the glass elevators that followed a longitudinal arc across the station. She jammed the button for her floor, tucked her bubble helmet neatly under one arm, and crossed her fingers.

Luck wasn't on her side today; it rarely was. At the mezzanine, six floors from her quarters, the frosted doors chimed and slid open. Audrey pasted on a smile and stared straight ahead as two guests stepped on and stood right beside her.

"Look, darling, it's one of those space workers -- the ones that swim around out there!" one of them whispered, not at all quietly. Audrey lowered her eyes to see if they were headed for an earlier floor; they weren't.

"They're called extravehicular engineers, dear," the other guest informed his partner stuffily. "I was reading about them on the way up, remember? Something about their unions..." Audrey could feel his skeptical gaze on her, and worked that much harder on her smile.

"I like how they swim around," the first one said, fortunately uninterested in weighing in on labor politics, but unfortunately very interested in Audrey. "It's nice to watch... like fish in a fishbowl, just for us!"

"Hm, I suppose."

"They should start wearing something brighter, like tropical fish. Plain gray's no fun. Don't you think?"

It took until the elevator slid to a stop at Audrey's floor for her to realize that the woman beside her had asked her a question.

The guest blinked her long lashes, smiling synthetically-brightened teeth at Audrey. "Don't you think that would be fun?"

"Ma'am," Audrey managed to smile, and marched away as quickly as she could to her quarters. None of the rooms on the station had windows; at least there no one could gawk at her.

* * * * *

"...like an animal in a zoo -- like a fish in a fishbowl! They think we're for their viewing pleasure, just like the stars they see from inside their bubble. Did you know they've added more constellations to the interior projections?
Management's responding to complaints. 'Adequate service, but disappointing view. Not enough stars.' That's a real review. I'll send you the link.

"Speaking of the view, I was scrubbing debris, and guess who I spotted fooling around in the café? Our friends from the elevator. And they talk about their view.

"The fishbowl's inside the station, not out here. Trust me, Merced. You can see everything from out here, whether you want to or not.

"I... guess that's all. And, uh... I'm sorry about earlier. Something came up. Let's talk about it. End message," Audrey enunciated into her helmet, and her communications display dimmed.

She was drifting again, but much closer to the station. She could see stars beyond the hazy horizon and several EVA techs in her field of view. She'd spent her entire shift bagging debris, despite the fact that a shuttle was disembarking; she'd have to clear that last citation from her record before management would put her on shuttle duty again.

"But from this perspective," she murmured into her muted helmet, and looked around: the supervisor was further out and facing away from her, tracking a shuttle waiting for an open airlock. She planted her boots on a wide girder between two floor, grimaced at the owlish faces on the other side of the glass, and pushed off.

She put the Moon in front of her as she spun away from the station, focusing on the twinkling lights of Tychopolis -- another facility turned luxury resort. Then she spun to face the station, a giant glass ornament suspended over the Indian Ocean, with a protruding shuttle blocking her view of Madagascar.

A cloud of fluorescent gases fanned out across Mauritius, coating the shuttle, the station's glassy surface, and the sharp-edged metal screws on the docking airlock.

"Chemical leak! Stop the launch!" Audrey screamed into her helmet as she vented air, floating away from the station far slower than her jetpack. It only took one spark to ignite a reaction, but if the shuttle made a clean break...

She saw faces in the windows, transfixed by the chemical rainbow venting into space as the docking seal broke. Autopilot didn't wait for the bolts to clear the sockets; the shuttle banked hard, and the station ignited.

*   *   *   *   *

Audrey drifted through a sea of stars.

There were more than she remembered, forming alien constellations no earthbound eyes would ever see. They spun in place, arced around her, and bounced harmlessly away from her suit; they sparkled silver-white as the glass caught the moonlight.

She swept the broken shards of Crystal Paradise away from her helmet and looked for something other than the stars.

From the size of the nearest gravity well gathering millions of pieces jagged debris, she was miles closer to Earth than when she blacked out. She checked her display, which took agonizing seconds to light up from idle. Emergency transponder active; no pending communications, no one on radar -- she must have drifted away from the survivors, if there were any; less than a quarter of her oxygen remained.

At least she was over Australia. She spotted Darwin by finding the shape of Beagle Bay and the trailer camps sprawling inland; somewhere down there was a trailer with her name on the mailbox, above M. Menendez.

"Direct communication from Darwin; identification not listed."

Audrey coughed hard, fogging up her helmet. "Accept," she managed.

"Hi there, love," she heard Merced's voice, nearly a coo. "I just got your message, and... do you have time?"

Audrey checked her display. Her transponder sent out a ping every minute; no responses yet; oxygen dropped to 22%. "Some... Listen... Merced -- "

"Me first," she insisted. "Look... Earth is awful. You're not the only one who hates it. I hate it too, and more because it hurts you. But Earth's not the only awful place that's got you in its gravity. You're right, that station's a glorified fishbowl, and that's no place for someone like you to be."

"Merced..."

"With the Exchange, there's no money, no debts, no birth restrictions... It's not light-years away, but it's something better, for both of us.

"We don't just need stars, Aubrey; we need a place that won't hold us down. We won't find it on Earth, and it's not up in orbit, either... but it's out there, somewhere. Even without Alpha Centauri. Let's find it together."

Audrey blinked rapidly, her eyes blurry with tears that wouldn't fall away in zero gravity. The stars were blindingly bright, and she squinted to tell the stars from the glass.

The blinking lights of a passenger shuttle steadied alongside her, and dozens of curious faces pressed to the windows to watch her drift closer. Her helmet chimed a response notification, belatedly. She grinned.

"Does it have to be Venus?" she asked Merced.

"Venus is just the first opening. Mars is next."

"Let's hold out for Mars. I hear they don't have fish on Mars."

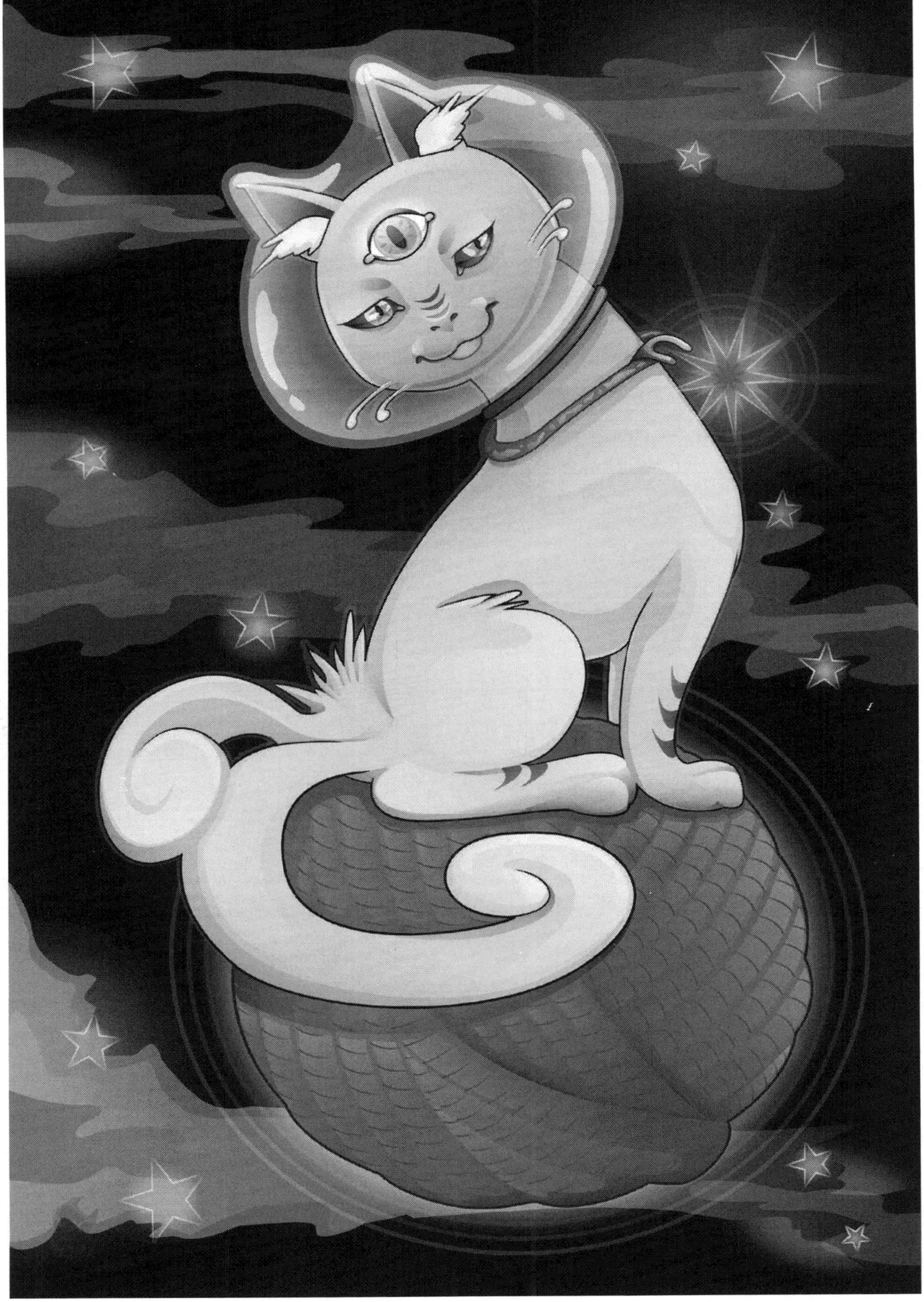

Kodi Kat

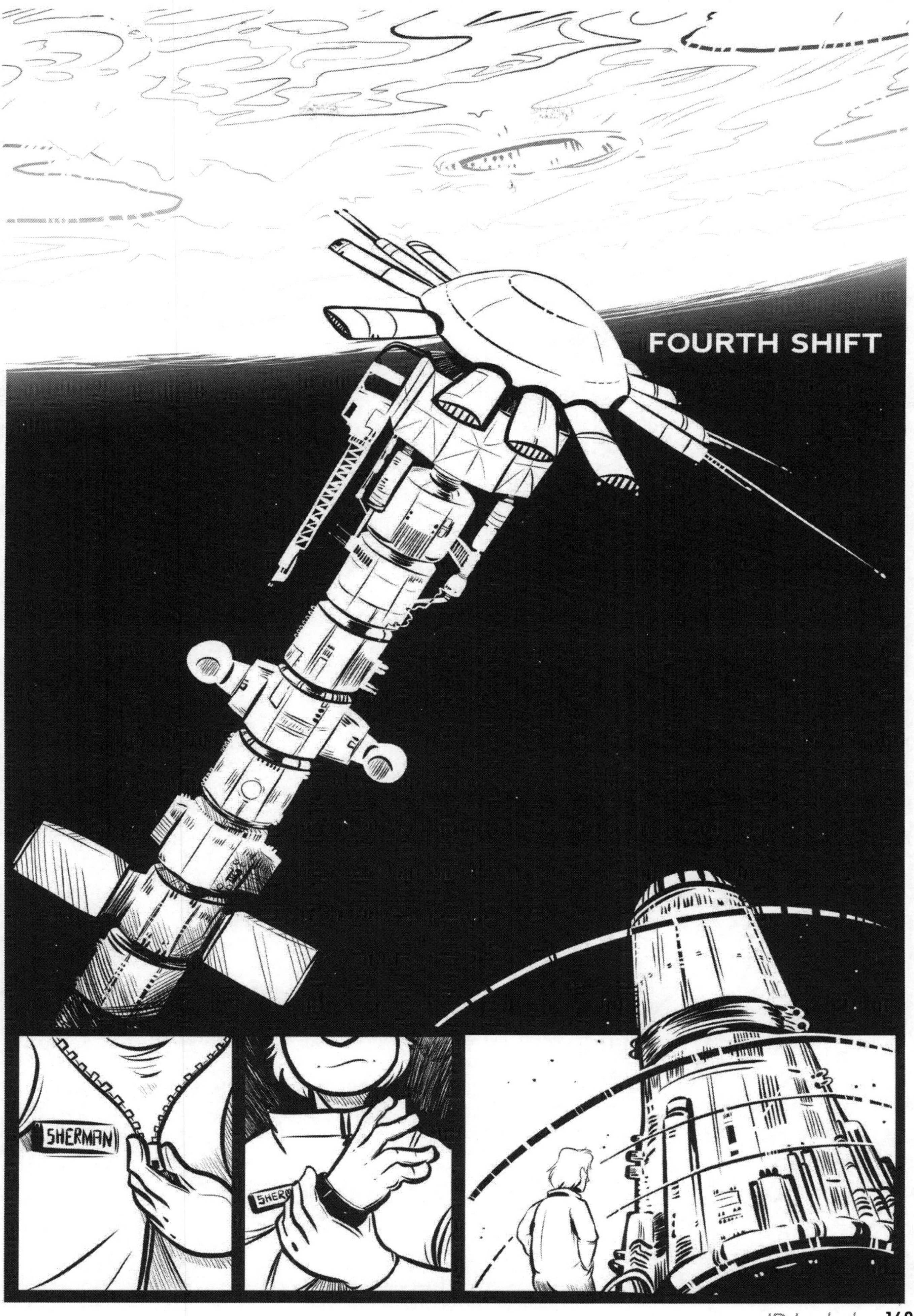
FOURTH SHIFT
SHERMAN
SHERM

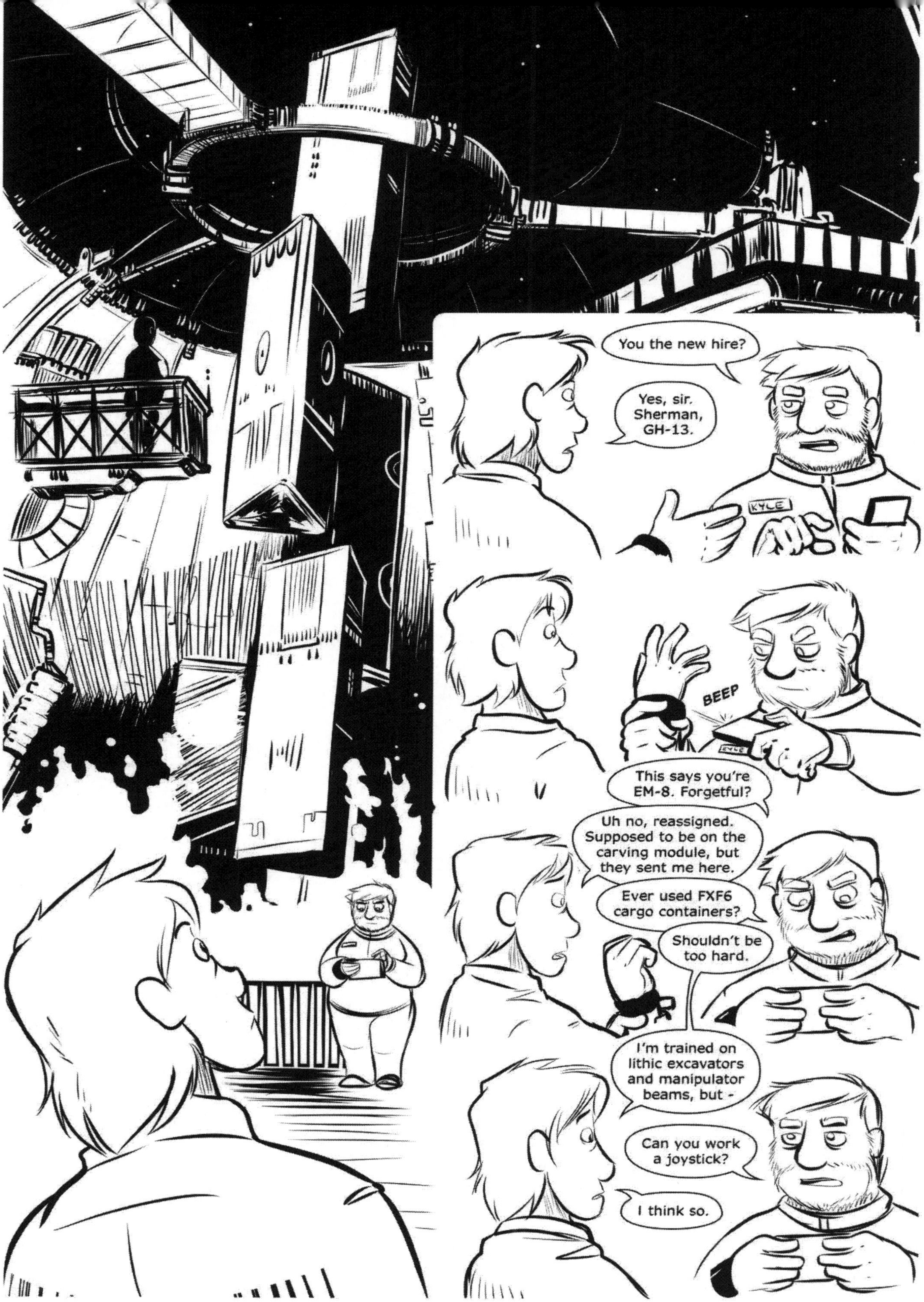
You the new hire?
Yes, sir. Sherman, GH-13.
KYLE
BEEP
KYLE
This says you're EM-8. Forgetful?
Uh no, reassigned. Supposed to be on the carving module, but they sent me here.
Ever used FXF6 cargo containers?
Shouldn't be too hard.
I'm trained on lithic excavators and manipulator beams, but -
Can you work a joystick?
I think so.

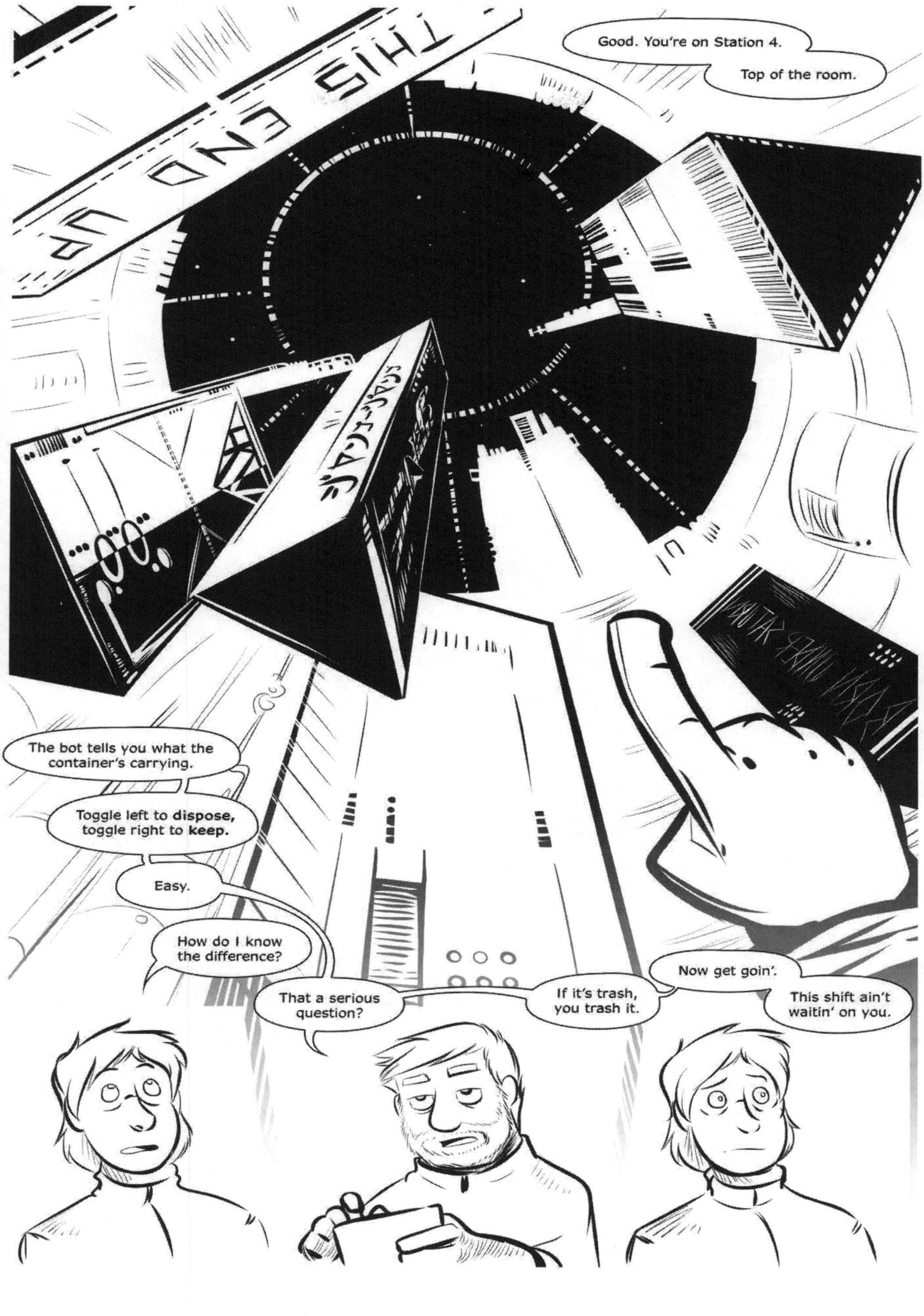
THIS END UP
Good. You're on Station 4.
Top of the room.
The bot tells you what the container's carrying.
Toggle left to **dispose**, toggle right to **keep**.
Easy.
How do I know the difference?
That a serious question?
If it's trash, you trash it.
Now get goin'.
This shift ain't waitin' on you.

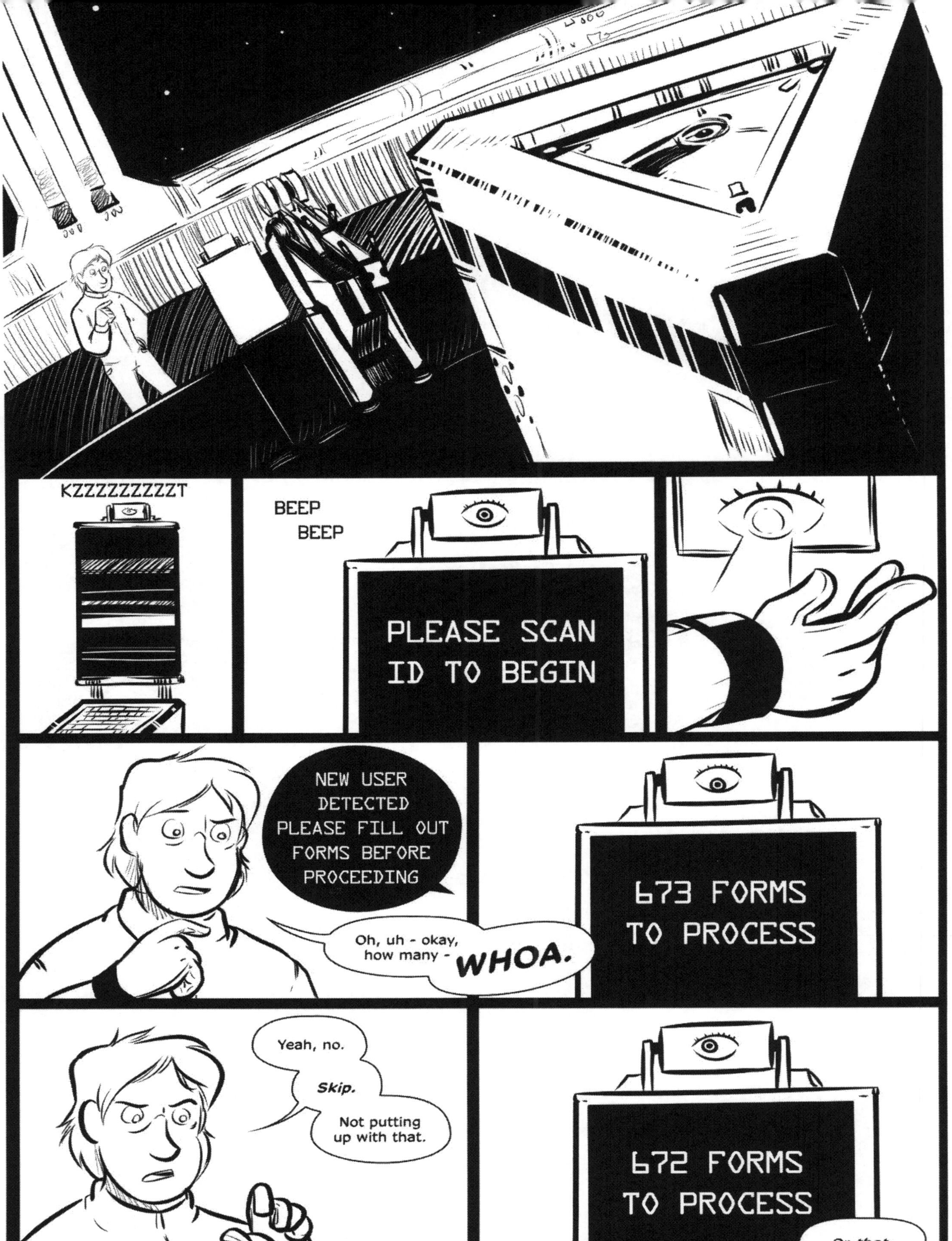
KZZZZZZZZZT
BEEP
BEEP
PLEASE SCAN ID TO BEGIN
NEW USER DETECTED PLEASE FILL OUT FORMS BEFORE PROCEEDING
Oh, uh - okay, how many -
WHOA.
673 FORMS TO PROCESS
Yeah, no.
Skip.
Not putting up with that.
672 FORMS TO PROCESS
Or that.

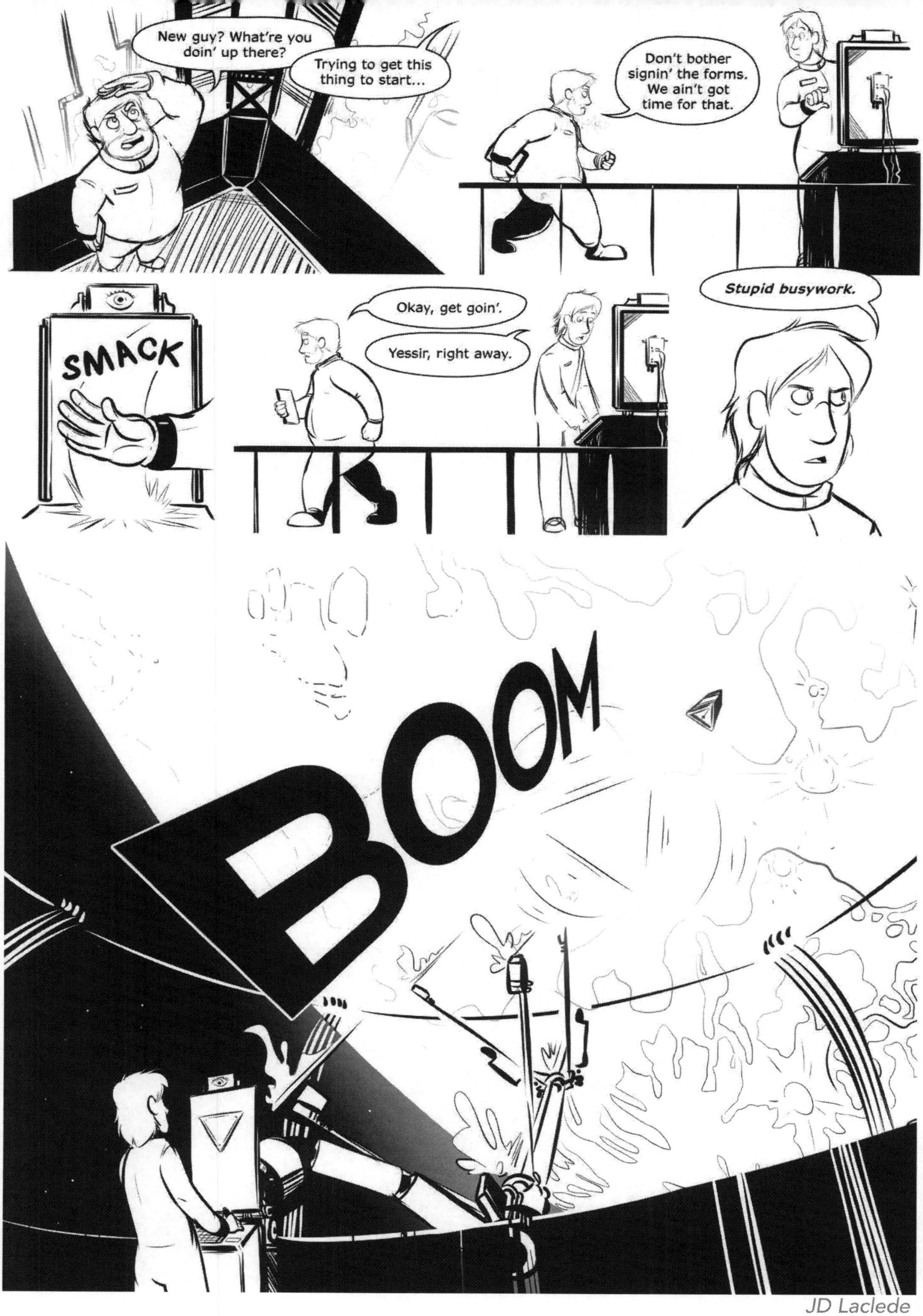
New guy? What're you doin' up there?
Trying to get this thing to start...
Don't bother signin' the forms. We ain't got time for that.
SMACK
Okay, get goin'.
Yessir, right away.
Stupid busywork.
BOOM

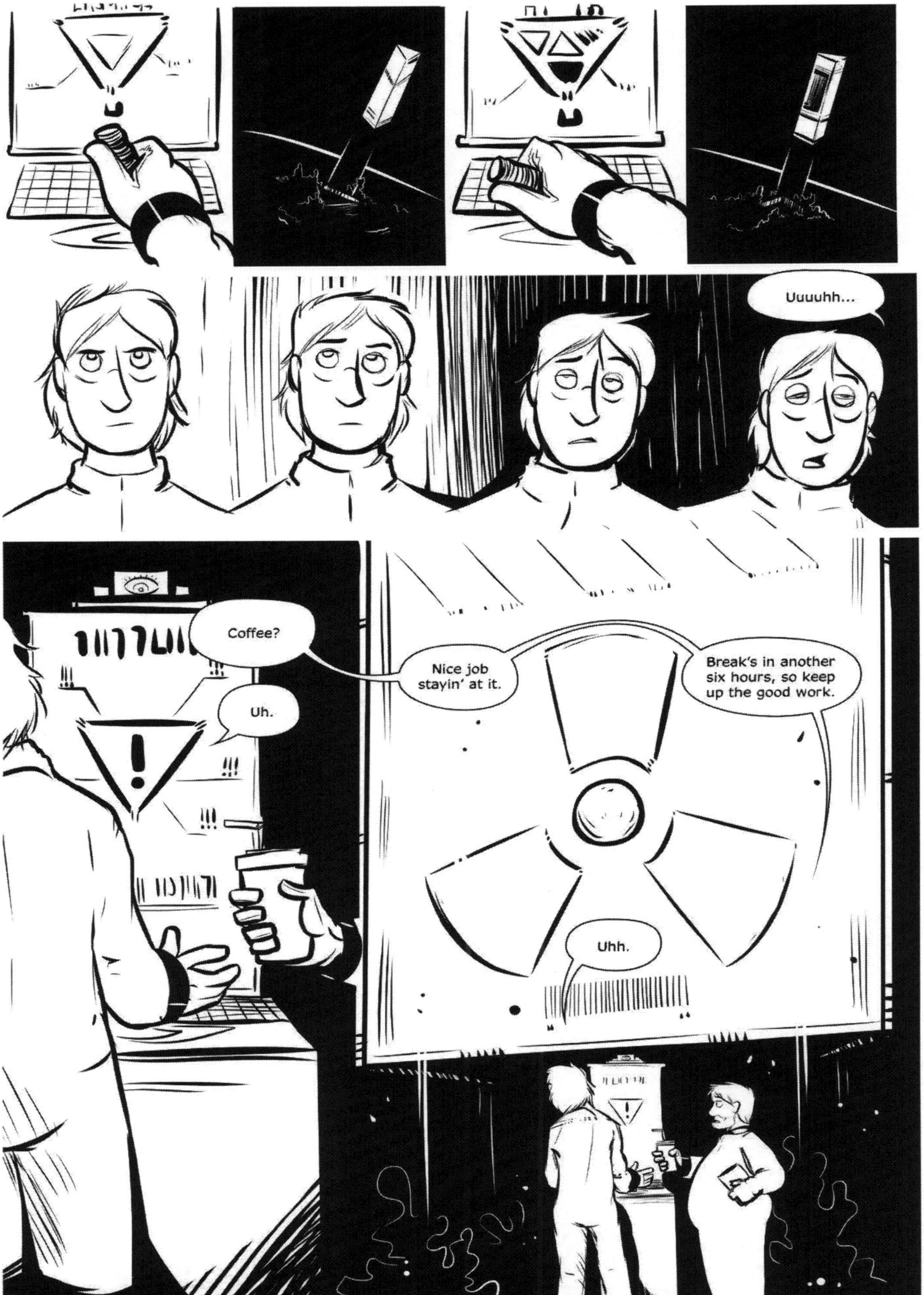
Uuuuhh...
Coffee?
Uh.
Nice job stayin' at it.
Break's in another six hours, so keep up the good work.
Uhh.

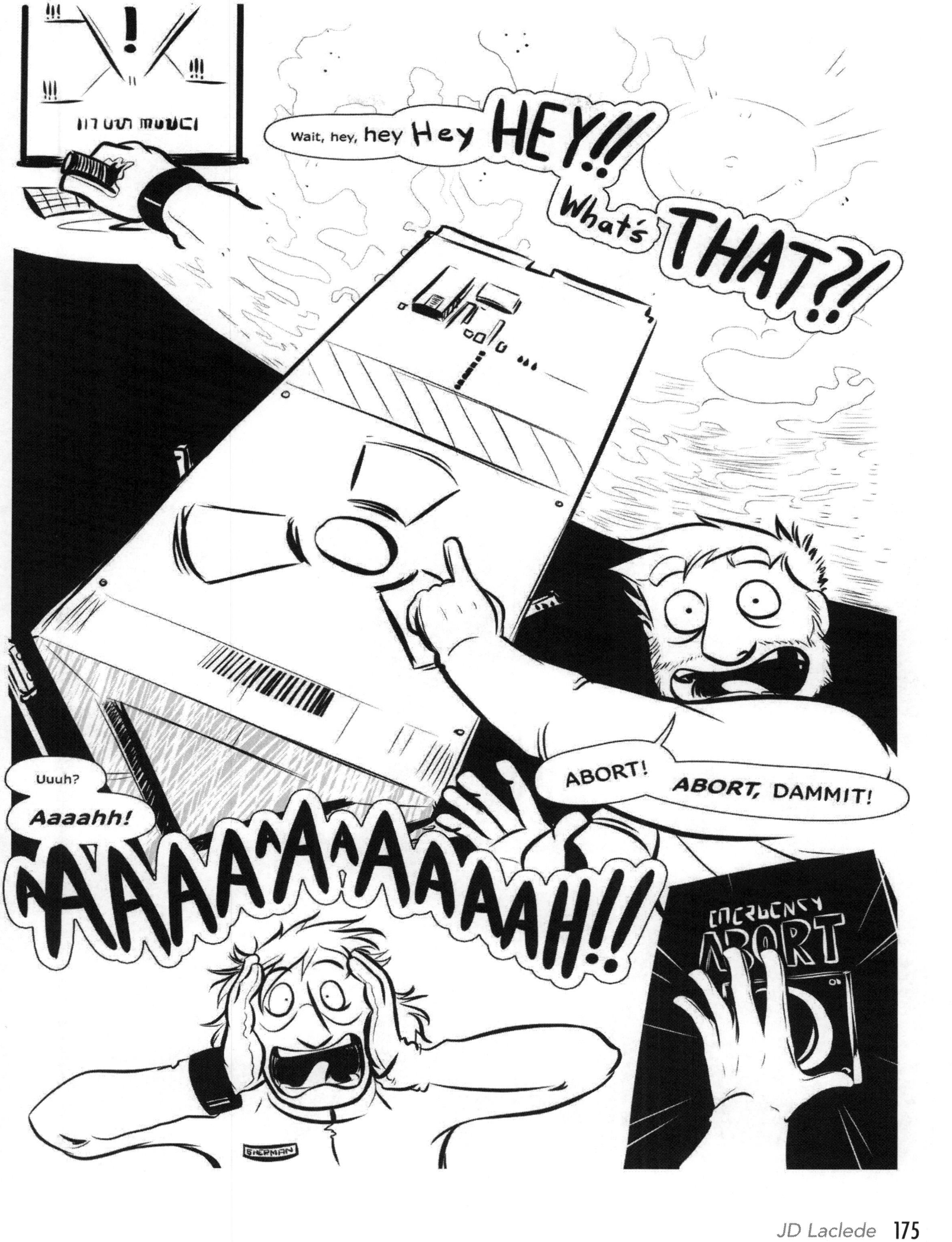
Wait, hey, hey Hey HEY!!
What's THAT?!
Uuuh?
Aaaahh!
ABORT!
ABORT, DAMMIT!
AAAAAAAAAAAH!!
ABORT
SHERMAN

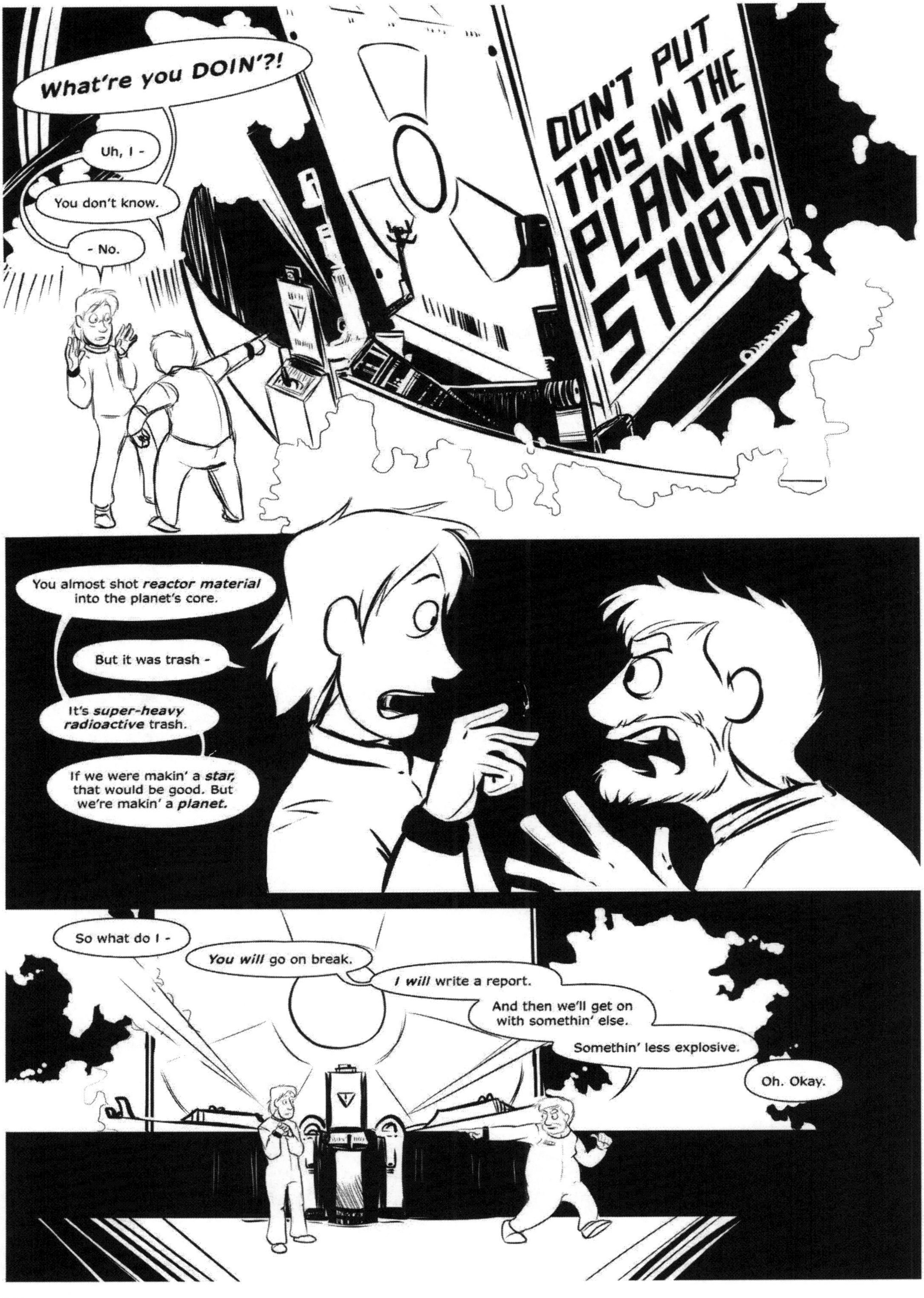
What're you DOIN'?!
Uh, I -
You don't know.
- No.
DON'T PUT THIS IN THE PLANET. STUPID
You almost shot reactor material into the planet's core.
But it was trash -
It's super-heavy radioactive trash.
If we were makin' a star, that would be good. But we're makin' a planet.
So what do I -
You will go on break.
I will write a report.
And then we'll get on with somethin' else.
Somethin' less explosive.
Oh. Okay.

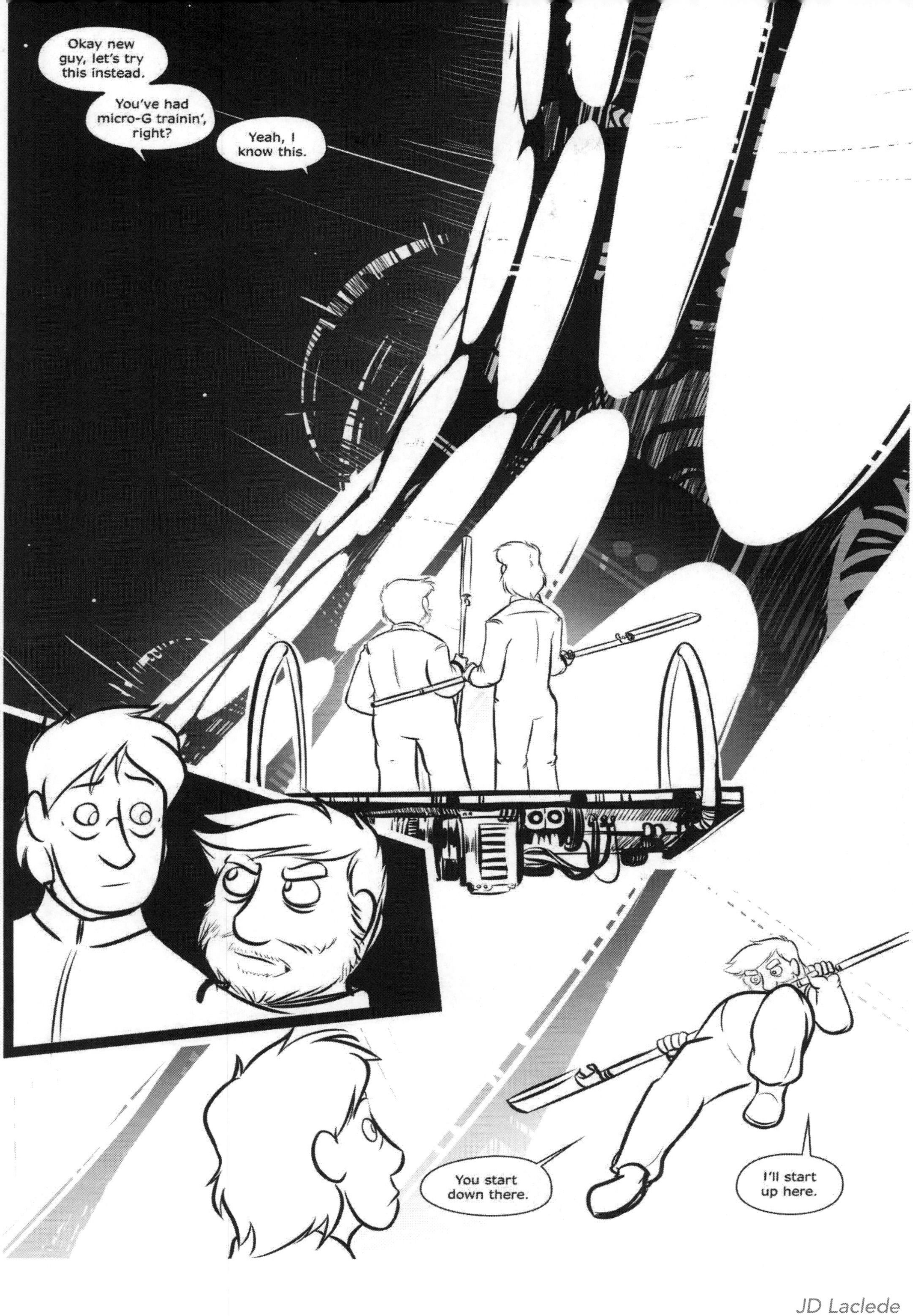
Okay new guy, let's try this instead.
You've had micro-G trainin', right?
Yeah, I know this.
You start down there.
I'll start up here.

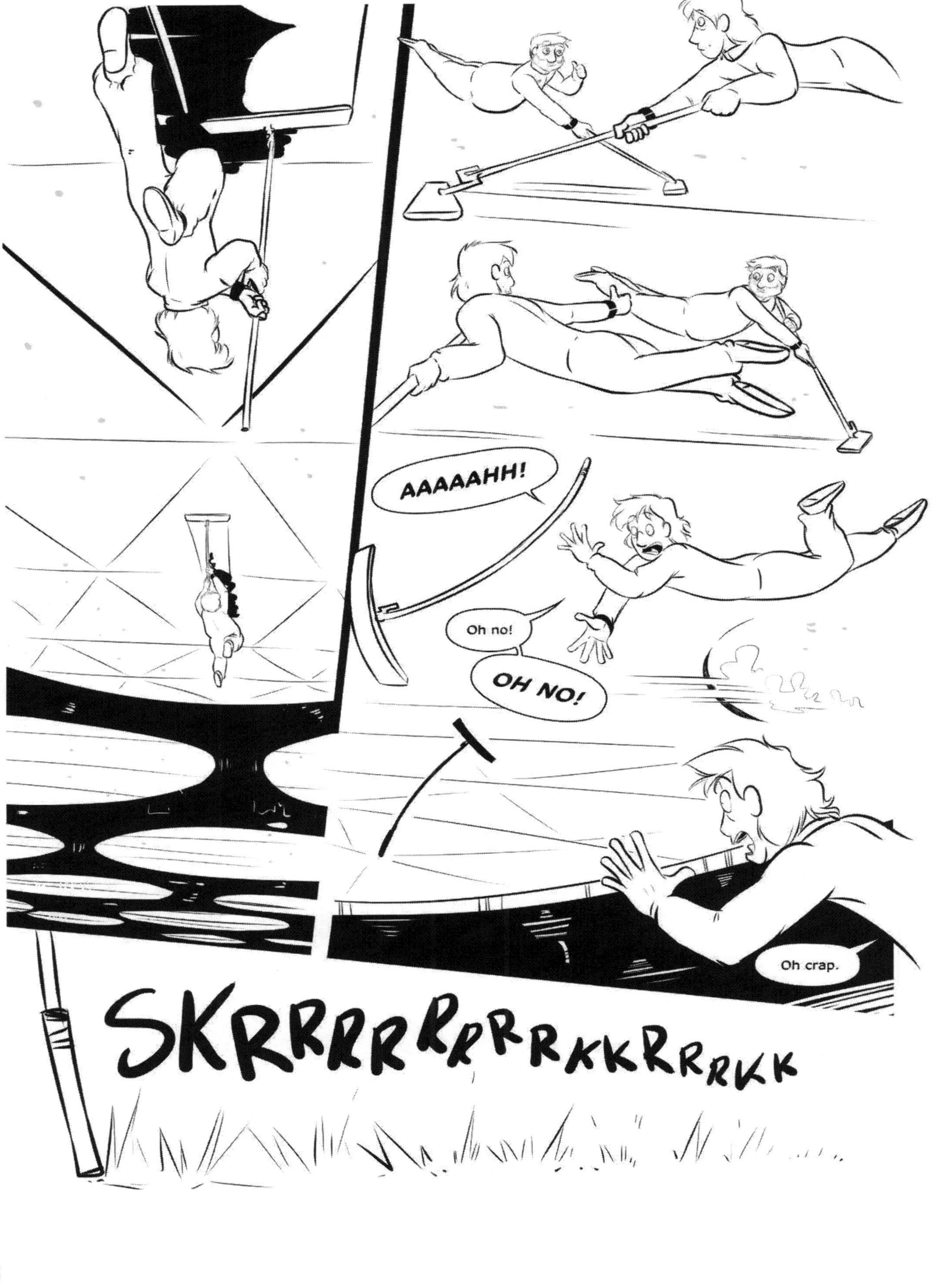
AAAAAHH!
Oh no!
OH NO!
Oh crap.
SKRRRRRRRRRKKRRRKK

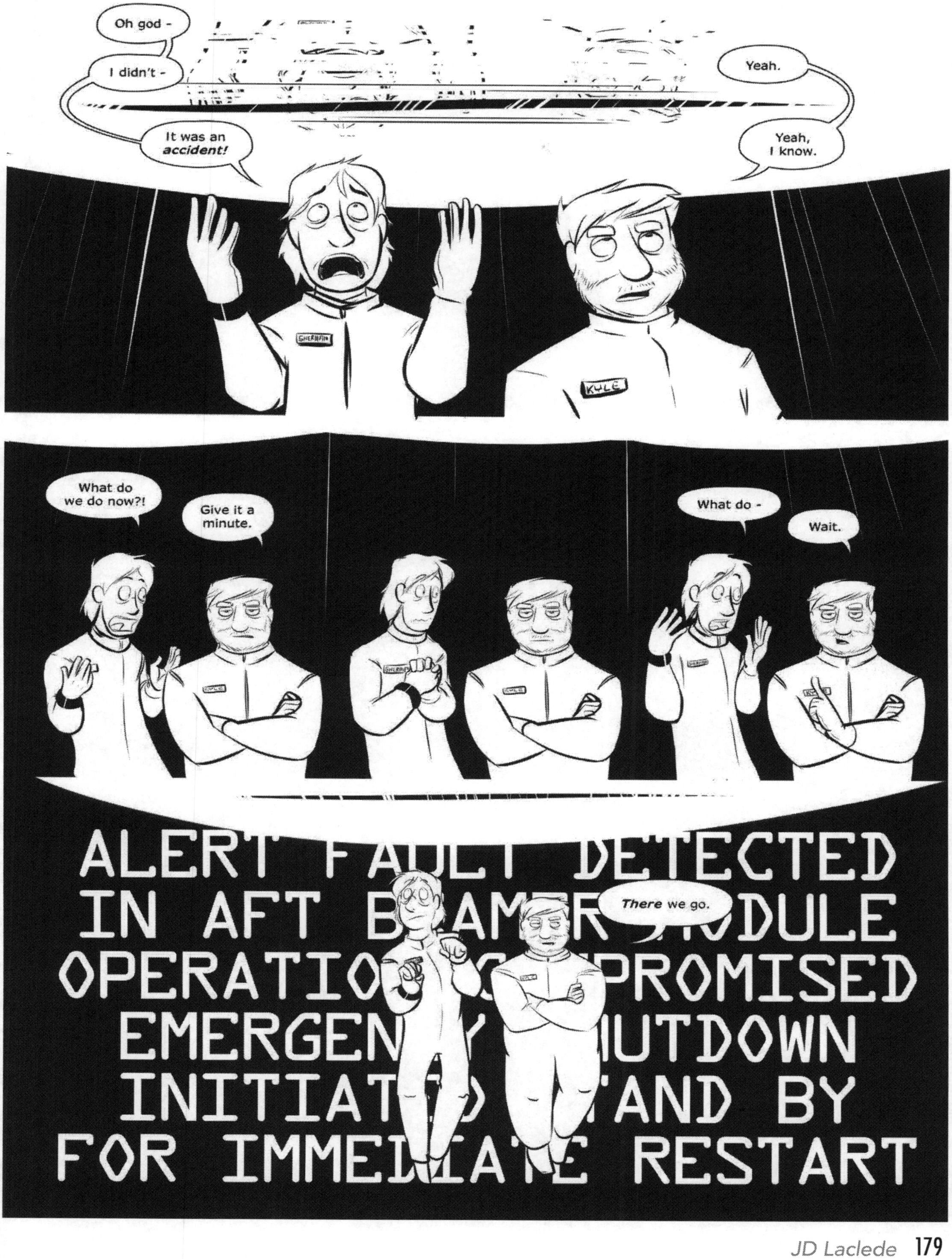
Oh god -
I didn't -
It was an *accident!*
Yeah.
Yeah, I know.
KYLE
What do we do now?!
Give it a minute.
What do -
Wait.
ALERT FAULT DETECTED
IN AFT B AMER DULE
OPERATIO PROMISED
EMERGEN UTDOWN
INITIAT AND BY
FOR IMMEDIATE RESTART
There we go.

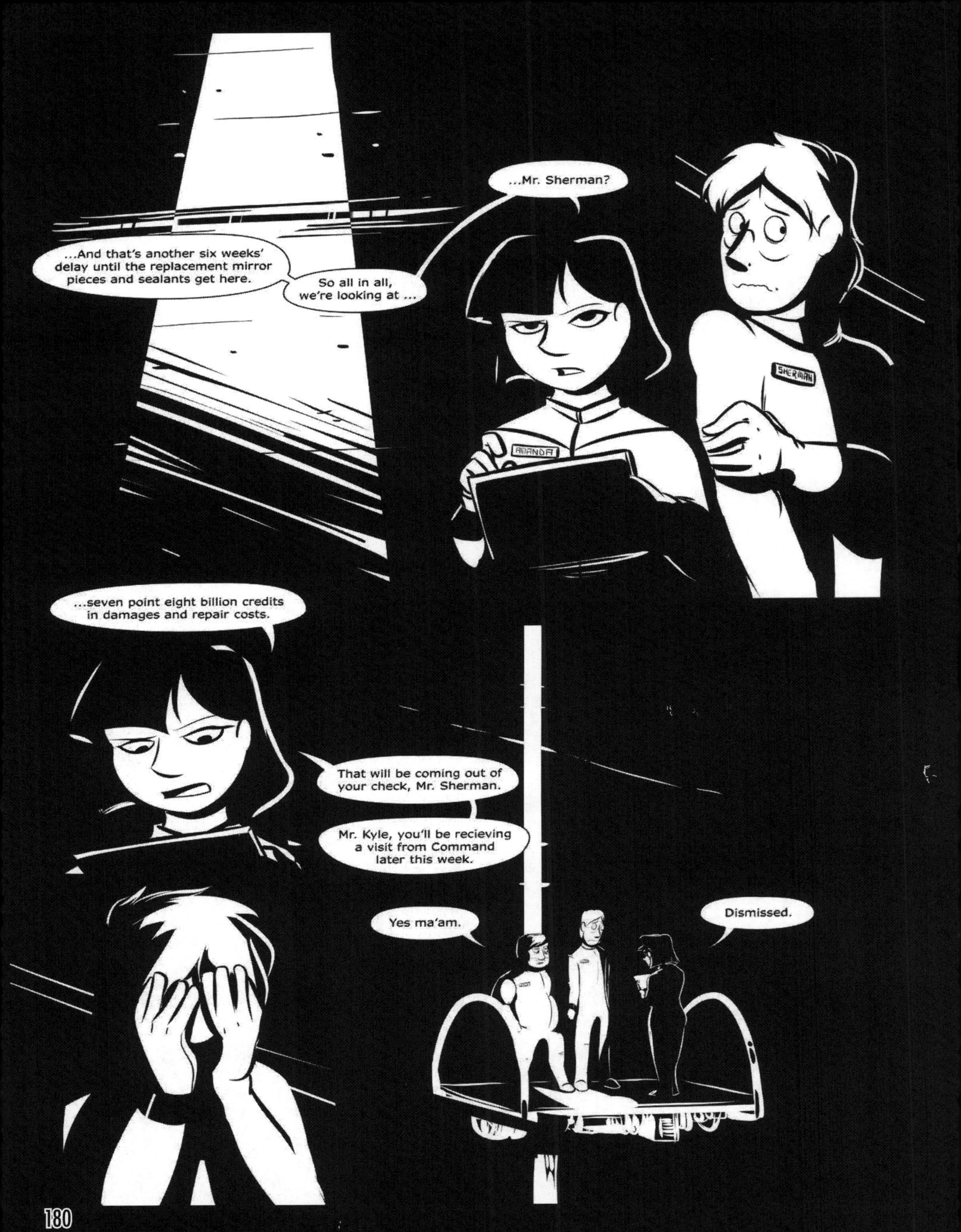
...And that's another six weeks' delay until the replacement mirror pieces and sealants get here.
So all in all, we're looking at ...
...Mr. Sherman?
SHERMAN
AMANDA
...seven point eight billion credits in damages and repair costs.
That will be coming out of your check, Mr. Sherman.
Mr. Kyle, you'll be recieving a visit from Command later this week.
Yes ma'am.
Dismissed.

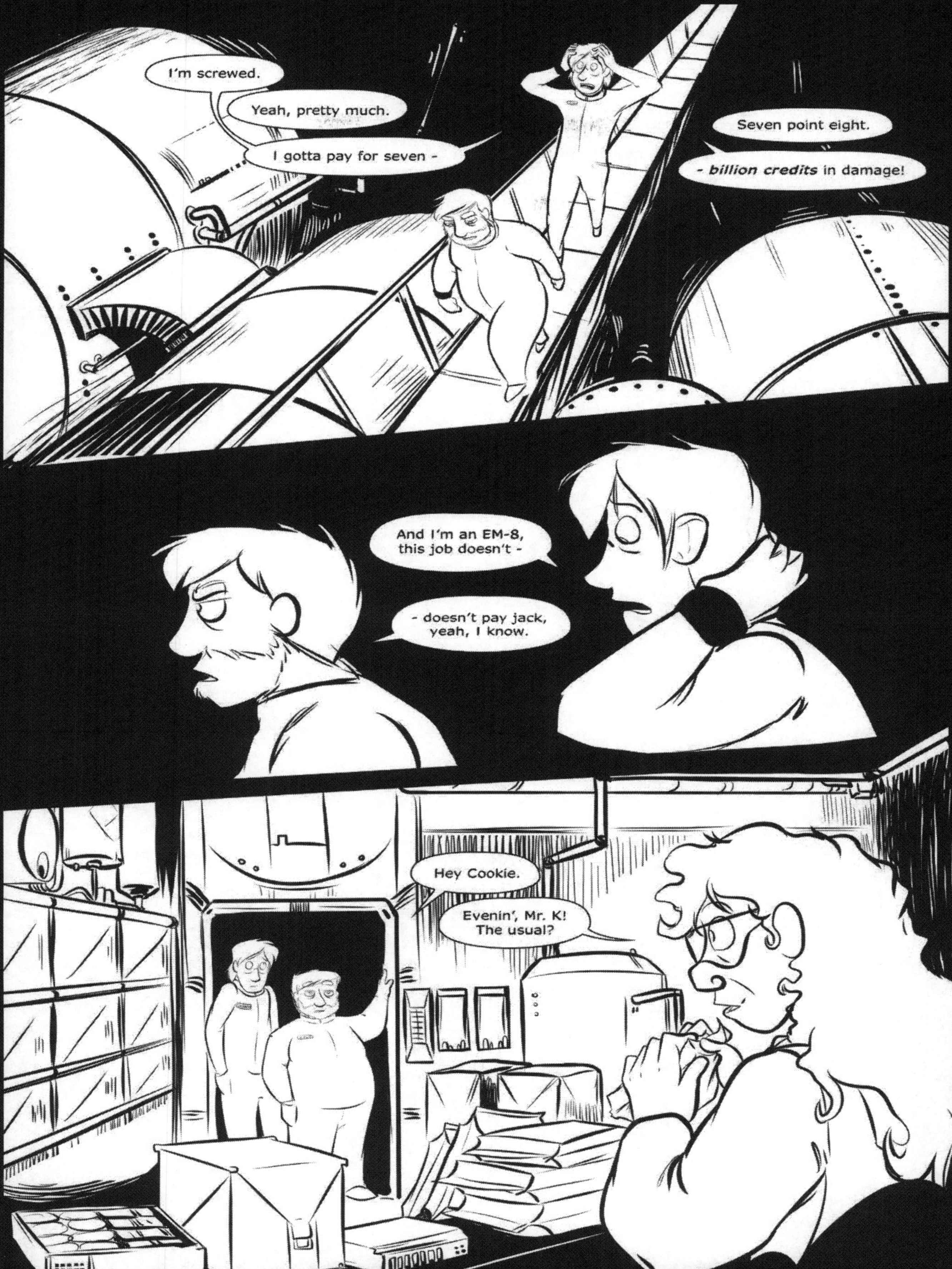
I'm screwed.
Yeah, pretty much.
I gotta pay for seven -
- billion credits in damage!
Seven point eight.
And I'm an EM-8, this job doesn't -
- doesn't pay jack, yeah, I know.
Hey Cookie.
Evenin', Mr. K! The usual?

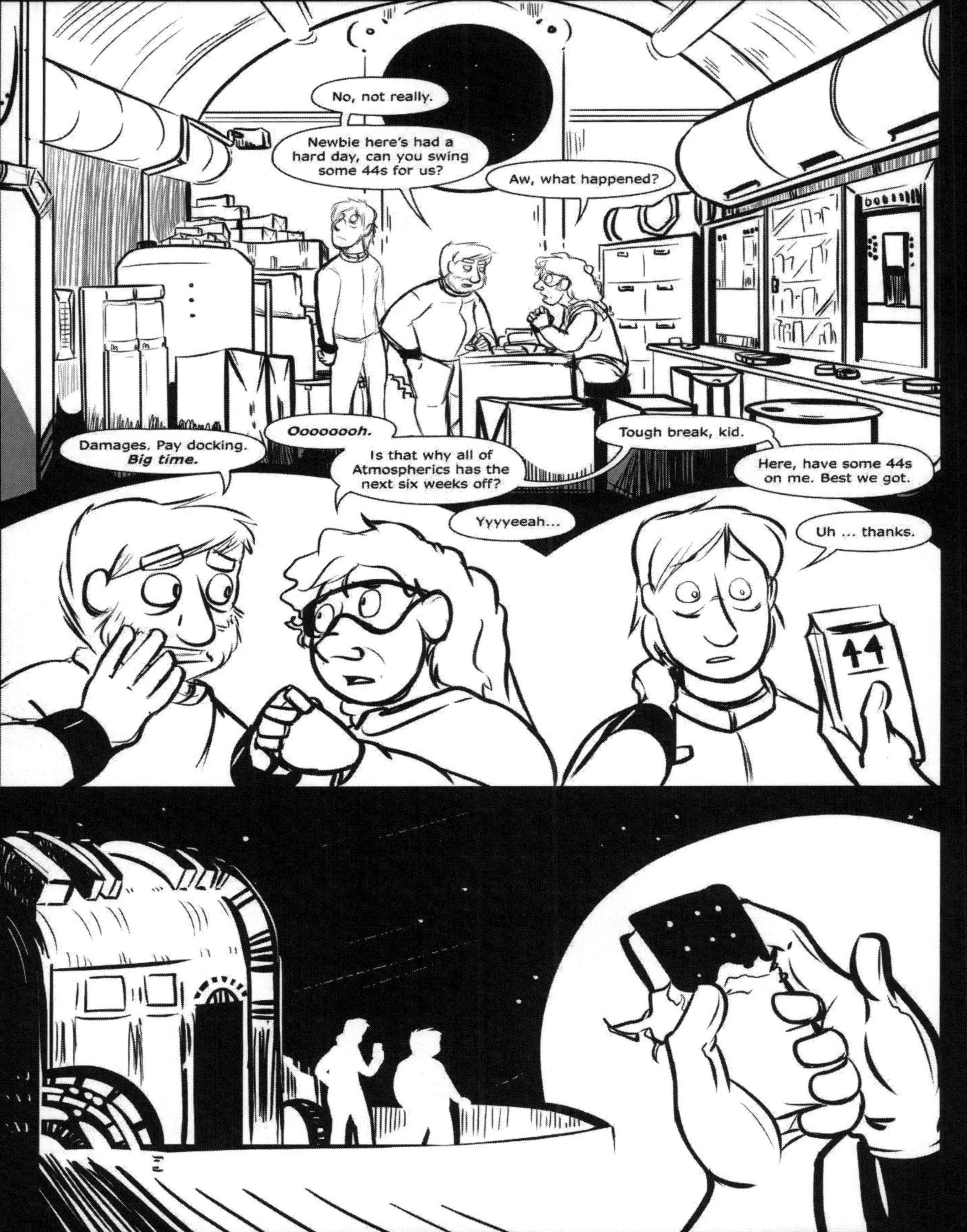

No, not really.
Newbie here's had a hard day, can you swing some 44s for us?
Aw, what happened?
Damages. Pay docking. *Big time.*
Ooooooh.
Is that why all of Atmospherics has the next six weeks off?
Tough break, kid.
Here, have some 44s on me. Best we got.
Yyyyeeah...
Uh ... thanks.
44

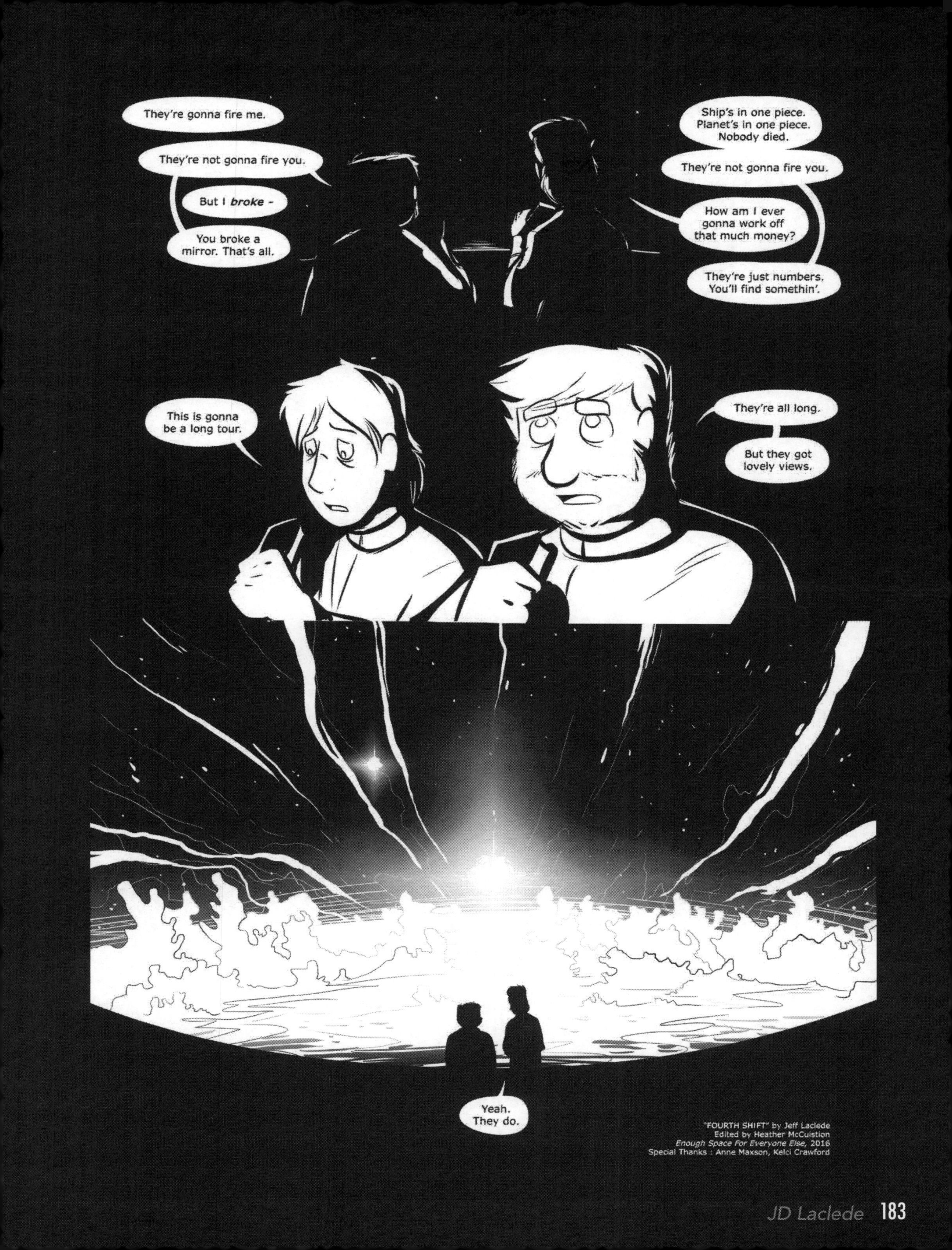
They're gonna fire me.
They're not gonna fire you.
But I *broke* -
You broke a mirror. That's all.
Ship's in one piece. Planet's in one piece. Nobody died.
They're not gonna fire you.
How am I ever gonna work off that much money?
They're just numbers. You'll find somethin'.
This is gonna be a long tour.
They're all long.
But they got lovely views.
Yeah. They do.

"FOURTH SHIFT" by Jeff Laclede
Edited by Heather McCuistion
Enough Space For Everyone Else, 2016
Special Thanks : Anne Maxson, Kelci Crawford

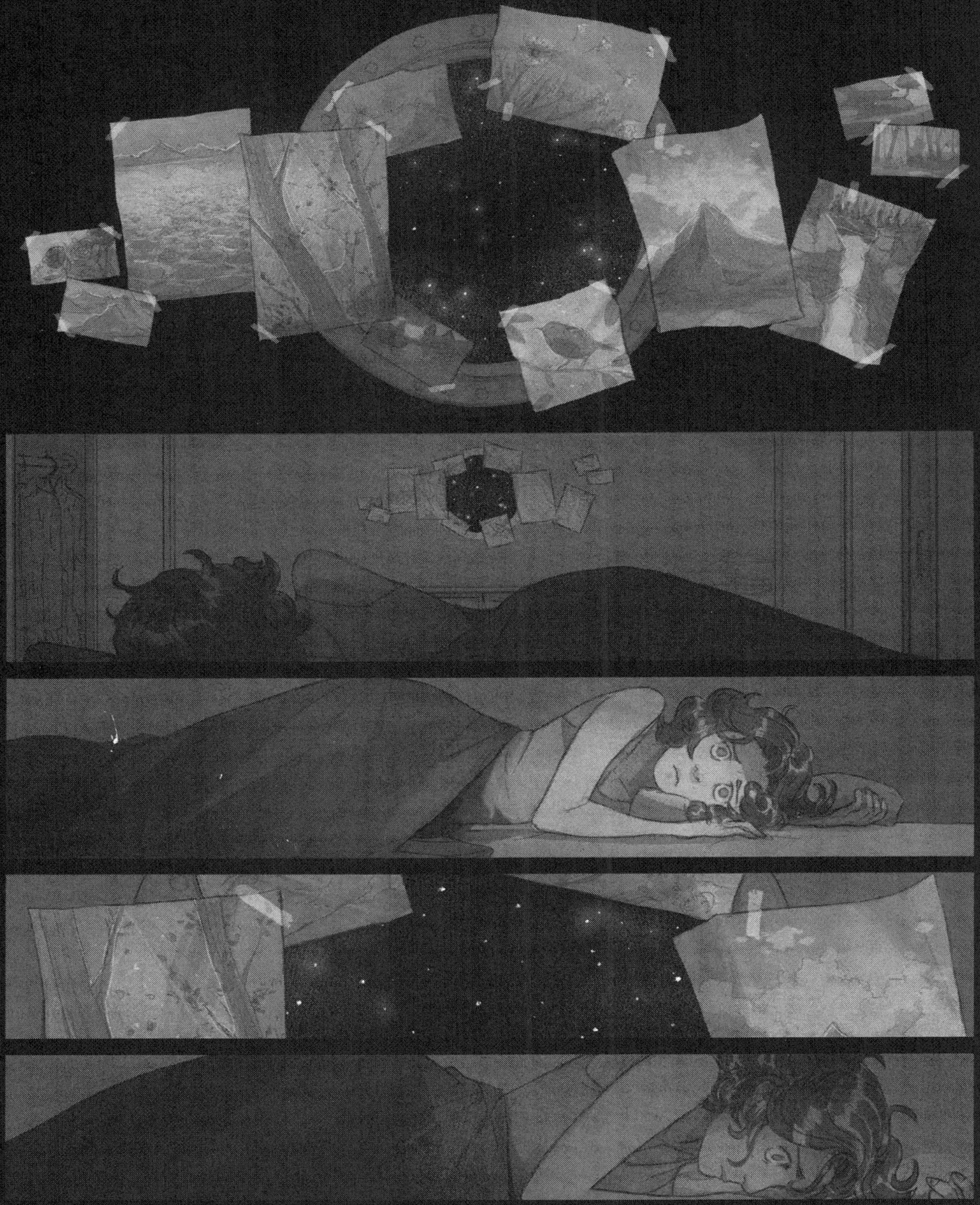

HABITUS

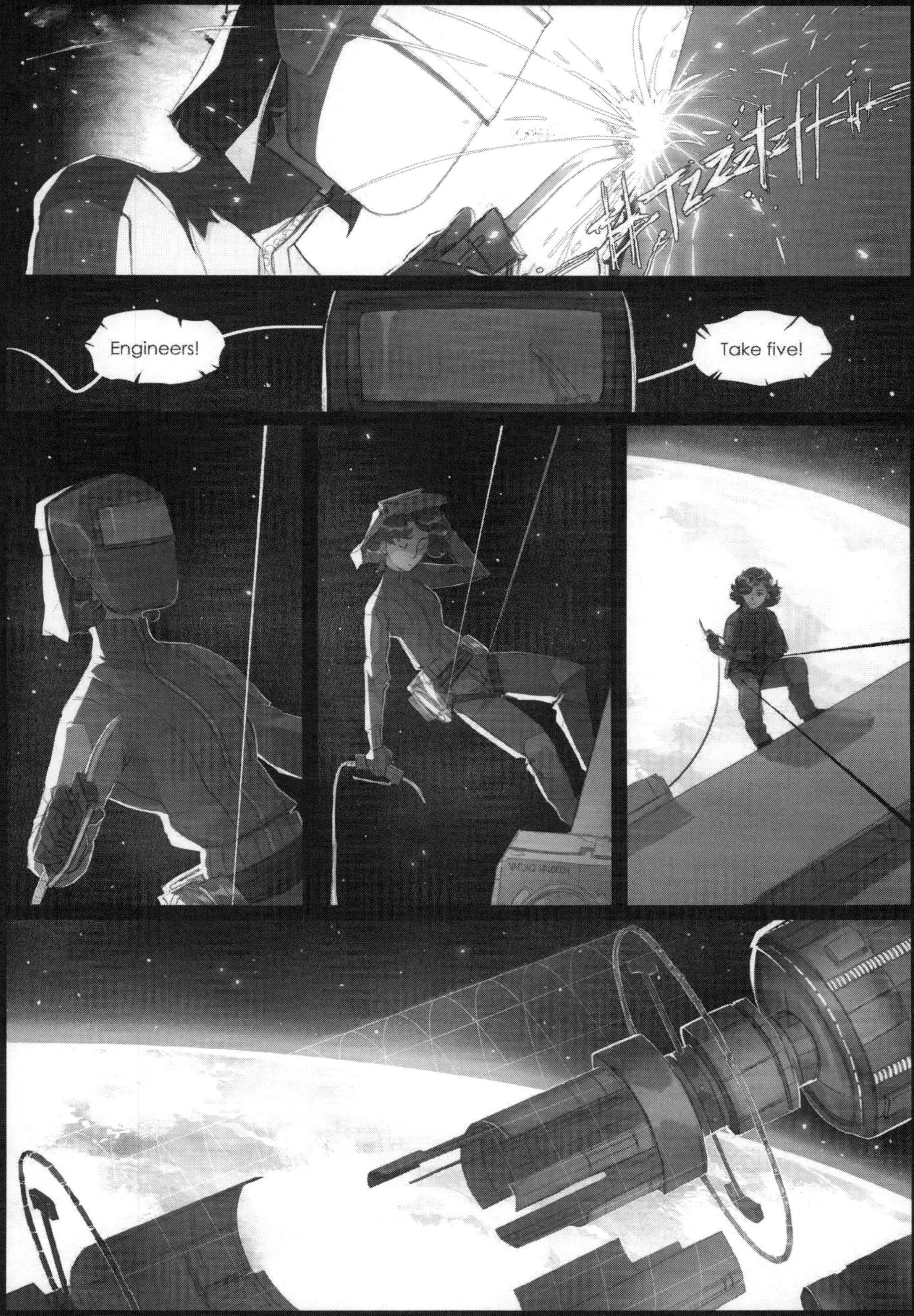

Engineers!
Take five!

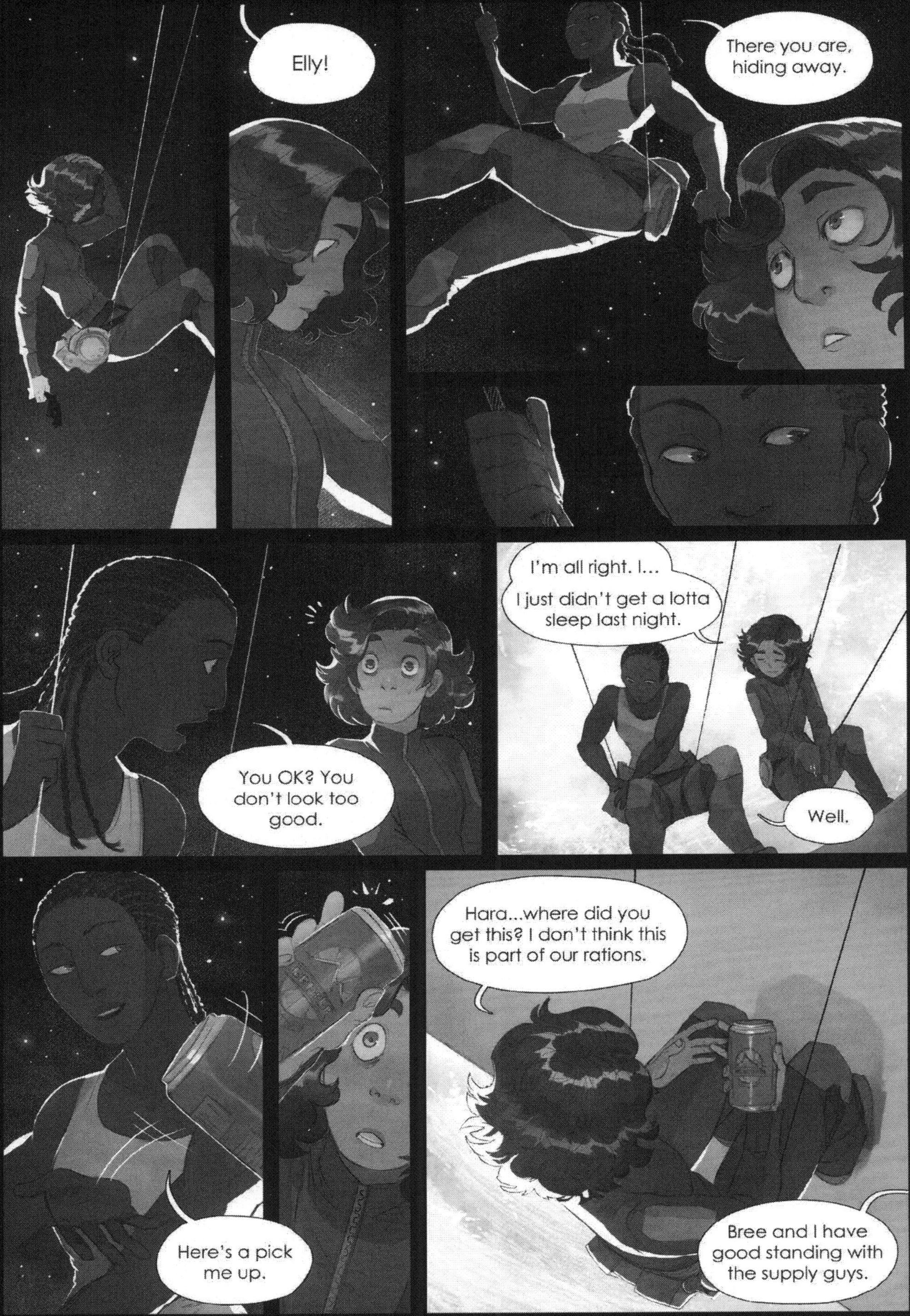
Elly!
There you are, hiding away.
You OK? You don't look too good.
I'm all right. I...
I just didn't get a lotta sleep last night.
Well.
Here's a pick me up.
Hara...where did you get this? I don't think this is part of our rations.
Bree and I have good standing with the supply guys.

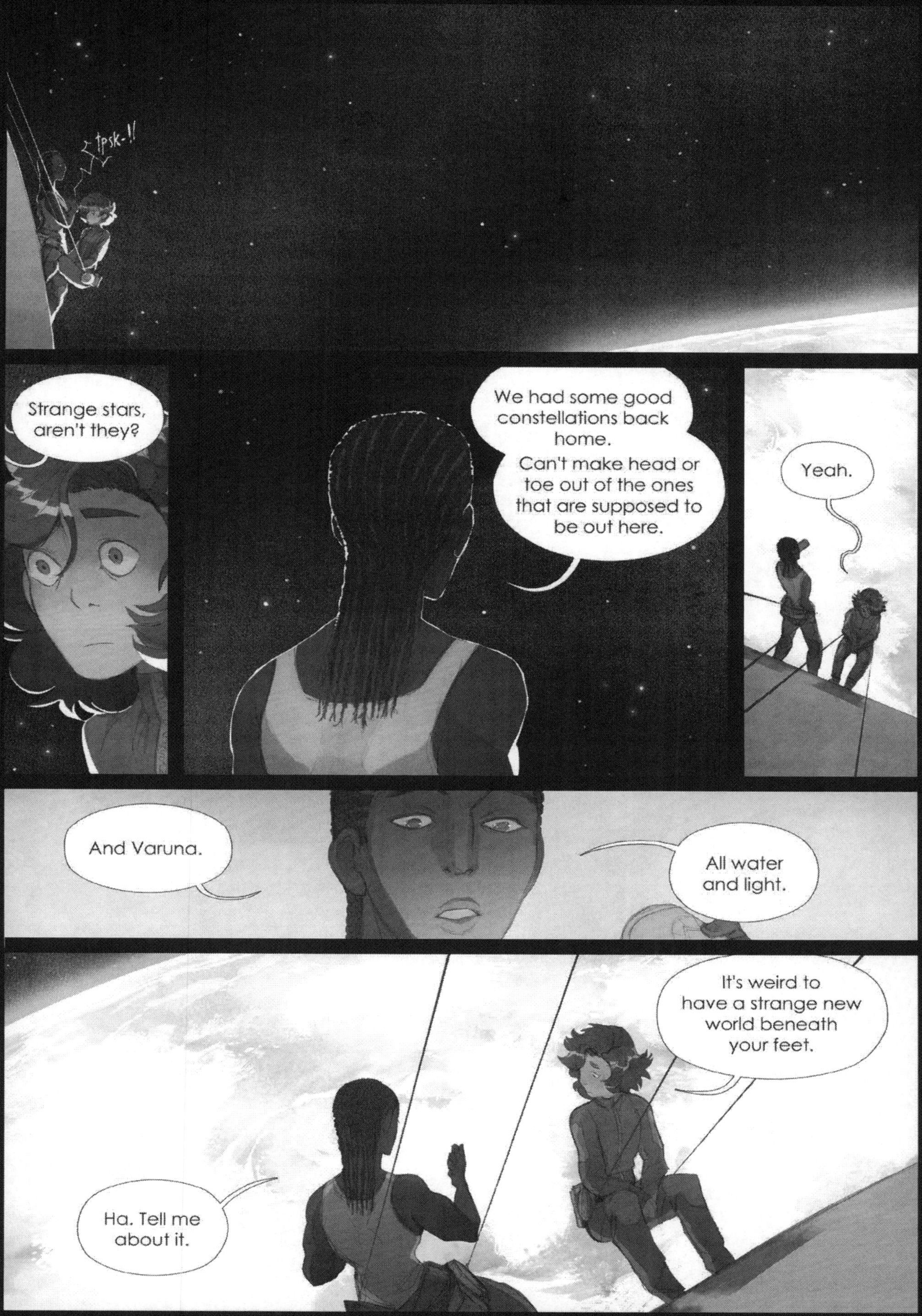
tpsk-!!
Strange stars, aren't they?
We had some good constellations back home.
Can't make head or toe out of the ones that are supposed to be out here.
Yeah.
And Varuna.
All water and light.
It's weird to have a strange new world beneath your feet.
Ha. Tell me about it.

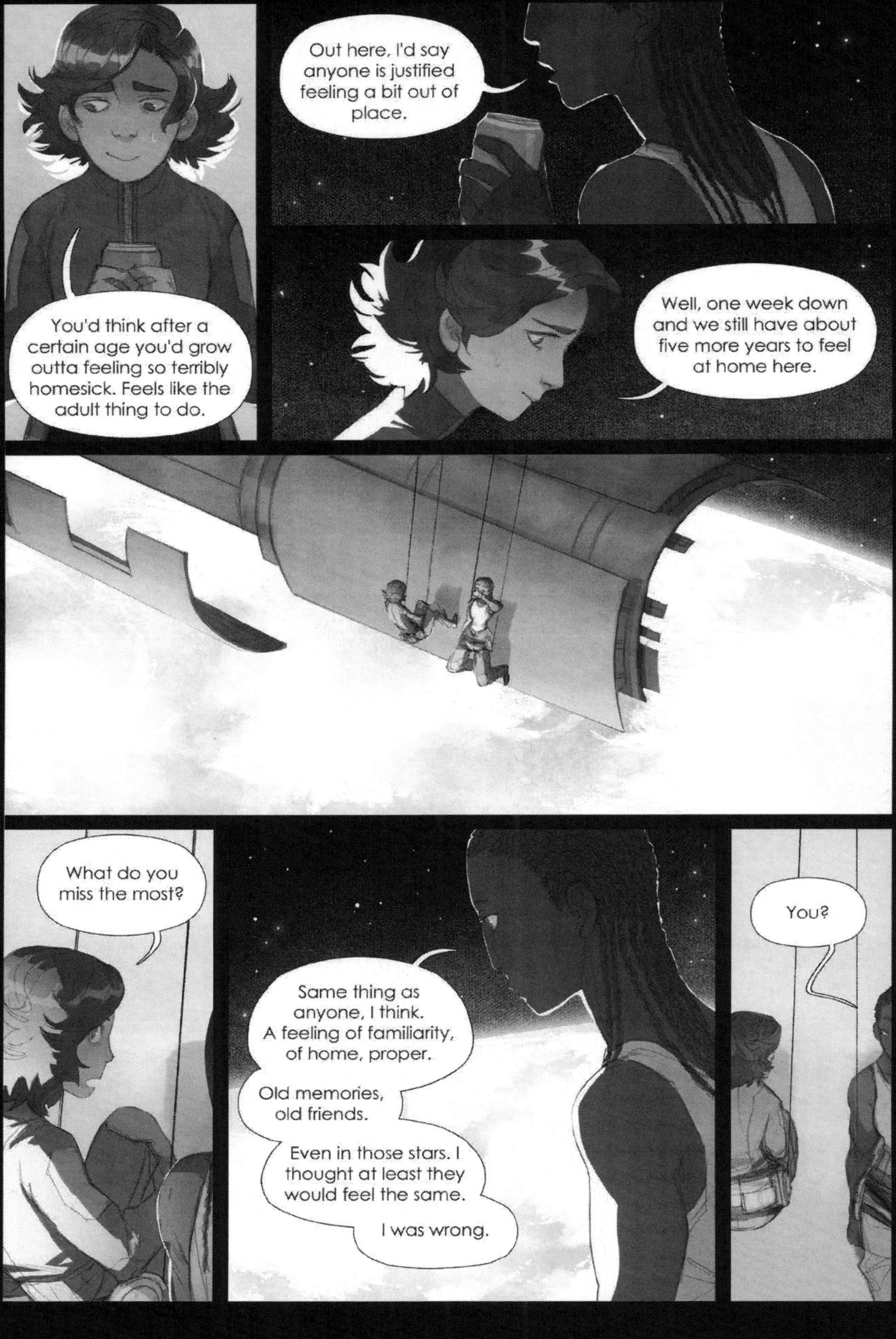
Out here, I'd say anyone is justified feeling a bit out of place.
You'd think after a certain age you'd grow outta feeling so terribly homesick. Feels like the adult thing to do.
Well, one week down and we still have about five more years to feel at home here.
What do you miss the most?
Same thing as anyone, I think. A feeling of familiarity, of home, proper.
Old memories, old friends.
Even in those stars. I thought at least they would feel the same.
I was wrong.
You?

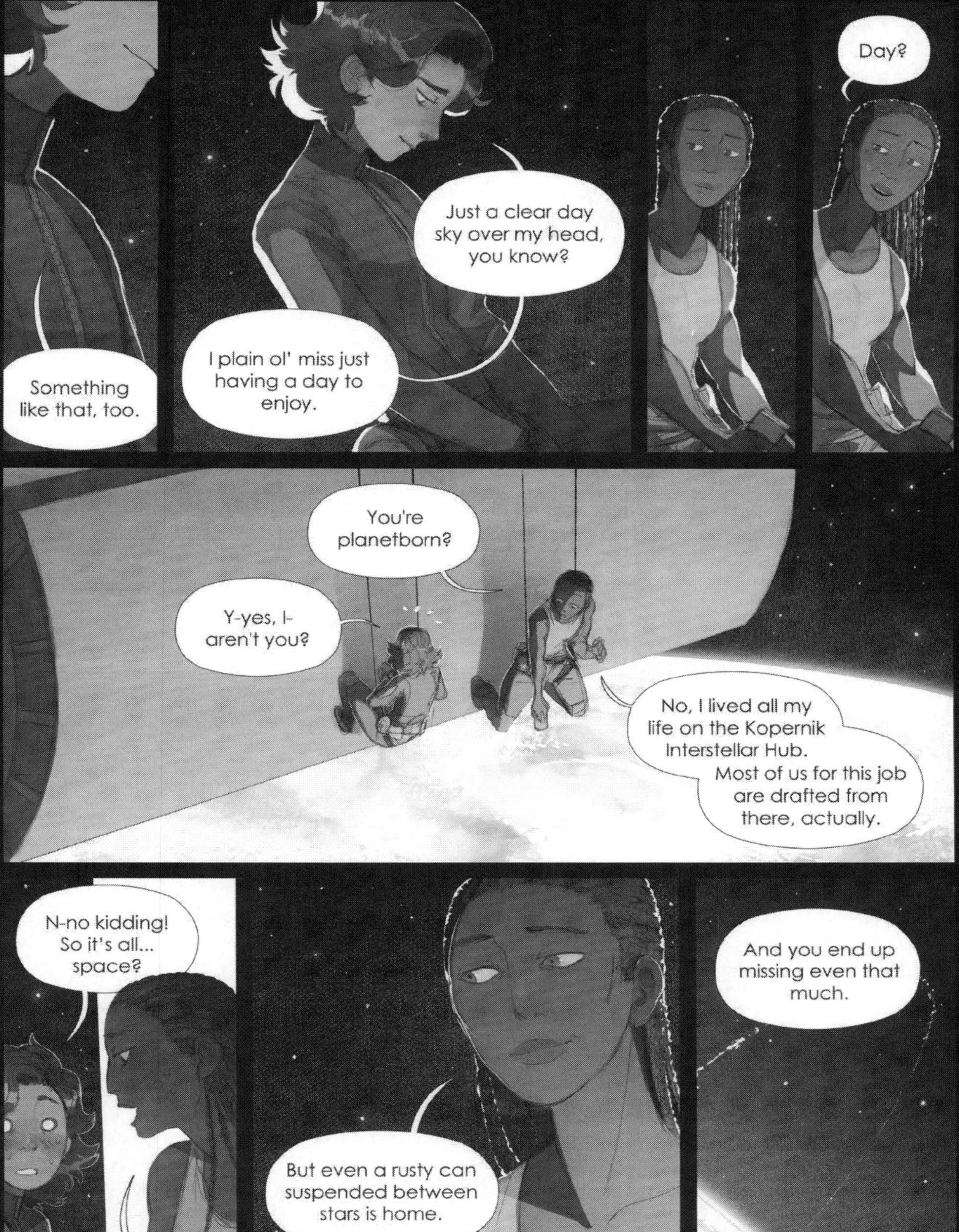
Something like that, too.
I plain ol' miss just having a day to enjoy.
Just a clear day sky over my head, you know?
Day?
You're planetborn?
Y-yes, I- aren't you?
No, I lived all my life on the Kopernik Interstellar Hub.
Most of us for this job are drafted from there, actually.
N-no kidding! So it's all... space?
You can't even have so much as a planetoid around Hubs.
But even a rusty can suspended between stars is home.
And you end up missing even that much.

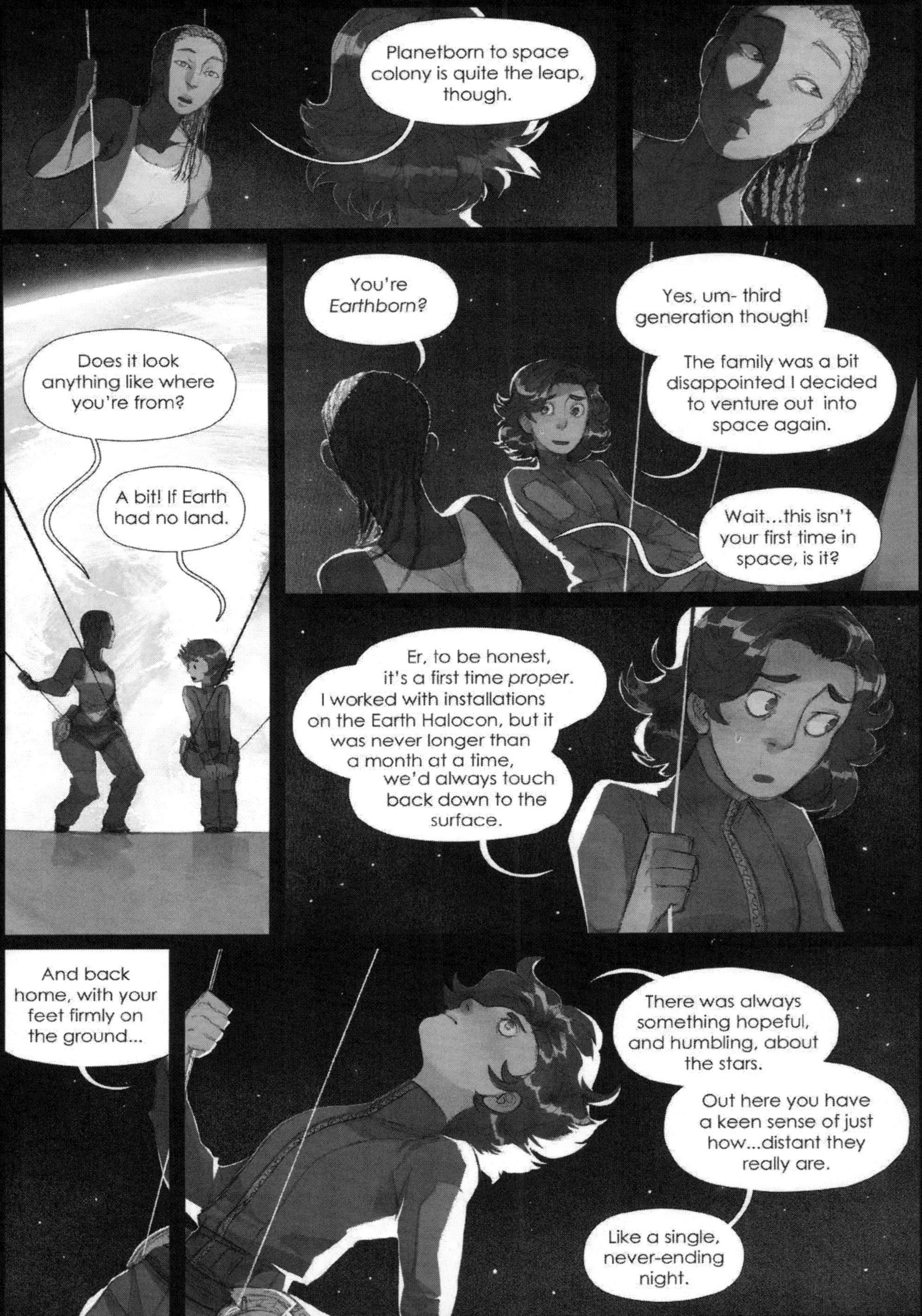
Planetborn to space colony is quite the leap, though.
You're *Earthborn*?
Yes, um- third generation though!
The family was a bit disappointed I decided to venture out into space again.
Wait…this isn't your first time in space, is it?
Does it look anything like where you're from?
A bit! If Earth had no land.
Er, to be honest, it's a first time *proper*. I worked with installations on the Earth Halocon, but it was never longer than a month at a time, we'd always touch back down to the surface.
And back home, with your feet firmly on the ground...
There was always something hopeful, and humbling, about the stars.
Out here you have a keen sense of just how...distant they really are.
Like a single, never-ending night.

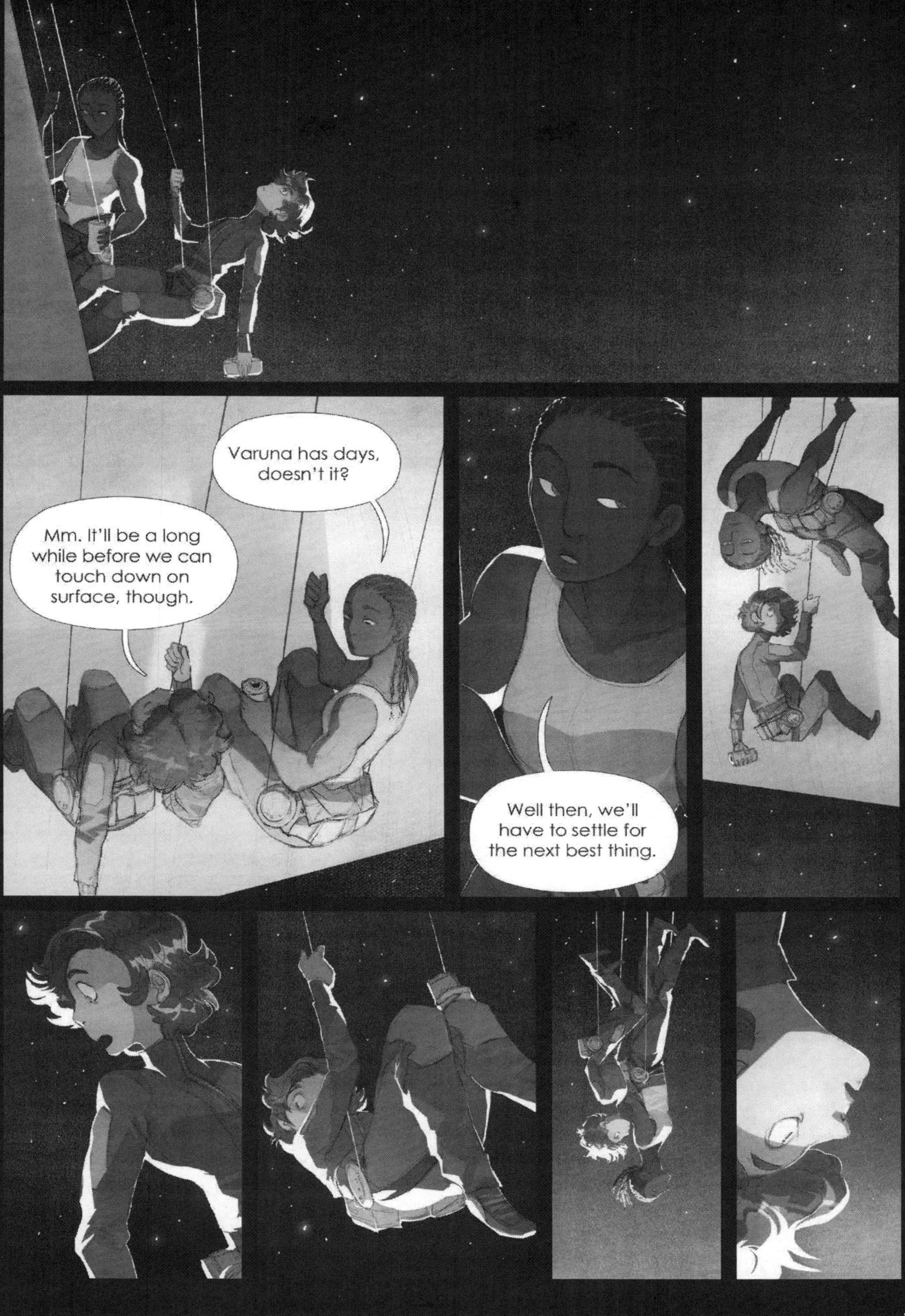
Varuna has days, doesn't it?
Mm. It'll be a long while before we can touch down on surface, though.
Well then, we'll have to settle for the next best thing.

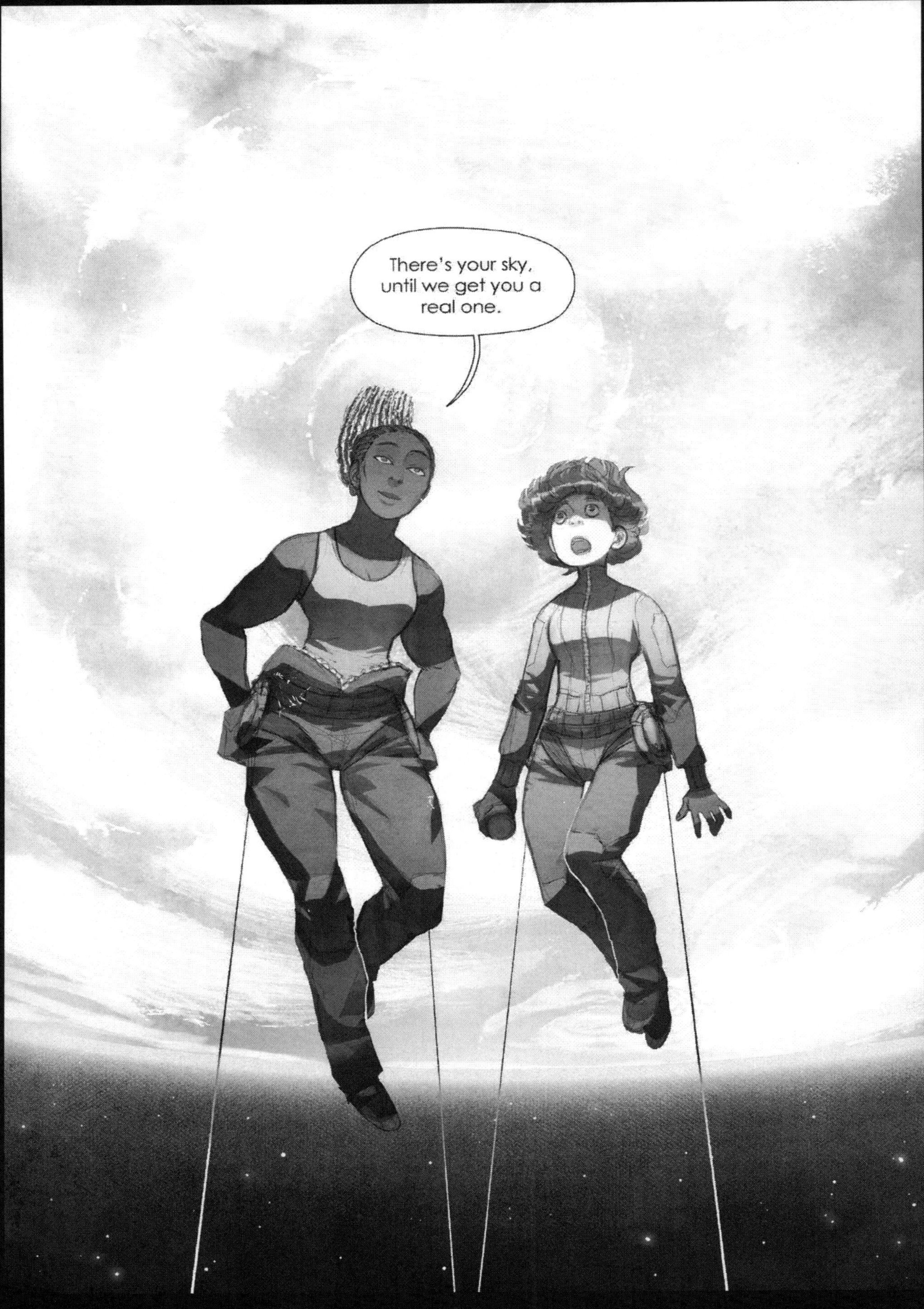
There's your sky, until we get you a real one.

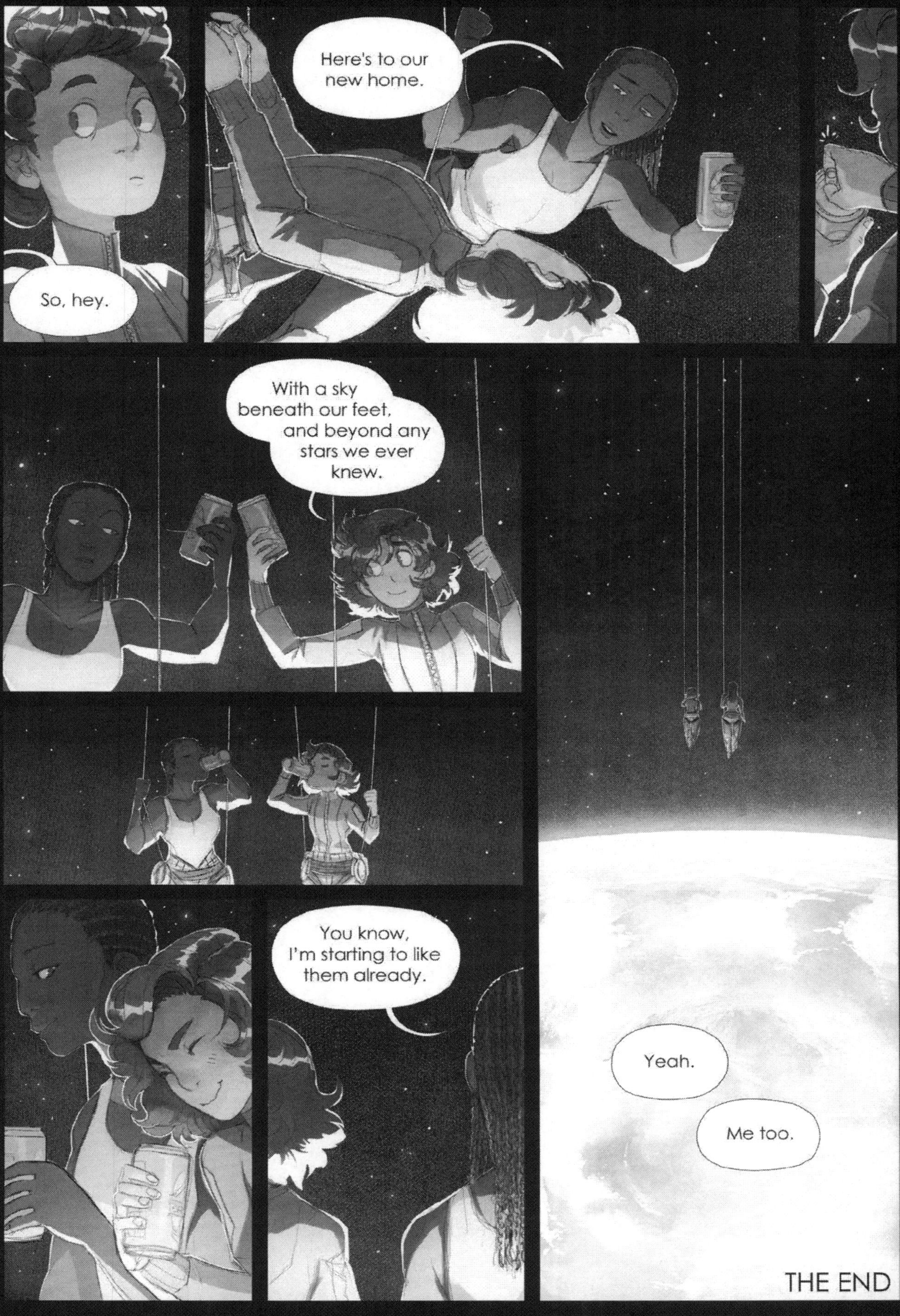

So, hey.
Here's to our new home.
With a sky beneath our feet, and beyond any stars we ever knew.
You know, I'm starting to like them already.
Yeah.
Me too.
THE END

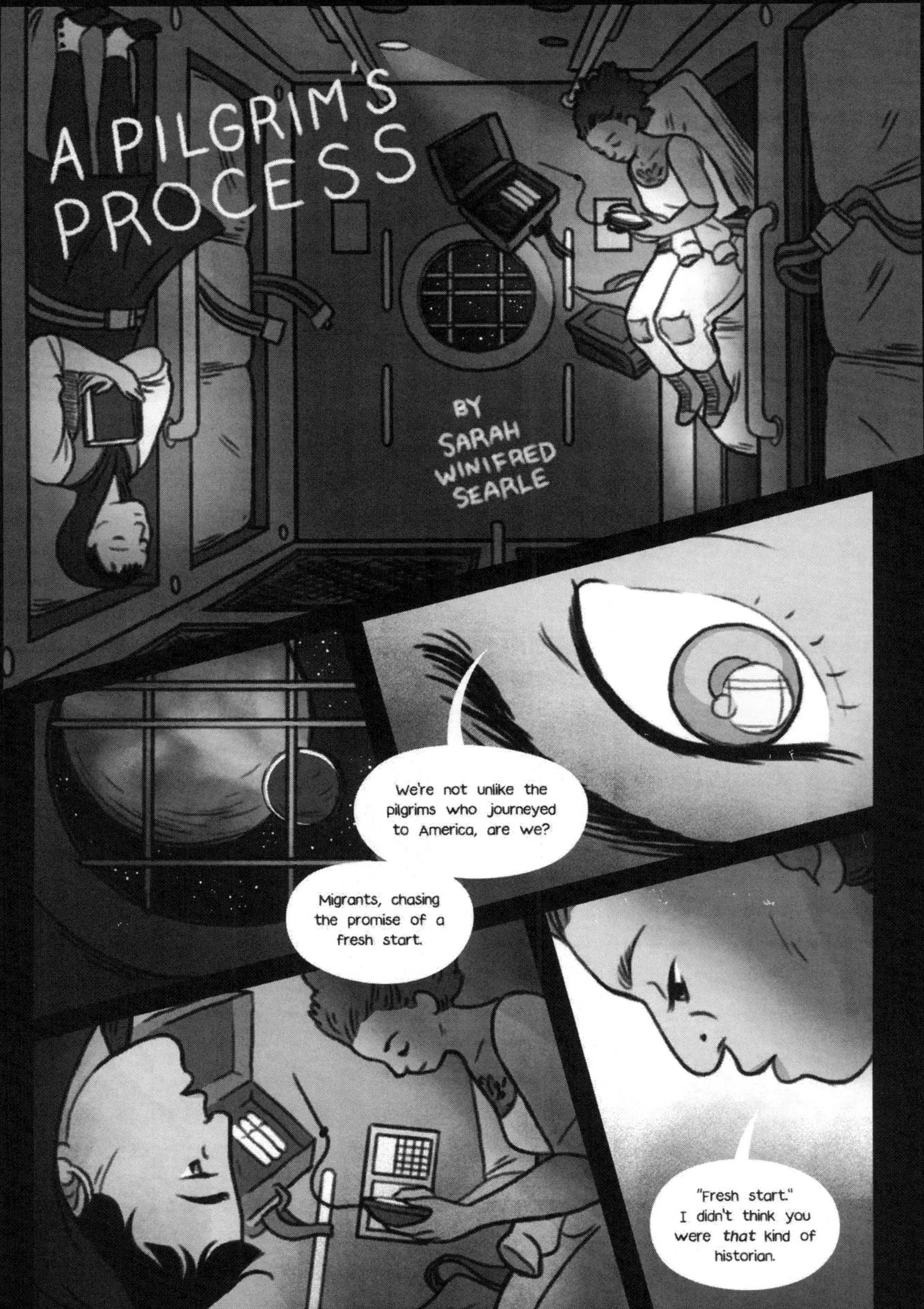
A PILGRIM'S PROCESS
BY SARAH WINIFRED SEARLE
We're not unlike the pilgrims who journeyed to America, are we?
Migrants, chasing the promise of a fresh start.
"Fresh start." I didn't think you were *that* kind of historian.

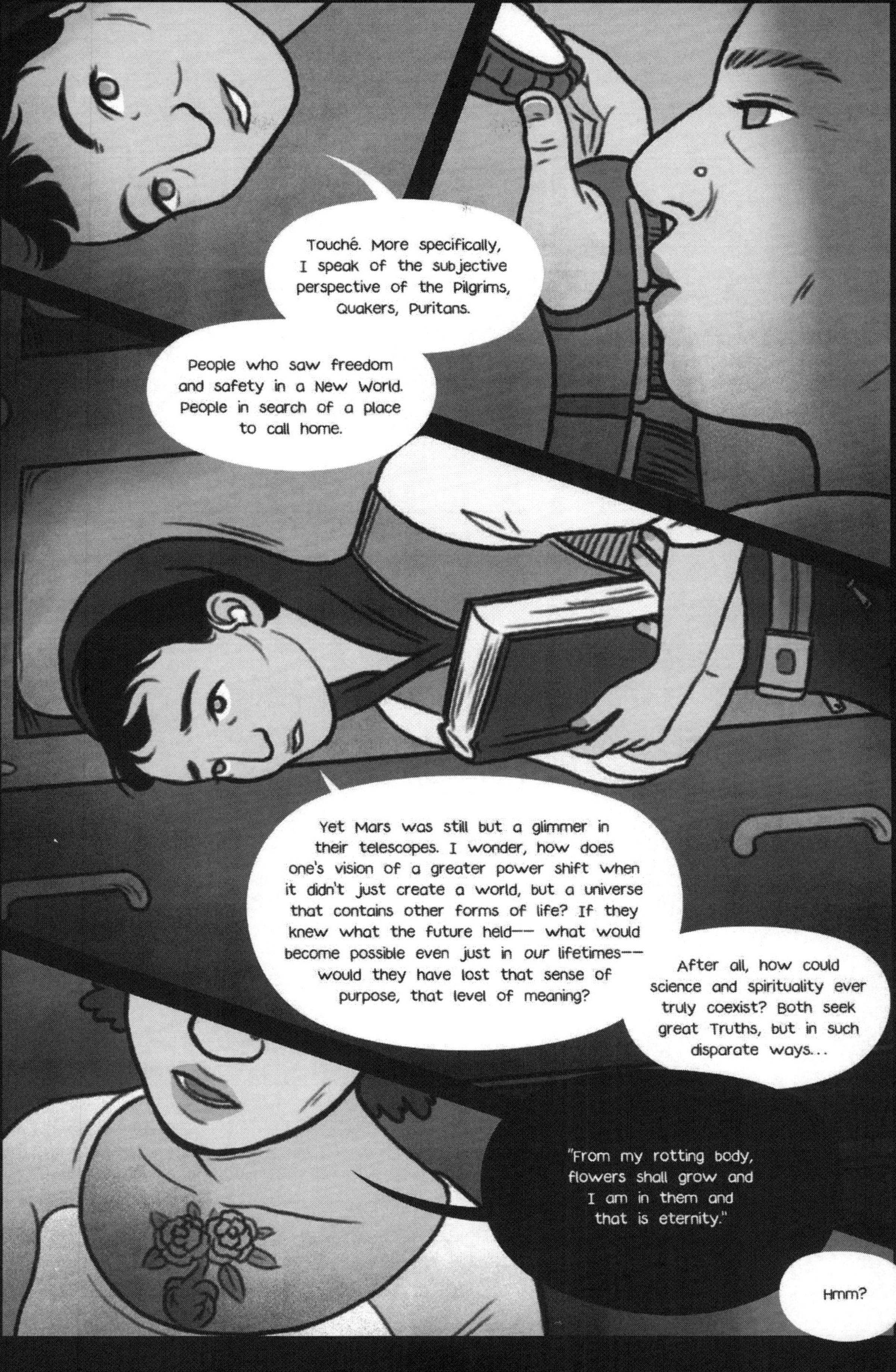
Touché. More specifically, I speak of the subjective perspective of the Pilgrims, Quakers, Puritans.
People who saw freedom and safety in a New World. People in search of a place to call home.
Yet Mars was still but a glimmer in their telescopes. I wonder, how does one's vision of a greater power shift when it didn't just create a world, but a universe that contains other forms of life? If they knew what the future held–– what would become possible even just in *our* lifetimes–– would they have lost that sense of purpose, that level of meaning?
After all, how could science and spirituality ever truly coexist? Both seek great Truths, but in such disparate ways...
"From my rotting body, flowers shall grow and I am in them and that is eternity."
Hmm?

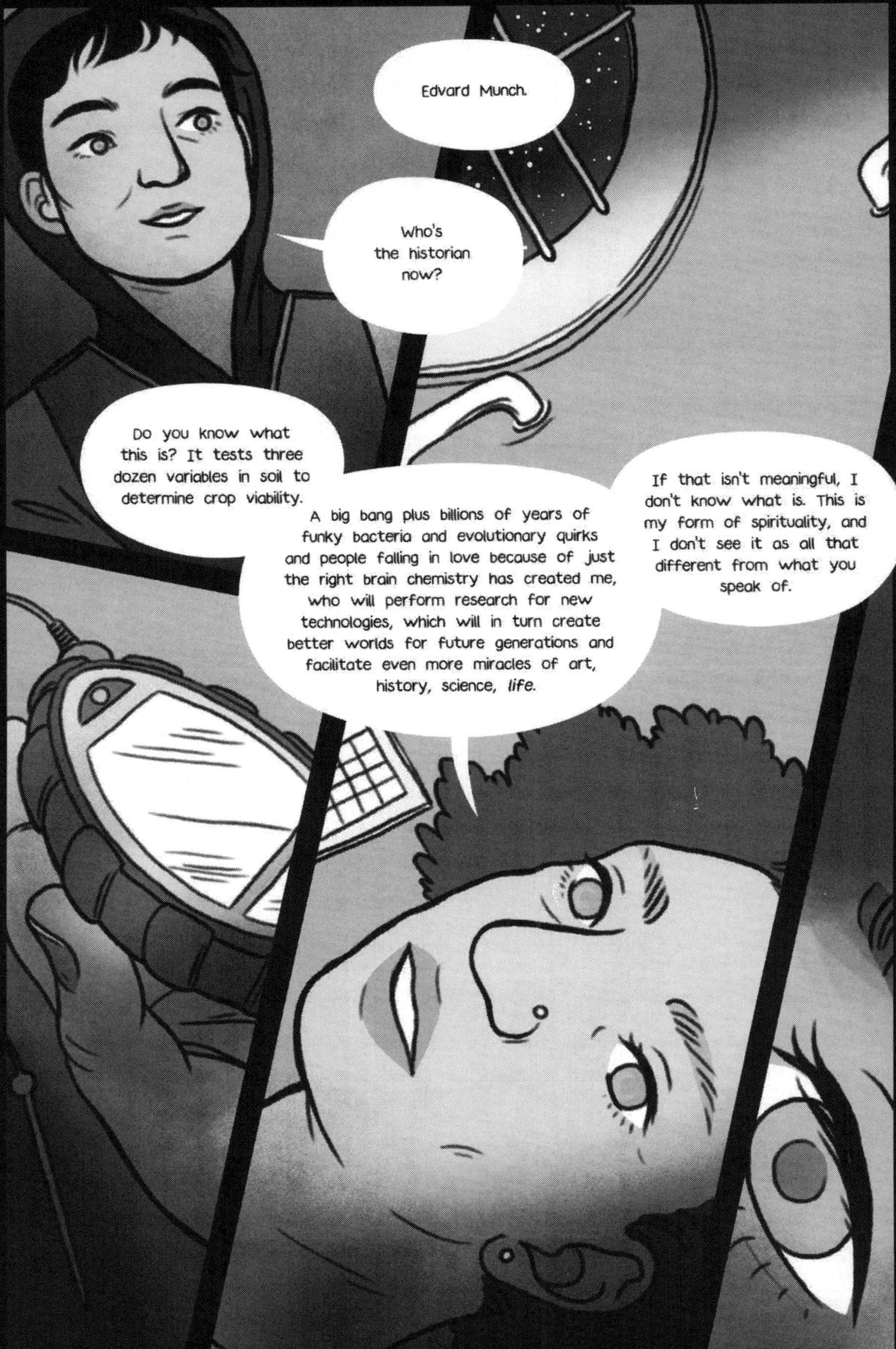
Edvard Munch.
Who's the historian now?
Do you know what this is? It tests three dozen variables in soil to determine crop viability.
A big bang plus billions of years of funky bacteria and evolutionary quirks and people falling in love because of just the right brain chemistry has created me, who will perform research for new technologies, which will in turn create better worlds for future generations and facilitate even more miracles of art, history, science, *life*.
If that isn't meaningful, I don't know what is. This is my form of spirituality, and I don't see it as all that different from what you speak of.

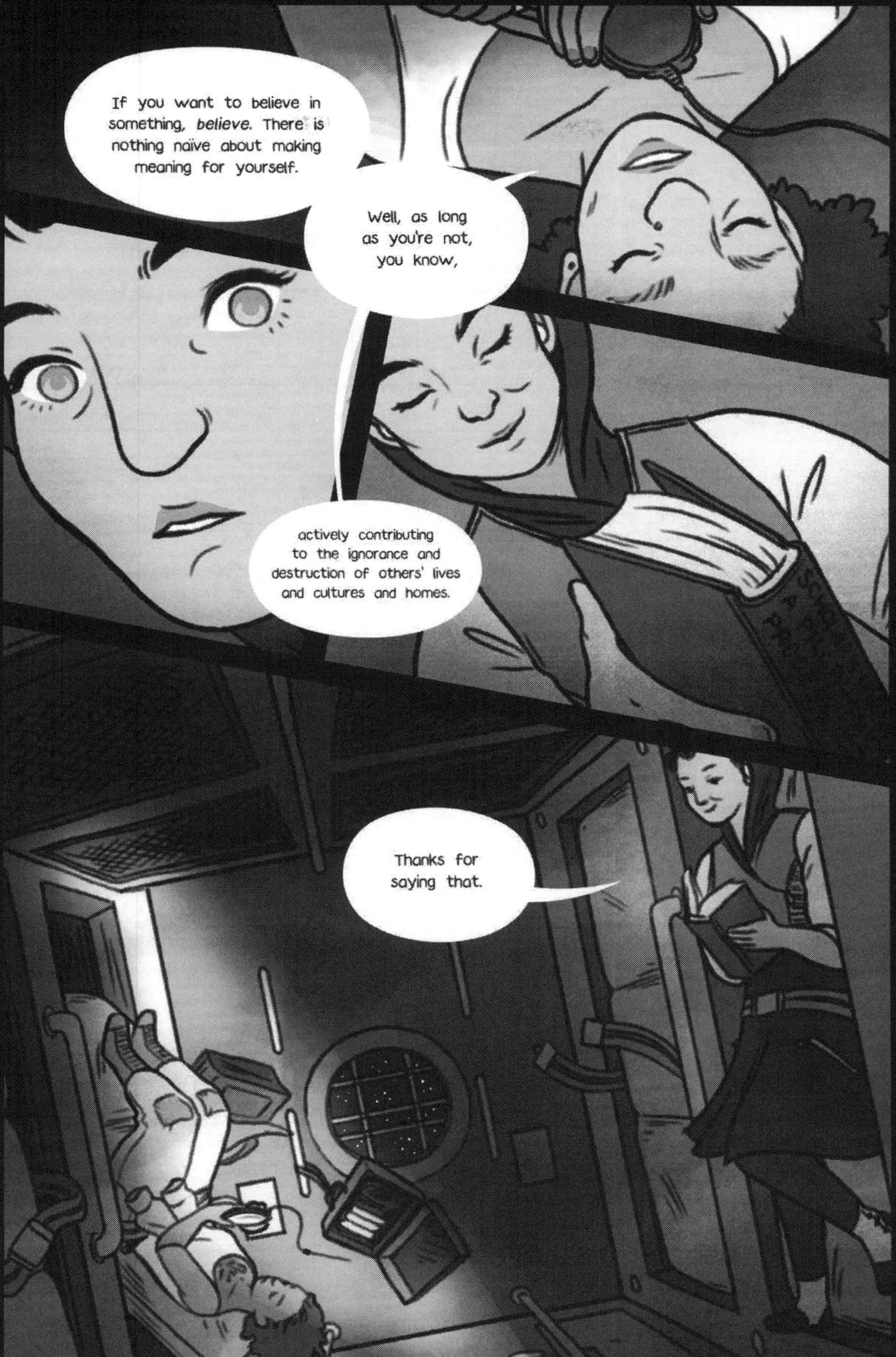
If you want to believe in something, *believe.* There is nothing naïve about making meaning for yourself.
Well, as long as you're not, you know,
actively contributing to the ignorance and destruction of others' lives and cultures and homes.
Thanks for saying that.

THE SKY IS FALLING

by Eryn Williams

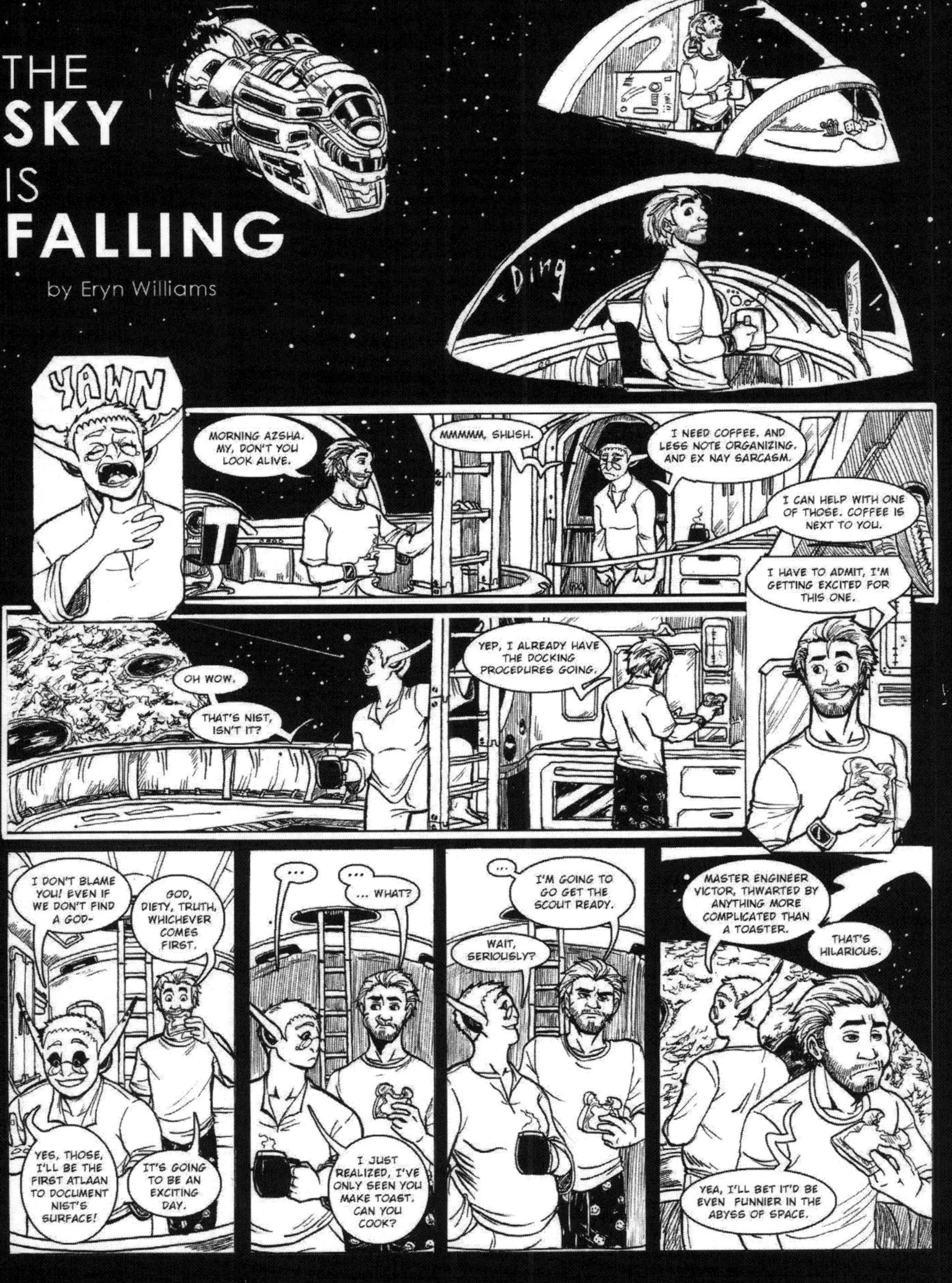
Ding
YAWN
MORNING AZSHA. MY, DON'T YOU LOOK ALIVE.
MMMMM, SHUSH.
I NEED COFFEE. AND LESS NOTE ORGANIZING, AND EX NAY SARCASM.
I CAN HELP WITH ONE OF THOSE. COFFEE IS NEXT TO YOU.
I HAVE TO ADMIT, I'M GETTING EXCITED FOR THIS ONE.
OH WOW.
THAT'S NIST, ISN'T IT?
YEP, I ALREADY HAVE THE DOCKING PROCEDURES GOING.
I DON'T BLAME YOU! EVEN IF WE DON'T FIND A GOD-
GOD, DIETY, TRUTH, WHICHEVER COMES FIRST.
YES, THOSE. I'LL BE THE FIRST ATLAAN TO DOCUMENT NIST'S SURFACE!
IT'S GOING TO BE AN EXCITING DAY.
...
... WHAT?
I JUST REALIZED, I'VE ONLY SEEN YOU MAKE TOAST. CAN YOU COOK?
...
I'M GOING TO GO GET THE SCOUT READY.
WAIT, SERIOUSLY?
MASTER ENGINEER VICTOR, THWARTED BY ANYTHING MORE COMPLICATED THAN A TOASTER.
THAT'S HILARIOUS.
YEA, I'LL BET IT'D BE EVEN FUNNIER IN THE ABYSS OF SPACE.

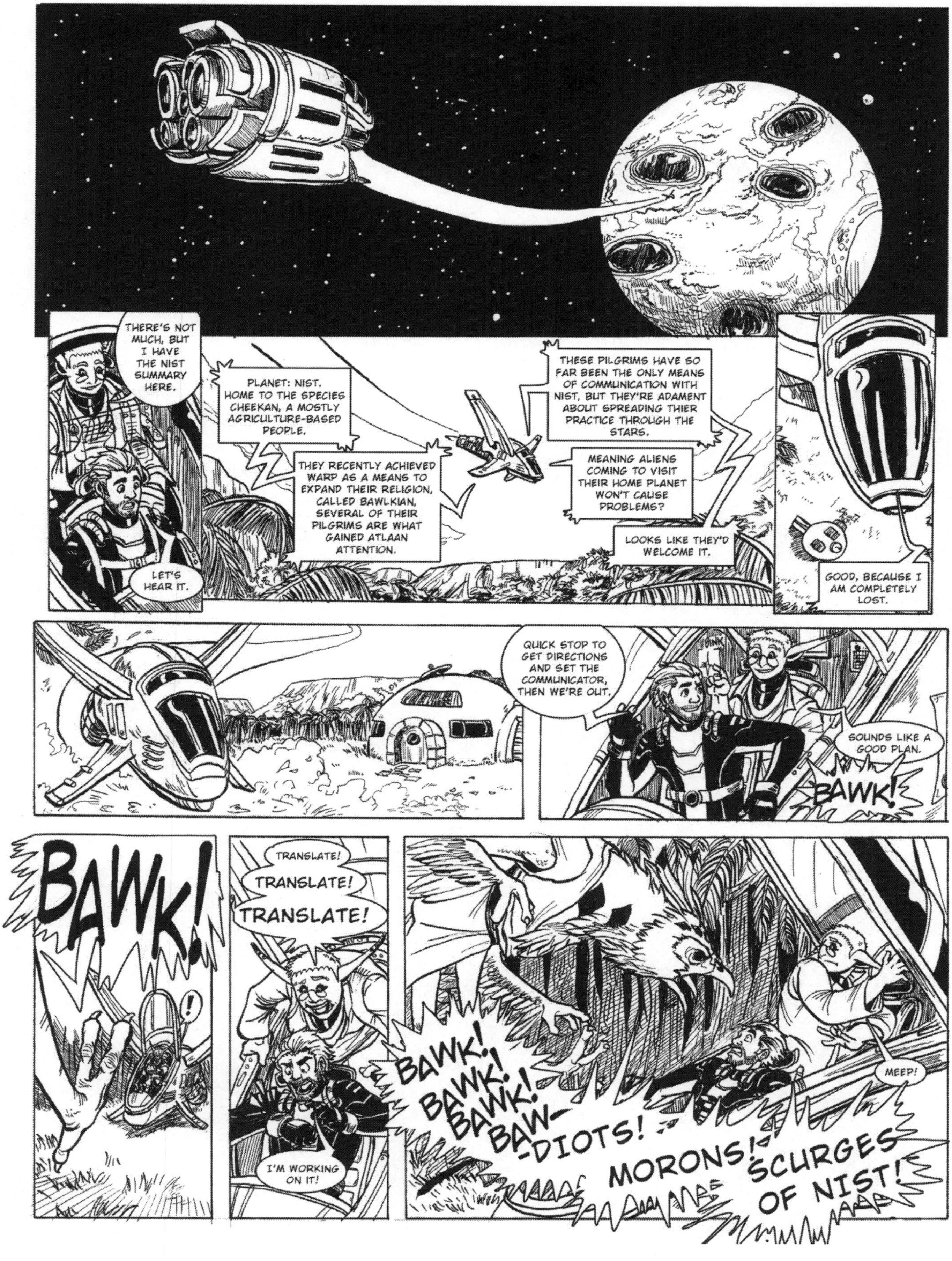
THERE'S NOT MUCH, BUT I HAVE THE NIST SUMMARY HERE.
LET'S HEAR IT.
PLANET: NIST. HOME TO THE SPECIES CHEEKAN, A MOSTLY AGRICULTURE-BASED PEOPLE.
THEY RECENTLY ACHIEVED WARP AS A MEANS TO EXPAND THEIR RELIGION, CALLED BAWLKIAN, SEVERAL OF THEIR PILGRIMS ARE WHAT GAINED ATLAAN ATTENTION.
THESE PILGRIMS HAVE SO FAR BEEN THE ONLY MEANS OF COMMUNICATION WITH NIST, BUT THEY'RE ADAMENT ABOUT SPREADING THIER PRACTICE THROUGH THE STARS.
MEANING ALIENS COMING TO VISIT THEIR HOME PLANET WON'T CAUSE PROBLEMS?
LOOKS LIKE THEY'D WELCOME IT.
GOOD, BECAUSE I AM COMPLETELY LOST.
QUICK STOP TO GET DIRECTIONS AND SET THE COMMUNICATOR, THEN WE'RE OUT.
SOUNDS LIKE A GOOD PLAN.
BAWK!
BAWK!
!
TRANSLATE!
TRANSLATE!
TRANSLATE!
I'M WORKING ON IT!
BAWK! BAWK! BAWK! BAW-
-DIOTS!
MORONS!
SCURGES OF NIST!
MEEP!

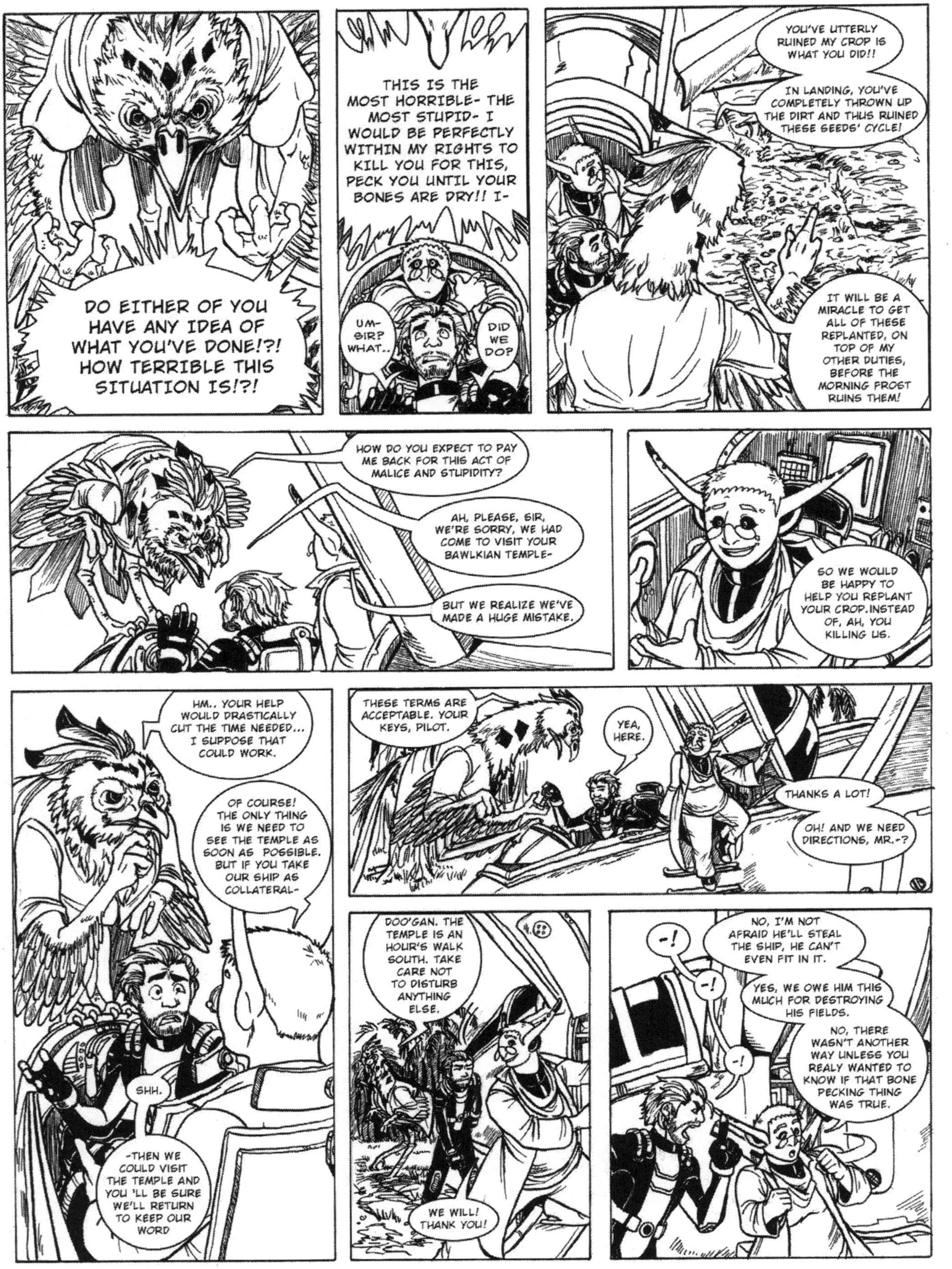
DO EITHER OF YOU HAVE ANY IDEA OF WHAT YOU'VE DONE!?! HOW TERRIBLE THIS SITUATION IS!?!
THIS IS THE MOST HORRIBLE- THE MOST STUPID- I WOULD BE PERFECTLY WITHIN MY RIGHTS TO KILL YOU FOR THIS, PECK YOU UNTIL YOUR BONES ARE DRY!! I-
UM- SIR? WHAT..
DID WE DO?
YOU'VE UTTERLY RUINED MY CROP IS WHAT YOU DID!!
IN LANDING, YOU'VE COMPLETELY THROWN UP THE DIRT AND THUS RUINED THESE SEEDS' CYCLE!
IT WILL BE A MIRACLE TO GET ALL OF THESE REPLANTED, ON TOP OF MY OTHER DUTIES, BEFORE THE MORNING FROST RUINS THEM!
HOW DO YOU EXPECT TO PAY ME BACK FOR THIS ACT OF MALICE AND STUPIDITY?
AH, PLEASE, SIR, WE'RE SORRY, WE HAD COME TO VISIT YOUR BAWLKIAN TEMPLE-
BUT WE REALIZE WE'VE MADE A HUGE MISTAKE.
SO WE WOULD BE HAPPY TO HELP YOU REPLANT YOUR CROP.INSTEAD OF, AH, YOU KILLING US.
HM.. YOUR HELP WOULD DRASTICALLY CUT THE TIME NEEDED... I SUPPOSE THAT COULD WORK.
OF COURSE! THE ONLY THING IS WE NEED TO SEE THE TEMPLE AS SOON AS POSSIBLE. BUT IF YOU TAKE OUR SHIP AS COLLATERAL-
SHH.
-THEN WE COULD VISIT THE TEMPLE AND YOU 'LL BE SURE WE'LL RETURN TO KEEP OUR WORD
THESE TERMS ARE ACCEPTABLE. YOUR KEYS, PILOT.
YEA, HERE.
THANKS A LOT!
OH! AND WE NEED DIRECTIONS, MR.-?
DOO'GAN. THE TEMPLE IS AN HOUR'S WALK SOUTH. TAKE CARE NOT TO DISTURB ANYTHING ELSE.
WE WILL! THANK YOU!
-!
NO, I'M NOT AFRAID HE'LL STEAL THE SHIP, HE CAN'T EVEN FIT IN IT.
-!
YES, WE OWE HIM THIS MUCH FOR DESTROYING HIS FIELDS.
-!
NO, THERE WASN'T ANOTHER WAY UNLESS YOU REALY WANTED TO KNOW IF THAT BONE PECKING THING WAS TRUE.

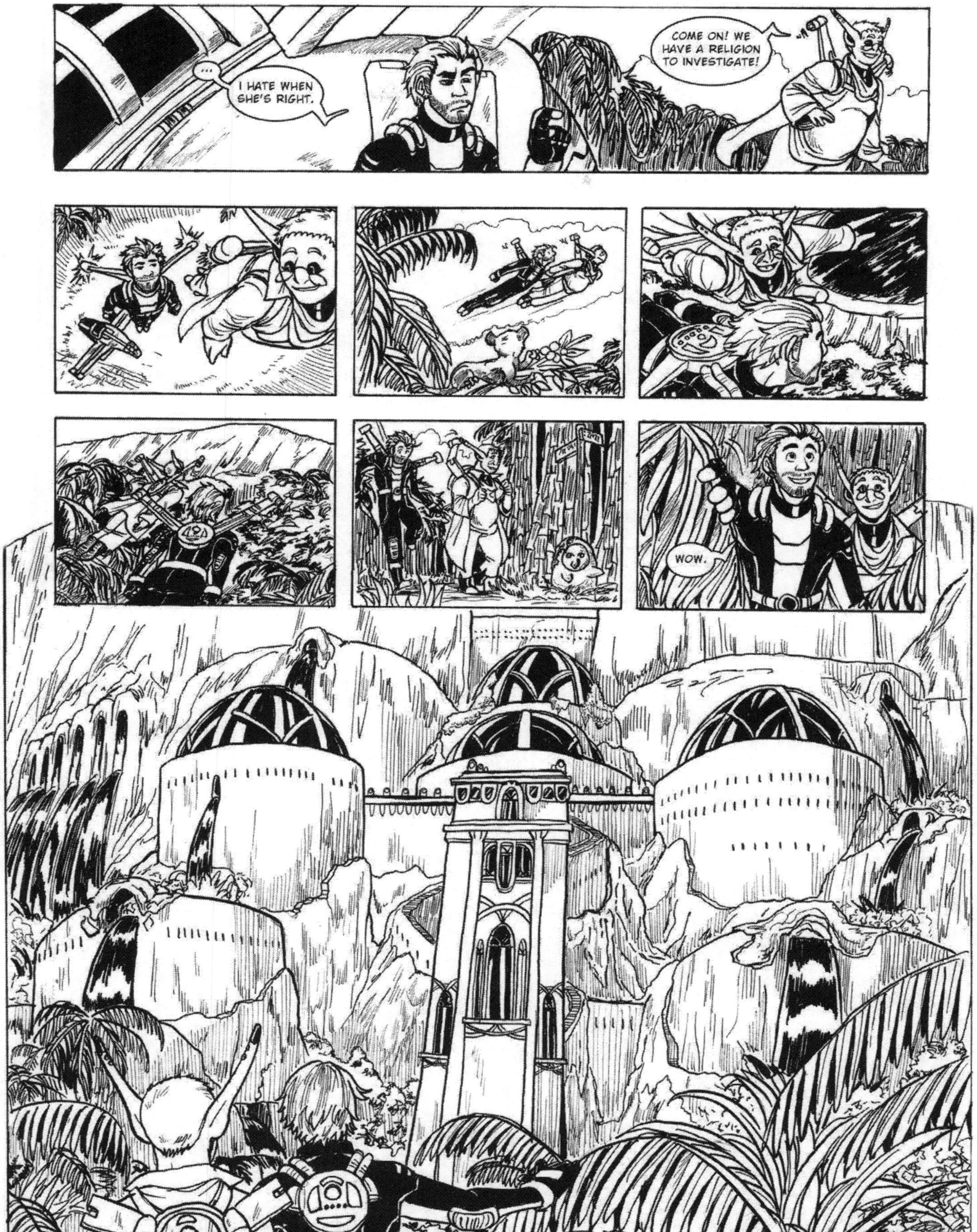
...
I HATE WHEN SHE'S RIGHT.
COME ON! WE HAVE A RELIGION TO INVESTIGATE!
WOW.

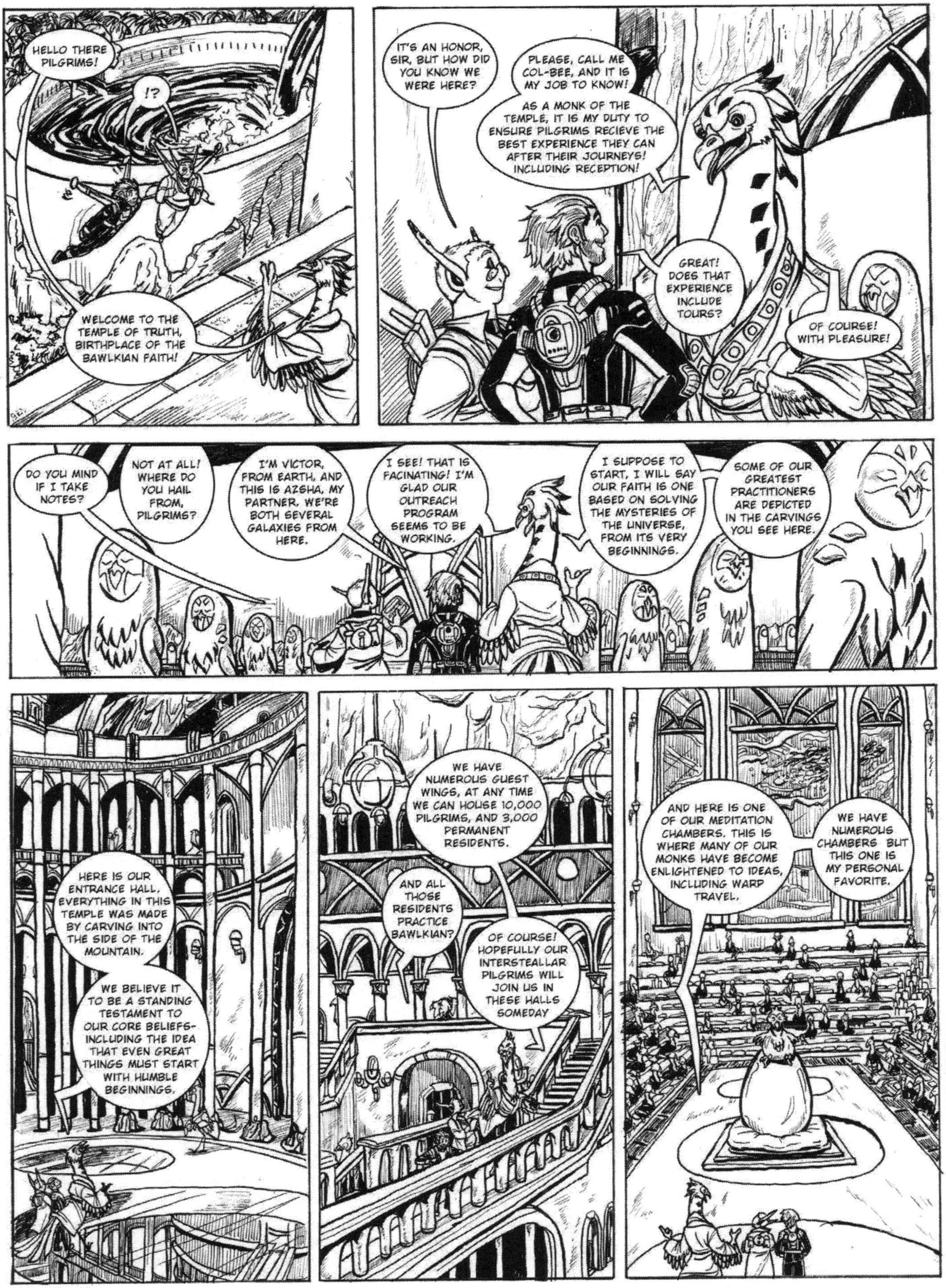
HELLO THERE PILGRIMS!
!?
WELCOME TO THE TEMPLE OF TRUTH, BIRTHPLACE OF THE BAWLKIAN FAITH!
IT'S AN HONOR, SIR, BUT HOW DID YOU KNOW WE WERE HERE?
PLEASE, CALL ME COL-BEE, AND IT IS MY JOB TO KNOW!
AS A MONK OF THE TEMPLE, IT IS MY DUTY TO ENSURE PILGRIMS RECIEVE THE BEST EXPERIENCE THEY CAN AFTER THEIR JOURNEYS! INCLUDING RECEPTION!
GREAT! DOES THAT EXPERIENCE INCLUDE TOURS?
OF COURSE! WITH PLEASURE!
DO YOU MIND IF I TAKE NOTES?
NOT AT ALL! WHERE DO YOU HAIL FROM, PILGRIMS?
I'M VICTOR, FROM EARTH, AND THIS IS AZSHA, MY PARTNER. WE'RE BOTH SEVERAL GALAXIES FROM HERE.
I SEE! THAT IS FACINATING! I'M GLAD OUR OUTREACH PROGRAM SEEMS TO BE WORKING.
I SUPPOSE TO START, I WILL SAY OUR FAITH IS ONE BASED ON SOLVING THE MYSTERIES OF THE UNIVERSE, FROM ITS VERY BEGINNINGS.
SOME OF OUR GREATEST PRACTITIONERS ARE DEPICTED IN THE CARVINGS YOU SEE HERE.
HERE IS OUR ENTRANCE HALL. EVERYTHING IN THIS TEMPLE WAS MADE BY CARVING INTO THE SIDE OF THE MOUNTAIN.
WE BELIEVE IT TO BE A STANDING TESTAMENT TO OUR CORE BELIEFS- INCLUDING THE IDEA THAT EVEN GREAT THINGS MUST START WITH HUMBLE BEGINNINGS.
WE HAVE NUMEROUS GUEST WINGS, AT ANY TIME WE CAN HOUSE 10,000 PILGRIMS, AND 3,000 PERMANENT RESIDENTS.
AND ALL THOSE RESIDENTS PRACTICE BAWLKIAN?
OF COURSE! HOPEFULLY OUR INTERSTEALLAR PILGRIMS WILL JOIN US IN THESE HALLS SOMEDAY
AND HERE IS ONE OF OUR MEDITATION CHAMBERS. THIS IS WHERE MANY OF OUR MONKS HAVE BECOME ENLIGHTENED TO IDEAS, INCLUDING WARP TRAVEL.
WE HAVE NUMEROUS CHAMBERS BUT THIS ONE IS MY PERSONAL FAVORITE.

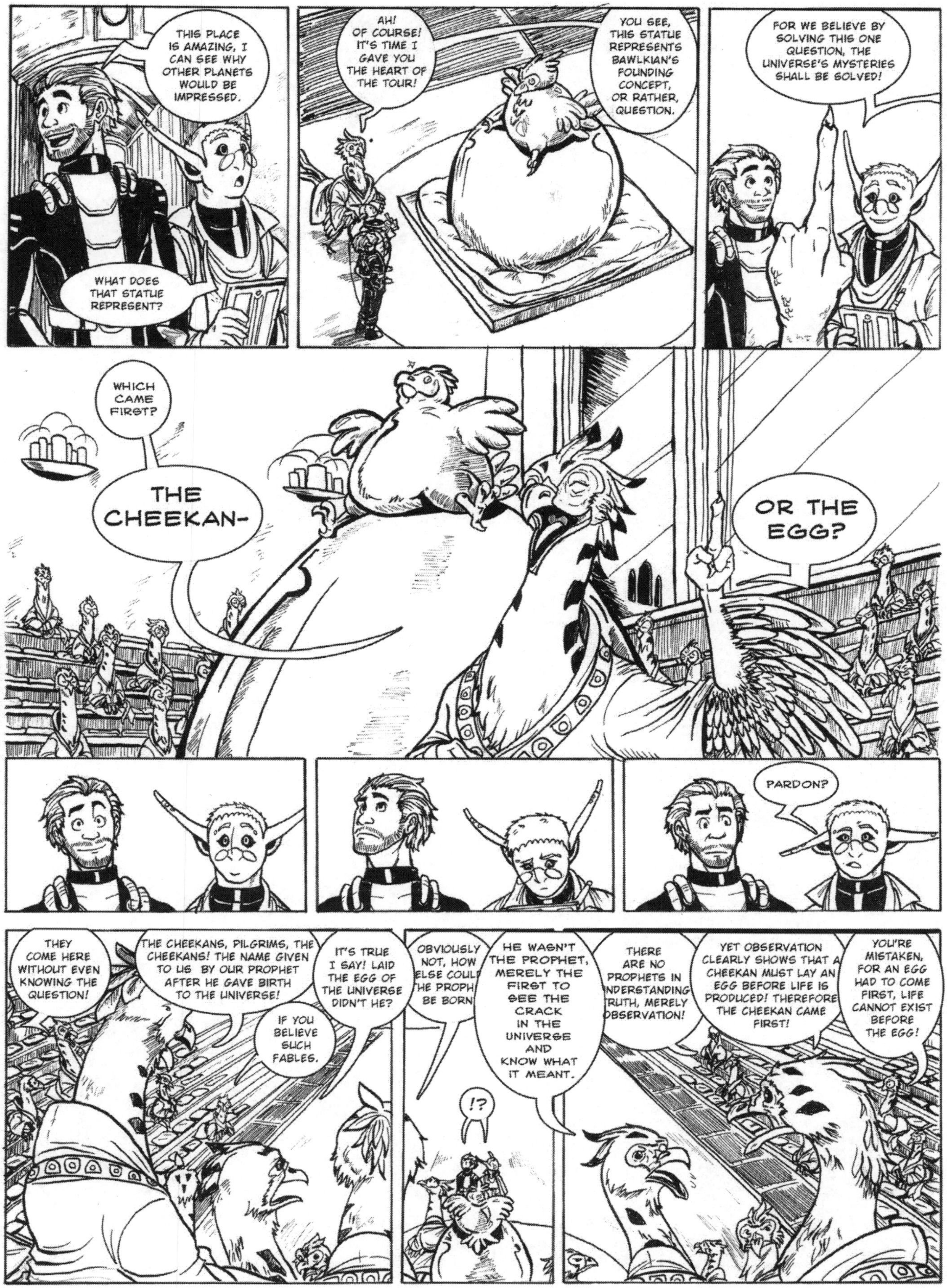
THIS PLACE IS AMAZING, I CAN SEE WHY OTHER PLANETS WOULD BE IMPRESSED.
WHAT DOES THAT STATUE REPRESENT?
AH! OF COURSE! IT'S TIME I GAVE YOU THE HEART OF THE TOUR!
YOU SEE, THIS STATUE REPRESENTS BAWLKIAN'S FOUNDING CONCEPT, OR RATHER, QUESTION.
FOR WE BELIEVE BY SOLVING THIS ONE QUESTION, THE UNIVERSE'S MYSTERIES SHALL BE SOLVED!
WHICH CAME FIRST?
THE CHEEKAN-
OR THE EGG?
PARDON?
THEY COME HERE WITHOUT EVEN KNOWING THE QUESTION!
THE CHEEKANS, PILGRIMS, THE CHEEKANS! THE NAME GIVEN TO US BY OUR PROPHET AFTER HE GAVE BIRTH TO THE UNIVERSE!
IT'S TRUE I SAY! LAID THE EGG OF THE UNIVERSE DIDN'T HE?
IF YOU BELIEVE SUCH FABLES.
OBVIOUSLY NOT, HOW ELSE COUL THE PROPH BE BORN
HE WASN'T THE PROPHET, MERELY THE FIRST TO SEE THE CRACK IN THE UNIVERSE AND KNOW WHAT IT MEANT.
!?
THERE ARE NO PROPHETS IN NDERSTANDING RUTH, MERELY BSERVATION!
YET OBSERVATION CLEARLY SHOWS THAT A CHEEKAN MUST LAY AN EGG BEFORE LIFE IS PRODUCED! THEREFORE THE CHEEKAN CAME FIRST!
YOU'RE MISTAKEN, FOR AN EGG HAD TO COME FIRST, LIFE CANNOT EXIST BEFORE THE EGG!

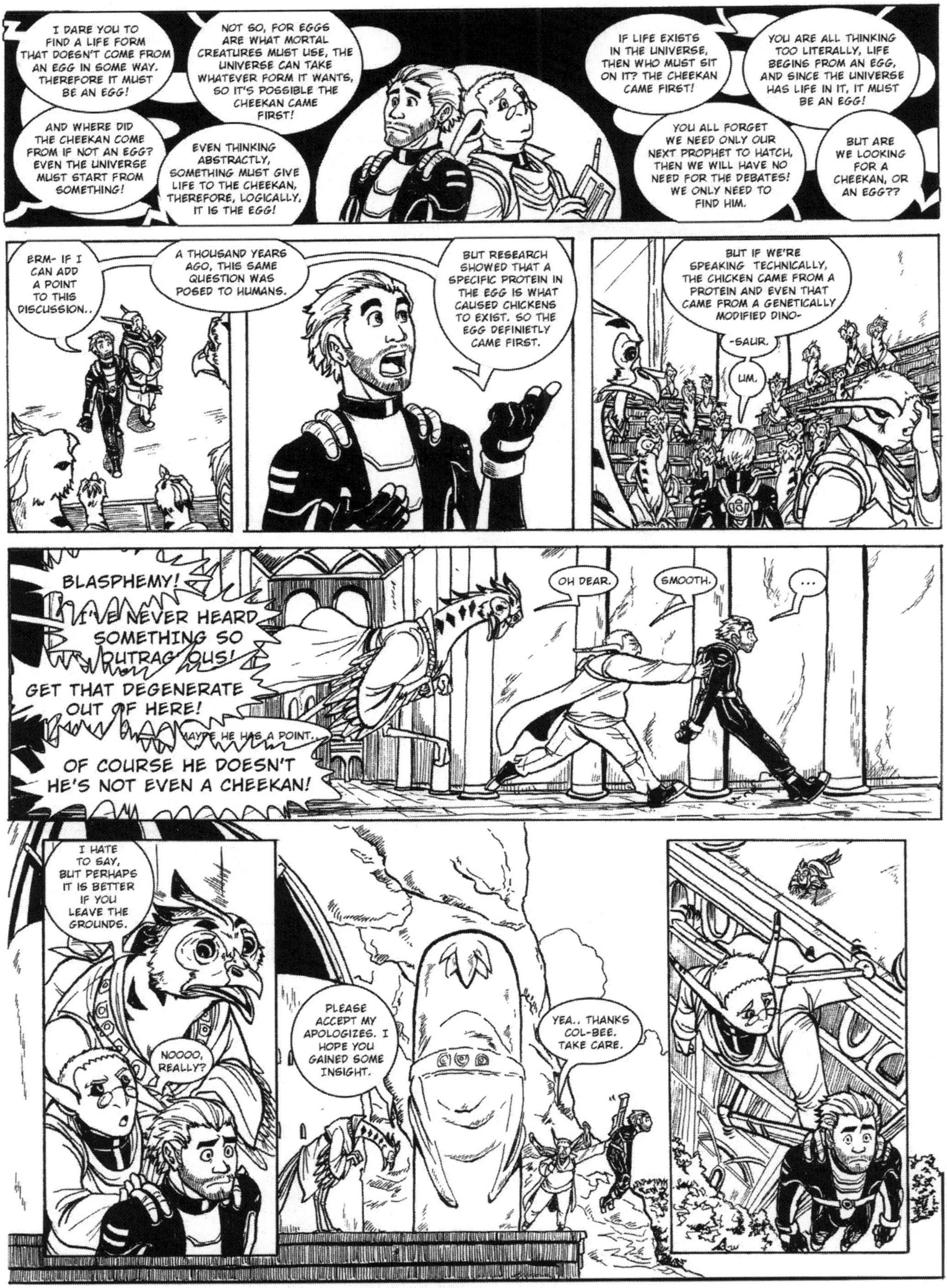
I DARE YOU TO FIND A LIFE FORM THAT DOESN'T COME FROM AN EGG IN SOME WAY. THEREFORE IT MUST BE AN EGG!
AND WHERE DID THE CHEEKAN COME FROM IF NOT AN EGG? EVEN THE UNIVERSE MUST START FROM SOMETHING!
NOT SO, FOR EGGS ARE WHAT MORTAL CREATURES MUST USE, THE UNIVERSE CAN TAKE WHATEVER FORM IT WANTS, SO IT'S POSSIBLE THE CHEEKAN CAME FIRST!
EVEN THINKING ABSTRACTLY, SOMETHING MUST GIVE LIFE TO THE CHEEKAN, THEREFORE, LOGICALLY, IT IS THE EGG!
IF LIFE EXISTS IN THE UNIVERSE, THEN WHO MUST SIT ON IT? THE CHEEKAN CAME FIRST!
YOU ARE ALL THINKING TOO LITERALLY, LIFE BEGINS FROM AN EGG, AND SINCE THE UNIVERSE HAS LIFE IN IT, IT MUST BE AN EGG!
YOU ALL FORGET WE NEED ONLY OUR NEXT PROPHET TO HATCH, THEN WE WILL HAVE NO NEED FOR THE DEBATES! WE ONLY NEED TO FIND HIM.
BUT ARE WE LOOKING FOR A CHEEKAN, OR AN EGG??
ERM- IF I CAN ADD A POINT TO THIS DISCUSSION..
A THOUSAND YEARS AGO, THIS SAME QUESTION WAS POSED TO HUMANS.
BUT RESEARCH SHOWED THAT A SPECIFIC PROTEIN IN THE EGG IS WHAT CAUSED CHICKENS TO EXIST. SO THE EGG DEFINIETLY CAME FIRST.
BUT IF WE'RE SPEAKING TECHNICALLY, THE CHICKEN CAME FROM A PROTEIN AND EVEN THAT CAME FROM A GENETICALLY MODIFIED DINO-
-SAUR.
UM.
BLASPHEMY!
I'VE NEVER HEARD SOMETHING SO OUTRAGEOUS!
GET THAT DEGENERATE OUT OF HERE!
MAYBE HE HAS A POINT...
OF COURSE HE DOESN'T HE'S NOT EVEN A CHEEKAN!
OH DEAR.
SMOOTH.
...
I HATE TO SAY, BUT PERHAPS IT IS BETTER IF YOU LEAVE THE GROUNDS.
NOOOO, REALLY?
PLEASE ACCEPT MY APOLOGIZES. I HOPE YOU GAINED SOME INSIGHT.
YEA.. THANKS COL-BEE. TAKE CARE.

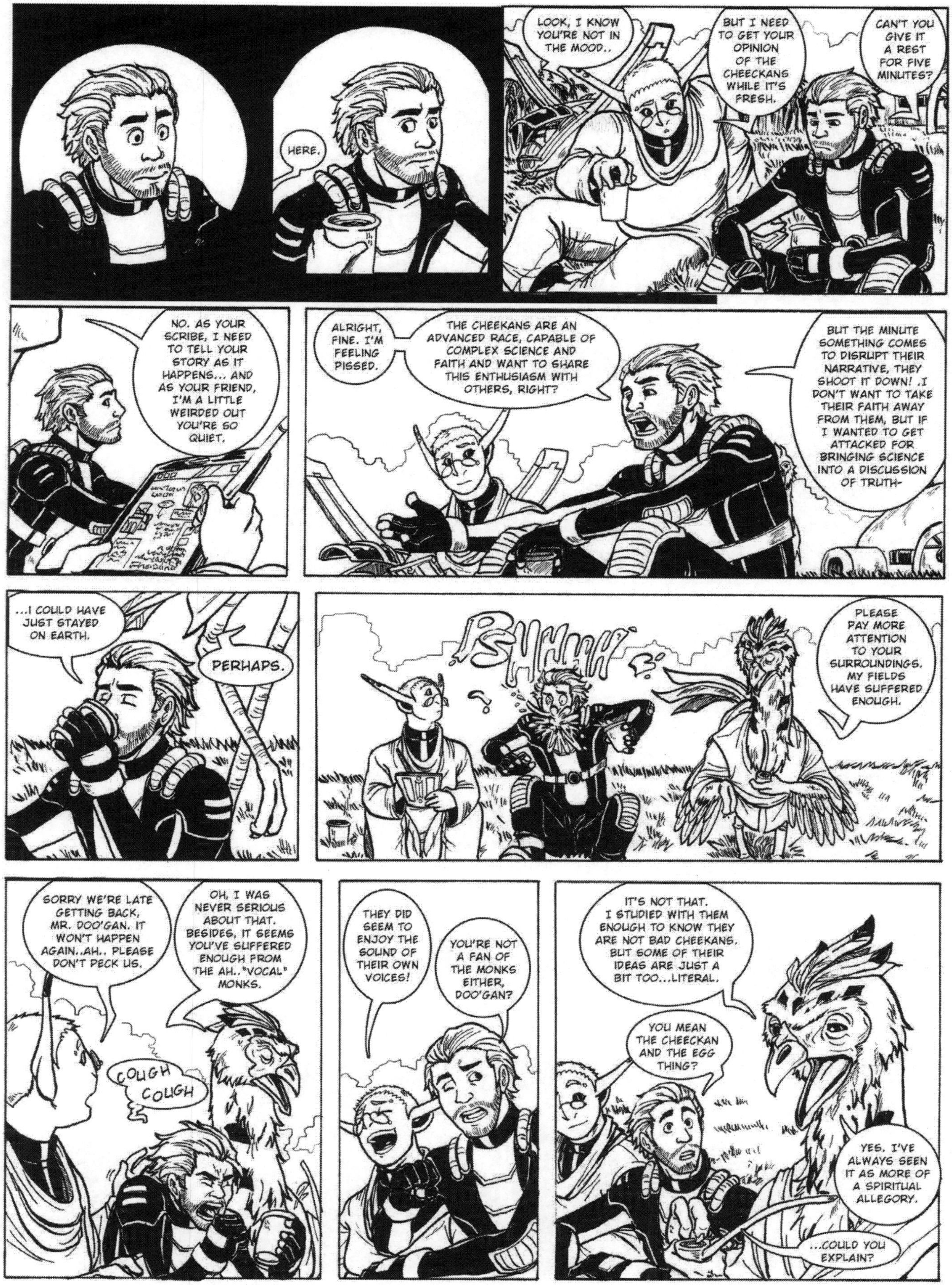
HERE.
LOOK, I KNOW YOU'RE NOT IN THE MOOD..
BUT I NEED TO GET YOUR OPINION OF THE CHEECKANS WHILE IT'S FRESH.
CAN'T YOU GIVE IT A REST FOR FIVE MINUTES?
NO. AS YOUR SCRIBE, I NEED TO TELL YOUR STORY AS IT HAPPENS... AND AS YOUR FRIEND, I'M A LITTLE WEIRDED OUT YOU'RE SO QUIET.
ALRIGHT, FINE. I'M FEELING PISSED.
THE CHEEKANS ARE AN ADVANCED RACE, CAPABLE OF COMPLEX SCIENCE AND FAITH AND WANT TO SHARE THIS ENTHUSIASM WITH OTHERS, RIGHT?
BUT THE MINUTE SOMETHING COMES TO DISRUPT THEIR NARRATIVE, THEY SHOOT IT DOWN! .I DON'T WANT TO TAKE THEIR FAITH AWAY FROM THEM, BUT IF I WANTED TO GET ATTACKED FOR BRINGING SCIENCE INTO A DISCUSSION OF TRUTH-
...I COULD HAVE JUST STAYED ON EARTH.
PERHAPS.
PSHHHH
PLEASE PAY MORE ATTENTION TO YOUR SURROUNDINGS. MY FIELDS HAVE SUFFERED ENOUGH.
SORRY WE'RE LATE GETTING BACK, MR. DOO'GAN. IT WON'T HAPPEN AGAIN..AH.. PLEASE DON'T PECK US.
OH, I WAS NEVER SERIOUS ABOUT THAT. BESIDES, IT SEEMS YOU'VE SUFFERED ENOUGH FROM THE AH.."VOCAL" MONKS.
COUGH COUGH
THEY DID SEEM TO ENJOY THE SOUND OF THEIR OWN VOICES!
YOU'RE NOT A FAN OF THE MONKS EITHER, DOO'GAN?
IT'S NOT THAT. I STUDIED WITH THEM ENOUGH TO KNOW THEY ARE NOT BAD CHEEKANS. BUT SOME OF THEIR IDEAS ARE JUST A BIT TOO...LITERAL.
YOU MEAN THE CHEECKAN AND THE EGG THING?
YES. I'VE ALWAYS SEEN IT AS MORE OF A SPIRITUAL ALLEGORY.
...COULD YOU EXPLAIN?

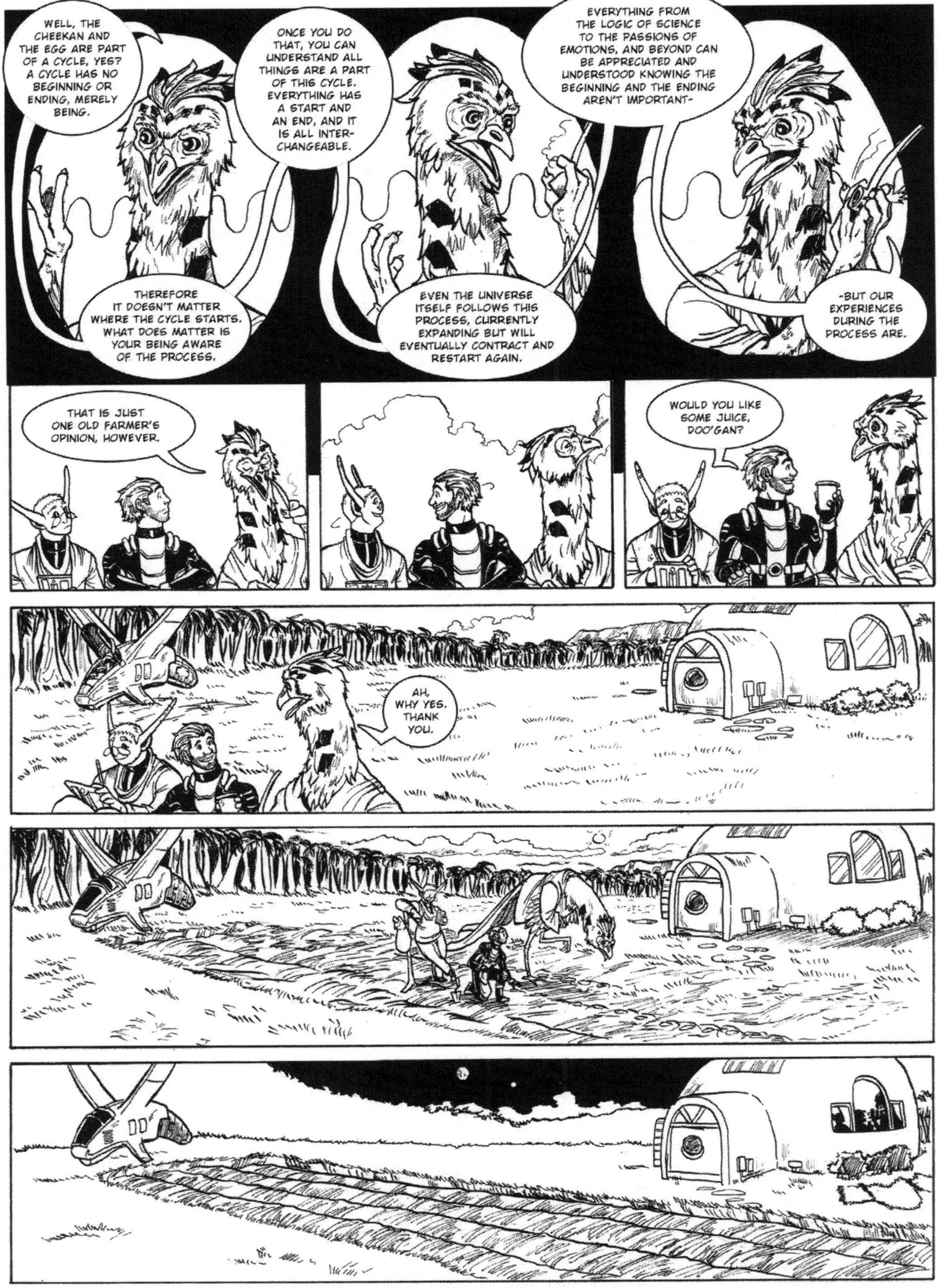
WELL, THE CHEEKAN AND THE EGG ARE PART OF A CYCLE, YES? A CYCLE HAS NO BEGINNING OR ENDING, MERELY BEING.
THEREFORE IT DOESN'T MATTER WHERE THE CYCLE STARTS. WHAT DOES MATTER IS YOUR BEING AWARE OF THE PROCESS.
ONCE YOU DO THAT, YOU CAN UNDERSTAND ALL THINGS ARE A PART OF THIS CYCLE. EVERYTHING HAS A START AND AN END, AND IT IS ALL INTER-CHANGEABLE.
EVEN THE UNIVERSE ITSELF FOLLOWS THIS PROCESS, CURRENTLY EXPANDING BUT WILL EVENTUALLY CONTRACT AND RESTART AGAIN.
EVERYTHING FROM THE LOGIC OF SCIENCE TO THE PASSIONS OF EMOTIONS, AND BEYOND CAN BE APPRECIATED AND UNDERSTOOD KNOWING THE BEGINNING AND THE ENDING AREN'T IMPORTANT-
-BUT OUR EXPERIENCES DURING THE PROCESS ARE.
THAT IS JUST ONE OLD FARMER'S OPINION, HOWEVER.
WOULD YOU LIKE SOME JUICE, DOO'GAN?
AH, WHY YES. THANK YOU.

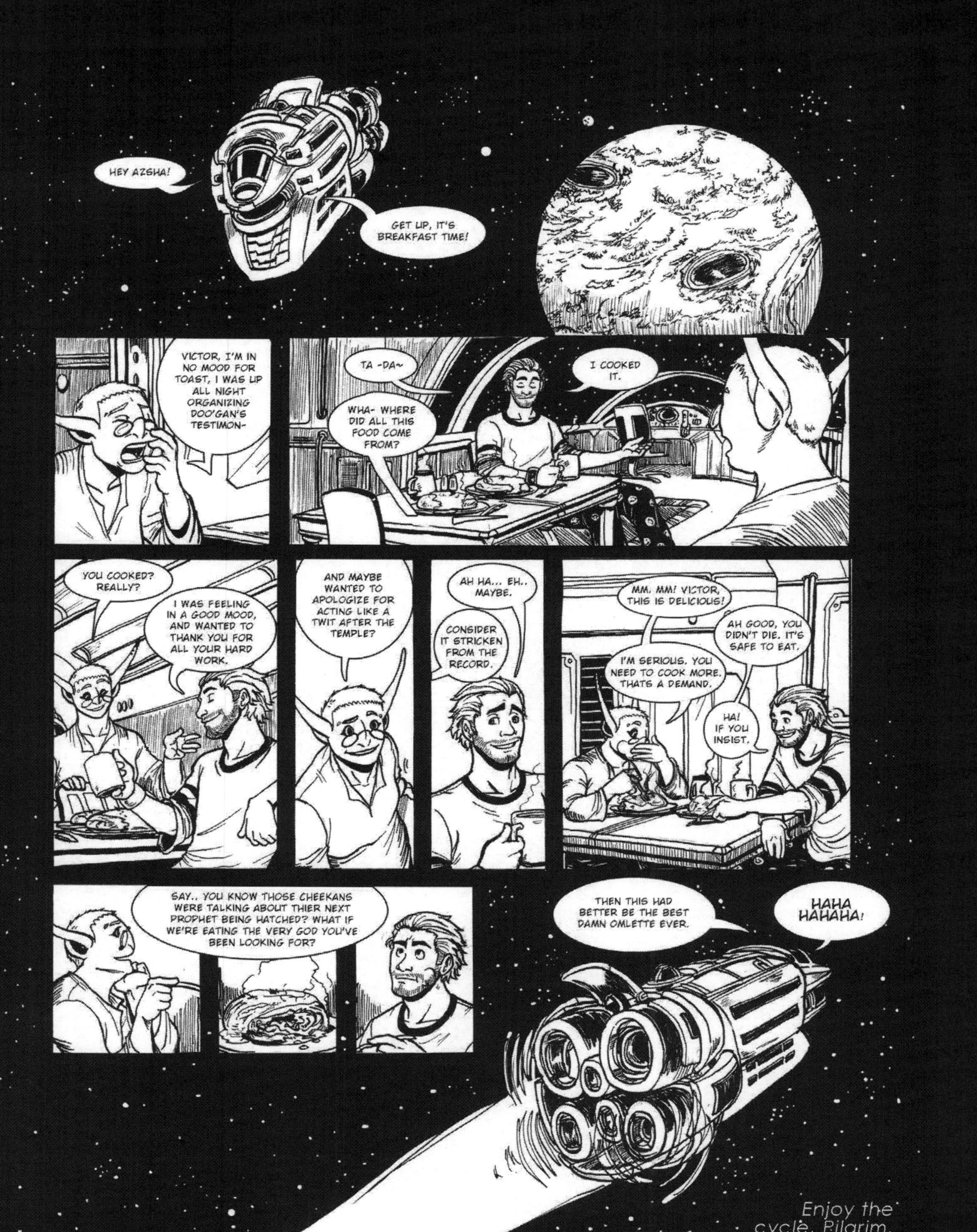
HEY AZSHA!
GET UP, IT'S BREAKFAST TIME!
VICTOR, I'M IN NO MOOD FOR TOAST, I WAS UP ALL NIGHT ORGANIZING DOO'GAN'S TESTIMON-
TA -DA~
WHA- WHERE DID ALL THIS FOOD COME FROM?
I COOKED IT.
YOU COOKED? REALLY?
I WAS FEELING IN A GOOD MOOD, AND WANTED TO THANK YOU FOR ALL YOUR HARD WORK.
AND MAYBE WANTED TO APOLOGIZE FOR ACTING LIKE A TWIT AFTER THE TEMPLE?
AH HA... EH.. MAYBE.
CONSIDER IT STRICKEN FROM THE RECORD.
MM, MM! VICTOR, THIS IS DELICIOUS!
AH GOOD, YOU DIDN'T DIE. IT'S SAFE TO EAT.
I'M SERIOUS. YOU NEED TO COOK MORE. THATS A DEMAND.
HA! IF YOU INSIST.
SAY.. YOU KNOW THOSE CHEEKANS WERE TALKING ABOUT THIER NEXT PROPHET BEING HATCHED? WHAT IF WE'RE EATING THE VERY GOD YOU'VE BEEN LOOKING FOR?
THEN THIS HAD BETTER BE THE BEST DAMN OMLETTE EVER.
HAHA HAHAHA!
Enjoy the cycle, Pilgrim.

THE EDGE

DEBBIE FONG

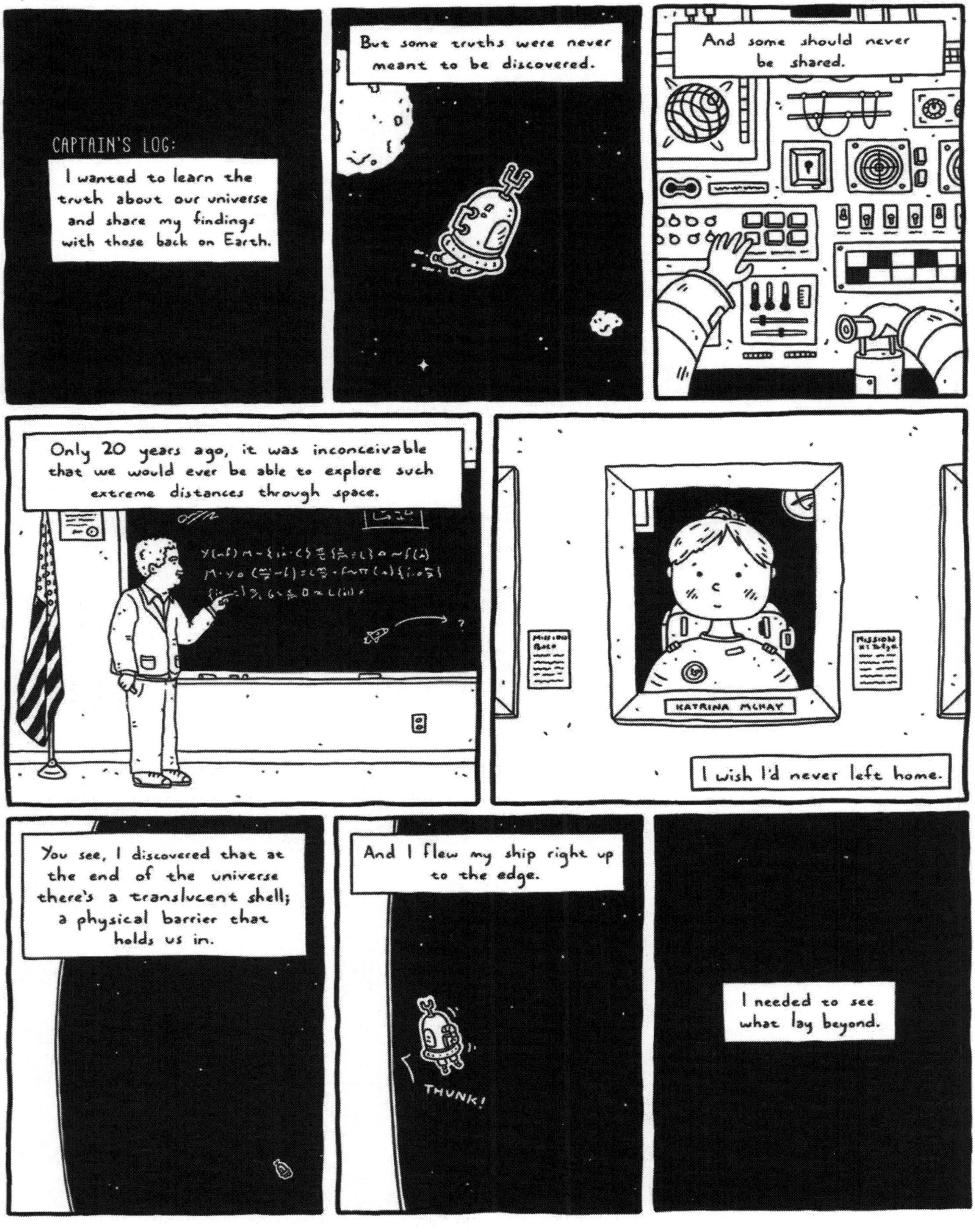
CAPTAIN'S LOG:
I wanted to learn the truth about our universe and share my findings with those back on Earth.
But some truths were never meant to be discovered.
And some should never be shared.
Only 20 years ago, it was inconceivable that we would ever be able to explore such extreme distances through space.
KATRINA MCKAY
I wish I'd never left home.
You see, I discovered that at the end of the universe there's a translucent shell; a physical barrier that holds us in.
And I flew my ship right up to the edge.
THUNK!
I needed to see what lay beyond.

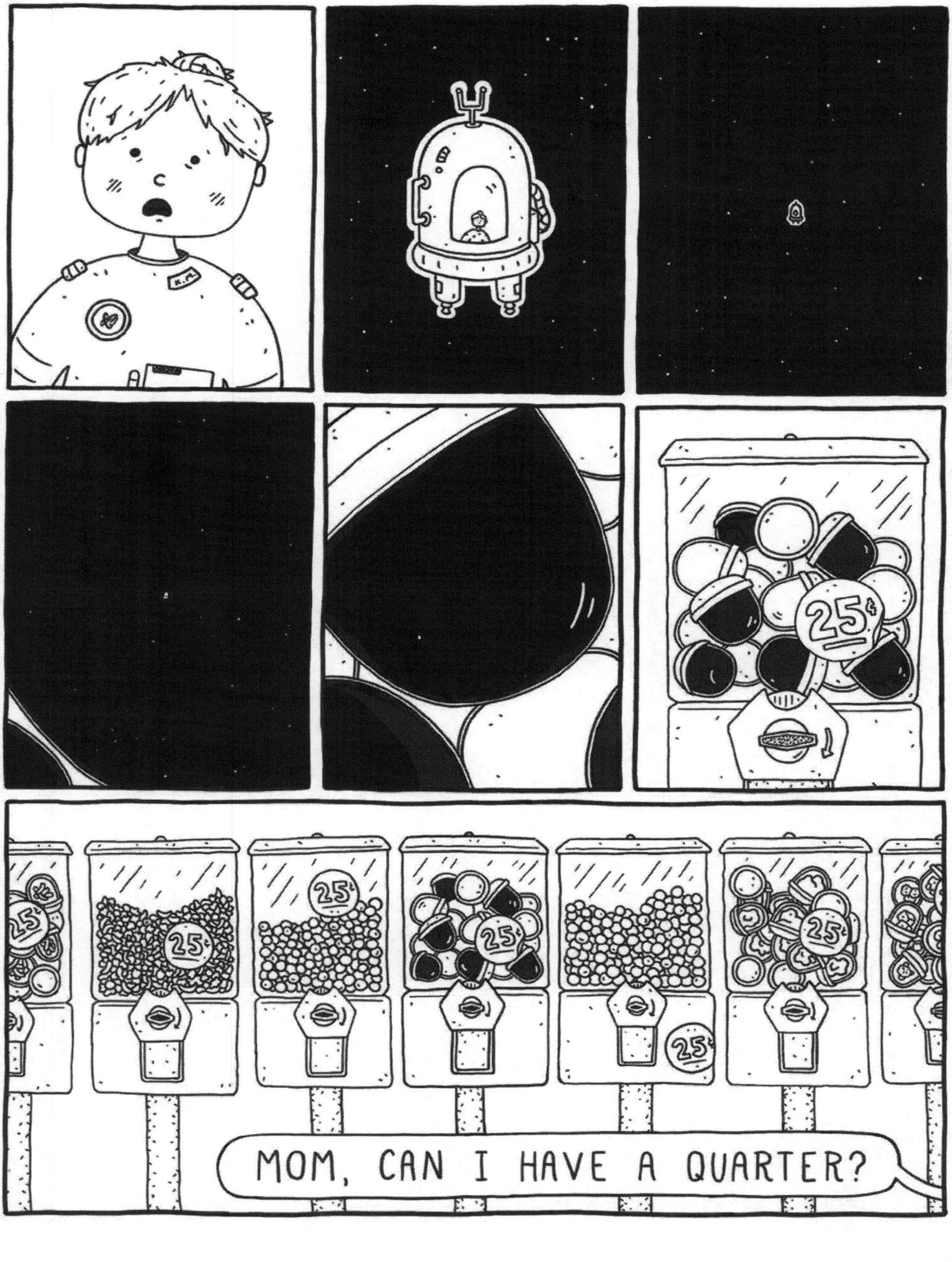
K.M.
25¢
25¢
25¢
25¢
25¢
25¢
MOM, CAN I HAVE A QUARTER?

PLATINUM

Abby De Vries

Alana Christie

Alondra Araujo

Amanda Kay Davison

Amy C

Anthony Miller

Åsa Roos

Ayla Cuda

baidarka

BeccaieJ

Ben Chilcoat

Bitsy

Bob Tienken

Brian Wilson

Bunni!

Callie Fox

Carl De Coster

Carol Smith

Cass

Chad Riley

Chas Lobdell

Chris Sarnowski

Cynthia Pollak

Dan Brewster

Dan Gonyea

David Lars Chamberlain

David S. Robinson

Debi Argust

Edward

Elisabeth Lindenthaler

Emma Rose

Eric Meadows

Eric Willey

Erin Bradley

Ezzy G. Languzzi

G. Willie Arnold & Kith Von Atzinger

Gabe Carino

Gage "CatComixz Studios" Lippolt

gameboygirl. tumblr

George Aspesi

Glen Brixey

Graphic Retellings

Hillary (Bee) Froemel

J.F. Wallace

James Rowland

Jennifer K. Koons

Julia Christianson

Katherine & Elizabeth Rowe

Kelsey Liggett

kungtotte

SPONSORS

Lennhoff Family

Leron Culbreath

Lisa Prime

Mark Skews

McAlister Grant

Michael Howell

Milou

Molly Sullivan

Morgan Thompson

Natasha R. Chisdes

Nicholas George

Norman Jaffe

Paul 'Smooth Head' Spence

Petrov Neutrino

Phil "Herr Direktor Funranium" Broughton

Rachael Badell

Rebekah Bernard

Rita Ficarra

Robert Early

Rose K. Goolsby

Ruben

Rydell-Sandgren

Ryan

S & M Cavanaugh

Sarah Hale

Seleweleboo

Shelley DeVost

Solveig Felton

Sophia Bisignano-Vadino

Stacey Morin

Star Nitori

Steampunk-Archivist

Strange Adventures Comix & Curiosities

Tammy Elliott

Tess M

The Dread Vixen Alinsa

"ToeJam and Earl" By: Greg Johnson

TreeNostalgia

TysonNW

"This section is for the wonderful people who went above and beyond the stars in funding the anthology. This book may not exist in parallel dimension, but thanks to your efforts, it exists in this one. Live long and prosper."

-ESfE Staff

BIOGRAPHIES

* * * *

PATABOT

Pat is the artist and creator of the webcomic BFGF Syndrome. She likes her dog, her guy, and drawing (in roughly that order).

ELEMEI

Currently a senior studying illustration, Elemei anticipates their post-school life with a mixture of surprise and mild confusion. They enjoy comics, RPG podcasts, and potatoes.

KRISTEN GUDSNUK

Kristen Gudsnuk is a comic artist/ writer living in Queens, NY. She's the creator of the comic series Henchgirl.

MARI COSTA

Mari is a gay webcomic artist from Portugal. She draws Peri-tale, Roji and a bunch of other stuff.
She also collects snowglobes.

ANNA LANDIN

Comic artist, illustrator, story teller, builder of imaginary worlds. Fascinated by everything. Lives in the far north-ern realms of the world (Sweden), in a town too small to show up on maps.

BENITO CERENO

A comics writer, freelance classicist, and professional Christmas ethusiast. He has written for Image Comics (Tales from the Bully Pulpit, Hector Plasm, Guarding the Globe), Dark Horse (The Adventures of Dr McNinja), and New England Comics (The Tick), among others. He is currently co-creating the webcomic The Mummy's Sabbatical with cartoonist Joel Priddy at rocketmummy.com, and is a regular contributor to ComicsAlliance.com.

CAITLIN MAJOR

Caitlin is an animation compositor by day and comic creator by night. She is best known for her webcomic 'Manfried the Man'. She lives with her partner Matthew in Toronto.

ALICE GAO

Mid-twenties something, she's a full time day-dreamer and currently doing schooling for a Real-JobTM. She loves reading comics and drawing in her free time, and pretty much anything else that's appealing to mind and the spirit. She hopes to be able to share even more of her pictorial shenanigans with the world in due course. Till then, she encourages readers to keep reaching for the stars!

COURTNEY HAHN

Courtney grew up in Indiana, teaching herself to draw and waking up before everyone else to watch cartoons. Focusing on all ages comics, Courtney has been lucky enough to work on a variety of projects from small comics to rebranding old video games.

SIGMUND REIMANN

Sigmund is an illustrator currently residing in Newcastle-up-on-Tyne in the United Kingdom. He specialises in illustrating animals; great and small, real and mythical. He also loves to tell stories and so creating comics was a natural progression in his artistic interests. He especially enjoys the challenge of telling stories using pictures alone, forgoing the crutch of words to convey meaning.

KODI KAT

Also going by Kodi Kat, Kodi is a graphic designer located in corn infested Iowa. She produces vector illustrations in her free time and is usually dabbling in dark and cute themes. Her works generally include cats (black cats in particular due to the passing of her family's feline). While she tends to be fascinated with certain subjects, exploring various genres challenges her ideas when creating pieces from her own perspective. She hopes her work will keep people curious.

Z AKHMETOVA

Z Akhmetova draws pictures and comics, including the webcomic Gods Can't Die. She was born in Russia and now lives in a hollow log, whispering arcane secrets to passers-by.

CLAUDIA RINOFNER

An artist hailing from Austria, that little weird country in Europe. When she's not scribbling, she's probably thinking about weird stories she wants to scribble later. When she grows up she wants to make money with her art.

TOD WILLS

Tod lives in the Pacific Northwest with three cats, nine chickens, some lizards, a dog, some roommates and a husband. He loves drawing all sorts of critters and friendly monsters, and was thrilled to have an excuse to draw goofy aliens for you!

DIANA NOCK

Diana is a cartoonist living and working in Minneapolis, MN, home of giant spoons and exploding flour mills. You can read more comics by her at wonderlustcomic.com and intrepidgirlbot.com. To view a broader portfolio of her work, check out: *diananock.artstation.com.*

LEE BLACK

Lee Black is a writer and editor who lives in Richmond, VA with some cats and a dude. When she isn't editing the Eisner nominated print/web comic Atomic Robo she's probably making a tofu scramble while half-watching a PBS murder mystery. Enough Space is her first anthology.

JON INAKI

Jon Iñaki is an Euskaldunak from Saskatchewan. He hopes linguistic diversity will get real wild, like a complicated but harmonious eco-system is wild. He is trying to maintain healthy gut flora by eating probiotic foods.

ZOE MAXINE

Zoe Maxine grew up in various parts Canada, and never stopped drawing pictures in the meanwhile. She particularly likes drawing robots, aliens and people in fancy clothes, all in bright colours. Her other specialties include "knowing more about supervillains than you, probably" and making bad puns.

S. PACE SMITH

S. Pace Smith was born in the underbelly of Moonbase 9 in 2099, to the king- and queen-in-exile of the Laser Kingdom. He was sent back to the year 1986 to elude the cabal of clockwork assassins that pursued his family, and has spent the intervening years learning Earth customs and adapting to this timeline. He lives among the Earth-dwellers with his wife, two cats, and more journals than you can shake a stick at.

MEGAN ROSE GEDRIS

Megan Rose Gedris, aka Rosalarian, is a comic book artist, burlesque performer, costume designer, and cheese enthusiast based in Chicago. She writes about women and queer people and surreal adventures and aliens and mermaids and sexy times and ghosts and feelings.

KORI MICHELE

Kori is a comic writer and artist from Maine, USA. They've drawn, written, and edited comics for a number of queer and progressive anthologies, and work regularly on webcomics and zines.

CONSTANZA YOVANINIZ

An Astronomy MSc student and comic artist based in Santiago, Chile. She works doing research on variable stars, doing science outreach activities, and making webcomics. She's a fan of both science-fiction and science-reality.

SARAH WINIFRED SEARLE

Originally hails from spooky New England but recently moved to sunny Perth, Australia, which confuses her gothic nature. She writes and draws comics inspired by history, feelings, and intimacy of all sorts. Read some over on *swinsea.com*!

DEBBIE FONG

Debbie Fong is a comic-maker, moleskine doodler, book-binder, and cat-petter from Brooklyn, NY.

MEGAN KEARNEY

Megan Kearney is a Toronto-based illustrator, and the manager of Comic Book Embassy, a small but cheerful co-work studio in the city's downtown core. When she's not hard at work on comic books, she's likely to be found lurking somewhere in the local library. She thinks that outer space is scary, and she's pretty sure it's just made up.

SAMANTHA RICH

Samantha Rich is a lifelong fan of superheroes, science fiction, and the supernatural.

Her work has appeared in the anthologies Sword and Sorceress XXIX, Accessing the Future, Defying Doomsday, and Monsters!. She lives in Maryland with a (grumpy) cat and a (nervous) dog.

JD Laclede

JD Laclede is a werewolf for a living. He is the author of El Indon, a fantasy webcomic, and Ask The Werewolves, a blog dedicated to asking a couple of werewolves about werewolves.

TS Porter

TS Porter is a tiny geek frequently mistaken for a collection of knobbly twigs wearing glasses. When not sleeping, they are usually found obsessively writing or baking sweet delicacies. TS' physical location and momentum varies, but home is always online. They can be found at *ts-porter.tumblr.com*.

Niki Smith

Niki Smith is an artist, writer, lover of fine comics (and some pretty trashy ones too). A recent expat, she lives in Germany with her wife. Her graphic novel, Crossplay, is about a group of friends exploring sexuality and gender identity through fandom, and will be out from Iron Circus Comics in 2017. Her work can be found at: *niki-smith.com*

SimonWL

Just a silly dude from Austria who has been drawing for as long as he can remember! Sometimes those drawings come out better than they did when he was still a kid. More of his comics, as well as other art can be found at: simonwl.com

Ver

Ver is a humble goblin from Eastern Europe. Their hobbies include writing stories and petting dogs. They live outside of their home country and try their best to balance simple day jobs and art. Results vary.

Eryn Williams

California born and raised, all natural illustrator and graphic designer. Requires minimal sleep and feeding, sustaining self through drawing, petting her silver tabby and watching horrible movies. To see her work, visit: *erynwilliams.com*

Made in the USA
Charleston, SC
23 February 2017